NORA KELLY

HOT PURSUIT

POISONED PEN PRESS MYSTERIES
published by ibooks, inc.:

Dangerous Undertaking
by Mark de Castrique

Spiked
by Mark Arsenault

Frostline
by Justin Scott

Old Wounds
Hot Pursuit
by Nora Kelly

COMING FEBRUARY 2005
Family Claims
by Twist Phelan

HOT PURSUIT

A GILLIAN ADAMS MYSTERY

NORA KELLY

ibooks
new york
www.ibooks.net

DISTRIBUTED BY SIMON & SCHUSTER, INC.

A Publication of ibooks, inc.

An ibooks, inc. Book

Distributed by Simon & Schuster, Inc.
1230 Avenue of the Americas, New York, NY 10020

ibooks, inc.
24 West 25th Street
New York, NY 10010

The ibooks World Wide Web Site Address is:
www.ibooks.net

The Poisoned Pen Press World Wide Web Site Address is:
http://www.poisonedpenpress.com

ISBN 0-7434-9817-8
First ibooks, inc. printing January 2005
10 9 8 7 6 5 4 3 2 1

Printed in the U.S.A.

PAPAGENO: What shall we say?

PAMINA: The truth! Though it be a crime.

—*The Magic Flute*

1

London was rousing from the brief, unquiet sleep of a summer night. Phones were shrilling, trains were thundering under the streets, delivery vans were hurtling through roundabouts. The earth thrummed, a muted roar and quiver rising through the pavement and vibrating in flesh and bone. As stragglers from after-hours clubs fell from taxis into unmade beds, the mercury climbed, and the soft, dusky faces of terraces and warehouses hardened in the daylight.

Gillian, only half awake, stood in the doorway of the smaller bedroom of the new flat, eyeing the stacks of cardboard boxes. Her cardboard boxes. They leaned crookedly, like doomed highrises financed by the Mafia.

"What was I thinking? That I was moving to Blenheim Palace? That I had to fill two hundred rooms?"

"This flat feels palatial to me," Edward said. He had already showered and dressed and had a coffee cup in one hand and a newspaper in the other.

"That's because your old one was so small we couldn't squeeze past each other without having tantric sex. Where on earth am I going to put all this?"

She'd shipped the boxes at the end of June and had been living with what she'd carried on the plane—summer clothes, her laptop. It felt like camping.

"Sod the boxes. It's too hot today to do anything," Edward said.

Gillian buttoned a sleeveless dress and decided she would have to buy a hat. Something to shade her face. It had never been this hot in London, and she wasn't used to it. Even the nights were heavy with heat. Her hair felt limp and gritty. "I'm supposed to visit Charlotte this morning. I wonder if she'll remember."

"You could ring her up."

"I could if she'd answer. She has the machine on half the time, and it doesn't work. It cuts you off before you can even leave your name."

"How is she, these days?"

"I'll find out when I get there."

"She's still in Fulham?"

"In her same old house. She hasn't moved an inch."

"Lucky Charlotte."

Gillian's boxes had arrived the previous afternoon. The men had carried them up the stairs, sweating. Fifteen hundred books, she'd packed. Half her library. Shoes, winter coats, sheets, wine glasses, china, CDs, pictures, papers, a pair of curtains made up from a fragment of Flemish tapestry, a dozen sweaters, and God knows how many other things that had seemed important at the time. It had been hard to strip down, even to this vast *favela* of boxes.

Edward had finished his coffee. He'd be off in a minute. She knew his route. He'd walk up through Warwick Square and across the Vauxhall Bridge Road, and wend his way past the playing fields and through the smell of frying chips in Strutton Ground to Scotland Yard. For more years than she'd known him, he'd been walking the same streets in Pimlico. The neighbours didn't set their watches as he passed, since he kept irregular hours, but the shopkeepers knew him, and so did the old ladies and the dogs.

He was wide awake in the mornings, while her mind was still clouded with sleep. In summer he was up before six, unless he'd been working late. Even in the dark of winter, he usually heard the clock's preparatory click and shut it off before the alarm sounded. He liked a smooth glide to the door, nothing in the way. He filled the kettle before he went to bed and set a new paper filter in place over the coffee pot. Over the years, he had honed his routine. Choice had been eliminated where practical, as in the matter of socks. His socks were all the same. As for his other clothes, they weren't literally the same, but they were similar. Well-made, unobtrusive, plain. They lasted. He still had—still wore—the same gray herringbone tweed jacket she'd seen him in when they first met. Never once had she caught him staring blankly into the cupboard wondering what to wear, a posture she herself was all too familiar with. He dressed, he drank his coffee and ate his slice of toast, and he was gone.

This morning, when she'd heard him moving about, she hadn't wanted to open her eyes. People who could rocket out of bed in the morning had an unfair advantage in life, she sometimes thought. What for the rest of humanity was a daily test of character—waking at the necessary hour, being efficient and cheerful—was automatic for Edward and his early-to-rise sort. Not that the difference mattered here and now. She had no need to race to the door, to think of six impossible things before breakfast. She needn't have risen from the bed. But she was used to getting up to go to work, and it was hard to settle back to sleep after twenty minutes of morning noises—water running, drawers shutting, the kettle blasting into outer space. Also, it felt indecently slothful to be still in bed as Edward left the flat. Demoralising. So she was up and dressed, and rewarded by a sense of rectitude and a view of the back of his newspaper.

"Maybe we should buy a cottage," she said.

"What?" Edward lowered the paper, looking startled.

Satisfied with her effect, she said, "I could put the boxes in it. Visit them once in a while. Like a museum."

He laughed, relieved, and went back to scanning the headlines.

The street was quiet, protected by traffic barriers. Edward had found the flat, in one of those buildings that were swathed in cream paint up to the knees and showed bare brown brick above. It had tall windows, two bedrooms, and a balcony off the sitting room just big enough for a dolls' tea party. When Gillian opened the French windows in the evening, she could sometimes smell the river. One of Edward's mother's friends had a son in the property business who'd had a word with some-one-or-other, and Edward had been the first to see the flat. It had been a distress sale, the renovations unfinished, otherwise the price would have been beyond their reach. It was still shockingly high, but that was the reality of property in London now. Gillian had listened and simply said yes over the phone.

The move had been hard for Edward. She knew that because he'd complained, and because she knew how hard she found it herself. "What have you got to grouse about?" she'd said one night on the phone. "You're moving from a small flat to a *larger* one. That's easy. I'm trying to shrink a big house into a couple of dinky rooms."

"I haven't moved since I was divorced."

"I've been in my house almost as long. And I have to cross an ocean. You're just moving around the corner."

"You have a heart of stone."

"Cardboard. As in box."

The new flat was hardly any further from the Yard than the old one. That had been Edward's only condition. Gillian hadn't contested it. The walk had an almost mystical power to put him in a good mood, whereas driving any distance through the congested streets of central London made him short-tempered. She didn't want to discover what he'd be like to live with if he were forced to commute by means other than foot. Besides, she liked Pimlico, its mix of the seedy and the posh, Regency terraces and council flats, flaking paint and lightning-strike reno jobs, its unassuming eclecticism.

She liked the Italian she heard in the streets, the old ladies emerging from their roosts, the cool young mothers reading on benches in the gardens while their children squabbled, the rows of quiet flats interspersed with Buddhist temples and language schools and little hotels. She'd stayed in one of the hotels once, in a room on the top floor. Her head had bumped the ceiling at the turn in the staircase. Pimlico felt a bit out of the way, tucked into a bend of the Thames. Nothing quite stood still, but the tidal race of London swept past, while Pimlico drifted a little.

"I'm off now," Edward said. "I'll be in court all day."

"Who's the judge?"

"Rankin. Just our luck. Will you see Olivia this morning?"

"Another time. She's away filming, Charlotte said."

He kissed her. "Don't fret about your boxes."

"I wish the ship had sunk."

She'd liked the flat, too. It was empty and light, Edward's spare living habits having made only a slight imprint on its neutrality. In the mornings, the kitchen smelled of peeled oranges and coffee. The paint wasn't even scratched yet. A few pieces of furniture stood where he'd put them but didn't look settled; they had a temporary air, as if they had unexpectedly found a pleasant little hotel. It was how she felt herself. All she'd had to do was move in.

He closed the door, quietly. If she were to list the things she liked about him, one of the items would be 'does not slam doors'. The list of deficiencies would include 'does not cook'. But she hadn't added up the pros and cons before moving. The conclusion hadn't been reached through a process of rational analysis. The analysis, such as it was, had come afterwards, as it tends to when we want something. She had wanted to be here, suddenly wanted it badly.

And now that she'd arrived? Today she could be in her own large, cool house, looking at reading lists for the fall semester. All her books would be on the shelves; her papers would be spread out across the desk. Her garden would be blooming outside the windows. Not that she'd ever been a real gardener, but right now the honeysuckle would be perfuming the back yard and the daisies and hollyhocks would be opening. She shouldn't think about them. The house had been bought by a Chinese doctor, daisies and all.

The long day loomed before her. Why had she shipped all these boxes? They would just remind her of everything she'd left behind. She was supposed to be starting a new life in London. Freedom. Janis Joplin's sorrowing, scraped-bare voice came to mind, though Gillian had plenty left to lose and thumbing rides in the rain was hardly congruent with her shipping bill and the pink-faced, sweating movers. The boxes looked stupid, comic in their inadequacy and excess, as if she'd thought she could drag her other life along and tack it on to her new life in London. But the boxes couldn't hold the spaces of the house she had loved, the blue-green Pacific-drenched light, evenings in the kitchen at Laura's house. The boxes were merely emblematic of the wrench of departure. They were funereal. They made her think of Egyptian tombs where the mummified dead lay surrounded by objects they were supposed to require in the next life. Well, at least she hadn't killed her slaves, too. Maybe the Egyptians were right: the contents of the boxes would come in handy in a few thousand years.

She washed her cup and dried it and read the headlines in the paper. The stories couldn't hold her attention; they were abstract tales, like gossip about people you hadn't met. Since the boxes had arrived, her move, her displacement, had become tangible. Why had she thought she could reinvent her life? Love. But now that she was here, she felt the immensity of London. It did not know her, and a new life seemed like a foolish enterprise. Perhaps it was the heat. Anyhow, this morning she was going out. She would shut the door on the idiocy of her boxes; she would visit Charlotte and look for a hat.

A few miles away, in Bayswater, a man leaned against the wall just inside the entrance to a dilapidated arcade of shops. Shoe repairs, key cutting, small print jobs and photocopying—businesses that couldn't afford to pay for higher visibility—clung to a few square feet of musty space in the dim passageway. The shops were empty, the windows still dark. On the corner, the Queen's Head pub was locked and silent. Only the Chagga, a coffee bar a few doors down, was open and busy. A stream of people flowed in and then briskly out, fortified with caffeine.

The man made no move towards the coffee bar, remaining in the shadowed entryway. He was big, with broad shoulders and a large round head, the scalp showing white through a brown stubble of crew-cut hair. His clothes hung loose, shirttail flopping, cuffs dragging over his boots. He slouched, his chin thrust forward, a fixed frown making him seem unaware of his surroundings until a sudden darting upward glance focused on a window across the road.

Not many people were about. Solitary men and women hurried along the pavement, intent on the day, their minds jumping ahead, already at work or skittering past it to the promise of the evening. They chatted into phones; they ruminated on shopping lists; they fretted about computer viruses or whether the escalators at their underground stops were still out of service. They knew their way and hardly saw the street's details; they responded to motion in the field of vision and then forgot.

For long minutes the man was still, framed in the recess like a statue in a niche. Only his eyes flickered over the block of flats across the street. Then he twitched, and his fingers stabbed into the pocket of his shirt. He lit a cigarette. A woman passing the arcade glanced sideways, startled to see him so close to her. She scuttled away, angling across to the outer edge of the pavement. Ignoring her, he resumed his surveillance of the flats, the cigarette pinched between his thumb and forefinger, his curled palm hiding the glowing tip.

Moments later, a figure appeared in the doorway of the building he was watching. A blonde in sunglasses. He started, straining forward. His pale eyes focused sharply as she stepped out into the light, but almost immediately he frowned and slumped back against the wall. The young woman, oblivious, slipped across the street to the coffee bar; his gaze tracked her briefly, then drifted away. He muttered and fidgeted, shifting his weight from one foot to the other.

He studied the building again. The window he was watching was on the fourth floor. It was open and the curtains were drawn; the folds of thin, cream-colored fabric hung limp in the humid air. The nearby windows, presumably belonging to the same flat, were also open, but the listless curtains revealed nothing of the interior. At night, he might have seen something, for there was a gap where the curtains didn't quite meet, but in the daytime it was only a triangular strip of darkness between opaque swathes of cloth.

Well down the street, a pair of constables moved steadily along, scanning the shop entrances and the weave of traffic, sorting the sample of humanity that showed itself at this early hour. They were relaxed, but seeing them, the crew-cut man withdrew deeper into the arcade.

An empty plastic flask of gin lay on the tiled floor beside a flattened nest of cardboard and newspaper. A dosser had been sleeping in the arcade, but he'd smelled foul, and the man had kicked him until he woke up, grunting, and staggered off. The sour reek of urine hung in the air. The man wiped his sleeve across his nose. A wad of gum was stuck to the edge of his bootsole. Irritably, he scraped his foot against the brick wall, missing the constables as they crossed the street. He was taken by surprise when they suddenly stood at the mouth of the passage, blocking out the light.

"Looking for something, mate?"

"Waiting for a friend." He turned away, staring sullenly at the cards in the window of the print shop.

Their eyes flicked over the arcade, registered the tattered cardboard.

The same one spoke again. "Been having a kip?"

"Do I look like it, for Chrissake?"

The other officer was studying the man. "I've seen you here before, hanging about."

"No you haven't."

"I know your face."

The man shrugged. "So? I've got a mate lives near here. We have a few pints at the pub."

"Pub's not open, son. What's his name, this mate of yours?"

"Piss off." Coppers.

"How long you been waiting?" the first constable asked, intervening.

"A while."

"On yer bike, then." The constable jerked his thumb, dismissive. "Go and wait where your friend can see you."

Stepping aside, the two officers waited while the man left the arcade and clumped along the pavement. Near the coffee bar, the people clutching their lattes in paper cups saw him coming, saw the wide-legged walk and the glare, and detoured out of his way.

"Right. Piss off," he repeated half aloud, halting outside the window of the Chagga. The blood was drumming in his ears. He peered in. She wasn't there, Olivia. Only a scrum of idiots dressed up for work, pouring coffee down their throats before they went to their robot jobs. Poncy blokes, girls with expensive shoes and wee tattoos on their shoulders. He balled his hands into fists. Sweat beaded under his arms and trickled down his sides.

The regal-looking black woman at the cash register saw him staring in. The lower half of his face was hidden by the swirl of gold lettering painted across the glass, but she recognised the big head, the eyes. Him again. She'd told him she didn't want him hanging about. Mechanically, she handed change across the counter, smiled, greeted the next customer in the queue. But she remained aware of the man outside, watching. Those two constables she'd just seen walking the beat, had they noticed him? She wouldn't mind having a word with them, but there were more people coming through the door; she had no time now, her busiest hour was just starting.

The crew-cut man squinted into the sun, checking the block of flats. The curtains on the fourth floor were still closed. The Old Bill hadn't budged from the arcade; they were alert, keeping him under observation. It would be stupid to wait about; he would have to come back later.

When the woman in the Chagga looked up again, he was gone.

On a cooler day, Gillian might have decided to walk, but not this morning. She went to Victoria Station and took the District Line. The passengers had a stunned look. Underground, the air felt greasy, like air that had spent the night spitting in a deep-fryer. Second-hand air. A mathematician had once told her that she had a 99% chance of breathing some of the same atoms that Aristotle and Caesar had breathed. Possibly she was breathing some of them at this very moment, but only after everyone else in London had had a whiff.

At Parson's Green, she got off, blinking at the milky blue sky and the glaring streets as if she'd been to a matinee. Charlotte's house was only a few minutes' walk. She didn't remember all this graffiti near the station. Behind a row of houses, vines spilled over the tops of high brick walls, hinting at hidden Edens. Lower down, the scrawls of paint writhed angrily. She turned a corner and the graffiti vanished. Rows and rows of painted front doors, clean and shining these days. The houses hadn't been smart in the early 1970s when Charlotte moved in. Gillian could remember the grimy brick housefronts and cracked pavements and litter. Also piles of sand everywhere, and cement mixers, and here and there a polished brass letterbox or a single strand of clematis tied to a bare trellis announcing the arrival of the middle classes. The neighbourhood had been on the way up. Now, in the late 1990s, it was up, indeed. All of London was up, even dingy lanes in Clerkenwell.

She rang the bell. Charlotte had been pregnant with Olivia when she and Tom moved to Fulham. Gillian remembered her coming home with shopping bags from Habitat, nervous and elated, determined to excel, every move a rebuke to the recollections of her mother and Mrs. Arthur. Olivia would be, what? Twenty-four, in a few months.

She rang a second time. The tiny front garden was dry and brown, and a few crumples of silvery paper festooned the leggy shubbery like forgotten Christmas decorations. The black gloss paint on the door was peeling, but the bell was in working order; she could hear it. She looked up and down the silent street. There was no traffic. She didn't see anyone on foot. But there wouldn't be that many people about; most would have jobs, unlike herself, who had no urgent purpose in life at present, no tasks to perform, except a duty to unpack her bloody boxes. There was her unfinished book, of course. You could always do more research. But you had to feel there was a point to it, and lately, she hadn't felt there was much of a point to anything. If the move to London hadn't been planned, the flat bought, the machinery already in motion, she wouldn't have been able to carry it through. Ever since her mother died, her own life seemed to have stopped; she had coasted to London on momentum, and now she had no vision of the future.

It was pointless to keep standing. She would ring once more and then leave a note.

"Who is it?" Charlotte's voice came through the closed door. She sounded annoyed.

"Me, Gillian."

"Oh." There was a pause, and then the sound of the door being unlocked. "I thought you were coming tomorrow,"

Charlotte said. She squinted at the sunlight.

"Today's Wednesday."

"Is it? I suppose you're right. Well, you'd better come in."

Charlotte shuffled ahead of her. She was wearing a red silk kimono and woollen socks. In the old days, Gillian had come here often. So many dinners, washed down with so many bottles of wine. Charlotte gestured at the door of the sitting room. "Go in and sit down. I shan't be a minute." She walked heavily up the stairs, easing her weight onto her right foot and gripping the bannister for support.

Not a promising start. Gillian stepped cautiously through the door into the sitting room and waited for her eyes to adjust from the blaze outside. All the curtains were drawn, and a disheartened light seeped through their dusty folds. The room stayed cooler this way, she supposed, but it was stuffy, with a smell of ashtrays, like an empty pub. She knew every table and chair and footstool—good Victorian pieces Charlotte had picked up years ago, when no one wanted them. They squatted contentedly in the gloom. A fine collection of botanical prints hung in closely-packed rows on the walls, trophies from the days when Charlotte, quick of eye and sharp of elbow, had jousted at bookstalls and jumble sales.

Gillian moved closer to look. Ragged robin, star-of-Bethlehem, snake's head, honesty, traveller's joy. Names that evoked a vanished rural world, though not one Charlotte had grown up in. Gillian's foot touched something that clinked and she looked down. A cup and saucer. The bottom of the cup was coated with green mold.

Charlotte was at the door. She'd combed her hair and put on a skirt and some lipstick. They kissed, awkwardly. Charlotte's breath smelled of toothpaste; under it Gillian recognised the sour chemistry of alcohol coming off the body. It wasn't a smell you could wash off, not when you'd pickled every cell.

"So here you are," Charlotte said.

"Here I am."

"You've really quit your job?"

"I've quit my job. I've sold my house, and I've come to live in London. It was an ordeal. I had to get rid of things, tons of things. I hope you never have to move."

Charlotte raised her thin, arched brows. "Where would I go?"

"What do you keep when you're starting a new life? You look at things you've completely forgotten about, and when you see them again, they bring memories back. They're your history. 'Oh,' you think. 'My father gave me that when I graduated.' You remember the moment. Then you make another donation to the thrift shop. It goes on and on, like some task in mythology, trying to empty the sea with a spoon. I'd keep thinking I was getting somewhere, and then I'd open a closet and there would be more stuff. I'm not a packrat, not like my mother. But, God almighty." She stopped. She was talking too much.

"And how is your mother?"

"She died."

"Oh. I didn't know."

Dammit. I sent you a note, Gillian thought. "Her heart gave out last spring. On the 5th of April."

"That's an easier way to go than some."

"Yes, but I miss her."

"You were lucky to have Estelle for so long."

"I know. And I was there, at least. I was with her for the last eight months."

"What have you done with the farm?"

"I haven't done anything. It belongs to my brother and me, and we want to keep it. He goes up there sometimes on weekends. It's only an hour or so out of New York."

"But you can't use it if you're living here."

"I don't care. I don't want to change anything. It's the only home I've got." She wouldn't say that to Edward, Gillian thought. It was true, however. She was living in Pimlico, now, but it didn't feel like home.

Charlotte lit a cigarette. "Coffee? It's real, not nescaf."

"Coffee would be nice."

Charlotte went into the kitchen. Gillian heard the tap run and the fridge open and close. She walked to the windows and lifted up the edge of the curtain. A thick layer of soot coated the sill. In the light, the room looked worse. The wooden tables next to both armchairs were scarred with overlapping rings. There were cigarette burns on the carpet and a plate with old crusts of toast.

"I hope you can manage without milk," Charlotte said, from the kitchen. "It's gone off."

There was a framed eight-by-ten photograph on the whatnot. Charlotte, Tom, Olivia. A picture from another era. Handsome Tom, Olivia at about six. And Charlotte, smiling. A bright, particular star—vital, quick, furious and sentimental, gifted and scared. The trio, close to each other, the child in the middle. Olivia had grown up and had her own life now. And Tom? Tom had gone, had removed himself from the picture. He was still in London, Gillian knew, but he'd left Charlotte and Fulham years ago.

"Thomas is married, did I tell you?" Charlotte came in with the coffee. She'd always called him Thomas, though everyone else called him Tom.

"Married?"

"Yes, and having a baby, if you please."

"Who told you? Olivia?"

"She went to the wedding. It was important to him, she said."

"How old is his wife?"

"How old do you think? Young. Boring, isn't it? But at least she's not twenty. Credit where credit's due. She's older than Olivia."

"Thirty?"

"And Thomas is fifty-five. I hope he enjoys having a teenager in the house when he's seventy." Charlotte lowered herself into an armchair. "The woman's name is Sybil. Really.

Sybil. He probably thinks the silly bitch'll wipe his bottom for him when he's eighty, but she'll be gone by then, I expect, unless she's stupid."

"What about Olivia? Will she be back in town soon?"

"Any day now. She's on location. She was sharing a flat in Bayswater with her friend Lisa, but she's given it up. She'll be staying at her boyfriend's while she hunts for a flat of her own."

"I hope I'll see her more often, now that I'm here. What's he like, the boyfriend?"

"He's an architect. At the moment he's off in one of those Arab oil states. He's away a lot, she says. I can't tell whether it's serious. I've never met him." One corner of Charlotte's mouth twisted downward in self-mockery. "She might think I'd scare him off." She drew smoke into her lungs as if it was hard to get enough. "He has a posh flat—there's always a porter on duty, Olivia says, and I'm glad. Some perverted fan was hanging about, sending her flowers and ringing up constantly. Importuning her on the street. That's why she moved so suddenly. It's a good time for her to be away from London, I suppose."

"What's the film she's making?"

"A silly comedy. Diamond smugglers in the Sahara, people falling off their camels. Frightful rubbish."

"You used to like comedies."

"They used to be witty. She has to do one scene with nothing on above the waist," Charlotte said. "I saw that in the script; she wouldn't have mentioned it." Her blue glance shifted to the shrouded windows, as though it could escape, could fly out and over rooftops and oceans and deserts, to land, unerringly, at whichever global coordinates Olivia had positioned herself. "At least she's not entirely naked. I tell myself it's acting, even stars take their clothes off nowadays, and she's being decently paid. But then there are these perverts. It doesn't bear thinking of when it's your only daughter."

Gillian said nothing. If you didn't have children, you didn't express opinions about them to anyone who did, not if you didn't like being told you didn't know what you were talking about. This went double for Charlotte. Nothing but eggshells in all directions.

"She wants to work, I know that. She says it's good experience. But why do these dopey comedies and nihilistic films about drug addicts? Bloody *Trainspotting* was a hit, so now we've got to see every auteur's vision of life and death in a crackhouse? She was such a lovely baby," Charlotte went on. "Two minutes into the world and she latched onto the breast and went about her business. She was never fussy. You don't think then what they might do later. You don't think about anything at all, just how beautiful they are."

Gillian's mind wandered. Baby Olivia was a favourite subject of Charlotte's; the same memories tended to be repeated in the same phrases. Gillian had her own fund of recollections, but Gillian had also known Charlotte long before Olivia was born, before Charlotte was married, had met her way back, in the year of *Sergeant Pepper*. Charlotte was living in Notting Hill Gate, then, and Gillian was staying in London for the summer, doing research for her thesis in the Public Record Office. She still remembered the white-haired man behind the wicket in Chancery Lane who'd inspected her reader's ticket on the first day and, like a Cockney St Peter, had called her 'luv' and let her in.

Charlotte, conversely, let her out. She took Gillian shopping at Biba and explained how squats were organized, and who Mary Whitehouse was, and what *Private Eye* meant by its inscrutable references to 'Ugandan Affairs'. She seemed to know half the population of London and all the gossip; when she talked, the city of monuments and museums and peculiar hours for pubs was only the background to endlessly unfolding human dramas. After a long day in the silent domain of the Public Record Office, with its smell of pencil shavings and whispers of turning pages that reminded Gillian of exams, or—even more—after a day in the newspaper archives at the Siberian outpost of Colindale, seeing Charlotte had been as exhilarating as a holiday.

"You're not listening," Charlotte said.

Gillian smiled guiltily. "I was thinking about the long walks we used to take when I first met you. When I fell in love with London."

"It was a city worth loving, then. I don't know why anyone would move here now. It's been spoilt."

"Do you think so?"

"Do I *think* so? It was a humane city then. Look at it now—the traffic, Gillian, the crowds, the rudeness. Crack addicts, same as America. And the greed: it's so expensive. On top of that, busloads of tourists jammed into all those hideous hotels. Eyesores! And the bloody Labour government gave grants to people who built them. Then there's the pollution. No more 'bright and glittering in the smokeless air.' We got rid of the coal fires, thank you very much, but we might as well not have bothered, now we're being choked to death by diesel fumes. There isn't a politician in the country who'll put a stop to it. The 'motoring public' has them by the short and curlies. Cool Britannia. What a larf."

"I don't know, the mood's certainly fizzy."

"Dizzy, you mean. A foul-mouthed brat opens a new restaurant and the media wet themselves. It's all right for the rich, they breathe different air—they can afford to."

"Well, I've moved. I'm here, now."

"But I don't understand why you burnt your bridges. Why didn't you take a leave of absence from your job, so you could go back? What if it's not the right choice for you? Or Edward finds some dolly-bird?"

"Dolly-bird?" Gillian laughed. "I can't quite picture him with a girl in thigh-high boots and a miniskirt. You're right, though, if we can't stand each other in six months, I'll wonder if I was mad to move. But I've made my bed, so to speak."

All she'd had to do was sell her house and say goodbye to her friends and her job and pack up her entire life and shift it to the other side of the globe. She might have confided in Charlotte, confessed her doubts, but not when Charlotte was in this unbending mood.

"He never thought of moving, of course."

"No."

"So you left your job."

"Well, Charlotte, I wanted to."

"Why?"

"Lots of reasons, but if you want the short version, the answer is too many meetings."

"Meetings?"

Gillian laughed. "You sound as if you'd never heard of them. I've developed a galloping phobia. I hear the word 'meeting' and I fall down and foam at the mouth. I've lost my zest for the battles. I'm tired of my colleagues, tired of students turning into consumers of education and the university acting like a struggling shopping mall, with special offers and discounts on grades. And I wanted to move to London, Charlotte, lunatic as that may seem to you. I want to live with Edward before I get old. The decision made itself when I was living with my mother last year, and I was reminded how short life is. So it's done, for better or worse. I won't say for richer or poorer—I know I'll be poorer. But it's still London, whatever they do to it. As long as I can breathe. Do you ever get away to the cottage?"

"Never. It's rented."

"You once loved that place. Who lives there now?"

"I scarcely know. The estate agency looks after it for me. It's not what it was, you realise. I couldn't bear to see it. A stockbroker bought the field next door and built a monstrous house. I'm told it looms over the hedge and is visible for miles."

"But you don't want to sell?"

"Not unless I must." Charlotte stood up. "I'm going to have a glass of wine. Would you care for any? The house white is Muscadet."

"No, thanks." The last time she'd been in London, they'd gone out to lunch, but it hadn't been a success. Charlotte had pushed the food around her plate and bitched about the effort, though they'd only gone as far as Chelsea. The bill had seemed like an expensive joke. It had been her fault, Gillian had concluded; she'd thought an outing would be good for Charlotte, and Charlotte had acquiesced, probably to please her.

"Thomas, that bastard," Charlotte said, coming back with her wine. Gillian guessed she'd swallowed a quick mouthful in the kitchen before coming back; she seemed more relaxed. "It was bad enough that he married again. But a baby—I could kill him. It's been almost eight years, Gillian. Eight years. I didn't believe he was never coming back until he married that woman."

"Does he see much of Olivia?"

"Hmph. He's frightfully busy, my dear. He has his own company now. Spinning gold from straw. Did you know that boards can be made from the chaff that farmers used to burn? That's the sort of thing Thomas is interested in these days."

"It sounds like good work he's doing."

"Oh yes. He always has done. He's nothing if not high-minded, our Thomas. He'll probably be a candidate for an OBE one of these years, if they persist with the absurd custom of handing them out." Charlotte lit another cigarette. "Sorry about the fag reek. I rather hope they're not what kills me, but I can't stop. Did I tell you, someone at Granada rang me a few weeks ago? Maybe it was a few months ago. About a job. I said no. I don't work any more. I could hardly believe they called me."

"Charlotte, your programmes were wonderful. Everyone said so. You might like it if you started again."

"You must be joking. Looking like this? Everyone in the studio will be twenty-two and as skinny as Kate Moss and perfectly certain they'll never look like me." Charlotte finished her glass and fetched another. "It doesn't matter what I do now. It's Olivia's life that matters."

"Charlotte, you're only in your fifties."

"Most people who ever lived died before they were sixty."

"Do you eat?"

"Not much."

"Do you ever see a doctor?"

"I wouldn't want to waste the NHS's money. There's not enough to go round as it is." Charlotte's voice grew sharp. "Don't tell me I should be taking better care of myself. You don't know a thing about it."

"Tell me, then."

"I can't. You've got Edward, so you can't understand."

"You and I go back a lot further than that."

"Give it a rest, Gillian. I don't want to moon over the old days when we hitchhiked around France and slept on the beach at Corfu and all that. Or what a brilliant producer I was. That's finished. All over now. I'm fat, I'm losing my hair, and I drink. My husband's having a baby with somebody else."

"You still have a daughter. A marvellous daughter."

"I've done all I can for her."

Gillian heard finality in Charlotte's voice.

"Charlotte, tell me whether I should come back. I'd like to see you, and Pimlico's not far, but I can't tell how you feel about it."

There was a silence. Gillian waited. Charlotte had her bad days and she'd been caught unprepared; that might have made her cranky.

"I don't know, seeing people. It's easier not, in a way. I'm out of the habit. But yes, do come. You're the only one I can speak the truth to. Parts of it, anyhow."

At the end of the afternoon, the crew-cut man stopped in front of a florist's shop. He ignored the brightly-hued arrangements in the window and peered through the glass to see who was inside.

A stout, graying, middle-aged woman was alone at the rear of the shop, stripping wilted leaves from the stems of daisies. He pushed the door open and she looked up.

"Kevin. What are you doing here?"

He came towards her.

"I thought I told you to keep out of this," she said. "I don't fancy getting the sack."

"I won't hang about, I just need a bit of money."

"I haven't got it."

"Of course you have. That old cow is paying you, right? All I'm asking for is twenty quid, for Chrissake."

"You had twenty off me three days ago. I haven't got it."

"I need it."

A terra cotta cupid stood on the counter, wings spread, one dainty foot cemented to a cast iron base, a pot of African violets in its arms. He flipped over the price tag. "Christ. Who'd pay 140 quid for that?"

"Plus VAT. You'd be surprised."

"They must be daft."

"Your shirt's missing a button, I could sew it for you at the weekend."

"Yeh, Mum, and bring me my tea. Never mind the bloody button. I need twenty pounds. Just the once. That's it, I promise."

"Until you're skint." Reluctantly, she opened her bag and fished out a ten pound note. "A tenner's all I can spare. You'll have to make do."

He took the money and moved over to the glass door of the chilled display cabinet and opened it. Olivia liked roses. He would probably have seen her this morning if it wasn't for those two coppers. They thought he was waiting to rob someone. Stupid gits.

"Leave the bloody roses!" the woman said. "Every time you nick one, I've got to pay for it. You think the old cow can't count?"

He removed a rose from the cabinet and shut the door. Then he tore a sheet of green paper from the roll behind the counter and wrapped the rose and taped it.

"Who's it for then? Some tart?"

Olivia. His mum would be pleased, all right, if he told her. But if she thought he had a girlfriend she'd be pestering him, wanting to meet her. A film actress, she'd go telling her friends. They'd natter.

"Kev?"

He shrugged.

His mother picked up the rose in its paper cone. "Look. I don't want to see you at this shop again. Where would you be if I had no bloody job?"

He reached for the rose and she let go. She was always on about her job. He was right not to tell her anything. You never told anybody what you were doing, what you were thinking. Not if you knew what was good for you. He turned towards the door.

"Please." Her voice was suddenly beseeching. "It's no good, the way you're carrying on."

He hunched his shoulders awkwardly. "I'm all right."

"You've no work. No money. Nothing to do with yourself except hang about in pubs and I don't know what."

"Work? Road-mending, like? Up to my armpits in dirty water in some fat-arsed bastard's kitchen?"

"If you'd go back to school! It's no good like this, Kevvie. You can't tell me it is, you don't even see your old mates. Please—go and talk to Dr. Paul."

"Oh right, you'd like that," he sneered. "Dr. Paul. Not a fucking chance." He yanked the door open and flung out.

The woman shut the door after him. She stood watching through the glass until he was out of sight. Her feet ached; she eased one out of its shoe and rubbed it against her calf. Then she walked back to the till. She looked sourly at the cupid, resting her elbows on the counter, pressing her palms to her temples. She'd had her own shop when Kevin was small. He'd liked putting flowers in vases. Donkey's years ago, that was. What did he want with roses now? He'd never had a girl. Wouldn't get one, either. Not with his stained shirts and his temper and his odd way of drifting into a dream. Sometimes, when he was home, he'd sit by himself in the dark. The TV might be on, but he wouldn't know what the program was, he'd be way off on some planet of his own. She'd practically have to shout to get his attention. Then he'd get stroppy with her. It scared her half to death, thinking what might happen to him; he couldn't manage. And he was stubborn—would never admit anything was wrong. Got that from his father, she supposed.

No point in thinking about all that. She used to get up in the night when he had bad dreams, sit by him until he fell asleep again. Well. He wasn't a child any more; there was little she could do except give him a few quid now and then and hope it kept him out of trouble.

It was time to close the shop. Before setting the alarm and locking the door, she rang up the sale of one rose, opening her bag again to take out the money.

Gillian was sitting on the floor when Edward got home. The French windows to the balcony were open and the fan was blowing the hot air around.

"Was London ever malarial?" he said, coming in from the kitchen with a bottle of beer and a glass.

"The quinine cure was invented in the Essex Marshes."

"In Essex?"

"So many people there had the ague. A man named Talbor concocted a patent medicine with cinchona bark and white wine, and Charles II made him physician royal. He got stinking rich and ended up curing half the crowned heads of Europe. Malaria was all over the place."

"I had no idea. But I believe you. I wouldn't be surprised to see crocodiles in the Thames."

"Sunning themselves beside the Houses of Parliament and snapping up the odd tourist?"

"Or MP. Might put everyone in a better temper."

"Uh-oh. You were in court today, weren't you? The rent boy who murdered the Soho landlord. What happened?"

"I cooled my heels all morning before being told they were going to adjourn and I wouldn't be needed today, thank you. The courts don't run on Greenwich time, they set their own clocks, and bugger the rest of us."

"I remember when doctors had their own clocks. You'd show up for an appointment at ten and be lucky to be seen by noon. It was maddening. Do you have to go back tomorrow?"

"In the morning. With any luck, I'll be free by Christmas." Edward watched the head of foam subside in the glass. "No, the judge is slow but the case should go smoothly. Prints all over the shop, blood on the shoes, wild-eyed exit from premises witnessed by shocked crowd at pub—not exactly a criminal mastermind at work. The hard part was finding him." Edward paused to swallow some beer. "That tastes good. The gym smelled like old socks today."

"*Il faut souffrire pour être beau.* Is Hilary still away?"

"Until Tuesday. Keith has told me at least three dirty jokes; they keep popping out as if he had Tourette's. And we had a budget meeting this afternoon."

"No wonder you want to feed MPs to the crocs."

"And just to make the day complete, there was the affair of the pen. Have I told you about Nick Bertuca's pen?"

"What pen?"

"He won it in a shooting competition last month. The cap is a copper—a little bobby in a helmet with a light on it. Bertuca never writes with it, he just likes to show it off. Someone borrowed the pen and forgot to return it, and Bertuca over-reacted. A storm in a teacup, but we're all feeling the heat. Bertuca's plump, and he turns bright red when he's upset. Keith said he looked like an apoplectic tomato."

Gillian laughed. "Did he get the pen back?"

"For the moment."

"He should chain it to his desk, like pens at the bank."

"That would be damaging government property. Did you see Charlotte?"

"Yes I did. It made me want to cry."

"What happened?"

"Nothing happened—not today. It's what's happened to her. I was thinking about who she used to be, such a bundle of talent and nerve. A real high-wire act. Now she's fallen off and is lying all broken at the bottom. It makes me sad. Everything she used to love has turned on her—or she's turned on them. Tom, London, her work, the cottage, even Olivia is off in Morocco. Charlotte's all alone."

"Why did she fall?"

"I don't know."

"You must have some idea—you've been friends for a long time."

"So we have, but I'm still mystified. She had everything she said she wanted, once, and I don't think she was truly happy then, either. I don't know why, maybe it goes back to the foster home. Never feeling she was quite secure where she was. But she seemed on top of the world, for a while. Remember those dinner parties? When I think of Charlotte, I think of her in long leather boots driving her TR3 like a rocket and throwing the speeding tickets in the dustbin. Christ, not someone who'd end up sitting alone in a dark room. She made all those programmes—she could talk to anyone! Now she says she's out of the habit."

"She was always mercurial."

"But when she went down she didn't stay down, not until the year her marriage fell apart. Before that.... You're right, though. Even when she was young it must have taken enormous energy to stay up on her high wire, because she was always looking down and seeing an abyss underneath. Maybe she just got tired and let herself fall. But I think there's something else. Something she hasn't told me."

Edward drank some more beer and closed his eyes. The fading pink light of evening gave his skin a rosy tone, as if he'd been to the beach, but Gillian saw how tired he was. Two vertical creases were permanently etched between the dark brows, and there were hollows under the cheekbones. His hair, still thick as a beaver's pelt, glinted gray at the temples. Was it going to work, this decision they'd made? He'd lived alone for twenty years, except for her visits. She'd stayed for months at a time on her sabbaticals, but they'd always known she was leaving again. She'd been a visitor, and now there was a lot of shared territory to negotiate. He'd wanted her to move to London, or he'd never have left the old flat, but it wasn't easy to change bachelor habits, not after twenty years. And now her boxes were here, like a shipload of reality. Not the Titanic, she hoped.

She couldn't picture him settling anywhere else. It was beyond imagination. He'd lived in London his entire life. Theoretically, she should adjust more easily; she'd moved before, and London was familiar. All the same, she felt deracinated, though probably less so than many immigrants or even their children, born in the city but thrashing about in a tumultuous confusion of parental customs and the ways of the West. The city was thronged with lost souls.

Edward was not one of those; he was rooted deep, five generations of Londoners. How would she have felt if he'd moved? Responsible for his happiness to an unreasonable extent. Was that the way he felt? These things weren't necessarily reciprocal. As he was male and English and more interested in concrete realities than wispy inner psychologies, he probably hadn't put the question to himself in quite that way. His solitary fortress had been invaded, but the rest of his life was still intact: he was still in his own city, mere steps from his old flat, and he still had his job, his colleagues. Even his mother was still alive. He'd dared to complain about moving a few hundred yards! The truth was, he didn't know what it was to move—to change cities, countries, continents. He would take her at her word that she wanted to live in London. Where else would one want to be?

He opened his eyes. "What are you going to do? Are you going to visit her again?"

Gillian went to the kitchen for more beer. "If she answers the bloody door. She forgot it was Wednesday and almost didn't let me in today."

They lay on the sheets naked, the fan humming, churning the thick air. London didn't cool off when the sun went down; the stones, the brick, the cement, the asphalt, had absorbed solar energy all day long, and now gave it back to the London night, which throbbed with the roaring, oily breath of a million restaurant kitchens, the toxic farts of the cars, the lights, the air conditioners, the boilers, the cookers, and the computers churning out data around the clock.

Edward slept. Gillian lay awake. At home, in the old house on Salt Hill Road, it would be evening now. Sleepy bird notes, dew on the grass. The house would be locked up tight. In the spring, she'd gone through her mother's clothes, given most of them to the shelter in Newburgh. She'd cleaned up the kitchen, thrown out the gummy jars of chutney and spice jars caked with pale, musty powders. The little bottles of pills, the creams, combs, hairbrush, ossified rolls of adhesive tape, these she'd dealt with easily. And she'd even laughed a little, finding one of her mother's old girdles in a bottom drawer, unworn for forty years. The elastic had crumbled when she picked it up, showering grit on the paper lining the drawer. But she'd left everything else alone. The photographs, the worn cushions, the clutter, they'd stayed. Even the stacks of old *New Yorkers*. She and her brother had agreed that eventually there would be changes, but not now. It wasn't much, but it was something, not to erase Estelle too quickly.

At least Estelle had lived to see the storm windows come down in the spring. It was one of her favourite moments of the year. Gillian lay still, feeling suffocated in the darkness, her throat aching. Both parents gone. It was like standing in a long line that shuffled imperceptibly forward, and now it was suddenly your turn. A door opened into empty space.

There was nowhere to hide. She'd stripped herself of more than possessions. She'd let go of every structure that propped her up: her house, her job, years of habits. Now what? She was supposed to be excited. But she longed to go back home, back to the house she grew up in, back to her own bed where she'd lain awake as a child and heard her parents' voices downstairs.

The next morning, the phone rang. It was Charlotte.

"I just wanted to apologise."

"For what?"

"I was rude. It's the booze that does it. It makes me feel depressed. I hate myself and then I get angry."

"Then what's the point? I mean, if it makes you feel bad?"

"It's worse without. Come and see me. And I want you to see Olivia when she gets back from doing that film. She'll be here in a day or two."

"I'd love to do that. I miss her, Charlotte. It's been ages. We used to take her to the movies, and now she's in them."

"Serves me right," Charlotte said. "Had I but known," she intoned sepulchrally, "when I took her to see *The Red Shoes*...."

"You took her to see everything, didn't you?" Gillian could hear Charlotte blowing cigarette smoke out in a long exhalation.

"Everything I liked." A pause. "Gillian." Charlotte's voice rasped, then she stopped for a small paroxysm of coughing. "You know me. It feels like you've always known me. You know my stories. You know about Beatrice Street, and the first boy I ever had sex with. All the rest of them, for that matter. There haven't been any new ones, not since Thomas."

"The first one, his name was Freddie, right? And you were so scared you'd get pregnant you practically boiled yourself in a bath afterwards."

"See? You know me. That matters, you know?"

"Sure. I'm a historian. The past counts."

"I knew you'd understand. Thomas doesn't, you see. He doesn't look back."

"He's probably too busy. It's the way we live now."

"Do you believe in destiny, Gillian? In fate?"

"You mean everything all mapped out before we're born? No."

"I didn't when I was young. I thought we made our lives ourselves. But now I see that certain things are there, waiting for us, and we can't avoid them."

"Things like what?"

Charlotte didn't answer. "Would you live your life over again?"

"Only if I could fast-forward through the bad bits. Or change them, like Bill Murray in *Groundhog Day*."

"What?"

"The movie," Gillian said.

"I never go to films now."

"A guy has to keep living the same day over and over until he gets it right. He starts off as your basic rat, and ends up more like a golden retriever."

Charlotte gave a rusty chuckle. Gillian heard the sound of a bottle clinking against a glass. "I'd like to make Thomas do that." Then she sighed. "If only we all could do it."

"We're going to the Norfolk coast for a couple of days—borrowing a cottage. If there's a breeze anywhere in the south of England, it'll be there. I'll call you when I get back. We can live our visit over again. I'll stand there and ring the bell, and you can answer before I've rung three times. I won't ask you about your doctor or your diet."

"We'll sit in the garden."

"Lovely."

"When are you leaving for Norfolk?"

"Tonight. We'll have two whole days. Coming back Saturday evening."

"You'll have a long drive."

"Yes, but the flat's so hot that if we stay here, we'll have to sleep in the park. But heat waves never last long in London, do they? I could come and see you Tuesday."

"What's today? Never mind. Tuesday's fine. Any day you like. I'll try to keep track of the calendar."

"Hey, Kev."

He knew that voice. He ignored it. He didn't feel like talking to anybody.

"Kev!"

Tim had a new girl. He usually did. This one had spiky hair and stared at Kevin, her eyes wide, her red mouth moving around and around. She was chewing gum; a stud glittered on her tongue. He could smell perfume.

"Where've you been? Under cover?"

Tim. Always joking. Kevin shrugged. He had nothing to say.

"I've got a new job, mate, selling CDs. Tell you what, come down the shop. I can get a discount for friends." He winked.

"Yeh."

"You don't know Kev, do you?" Tim said to the girl. "His girlfriend's a film star. Right Kev?"

Kevin glared. He'd once mentioned Olivia to Tim, just once, but Tim could never leave it alone. Had to play the bloody comedian.

"What?" The girl laughed. "Who?"

"Katie here reads all about film stars. Her name's Olivia, right, Kev? Olivia Bening, isn't it?"

"Olivia Bening!" the girl screeched. "You're joking. She's in a magazine. She's in *Screen* with Bobby Carr." For half a second she looked at Kevin with awe and then she dismissed him. "You think this is funny, right?" she said to Tim.

"Buy us a pint, Kev?" Tim said.

"Piss off." Kevin walked away. Bastard. What was the name of the magazine? The girl said it. *Screen*? He had to find it immediately. See if Olivia was in it.

The newsagent was suspicious. He didn't like the way the big lout with the crew-cut was drifting aimlessly along the magazine racks. He'd bought a phone card and a packet of cigarettes at the counter, but then he hadn't gone out again. He seemed to have time to kill. One or two cover photos in the sports section caught his attention, but he didn't take anything off the rack. He paused and turned his head casually towards the front of the shop as another customer entered.

What was he looking for? The newsagent wondered about robbery. He kept half an eye on the man, but the shop was busy: someone buying Twix and peppermint gum, then a woman coming in, a regular.

"Hotter than yesterday," she said. "How are you, Charlie?"

The man drifted further, he was scrutinizing the film magazines now, looking at the photograph on the cover of *Screen*. He reached for it, flipping quickly through the pages. As the newsagent bent down, riffling through the stack of reserved papers for the woman's copy of the *Times*, the man slid the magazine under his loose shirt, into the waistband of his trousers.

Out of the corner of his eye, the newsagent caught the blur of movement. He hadn't quite seen it, but he knew what theft looked like and that the man had the magazine under his shirt. He banged the cash register drawer shut.

"Hey mate, put it back," he said. He'd dealt with this sort of nonsense before. He was a short, burly man whose father had run the shop before him, and he had no patience with thieves.

The woman buying the *Times* and a packet of lemon drops turned and stared. The crew-cut man strode towards the front, his long arms swinging.

"Hey," the newsagent said. He lifted the counter flap and stepped forward, moving to block the door. The woman backed away, alarmed. Planting his feet apart, the newsagent thrust his palm out. "The magazine, son," he barked.

The man held up his hands, empty. "No magazine, squire."

The newsagent made a grab for the man's shirt. The man's long arm whipped up and out, shoving him hard in the chest so that he lost his balance and fell against the counter. The woman gasped. The crew-cut man barged through the doorway and out into the street.

"Gracious, Charlie," the woman said shakily. "Are you all right?"

He pulled himself upright, shooting a look of contempt in the direction of the street. "Thieving bastard. Off his nut with pills or something. I hate punks."

A few yards along the pavement, Kevin halted and yanked the copy of *Screen* from the front of his trousers. He stared at the cover. Bobby bloody Carr, in a half-unbuttoned white shirt, teeth gleaming. He flipped open the magazine. Yes, it was her. It was her absolutely. Olivia Bening. There was her picture, she was right next to Bobby Carr. Kevin stood motionless, gripping the pages; people walked around him. The story said she was filming in Morocco. With Bobby Carr. Morocco. It wasn't true. He breathed hoarsely; the pages crumpled under the pressure of his fingers. He slammed them shut and went to find a phone.

2

Olivia woke at nine o'clock on Saturday morning, wondering where she was. Raymond's flat. Pleased, she fell asleep again until nearly noon. When she woke the second time, she was hot and thirsty. She climbed out of bed, stretched luxuriously and walked to the kitchen, where she stood naked in front of the open door of the fridge, feeling the cool air on her body and drinking orange juice straight from the carton, a thing she could do because Raymond was away.

London. Heaven. No dust, no staring men, the camels in the zoo where they belonged. A river outside the windows, instead of the desert. Home. The past seventeen days hadn't been *Apocalypse Now*, but they'd been the hardest and most uncomfortable work she'd ever done. Everyone on the set had complained. Had she been any good? Sometimes she knew, but *Rough Diamonds* was Bobby Carr's picture, a laddish comedy, not like anything she'd done before.

She'd been so tired when she got off the plane Friday evening, she hadn't called anybody. Only Wanda, her trainer, to leave a message confirming an appointment for this afternoon. Wanda the Cruel, who would see instantly that she'd abandoned her routine, and who would say: do you want to look like a flabby-arsed shopgirl? A dismal truth: if you worked out constantly, you could tell the difference right away when you stopped. Olivia had looked like a racehorse at the beginning of the shoot, but not now. She would tell Wanda about the heat and the dust and the broken air conditioning in the hotel, and the plumbing that left her stranded under a drip with her hair full of shampoo. You shouldn't expect a lot of water in the desert, but if you saw a showerhead, you did think water would come out of it.

Olivia wandered back to the bedroom to find her phone. She cradled it lovingly in her palm. For two weeks, she hadn't been able to use it; in the desert they were beyond the blanket, or the net, whatever it was called; they were on a planet where mobiles didn't work. She rang Nicky.

"Nicky, it's me. I'm back."

"You're in London? Brilliant. Guess what, sweetie? While you've been rubbing shoulders with the famous Bobby Carr, I've found a perfect location for the squat in Acton. Sheila's ecstatic—four filthy mattresses in it already, so she doesn't have to round them up in her van. The landlord's letting me have the house for a hundred quid and a line in the credits, so we're doing set dec all day Wednesday. I've been going mad for weeks. Why did I want to do this film? Remind me. How was the desert?"

"I can't wait to curl up on a pee-stained mattress in Acton."

"Must have been fabulous."

"I learned a lot. Including how everyone really smells."

"Good training for the squat. Seriously, what was it like?"

"Hot. Seriously, think of dust—in the camera, in your eyes, in your hair. Mine was like broomstraw the whole time. If I made a film about the desert, it would be called 'Dust'. I drank water all day long, and my throat was always dry. I probably sound like I've had a tracheotomy."

"You're a little raspy. Did you smoke?"

"Not one. I'm still pure."

"You're my idol."

"Yeh, yeh. You don't even *want* to quit."

"But I admire your will-power. It's gotten you where you are today—working for me."

"You promised you'd make me rich and famous."

"I lied. How was Bobby?"

"He's a hard-working peacock. You never saw such feathers."

"The audience loves that tail. Daft buggers. What about the shooting schedule? When are you finished?"

"Three more days, here in London. Then I'm all yours."

"Are you free Monday night? I want you to know what I've been thinking. I'm up to my ears, mind. What about a rehearsal Wednesday evening? A run through?"

"Fine."

"Olivia, you know what's good about having too much to do?"

"You're too busy to get nervous."

"Exactly."

Is Martin being nice to you?"

"I haven't had a minute to see him. This is Nicky the writer-director-producer. No time for men. Not like you, lolling about in the desert with Bobby Carr."

Olivia laughed. "Nicky, I've missed you."

"Me too. Are you at Raymond's?"

"Yes, it's like the Savoy, after the desert. I look out at the river and London's paradise. My only problem is Kevin. Oh Nicky, I know it's silly, but when I got off the plane I actually looked for him at the airport. I was pushing my cart along, going towards the doors, the ones you go through and everyone's out there waiting for the passengers? I didn't want to go out. He could be there, I thought. I almost had a panic attack."

"Hey, if a nutter was after me, I'd want a couple of bodyguards with Uzis. Is Raymond back? Are you okay in the flat?"

"I only got in last night. He's still away, but I feel safe here on my own. Better than in Bayswater, anyhow. And I'm not planning to stay here very long."

"Good luck. Flat-hunting is murder. Has Lisa seen Kevin since you left? Like, lurking in the coffee bar?"

"Bibi doesn't let him lurk in there. I don't know what's been happening; I don't want to. It was such a relief not to think about him when I was away."

"Yeh. Well, better ask Lisa. And be careful. You're my star."

"Your unpaid slave."

"You can afford it this week."

"Yes, isn't it fabulous? Nicky, I actually have some money in my bank account!"

"Oooh, darling! Can you spare twenty-five thousand quid?"

Olivia stood under the shower and scrubbed herself all over with a brush, as if some of Morocco's dust might still be lurking in her pores. The jets of water cascaded through her hair and ran deliciously down her back. It was a miraculous luxury, water that kept coming and stayed at the same pressure and temperature. She hadn't had that in her own flat; she and Lisa always had to take baths.

The desert would probably look magical in the film: blue skies and rippling dunes, pink and gold light. Bollocks. The audience wouldn't smell the camels, or breathe the parched air; they wouldn't feel the dust coating their throats and the insides of their eyelids, or see the ugly, flat baked earth stretching for miles around the little town. The water in the hotel swimming pool had been so cloudy with algae that she couldn't see the bottom. She'd liked the coffee and the fresh figs for breakfast, but outside, wherever she went, there were skinny, staring little men, watching and watching. You'd think they'd never seen a blonde before. She couldn't go anywhere alone, or they'd walk up behind her and grab her bottom. And where were the women? Locked up, probably, you didn't see many of them.

Reluctantly, she shut off the flow of water and reached for a towel. Every shoot, she'd decided in the desert, was its own version of collective insanity. When you signed, it was like volunteering for the Foreign Legion.

Now she took inventory in the mirror, looking for damage. 'Item, two lips indifferent red; item, two grey eyes, with lids to them; item, one neck, one chin, and so forth.' Charlotte had repeated this to her so often after her evening bath when she was a child that she automatically thought of it after nearly every bath or shower. Her eyes were grey, in fact, and heavy-lidded, and the part of herself she liked best was her neck, which was long, like Audrey Hepburn's.

When had she last trekked out to Fulham? More than a month ago. She seldom let that many weeks slip by, but she wasn't usually away from London for long. She would ring today, but she wouldn't visit. Afternoons weren't the best time of day, unless Charlotte knew in advance. After *Rough Diamonds* was finished on Tuesday, she could go. Olivia sighed, thinking of the dark house and of her mother waiting for the telephone to ring. What sort of humour would she be in? Sometimes seeing her was all right. On other days it was painful and depressing. This time, Olivia would have stories to tell about the desert; Charlotte would be happy she was back, would be wry and interested. She might not even slag the film, the way she had last time. If she wasn't in one of her black moods, when she saw everything as a catastrophe, they might have a good giggle about Bobby Carr and his twig tea. As long as she didn't get on to Daddy and Sibyl. Then it would feel like the quicksand scenes in old movies, with Charlotte sinking and Olivia lying on the heaving earth, trying to pull her out.

Olivia rubbed cream all over her body and then picked her phone up and dialled her mother's number. She got the answering machine. "Hello Mummy," she said, and was cut off. Jesus, she thought. Why doesn't she get one that works? She was probably sleeping now. It was better to try her in the mornings.

Another assessment in the mirror, and then she lifted a magnifying glass out of her case and examined her face for lines. She'd used enough sunscreen to fill a bathtub; it had become a running joke that the pool was cloudy because she'd filled it with number thirty and swam in it every morning. She was not, in her view, neurotic about her body. She didn't go on mad little diets, or smoke to stay thin, or stand in front of the mirror for a half-hour at a time, criticizing parts of her anatomy. Not like Lisa, her former flatmate, who had even had a week of hating her elbows.

But she looked for damage. The sun had been so strong, it was hard to believe that any amount of screen was enough. She'd had to do that scene at the oasis, where she was alone and bathed herself. The water felt good, but after three takes she'd been desperate to be finished; she'd imagined her smooth white breasts turning freckled and lizardy after about five minutes of exposure. 'These are perishable assets!' she'd wanted to shriek. The cameras devoured her clear, luminous skin; directors and producers responded; they saw her image on screen and liked her cheekbones, her eyes, her neck. The body helped, too: her long, smooth legs, trained, toned, nice swell of calf muscle above the ankle, arse looked good in whatever she wore. They'd like the breasts, when they saw them. High white breasts like two plump birds. 'The package,' Wilder, her agent, called it, her ice-queen blonde look. But Wilder said it with an ironic inflection that she liked. It was conspiratorial, offering a shared understanding of the world, in which 'the package' was not what mattered. You have to be aware of this, the inflection said, but we both know it's not why you're here. She trusted Wilder; he was her stroke of good luck. Everyone needed luck, whatever talent they had.

'The package' had gotten her the part in Bobby's film. They'd seen her film clips, they knew she could do the part, but so could other actresses. They'd chosen her for her particular look, a 'pure' quality that they thought was a visual fit for the role. She had a short window when roles would come her way for that reason, when her looks might help launch her talent, give her more chances to be noticed. She hoped so, anyhow, though in Bobby's film it made her feel as if her body was like an expensive piece of furniture she owned and rented out as set dec. But Nicky didn't give a monkey's, and in Nicky's film she wasn't going to play a beauty.

She heard a buzzing sound. The entry phone. Who? It was too early for Wanda and no one else knew she was here. She stood still, listening apprehensively. Kevin? How could he have found her? She'd only arrived last night. Throwing on a dressing gown, she hurried to look at the video screen mounted in the wall beside the entrance to the flat. In her mind, she saw the round, close-shaven head and hulking shoulders she'd been watching for at the airport. The buzzer sounded a second time.

"Please let it not be him," she prayed, her stomach knotting. If it was, she wouldn't answer, but then what?

The screen showed no one at all, just a section of the empty pavement four stories below. She realised it was the porter at the front desk who was buzzing.

"Hello?" she said into the intercom.

"Miss Bening? A parcel was delivered earlier; I have it for you at the desk."

"Who sent it?" Her voice was sharper than she meant it to be.

"I'll just have a look." He turned away from the video screen, and she could see him pick up a thick, flat envelope. Not flowers, then, but Kevin had also tried chocolates. The porter came back.

"It says here, Sampson and Penn."

The parcel was from Wilder. A script. Oh thank God. "I'll come down and pick it up in a few minutes," she answered, weak with relief. She breathed slowly in and out to calm herself. It was not from him, not from Kevin; she'd been silly to be so nervous. He couldn't know where she was; surely he believed she was still living at Lisa's, even if he hadn't seen her recently. Why not, since her answering machine was still receiving messages there, and she'd only taken three suitcases with her? She'd told Lisa she'd pay her share of the rent until she found a flat of her own and could move her things into it. For the hundredth time, she thought about the day Kevin talked to her in the coffee bar and wished she could replay that morning and edit out the minutes in the Chagga. But would anything have turned out differently if she hadn't stopped in on that particular day? Probably not. Kevin would have been waiting for her the next time, or the time after that.

She dressed and combed her wet hair and took the lift down to the lobby.

"Sorry, Mr. Field, I'm a bit jumpy about parcels," she said to the porter. "There's a man who's been bothering me—he sends things. Flowers, mostly," she added.

"You don't like flowers?" he said, puzzled. "There are no flowers, miss."

She went back up to the flat. Lisa would know whether Kevin was still hanging about in Bayswater or whether his pattern had changed, but Olivia didn't want to ask her yet. She would ring Lisa in a little while.

The parcel. Her next part could be inside it. She ripped the envelope open and read the note from Wilder. Something about *Rough Diamonds* and the piece in the current issue of *Screen*. He'd enclosed a copy. The piece was about Bobby Carr, of course, he was on the cover. But she was in the article. With a photo. Olivia snatched up the magazine, flipped it open and scrutinised her photograph. It wasn't very large, but it looked okay. And, oh, there was another, a bigger one of her and Bobby. She'd been mentioned in reviews before, her picture had been printed, but she'd never been in a glossy piece about the making of a film.

She rang Nicky back. "Hey, I'm in *Screen*, with photos. I want a percentage of the gross."

Nicky laughed. "You can have a percentage of anything gross you want—try my fridge."

The enclosed script was about Byron. That could be interesting, and there ought to be juicy roles for women. The casting director was thinking of her for Teresa. A minor role. Who was she, Olivia wondered. Mummy would know; she always knew things like that. In the note Wilder said there was another period piece in the pipeline as well, a television movie about a family inheritance. That meant big houses and lawns. Horses, probably. They'd be a step up from camels. He hadn't read the script, just a synopsis. Charlotte would be happy—she'd like seeing her daughter in hats and gloves, in Merchant-Ivoryish elegance. There would be a conflict between love and money, Olivia guessed. What else? If she had to kiss anybody in a conservatory, though, it wouldn't be Bobby Carr. Olivia grinned to herself. It was inconceivable that any director would cast Bobby in a costume picture. He'd be about as convincing as ye olde Tudor pub with plastic oak beams.

He was good at what he did, though, and he had fans. Enough totty for a pig to roll in. It hung about in hotel lobbies hoping to jump him. What did he do with all those girls? Probably flexed his pecs in front of the mirror while they watched. She knew that if Bobby had said no, she wouldn't have gotten the part. He wasn't a huge star, but on the set the hierarchy was blatant. What was it like to be a bankable star—not to wait and hope for chances to act, but to have the best scripts sent to you? You'd pick and choose. There would be films with great directors and actors, the ones you'd die to watch when they were working. A dream, she thought, and as far away as the moon from where she was now. Reality at this moment was a part in Bobby's film. She certainly hadn't longed to see Bobby Carr at work, though he had something on screen that drew the audience. Never mind. She had the kiss scene to get through, but it shouldn't be a problem. She wouldn't enjoy it, but she'd do the shot as often as they wanted. She would be technical and inwardly remote, at the edge of the universe, too far away for a big telescope to find her. She'd done kiss scenes. She would let her eyes look limpid, her mouth go soft and blurry, while she did the multiplication tables.

Coffee, that was what she wanted. She'd been about to put the kettle on when the buzzer made her jump out of her skin.

While she waited for the water to boil, she looked at her diary. The tunnel, tomorrow. On Monday, they would do the scene when she went through British customs carrying the diamonds, and the kiss. Then, on Tuesday, there was only the bit in the alley. At some point, she'd have to dub her own voice over the footage in the souk where they'd had problems with the sound, but that would happen later. So Tuesday would be her last day of real work on *Rough Diamonds*. Wednesday, a meeting with Wilder. And on Thursday, her first day on Nicky's film. Nicky would be over the moon, finally in production after months of planning and more than a year of relentless wooing for funds, which she described as a cross between converting the heathen and selling shares in a swamp. It was almost a joke, how different Nicky's film would be from Bobby's. No budget, no stars, just an intense fifteen-minute black and white short from a script Nicky had written based on her dead half-sister. Olivia badly wanted to do it; she could taste the part. And the timing was perfect; she could afford to work for nothing. It would be one of those mouldy-sofa, cold-pizza shoots; she would know everyone on the set, she thought happily.

Wanda came promptly at three; she worked through a series of stretches and invented a new routine for Olivia to torture herself with for the next month. When she'd gone away again, Olivia sluiced off in the shower once more, ate a container of non-fat yoghurt and finished off the orange juice. Then she took her mobile out to the balcony and rang Lisa.

"Olivia? Where are you? Are you back?"

"Yeh, back where there are phones and running water."

"Brilliant. But isn't it hot? I'm losing weight just sitting here. And you know what I had to do this week? Furs. Full-length mink coats. It made me nearly die of heatstroke just to look at them. They wanted me to jump. Like so the fur swishes about? Do you have any idea how heavy a goddam mink coat is? The photographer goes, 'Look weightless, luv, like you're in outer space.' He's *from* outer space. He gets on my tits. The furs were awesome, though. I'd love to wear one when I go out with Johnny. In the winter, of course."

"Oh, furs, right. Lisa, you know you don't want them. Traps are cruel, and you'd be sprayed with red paint. So you're still going out with him?"

"Yeh. I'm seeing him tonight. Nothing's changed—it's like before you left. We'll go, we'll have a fabulous time, then he won't ring me for two weeks. Sometimes when I look at my phone and it's not ringing, I want to kill it. I could choke it to death."

"Then you should go out with someone else."

"I know, I know."

"You're gorgeous and you're fun. There'd be blokes queueing up." Olivia stopped, conscious of having said almost the same words before she'd moved out of their shared flat.

"I'm gorgeous and I'm stupid. If you'd ever met him, you'd know why."

"If I met him, I'd tell him to treat you better."

"He treats me fine," Lisa said, snickering. "That's the problem. I read my horoscope for this week, and it says it's a good time for love if you're a Gemini. Maybe my luck will change."

"It says that every time you read it."

"It does not. You want to know about Libra?"

"Only if it says that I'm going to sign a contract to be in the next Stephen Frears film."

"Then I won't tell you. You think it's rubbish, anyway. How's Raymond?"

"He's not here."

"God, Olivia. The man lives on airplanes. He should buy one, instead of a building."

"We're going to meet in Paris next week."

"Blimey. Three days of mad passion between flights, huh? Maybe *you* should go out with someone else."

"But I don't want to strangle my phone. Lisa, listen. I've got to know about Kevin. Have you seen him?"

"I haven't seen him, but I know he's been around. The roses."

"When?"

"The last one was on Wednesday."

"I thought he'd sent me a parcel here, but it was a false alarm. What about the phone?"

"God. He's been driving me bonkers. Silly bugger. Yesterday there were like ten calls in a row. Sorry, Olivia, but I have to tell you. I got brassed off. I picked up the phone and told him to give it a goddam rest because you were away on location. It was weird. He started screaming at me. He wanted to know when you'd be back. Of course I wouldn't tell him, so then he called me a bitch. I said he could sod off because you weren't going to live here any more, you were moving in with your boyfriend. I thought that would make him chill out."

"Oh God, Lisa, why did you do that? What if he finds out where I am?"

"How would he?"

"I don't know, but you shouldn't have talked to him. The police said not to."

"They said for *you* not to."

"But I wanted him to think I was living there, so he wouldn't try to find me."

"Right, right. I'm sorry, luv. I blew up. I think it worked, though, telling him off—he's stopped ringing."

"He scares me."

"Yeh, but didn't the police say he was just a geek?"

"They said he was probably harmless, but it's not them he follows to the tube station, is it? If you see him, or he calls again, *please* ring me right away. Okay?"

"Yeh, of course I will. How was your shoot?"

"Like jumping up and down in a fur coat for weeks."

"Did Bobby Carr try to shag you?"

"No, I was in luck. He brought a personal assistant with a suitcase full of lace knickers and kneepads."

Lisa giggled. "Olivia! I thought the desert was supposed to be romantic."

"Huh. The dunes are beautiful, but I worked like a dog. Oh God, you wouldn't have believed it. The pool at the hotel—there was green slime floating in it. The camels spit, there's dust in your hair and men everywhere trying to crawl up your skirt."

"Sounds like half the clubs in London. Listen, why don't you come tonight? There's four or five of us already. You haven't been to a club in months. Come and have a good time."

Olivia hesitated. She deserved an evening out, no question. She'd been working non-stop for more than a fortnight, and tomorrow she'd be on another long shift. A sensible person would stay home and go to bed, but you couldn't be sensible all the time. She hadn't seen Lisa in weeks. Besides, she was curious. Lisa said it was fun to go clubbing with Johnny. Everyone paid attention, the doormen, the bartenders, the women. Olivia knew how that felt: like walking a path across a set, aware that the camera was tracking you, keeping you in the centre of the frame. She'd only glimpsed Johnny from the window once, by chance, in his white car, when he'd been dropping Lisa off in the morning. He didn't come into the flat, or never had when she was home. "But I'm working tomorrow," she said, temporising.

"Come on," Lisa said. "You're so focused you're going to go cross-eyed. We're having dinner and then we'll go to the Paradise."

That was the club Johnny owned, Olivia remembered. She would love to go out, she would really feel she was back in London. Besides, Raymond never went to clubs; he said the music was too loud. "Won't it be too hot to dance?" she said, weakening.

"Zombie Kiss is playing."

"Ooh. Zombie Kiss? Yeh, okay, I'll meet you. But don't be cross with me if I don't stay out late."

"Do you want Johnny to bring a date for you?"

"Whatever. But I've got a boyfriend, so if he brings somebody for me, he shouldn't think I'm available. Like I'm not dating—I'm just going out."

"Fine. Don't get your knickers in a knot."

Olivia took the phone out to the balcony and sat under the umbrella looking at the river and doing nothing. It was bliss to have Raymond's flat to herself, the big bed and the shower like Niagara Falls. She would see him in Paris next week; that would be soon enough. Perhaps she ought to miss him more, but he was often away from London, and she was used to it. For her part, she preferred this intermittent pattern. They never discussed their relationship; it had no big ups and downs. Whenever Olivia listened to Nicky, whose love life made her think of crash test dummies, she was relieved to be where she was.

Not that the affair was free of stress. When Raymond was in London, and they went out, he liked to show her off. He was exacting, in his way; he wanted life to be streamlined and elegant, like his designs. He said her looks were flawless, and he expected polished behaviour to match. From the outside, their affair probably looked like another performance: Olivia as trophy, Raymond as man of discriminating tastes. It wasn't true; Raymond wasn't a heartless egotist, he was in fact very nice. Also witty, considerate, and expressive when he chose to be. When he talked about things or places he loved, like Vienna, she felt a warm affection for him that made up for the other times when she felt distant and lonely. Even so, she couldn't imagine living with him, now or ever. Raymond never saw her in an old T-shirt eating crisps out of a packet, and his taste in films was too austere. Besides, sharing a flat with him would mean sharing the same bed every night when they were both in London. The thought of it made her want to bolt.

Bed. Now that was a performance: acting, simulating a pleasure that was calibrated to his. It wasn't that she disliked sex with Raymond, it was all right, though sometimes she forgot to pay attention and started thinking of something else. She never particularly wanted it. He needed more than passivity from her, though, and she obliged. She'd done it before. Her other boyfriend had had the same need, and he was shaggy and silent and only twenty-five, while Raymond was thirty-eight and never at a loss for words, so men could be very different and still be the same about that. Better than the other ways they could be, the ones who didn't take any notice of how women felt, or wanted to hurt them. Raymond treated her with respect, he was generous, he never complained about her erratic schedule. When Nicky asked her whether she loved him, she said she was fond of him and Nicky groaned. But she felt safe when she was with him, and she liked being in the middle of a relationship; beginnings were tense and endings were sad.

Olivia scratched her bare ankle and shifted her thoughts to buying new shoes. Perhaps in Paris. It was lovely to have a bit of money for a change. So much more than she'd ever been paid before. But could she afford to spend it? After Nicky's film, she had nothing but tantalising possibilities and one little contract in September. She might have no work that paid well, or paid at all, for weeks, or even months. On location, it had felt as though they'd be working forever, but unemployment was close, only a few days away. She had her rent money in the bank, a big improvement, but still.

In the evening, she spent a long time choosing which dress and shoes to wear and putting on her minimal make-up. You never knew who might be at the next table. She had a little white silk dress with spaghetti straps, dead simple, the one she'd worn for her last set of publicity shots. When she looked out at the city, her mood grew sparkly, like the lights across the river. London on Saturday night was like one big fabulous club, everyone dressed up in their costumes, hopping in and out of taxis, dancing and drinking and forgetting who they were all week.

Then it was time to leave, and she was nervous about going out alone. Before she opened the door of the flat, she checked the video monitor. Her fright over the package had been a waste of time; it wasn't likely that Kevin had discovered where she was. But he must know by now where she'd been on location—he'd only have had to pick up a copy of *Screen* to find out. He might well be aware that the crew had packed up and returned to London. Anyone could get their hands on that kind of information. He might even be able to identify Raymond, if he knew how to search. She and Raymond had been photographed at openings and wrap parties a few times, and their names had been linked in print.

If only Lisa hadn't said anything about moving, or a boyfriend. But Lisa was like that: she lost her temper and was sorry afterwards. It would be wonderful, though, if she was right, if what she'd said made Kevin go away. He was only a fan, Olivia supposed, spying on her and pretending he knew her. But buying all those roses and leaving them about, and filling the tape on the answering machine with his horrible breathing and mumbled messages! She shivered in the warm summer air. She never knew what he was saying. The few audible words were like stray fragments of a bad dream.

Resentfully, Olivia plotted her exit from Raymond's flat. Going out ought to be simple: take the lift, cross the lobby, and walk through the courtyard to the street. The road was a busy one; scouting for a taxi wouldn't be like standing under Blackfriars Bridge waiting for Jack the Ripper. The porter kept an eye on the courtyard. But she was still nervous. If Lisa was wrong, Kevin would be trying to find her. From tonight, she would have to be watchful every time she went in and out. She rang for a taxi, locked the doors to the balcony and went down in the lift. In the lobby, she hesitated, looking out at the shadowy arch that led to the street. Then she crossed to the front desk and waited with the porter, impatient for release. The traffic crawled, and when the taxi at last arrived, she fairly leapt into it. London wheeled past the windows. She was extraordinarily happy to be out.

The Norfolk coast had been lovely, actually cool, with a breeze off the water that let them sleep at night. Not until they had crossed the M25 and were burrowing into the heart of London did Edward flick the button to activate his phone.

"On the leash again," he said. It beeped almost immediately.

"That must be Big Brother," Gillian murmured. They'd read and walked and admired expanses of sea and sky and rippling grasses, looked at bits of coast that were like paintings by Crome. Did she want to own a cottage? They wouldn't have many weekends, not with Edward's schedule. There would be plumbing and the roof to fuss about. But her memories of weekends at Charlotte's cottage were tempting. Charlotte's cottage was in Hampshire, lovely country. Possibly they could rent it, if her current tenant ever decided to leave. It was tiny; it couldn't be too expensive. A kitchen and a parlour downstairs and two small bedrooms up. That was all, except for the loo tacked on to the back. There was a hedge, and a little gate, and Charlotte had planted a vegetable garden. The garden might be gone by now, of course. Around it were open fields, and hedgerows, and a barn in the distance. A farmer kept cows in the pasture across the road—Jersey cows with huge brown eyes and thick lashes. They'd sometimes had cream and hand-churned butter from the farm. There'd been no central heating, and in winter you crawled into bed under twenty pounds of wool blankets. It was at

Charlotte's cottage that Gillian had had her only experience of sleeping on a straw mattress. The bedsprings were shot, and the straw prickled through the sheet as she sank towards the floor. It was like sleeping in a bird's nest. How long ago it seemed. It was too bad about the house next door. The view had been so unspoilt.

Edward was still on the phone. The traffic was heavy, as she'd known it would be. She wasn't used to driving on the left, and her hands and shoulders were tired from gripping the wheel too tightly. The light was slowly fading, the sky turning a violet pink. It would have been nice to have another day, but the owners had arrived as arranged, loaded with food, bright plastic toys, and numerous grandchildren. She and Edward had driven away after tea.

"I'll have to leave early Tuesday morning," Edward said.

"I thought your meeting was on Wednesday."

"It is, but I've got to go to Liverpool first. They're holding a man there we've been after for months."

"What's he done?"

"They've nobbled him for importing a load of heroin from Afghanistan via Turkey and Bulgaria, and we want him for using a machine-gun to express his dissatisfaction with a former business partner. He skipped the country—wasn't here legally in the first place—but he's come back."

"A machine-gun? It sounds like *The Godfather*."

"London's chock-a-block with guns. All sorts. Armed robberies used to be rare. Now we have them every day. Guns and drugs, guns and drugs. Keith says London's turning into the Bronx."

They paused, caught in a clot of traffic. The sun glared on the windows and the shiny curves of the cars. Gillian's skin was salty with sweat.

"Not the Bronx. Miami." A man was walking along with no shirt on. Through her sunglasses he looked almost purple.

"That reminds me," Edward said. "What happened to all that malaria? Why don't we have it any more?"

"Drainage, mainly. DDT. You're coming back Thursday night?"

"I hope so."

"I'm having dinner with your mother on Wednesday."

They crossed the Holloway Road. Gillian glanced at Edward. He was frowning. She went back to scanning the traffic. "You're thinking about Mrs. Wayland, aren't you?"

"The Holloway Road always reminds me. I must have told you that. It's odd, the way some cases stay with you forever. You dream about them. Others, like that Soho file we just closed, are all in a day's work. You don't forget, but they don't follow you about."

"From what you said, Soho will be better off without that landlord."

"He'll be replaced. His sort always is." Edward swatted the air. "Like fruit flies around fruit."

"Who sent you? To tell Mrs. Wayland that her son had been murdered, I mean."

"Sandy Ross, the Detective Sergeant. He's retired now. He was in a tank at the Battle of the Bulge and he liked to call any villain he was after 'the Hun'. So far as he was concerned, murder was just a fact of life. Albert Jones killed Jimmie Wayland—stabbed him to death in an argument over money. A quid. That was that. But I was young, and it was a shock. Did I never tell you? It was in the toilets at the back of a pool hall, and there was a lake of blood in the urinals. I can still see it. And I can remember Ross barking at me, 'A quid, laddie? I've seen people killed for tuppence. For nothing. For Happy Christmas.'"

Gillian braked. Horns were honking. A boy wearing earphones wove across the street, oblivious of the traffic. "Happy Christmas?"

"Ross had a case once, the victim said 'Happy Christmas' in the wrong tone of voice and was pushed out of a window. But Albert and Jimmie, they were a lovely pair of louts. They'd both been up on assault charges before. It was nothing out of the way—they don't haunt me. It's Mrs. Wayland: I didn't know how to face her. I'd never had to do anything like that before. It didn't seem possible to say to anyone's mother, 'It's my unfortunate duty to'—and so on. I tried to recite it to myself on the way, and my voice dried up. When I got to the front door, I was so nervous I could hardly ring the bell. Then Mrs. Wayland came, and she looked at me and she *knew*. I didn't have to say a word. She said, 'He's dead, isn't he?' I just nodded. Then she said, 'I knew it,' and she turned and walked away. Her eyes went blank, like a sleepwalker's."

"Maybe Ross shouldn't have sent you."

"Oh, Ross was all right; he taught me a lot. He was a talker, a theoretician. Opinions about everything." Edward laughed. "The Wayland murder happened three days before Christmas. Ross had a theory that Christmas was a bad time of year for the police. As soon as the decorations went up in the shops, he'd be in the pulpit about it. He hated giving anyone Christmas leave; he thought we needed every man, because people were crazier at Christmastime. More unpredictable, more violent. He had a hundred stories to prove it. The Wayland case was more grist for his mill."

"I think summer's worse than Christmas. I always feel more homicidal in the heat."

"Do you have anyone in mind?"

"Right now? The man in front of me. He's making an illegal right turn and I'm going to miss the light. Pass me the Glock, would you?"

The taxi set Olivia down outside the Roma at eight. Afterwards, when she remembered her arrival, she would always see it like a scene in a movie, a visual sequence with a soundtrack of street noise.

> *First, a long shot as she steps out of the taxi and it pulls away. There's an awning over the entrance to the restaurant. She sees a man standing under it, casually scanning*

the street. He's dark and beautiful, like a figure from mythology set down in her path. Dark suit, dark hair, olive skin. He drops the end of a cigarette, grinds it out under his heel. The camera zooms towards him. She steps onto the pavement and he sees her. He stands absolutely still; she almost has to ask him to move so she can get to the door. But at the last moment he steps aside and opens the door for her. She looks up, and his face fills the frame. The eyes, set wide apart, deep brown. They meet her gaze, and hold it, and she's suddenly not breathing. Everything stops. It feels like the time she was ten years old and lightning hit the cottage, running down a tree and back up through the floor in a single second, setting a mattress on fire and bouncing cups off the shelves. The traffic's roar fades, she's going deaf. When she was ten, she went deaf for two days, but now she recovers in a few seconds. The sound, the action start up again. He's a stranger, so she doesn't speak to him. She walks past him into the restaurant as if nothing has happened.

The room was large, full of noise and bustle. A plump man in a dinner jacket was in charge, greeting another pair of diners, so she halted, waiting her turn. The man with the brown eyes, who'd come into the restaurant behind her, caught up. He stopped beside her and smiled. Her blood was still racing; her feet felt light on the ground. She was startled by her own elation.

"I'm glad I wasn't driving a minute ago," he said. "I would have hit something." He had a Londoner's twang in his speech, nothing mythological about it.

At that moment, the plump man turned to them. "Hey," he boomed, his face splitting in a grin. "Gina said you came to see her yesterday. She was thrilled." He surged forward and embraced the brown-eyed man, kissing him on both cheeks.

"Gina's my girl," brown-eyes said.

The other man looked happy. "She's going to be fine, she'll be home in two days."

"That's brilliant, Tony." Brown-eyes clapped the plump man on the shoulder.

"And she's hungry. I brought her a beautiful dinner tonight," Tony went on. "Your table is ready, I'll take you myself," he announced, his smile including Olivia now, as though she and the beautiful brown-eyed man were of course dining together.

"Erm," Olivia began, her heartbeat revving, but she had no chance to speak. The door opened, and Lisa, all long legs and glittering tank top, sailed rapidly through.

"Johnn-ee!" she yelped, and gave the man with the brown eyes a kiss. "Olivia! You're here, you've already met. Brilliant."

"Sort of," Olivia said.

Lisa hugged her.

"I brought you a present." Olivia dug in her bag. "You can open it later."

"Ooh, you are sweet."

"Two beauties," Tony said to Johnny. "I don't know how you do it."

Olivia stiffened. Nudge, nudge, wink, wink. Stupid remark. Oh God. She had to pretend everything was fine. And Gina, who was Gina?

"Shut up, Tony," Johnny said amiably.

They followed Tony past a table loaded with flowers and fruit to the far side of the room, where another couple was already seated. Lisa squeezed Olivia's arm, rattled off names and information before they got there: Olivia had met Rachel before; she was another friend of Lisa's; her date had some business connection to Johnny. Olivia was too preoccupied to pay attention. Then the wine waiter brought a bottle of champagne to the table, on the house, he said. He opened the bottle and poured. "Tony's celebrating," he said. "The doctors said Gina's going to be fine."

"Is that Tony's little girl?" Lisa asked.

"Yeh," Johnny said. "She was hit by a car two days ago."

"Oh! Poor thing."

"Tony says she's all right." They drank to Gina, and Olivia felt her eyes moisten, although she'd only heard Gina's name and didn't even know how old she was. Some Italian opera or other was playing in the background. Olivia had hardly ever listened to opera, but now the voices pierced her, through the clatter of the restaurant. She recovered her poise gradually. Later, she could remember the food and the music but hardly any of the conversation, only a great deal of banter and a jumble of fragments—stories about bands and clubs, the wiles of music promoters, the trick cyclists and snake charmers she'd seen in the square at Marrakesh. If the moment outside the restaurant had had any effect on Johnny, it didn't show. Only once when their eyes met did she see something beneath the surface, but she looked away quickly. He treated Lisa in a friendly, rather than a romantic way, and Lisa seemed not to find anything unusual in this. She was in a frolicsome mood and drank a lot of champagne. They ate salad and then pasta, and Tony stopped again to ask how they liked the food. Despite her overheated emotions, Olivia was hungry and the squash ravioli tasted divine.

"I wish I could have dinner here every night," she said happily.

"You'd get fat," Rachel said. "Wait till you see the trolley."

Johnny grinned and Lisa tossed her syrup-gold curls at him.

"Johnny comes here all the time," she murmured, after Tony had moved on. "I said we should try a new Italian place I heard about, and he goes, 'No. Tony would be insulted.' I mean, really. How would Tony know?"

Later, they walked a short distance through thronged streets to the Paradise Club. A huge neon palm tree was mounted on the dark brick outside. Before they reached the door, Olivia could hear the music pulsing in the night air.

There was a queue outside, but they sauntered past it like diplomats going through customs.

The club was already crowded. An enormous vine twined over the entrance, hung with silvery pinpoints of light. The band was playing on an island in the centre of the big room, a turbulent surf of dancers rising and falling around it. Lisa instantly saw several friends and announced she would find Olivia someone to dance with.

"Would you like a drink first?" Johnny asked.

"No, we want to dance," Lisa said pertly. "You can go be a club owner now. I know the drill."

"Fine. I'll be at the bar if you're thirsty." He moved away, through the crowd.

Lisa was already waving to her friends. "He'll have to talk to the bartenders and the doormen, and half the blokes at the bar will want to have a word, blah, blah, blah, and we won't see him for half an hour." She ran her eye over the men at the bar. "And Max is here, so it'll take longer."

Olivia's eyes followed Johnny. "Who's Max?"

"The big bloke near the end there, with the girl in the green top."

"Him? God, he looks like a Picasso." It was because his eyes were set askew: one slanted downwards beside his mashed nose.

"He has a glass eye," Lisa said. "And he picked a different colour from the real one. He's Johnny's mate. He handles the security for the Paradise and some other clubs. The doormen. They're tough blokes."

The other couple they'd had dinner with were already on the dance floor, disappearing into the heave of bodies.

"Come on," Lisa said. "And if you want a drink, you don't have to queue. Just ask Johnny."

They wriggled their way to the table Lisa had waved at. She shouted a number of introductions, and Olivia danced with two men whose names she'd barely heard. The music engulfed her. The room grew hotter. It was jammed, packed solid with glistening, undulating flesh, narcotized by heat and the dreamy lines of Bukem-style drum 'n bass, as well as alcohol and other chemicals. The complex rhythms of the music thrummed in the bones of her head, pulled and kneaded the crowd. Speech was reduced to monosyllables.

After a while, Olivia could feel a fever in her skin almost like sunburn. She was parched. She maneuvered her way toward the bar, wondering how long she'd been dancing. In the morning, she had to be at work by 8:00 and in a resilient mood, because it would be a long day. She didn't want to be out too late, but it was hard to see her watch, or even remember to look at it. In the dark, steamy, glittering wonderlands of the club interiors, time elasticized, notes vibrating in the air for decades, an hour passing in a minute.

She joined a bar queue, squeezing in beside clusters of people cheerfully yelling and drinking and registering the music with rhythmic nods. Despite Lisa's advice, she didn't want to push past people who'd been waiting. Not far away, Johnny leaned an elbow on the bar, chatting and scanning the room at the same time. She caught a glimpse of the blunt profile, the muscled curve of shoulder, a strip of white collar touching the throat. Then her view was blocked, but the next convulsive movement of the queue carried her closer. He stood at the centre of a little group, the men chatting, relaxed and amiable, the women flirting their hair about, smiling toothily. Hundreds of pretty women came in to the club every week, she supposed. Schools of pretty women, like tropical fish. He'd just have to dip his net in and scoop out the ones he wanted.

The music drifted into a quiet, insinuating mode, like someone whispering in your ear. She spied Lisa, dancing with Max, now. Rachel and her date were at the far end of the bar. The queue moved once more, and then the crowd in front of her parted, and Johnny was there, with a glass in his hand. He was looking right at her. She had a sudden wild impulse to run away—the composure she'd summoned in the restaurant had deserted her.

"I've got a drink for you," he said. "Come on, let's go sit down."

"What is it?" It looked very silly, decorated with a little umbrella and a plastic Polynesian girl skewering bits of fruit.

"The house specialty. Mango and pomegranate and passion fruit juices, and rum."

She took an experimental sip. "Mmm. Thank you." She habitually drank very little but had had just one glass of champagne in the restaurant, hours ago; since then, she'd been content with mineral water. One drink with rum wouldn't hurt.

She followed him away from the fringe of the dancers to an empty table next to the wall. A wide section of floor all along the rear wall was raised, so they could see right across the room. He sat down on a leopard print sofa, and she perched on the edge, drawing herself together like a cat on a narrow windowsill. His left arm lay across the back, only a few inches from her bare shoulders. The skin on the nape of her neck and down her spine instantly acquired a whole new set of nerves that measured the distance.

"You've never been to the Paradise."

"No."

"Like it?"

Palm fronds rustled over their heads, stirred by a hidden fan. In the middle of the dance floor, a huge snake glowed green, suspended from a bough above the bandstand. Pink neon stars hung over the bar, and one of the barmen had a live monkey on his shoulder. The smell of gardenias was in the air.

"It's wicked," she said. Her drink was delicious.

"I'd like you to come with me another night." He said this as though it was the most natural thing in the world.

His sleeve brushed her arm as he reached out to set down his drink, and the place where he'd touched her skin lit up in her brain as though dipped in fluorescence. Her mind seemed to be entirely occupied by the geography of the sofa and his body and hers and what would happen if they touched. She had the impression that her dress had shrunk and resisted tugging at the hem where it lay across her bare thighs. In front of her, the dancers were a blur.

The glass felt cold in her hand, a barrier of sorts. She tilted her head so that her hair swung forward and hid part of her face.

"I have a boyfriend," she parried.

"That's interesting." There was a laugh in Johnny's voice, now. "Where is he? You got him in a pocket somewhere?"

"In Abu Dhabi." It sounded nonsensical, a musical comedy country.

"And you're here."

"I'm going to Paris in a week."

"Another film?"

"No. A holiday with Raymond." There. She'd made that clear.

"You're a good dancer," he said.

"The floor's so crowded, how could you know?"

"It's Saturday. Come with me another night, there'll be more room."

"But you're Lisa's boyfriend."

"Is that what she says? We go out sometimes, that's all. I like her. She's fun."

Johnny leaned back and lit a cigarette. Out of the corner of her eye, she watched the motions of his hands, as he placed it between his lips and flicked the lighter, the sudden flare illuminating his face from below. "I was in Paris once," he said lazily, "when London was bloody cold, not like now. I went to Paris because I heard it was warm there. It was. You could sit outside, late at night."

"You liked it?"

"Not the French."

"They're nicer if you speak their language."

"Do you?"

"Yeh. Mummy made me learn. I thought it was stupid before I went, but now I don't."

"Then you should go with me next time. Teach me some French."

She wasn't looking at him, but she could tell that he was smiling again, waiting to see what she'd say. A cliché Paris immediately leapt into her mind—walking along the Seine, cafés, the romantic little hotel. She shook her head to dislodge it. How had the conversation ever gotten to this place? Talking to Johnny was like riding in a car without brakes.

"Did we skip a reel?"

"Yeh, maybe." He laughed. "Want to go back to where we just met and I said 'this woman is so beautiful I'm going to die right now'?"

She turned to look at him. "You did not!"

"Oh, didn't you hear me? The Roma's kind of noisy."

"Huh. Are you sure which of your two beauties you said it to?"

He laughed again. "Oh, Tony. Don't let anything he says bother you. Can we go out tomorrow? Dinner?"

"Certainly not."

"No? Why? Aren't you having fun?"

"I'm busy tomorrow evening," she said with asperity, "and, besides, you shouldn't be asking me when you're on a date with Lisa. She's my friend."

"Then I'll ring you tomorrow when I'm not out with Lisa."

"I'll still be busy. And you don't have my number."

"Aren't you going to give it to me?"

"No. I have a boyfriend."

"You said that. We must have seen this part already."

She'd been almost angry, but now she couldn't help laughing. Her defences, rickety to begin with, were a shambles. The glass was so slippery in her hands she was afraid she was going to drop it. She flicked a glance at him sideways and was caught. Her heart began to beat right up in her throat.

"We can't talk now," he said. "When can I see you tomorrow?"

"You can't, I don't have any free time. And besides—"

She wasn't going to explain her reluctance to him; she wasn't sure she could explain it to herself. It went beyond the complications of Lisa and Raymond. Why not go out with him? Nicky would. But Nicky could handle herself; she'd had plenty of practice.

"You're working?"

She nodded. "I have to be there at eight."

"Talk to me then. I'll ring you."

"All right."

He reached into a pocket and pulled out his phone. "Troy."

She hadn't heard the beep over the music, but maybe he had set it to vibrate. He listened for a second, then flicked the phone off. "Shit," he muttered, and stood up, looking towards the entrance.

"What?" she said, startled.

"Where's Max?"

"On the dance floor, with Lisa."

He was talking into the phone. "Max? Connors is here. All charlied up. Right." He put it back in his pocket. "There's going to be trouble. What's your number, Olivia?"

She heard herself give it to him. "I have to go," she added.

"I'll call you tomorrow."

"You'll get my answering service. We're shooting in a tunnel all day."

"Monday, then. Bloody hell," he said, not looking at her. "I don't need this."

A big square blond man was ploughing across a corner of the dance floor towards the bar, shoving the dancers out of his way. Olivia looked in the same direction and saw the woman in the green top who'd been with Max earlier. She had frizzy chestnut hair and a wide red mouth, and she turned about on her barstool and watched the blond man come towards her. Then she yelled something at him. Olivia couldn't hear her over the music, but she saw her lips forming the word 'you.'

Max was moving towards the woman, too; Olivia saw Lisa standing alone with her mouth open. Johnny had left the table and was trying to slide through the crowd. The nearer dancers heaved, oblivious, but the blond man, Connors, left a wake behind him, and the people in front of him were backing away, squashing up against other people who couldn't see what was going on.

Suddenly, he arrived in front of the woman. He shouted, she slapped him, and Olivia saw him draw back to take a swing at her. Max stepped between them and blocked his arm, then pushed a melon-sized fist into the blond man's chin. Women screamed. The blond man crashed over backwards, knocking over a couple of people. Then he was up again, as though Max hadn't hit him at all. He ran at Max, head down, and Max grabbed him and picked him up and threw him a few feet. By this time there was a wide circle, as people gasped and shoved to get out of the way. The DJ looked over his shoulder and stopped playing. Olivia watched, frozen.

Incredibly, the blond man got up once more and swung blindly in Max's direction. Max kicked him in the solar plexus, and he jack-knifed, staggering backwards and then falling head first to the floor, where he lay still. Johnny forced his way through the packed ring of spectators, to where Max stood over the blond man, glaring, his mouth open in a snarl. Max's head came up. He saw Johnny, and the glare slowly died out of his eyes. His hands unclenched.

It had all happened in less than a minute. Johnny bent down to look at the blond man, and then the crowd pressed in around them and Olivia couldn't see. The woman in the green top was tilting a glass down her throat, her eyes stretched wide. She emptied it and the bartender handed her another. Then a couple of bouncers shouldered their way through and carried the blond man off the floor, through a door near the end of the bar. Olivia became aware that her right hand was still pressed to her mouth. She dropped her arm. Everyone was jabbering. Then the band started playing again, and slowly the crowd spread over the floor, filling in the space where the men had been fighting.

The adrenalin that had rushed through her body was gone, leaving her cold and a little sickened. She'd never seen a real fight before, and she wanted to go home. Her drink was still on the table where she'd put it when Johnny stood up. She left it there and struggled through the mob to find Lisa. The music had gathered force again; it was like golden hammers rapping on her skull. She was almost dizzy with shock, with the heat, the lights, the shiver of angry excitement running through the room.

Lisa was looking for her. They found each other near the loos.

"I'm going home," Olivia said. "Where's Johnny?"

"Over there. Talking to Roy Connors's ex. He says I should take a cab, he has to deal with this. I was scared—I was dancing with Max, you know, when Connors came in and it started."

Johnny came towards them followed by a big bald man who looked as if he'd been quarried rather than born.

"Sorry," Johnny said. "That wasn't part of the plans for the evening." There was no amusement in his voice now. He was distracted and in a hurry. "Lisa, you'll be all right?" He gave her a twenty pound note. "Andy will get you a cab."

"Yeh, fine," she said gruffly, as he kissed her on the cheek. Looking strained, he said a brief goodnight to Olivia and left them.

They followed Andy across the room and down the stairs. Outside, the night air was still warm, but much cooler than in the club. The street was full of people. Two gay men ambled towards them, tanned and fragrant, muscular in their perfect jeans, their pretty shirts. They looked with interest at Andy, for whom a path opened along the crowded pavement as if it belonged to him.

The traffic moved sluggishly past. Olivia was about to suggest that they walk to Charing Cross Road, when a taxi angled towards the opposite curb and stopped to let passengers out. Andy sprinted across the street, moving with surprising speed and grace. Horns honked. Olivia and Lisa waited for the light, crossed, and Olivia climbed in and gave the driver her address while Andy held the door. Lisa slid in beside her.

As soon as the door was shut and the cab moved off, Olivia said, "Have you ever seen a fight like that before?"

"Jesus, no," Lisa said. "I mean, I've seen some blokes get a little ugly, but—"

Olivia shivered. "Is Max that woman's lover?"

"Must be, what else? He gets about. Johnny's upset, that's all I know. I've never seen him so angry at Max."

"Who's the other man?"

"Connors? I'm not sure. Max knows some very rough people." Lisa crossed and uncrossed her legs and made an exasperated little noise. "It's just my bloody luck that this would happen tonight." She turned to Olivia. "So, did you like him?"

"Yes."

"Hah. I knew you would. Isn't he sexy?"

"Mmmhmm."

"Well? You still say I should go out with somebody else?"

"Why would I change my mind?"

"You must be blind."

"I can see perfectly. That club is full of women who see, and he knows it."

"Okay, yeh, he's a flirt," Lisa said, "but he's not a slut. I've been there; I can tell the difference."

Olivia was silent. She shouldn't be having this conversation, not when she'd just given the flirt her phone number.

"I know what you're thinking," Lisa said, inaccurately.

Olivia shrugged.

Lisa looked soulful. "But I'm in lurrrve."

"Well, he's not," Olivia said bluntly.

"I know that." The cab halted at an intersection. Next to them, a car was bouncing to a thunderous drumbeat, with the windows rolled down. Lisa glared at it. "Men," she said. "Look at them. They're morons."

Olivia glanced sideways at the car and the occupants bobbing up and down in unison with their mouths hanging open. She giggled.

"Wankers, the lot of them," Lisa said darkly. "You know who Johnny loves? Max. They should get married." She squeezed her eyes shut. "I'm getting a headache. Deadly stuff, champagne, God knows why it's legal. So, what should I do?"

"Oh, Lisa, I've told you what I think. Anyway, I'm the last person you should ask."

Olivia said nothing about the scene on the sofa. She felt like a traitor, but she couldn't bring herself to talk about it. Her skin flushed in the darkness of the cab. Thought and feeling spun together, then flung outward again, incoherent. And what had happened, after all? Some ridiculous conversation. Lisa would want her to repeat every word. She would want promises. Olivia couldn't make them. She was excited and at the same time suspended in doubt, mistrustful. Angry at herself. She didn't know what she was going to do. Yes or no. *Oui* or ***non***. 'Teach me French.' Huh. That kind of French he knew a lot better than she did. He undoubtedly had vocabulary she'd never heard of.

3

When she got up, Charlotte turned on Radio 4 to make sure it was Monday. The air was already stifling upstairs. She ran the cold water tap in the bathroom sink and cupped her hand under it, then let the palmful of cool water sluice over her forehead and run down her face. It didn't help much. She had a headache, and her brain had gone small and fuzzy. Felted, like a mitten that had shrunk in the wash. She struggled into her kimono and limped downstairs, clutching the bannister.

All the cups were dirty. The wine glasses, too. She eyed the door of the fridge but didn't open it. She wouldn't have a drink yet, not today. Today she would dress first and tidy the garden and do the washing up. She would do all that before she drank a drop, because she'd promised herself, and she would keep her word. The po-faced bottle-counters next door could say what they liked.

The wine was in there, waiting for her. Well, she could wait, too. She could discipline herself. When she was young, she'd taken ballet lessons twice a week for eight years. Practised every day, all through her teens. That had been discipline: the single-minded pursuit of a perfection never to be reached. She hadn't danced professionally. Too big, they said. She hadn't been quite good enough, she knew that. But she would have liked that life, the endless days at the barre, mending her toe shoes and washing her tights in the evenings, going to bed early. There was no lying awake, thinking. You were too tired. You danced in your sleep. She still did, sometimes, as ghostly as Giselle, her body weightless, her arms unfurling like new leaves. What a laugh. No one meeting her now would believe what her body had once been. She'd draped cloth over the mirrors so she would never see herself by surprise, but she knew how she looked.

She would have to dress. You couldn't garden in a silk kimono. But it was a nuisance, dressing. When she didn't need to go out, which was most days, she wore a dressing gown. Wool in winter, the kimono in summer. With the curtains drawn, she could hardly tell the difference between night and day, anyhow. What did it matter? To dress merely because another morning had begun was an idea that had come to seem strangely artificial. Genteel, like blue water in the loo.

The electric clock on the wall in the kitchen said ten minutes to ten. The others didn't, but they'd stopped. She'd stopped them. She didn't mind the one in the kitchen, because it was silent. The ticking was what she hated. The ticking prevented time from sliding past. She liked to fall asleep in the afternoons, when the streets were quiet, all the worker bees out collecting pollen. The days often dwindled into evenings before she woke.

She could have a cigarette before she dressed, but it was important not to have a drink, or she might have another and forget what she meant to do. The first mouthful was so seductive. Warmth hitting that cold pit in the belly. The first few mouthfuls would swim through her veins; she could almost feel the wine moving in her body, rising to her head. When it reached her brain, she would open her mind to it like opening her legs for sex.

The cigarettes were on the kitchen table. The packet was almost empty. She shook the last cigarette out, found a book of matches, lit up, and opened the back door, squinting at the blazing sunshine. Funny. She was like a vampire now, didn't like the sun. But she'd told Gillian they'd sit in the garden tomorrow. She'd forgotten what a mess it was. She'd suddenly had a picture in her head: the green grass, Olivia as a child. They'd sat outside in the garden while Olivia played with her dolls.

She'd had a farm—a little wooden barn, horses, cows, tiny people: lead figures, painted with shining enamel, none of your plastic rubbish. She'd planted beads in the dirt while Charlotte deadheaded the roses. Red beads were strawberries. Before the cottage, that was.

Christ, she was going dotty. What she wanted was a bath, a long, deep, soak. Maybe later she would sit in the tub with her second glass of wine and let the heat expand her blood vessels, moving the wine along, until it finally reached every part of her, even her feet. Her feet which were always cold, even in summer. Where had those feet come from? It was one of the things you didn't know, if you didn't know your parents. Her feet, like her height and her awkwardness, had seemed like arbitrary penalties inflicted by God, until the ballet lessons took hold, and she learned how to move, how to stand still.

Her mother had given her the name Charlotte. She'd hated it when she was young, even more when people tried to call her Lottie. She hadn't let them. But now Charlotte seemed to fit. It was a name for a fat, middle-aged woman, not a girl. She'd called her own daughter Olivia, a delicate name, a name for someone thin and graceful. The Princess of Parson's Green, Thomas had called her. Olivia. She was back in London; there'd been a message from her on the machine. It wasn't working properly, but she'd heard Olivia's voice. She'd thought they might have a visit yesterday, but Olivia hadn't come. Just as well. It had been an odd day, her head had felt queer, and she wanted to be alert when Olivia came to see her.

She got on all right by herself. She could manage. Sometimes she worried about money. It was a good job she owned this house. She'd have been out on her ear, the rents they wanted now in London. Men in shiny shoes always prowling, buying up flats, throwing old cows like her into the street. She didn't want to know how much she had left in the bank. She was good at not thinking about money, or about being lonely. At not seeing things. Sometimes you had to, but not often, not if the wine was doing its job. Sometimes, though, it turned on you, and you saw everything. The barn. And the figure suddenly there, in the road. His eyes, just before the impact. Then his body, sliding down, twisting, crumpling. Bright red blood splashed on the weeds. The barn again.

Another cigarette, that was what she wanted. She dropped the empty packet and wandered into the sitting room. Someone was talking on the telly. Had she turned it on, or had it been on all night? She couldn't remember. A woman was speaking. Her hair was sleek, her lips moved, displaying even, white teeth. She was speaking English, but what was she talking about? A man looked into her eyes, took her hands. It was like watching monkeys at the zoo. Sometimes she would fall asleep with the screen on and wake to voices murmuring, like doctors consulting in the doorway while the patient lies still, eyes closed, breathing. It was funny how she never read any more. The house was full of books. Half of civilization crammed onto the shelves, for all the good it did anyone. She didn't read at all—couldn't. She lacked the concentration. Anyhow, she didn't want to. She had her ways of making the time pass, her bottles of Muscadet, her crosswords. Finishing a crossword felt good. And she liked sitting and watching the exercise programmes. They reminded her of ballet classes. She didn't need more.

There must be some bloody cigarettes somewhere. She liked to keep two or three extra packets about, so she wouldn't run out when the shops were shut. She got down on all fours and scrabbled under the chair she usually sat in. A wine bottle, empty. No cigarettes. It wasn't worth looking upstairs; she never smoked in bed, she knew that bloody much. Kneeling down was a mistake. Her mouth opened, then clamped shut. Painfully, she hauled herself up, clinging to the arm of the chair. She wouldn't want Thomas to see her now, or any other man. Sometimes she thought a man would be nice, a warm body next to hers, someone else to be hungry so she'd feel like cooking, but it wasn't going to happen. Never again. And anyhow, she didn't really want it, not all of it, not the part when you met one of them and had to undress. It was only Thomas she wanted. Another thing that didn't bear thinking of.

She stood up. Some wine would steady her nerves, but she wasn't giving in. She'd get rid of this empty bottle and then go buy some more cigarettes. But first she'd have to dress and put on her face. She was still a dab hand with the lipstick. No clown mouth for her, with bits of red on the teeth. Really, she ought to do her face every day, in case she fell over and died, the way Mrs. Arthur used to say she should always wear clean underwear, in case she was hit by a bus.

The silly kimono had slipped off her shoulder. She pulled it up. The texture was like the sleepy warm smoothness of skin when, in your marriage bed, you turned over at night and brushed against each other. Such a long time now since she'd had that warmth. Years, too, since she'd felt desire, but she could remember what it was like. When she'd felt it, there was anger as well. Had that been true only after Thomas left? She didn't know any more. Now he lived in Maida Vale with his new wife.

Keys, she'd need her keys if she was going out. They weren't on the hook. She told herself to remember, but she forgot. Keys were a bother. She'd hated fussing with keys, ever since she was a girl. There'd been three locks on the door to the house in Beatrice Street, and four Bibles, one for each child. The Arthurs thought the ones who passed on watched from above. She didn't believe it, and when she said so, she was smacked. There was something after death, that much she believed. And she was still married to Thomas, whether he thought so or not. Whatever there was, after, they'd be together. But she wasn't one to imagine the Arthurs were watching her, peering over the rim of a passing cloud. The keys could be in a pocket, but the cupboard was hopeless, everything jumbled. Was it warm or cold when she'd last gone out? Warm. It was summer now, nearly August already. They'd said that on the radio.

Her hands shook. A drink would calm her down, just a small one, to drive off the devils. Now and then she actually saw them in her mind, little figures with grinning medieval faces, swarming like flies. Her demons. Concentration was what she'd lost. She was looking for her keys. Once or twice, she'd gone out without locking the door because she couldn't find them. It was all right, she hadn't been gone long. But she didn't want to make a habit of it. She was always frightened, thinking there might be someone hiding in the house when she got back, someone waiting. Perhaps she'd worn her mac the last time she went out. She remembered now, she'd put it on because it had looked like rain. Here it was. It had a button off. She would have to sew another. They had spares inside, coats like these. She'd bought it years ago, before the Japanese tourists came and everything started to cost so much. Burberry—she liked the sound of it, like an electric kettle starting to warm. But there were no keys in the pocket.

Why was she going out? Oh, for more fags. Perhaps there were some on the kitchen counter. She went back to the kitchen, carrying the empty bottle. If only she could find another packet, she wouldn't have to go out. She didn't like going out any more. If her coat didn't have any spare buttons, she'd have to go to the Button Queen. She used to like to do that, looking at the buttons salvaged from the wrecks of old finery—jet buttons and gold buttons and mother-of-pearl, vegetable ivory and jade. She would buy them even when she had nothing to sew them to. Who knew if the Button Queen was there any more? So much was gone, torn down, erased, ground under. Her old favourites had been gone for years. San Frediano. She'd loved that restaurant. She didn't know the right places, now, and anyway they were too expensive and the food was silly—piled up in little towers like children's blocks.

And she didn't like seeing her neighbours. They disapproved of her. They were probably hoping she'd drink herself to death one of these days, so someone could buy the house and tidy it up. Property values were threatened by her mangy lilac and the sweetie wrappers that blew into the hedge. Probably by her old mac, too, and her shoes that wanted polishing. A good job they couldn't see the bottles in the shed.

No fags anywhere. She was really going to have to face the shops, and without a fortifying glass of wine. The garden would have to wait, but this afternoon she'd give the table a scrub. That would make a start.

Kevin drained his third pint. He'd woken with a hangover, but he'd killed it now. Was Olivia back in London yet, or was she still in Morocco with Bobby Carr? He hadn't gone near her flat all weekend. He didn't care. If she wondered why he'd stopped ringing her up, why he wasn't sending her bleeding roses, then let her fucking wonder. He was finished with her. Girls were all the same, end of story. If she had a sodding boyfriend, he didn't want to know. He ordered another beer.

The game was nearly over, or he thought it was. He hadn't been watching. The TV was loud but he could hardly hear it over the screeching at the next table. Five girls. Knocking back the pints, laughing, yelling louder than any bloke. The one with the long dark hair hanging down her back. She looked foreign, but she was shouting in English.

"Wankers! Show us what you've got!"

He stared at her. Her bare shoulders gleamed. The top she was wearing, it was low cut and loose. When she leaned forward, he could see the lacy edge of her bra, the flesh jutting out. She wasn't looking at him. Girls like her didn't. They looked right past him, like they couldn't see him, or if they saw him they pretended not to. The bra was reddish-purple. Plum, or something daft. She had short legs. That was okay, he didn't mind short legs. High-heeled sandals, round, shiny knees. Fat thighs. Her skirt wasn't covering much. That shadow he could just see, where the hem was riding up, he couldn't be sure about it. He shifted his angle a little; his pint of lager stayed full, sweating in the humid air. The girl smiled. She tossed her hair back. She was on his bed, on her back, skirt off, plump white thighs spread wide, mouth open. Wanting it.

"Hey!"

He jerked, startled into awareness of the room. The noise. She was glaring at him. The others were nudging each other. She pulled the two halves of her neckline away from each other, exposing the tops of her breasts.

"Have a dekko, whyncha?" She spat the words out.

The girls giggled. Then, as if they'd practised, they all made a gagging gesture and turned their backs.

His face flamed. He poured the beer down his throat and left.

It wasn't like he'd done something, for Chrissake. He hadn't done anything. Hadn't said a bleeding word, had he? He'd just been sitting there, minding his own business, drinking his pint. A bloke had a right to sit in a pub. The girl was mental.

He crossed a street against the light and barely heard the horns honking.

After four takes of the kiss, Olivia could hear a pinched, nasal note of impatience in the director's voice.

"This is a simple scene, Olivia. Let's just run through it once more."

Olivia was stiff, and unhappy because she was stiff. Her gestures were clumsy and self-conscious. They weren't her own natural movements, but they didn't belong to the character she was playing, either. She'd lost her link to Bridget, an underwritten role in the first place, and couldn't believe for a moment that she would melt into this surprise embrace. Her throat was dry; she stammered her lines.

She was conscious that Bobby was already on his marks, waiting. She tried to focus her attention. Out of the corner of her eye, she saw the lamp ops checking their watches and yawning; she was holding everything up. A drop of sweat trickled down her neck. She rubbed it away and stepped into position.

"Bridget," Bobby Carr murmured, with precisely the same inflection as before. His arm slid around her waist, his mouth pressed on hers. Her body was inert, like a piece of china being glued.

She could blame it on the script, or on Bobby, with whom she had no helpful chemistry, but Bobby wasn't having any trouble. The director was right, the scene was simple. She should be able to do it easily. Bobby was supposed to discover that he cared about her more than the diamonds, and she was supposed to fall into his arms. That was all there was to it. She tried again to relax. The camera operator made a small adjustment. The assistant PA was now hovering with a towel. She blotted the sweat from her neck and handed it back.

"Take five." The clapper board snapped.

"Rolling," she heard, and then, right way, "Cut."

"Olivia, it's a passionate kiss," the director said. "Sweetheart, you look like a maths teacher being given an apple. What can we do to raise the temperature a few degrees? Do you need a break?"

Christ. They must be thinking she was totally incompetent. But she could do this. "No," Olivia said. "Just give me a minute." Distancing herself wasn't working at all. She would have to find her way into the scene instead of trying to be aloof and technical. Turning away, she stepped out of the glare and shut her eyes. Deliberately, she placed herself in the Paradise Club, next to Johnny on the sofa, recreating the moment through the details—the leopard print pattern and velvety nap of the fabric against her bare thighs, the damp heat at the back of her neck, the precise position in which she'd sat, the flare of the match, how the glass had been so cool and slippery in her hands. His sleeve, brushing her arm. Remembering, she summoned the awareness in the skin, the eyes, the hot core of her body. The feeling shimmered inside her, like an interior mirage. As soon as she had it, could taste it, the stiffness went out of her. Her body was light, fluid, filled with energy. Confident, she moved back under the lights. She stepped into take six as Bridget, and the energy flowed into Bridget's body. She knew what to do. It was as simple as pouring syrup from a bottle.

"Beautiful," the director said. "That was totally different. Let's move on."

Bobby gave her an appraising look. "That was okay. What was the matter with you?"

"I was nervous."

"I'll show you how to relax sometime," Bobby said and walked away, smirking.

Egotist, Olivia said under her breath. But she didn't care, because she'd done well. She went off to change for the next scene and examined herself in the mirror, silently exulting. Using those raw, new feelings had been a risk, and it had paid off. Furthermore, she knew she could use them again. The power to be able to do that! To take what was wild and uncontrolled and possibly foolish, and channel it into emotion on the screen, when you were somebody else, was a kind of alchemy of the soul. You could turn everything to gold.

She worked through the afternoon, and when they were finished for the day she called Nicky and arranged to meet her for dinner at Tutton's. As she was stuffing her phone into her bag, it beeped again. Thinking it was Nicky ringing back, she flipped it open again and said, "What?"

"Do you always answer the phone by saying 'what'?"

"Oh." At the sound of Johnny's voice, the image of him that had been in her mind since Saturday evening was instantly more vivid, the brightness turned way up. "I thought you were Nicky." She wasn't prepared.

"You got home all right? Sorry about the scuffle at the club. Usually when there's any trouble, it's outside, in the street."

"Yes." She drew a breath. "The blond man, is he okay?"

"No bones broken. He was too out of his nut to feel anything when Max hit him. He shouldn't have come to the club, the condition he was in," Johnny said curtly. Then his voice lightened. "I was thinking about you yesterday—what were you doing in a tunnel?"

"Being chased, like Orson Welles in *The Third Man*, but it's crooks who are after me. I haven't done anything quite as athletic as that on film, so it was interesting. I had to climb up a metal ladder and then jump down and land at exactly the right spot, then run. Ten times." He was thinking about her, he'd said. She perched on the arm of a chair and swung a foot back and forth.

"You must work out, if you can do that."

"Yes. And I go to dance classes."

"You're a dancer, too?"

"Not really, but I love taking the classes, and you can't act anything, even lying down, without knowing how you want to move. Dancing helps me learn how to move through space. Anyway," she added a little drily, "actors work on their bodies—expectations are high." She waited to see if he would make some goatish comment and found herself relaxing when he didn't.

"How did it go today?" he asked.

"Fine. I was smuggling diamonds through customs."

"Hang on, I thought you said you played a tourist. Why've *you* got the diamonds?"

"I don't realise I'm carrying them. It's a comedy, you know?"

"Hmm. Switched bags? That sort of thing?"

"You want me to give away the whole plot?"

"Yes, over dinner tonight."

"I'm not free for dinner."

"But you're keeping me in suspense."

"Go see the film when it comes out. See me run, see me jump, see me kiss Bobby Carr," she retorted, seizing a chance to thrust rather than parry.

He laughed. "Minx. You'll have to come with me and hold my hand. Tell me when the kiss is over, so I can open my eyes."

"Rent the video. Then you can fast forward." Olivia looked at her watch. "Oh my God, I'm almost going to be late. I've got to go. I'm supposed to meet Nicky."

"Nicky?"

"Chandler. She's a film-maker. And she's my best friend."

"I'd ask you to meet me afterwards, but I can't do it. What about tomorrow night?"

"No, the producer is giving a party, and I have to be there. This week is absolutely mad. I'm supposed to be flat hunting, too, and I'll hardly have a minute. It's not always like this," she added, not wishing to sound busily self-important.

"What are you looking for?"

"A miracle. I need to find a flat in a building with really good security, not one where anyone can get in by ringing all the doorbells or waiting about until some polite idiot opens the door for them."

"You're talking about staff, then. A porter, guards, maybe."

"Yes, but I can't afford that kind of flat."

"I see. It's because you're in the movies, you need it?"

"In a way. I can't explain it now, I have to go."

"Tomorrow, then. What time can I ring you?"

"In the afternoon."

She held her little phone in her palm for a moment, reluctant to put it away, as if, even after the connection was broken, it had trapped some essence she could still breathe. Oh God. What a fool she was. Before she knew it she'd be mooning about like a teenager, waiting for it to ring. He was so easy to talk to, but now that he'd actually called and said he wanted to take her out, she was in a fever of indecision. Why did it have to be complicated? Why him? What would happen? The thought of seeing him was like a drug flooding her brain, whatever was left of it.

He was definitely going to ring her again. He said he was thinking about her. There was Lisa, though, what about Lisa? When she talked to Johnny, she forgot Lisa. The blond man, what had Johnny said? The man had frightened her, the sight of him ploughing through the crowd in the club to get to the woman. He'd been out of control. She shivered; she didn't like people to lose control, she didn't want to be around them; she didn't want to be out of control herself. It would be safer to stay away from Johnny. But she'd loved talking to him, hearing him laugh.

Olivia had a fluttery sensation in her ribcage. If she let anything start it would be hard to stop. Or maybe it had already started. Maybe, maybe not. She dumped the phone into her bag. Dammit. Pretty soon she'd be reading her horoscope.

On Tuesday, Edward's alarm went off at 5:30. Through a confusing layer of dream, Gillian heard it, thought it was the telephone. The bed creaked. She heard his footsteps and then the roar of the shower. Unwillingly, she opened her eyes. Light seeped through the curtains, but the air was still cool.

She staggered off to the kitchen to make coffee, knowing she wouldn't be able to sleep again even if she stayed in bed. When he'd gone, she sat by the open doors to the balcony with the morning paper on her lap, watching the city come to life, as the sun hit the brick facades of the buildings, and the slight coolness in the air fled back to the river. HEAT WAVE CONTINUES, today's headline announced, as if its readers had been on Mars and might not know. There were reports of water shortages. Cumulus clouds had been sighted by sharp-eyed meteorologists, but, cagily, they refused to predict rain. On the letters page, a fierce correspondence had erupted about dogs left in parked cars.

Every leaf hung still, as if time had stopped. But the minutes ticked sluggishly on; in the early morning silence, Gillian could hear separate noises—the squeal of brakes on Belgrave Road, footsteps hurrying along the pavement, the slam of a door. Idly, she imagined Edward's crocodiles lurking in the Thames. HAVOC AT HENLEY. Not bad. But there were the toothsome little coxswains in the Oxford and Cambridge boat race. Perfect for the tabloids: CROCS CHOMP COX.

The crowds boiled through Victoria Station, Londoners surging purposefully past hesitant eddies of tourists. The underground platforms were packed, and the air had a humid smell of the herd, with top notes of mouthwash and smokers' effluvium. Passengers stood in a trance of waiting, their faces glazed with moisture and the effort of remaining inoffensively enveloped in separateness. When Gillian had landed in London, earlier in the summer, it had taken her a few days to recondition herself, to activate the filters that prevented sensory overload in the city's swarming, noisy, exhausting public spaces. She was in her own bubble zone now, like everyone else, able to thrust her way through the mobbed platforms or lurch and sway on the crowded cars, silently bumping bottoms with total strangers, avoiding eye contact and pretending to be deaf. Londoners were good at this, but it took something out of them, all the same. To suppress all normal reactions, they had to pretend that the others weren't there, or that they weren't there themselves. Or both. Everyone stood jammed together conspiring to behave as if nobody was there at all. It struck her anew as an astonishing fact of urban life that millions of people did this every morning. "Mind the gap," the recorded voice intoned hollowly. Well, exactly. A mantra for mass transit.

The Wimbledon train squeaked and rattled eastward until it approached Earl's Court. Then it slowed to a crawl and stopped, outside the station. It sat for five or six minutes. Maddening minutes, like the ones at traffic lights. Finally it gave a martyred sigh, as if about to sacrifice its deep need for rest to the absurd demands of the schedule, and limped forward again. Gillian fumed, which made her hotter. It wasn't even ten, but she already felt scuffed by the day.

In Parson's Green, the side streets were quiet. She passed a florist's and felt a cool green breath of earth and water, and caught a whiff of freesias. The parked Rovers and Peugeots dozed in the sun like cats. She was carrying a slab of Roquefort cheese from the shop in Neal's Yard. The shop was a delight, even the sight of its windows. That was what you lived in London for, what its fearsome hugeness permitted: this fantastic jumble, this excess—a window stacked with golden wheels of cheese big enough for Cinderella's coach.

She rang the bell and waited. Charlotte had once loved good food, spicy tastes, rich, smelly cheeses, fruit tarts barely sugared. Antidotes to the bland food of her childhood. Mince, boiled potatoes, tinned peas. Mrs. Arthur's cooking. Charlotte always referred to her as Mrs. Arthur. "She didn't starve us, but she never thought, was there something we might like. Food wasn't about pleasure." Now Charlotte hid behind her door as if London no longer had any pleasures to offer. Yet London had everything. It was a midsummer fair, a palace stuffed to the rafters with the loot of empire, a carnival hawking cows preserved in formaldehyde and shares in insurance policies on movie stars' teeth.

Admittedly, the faces Gillian saw on the underground didn't register anything about London except the fatigue of coping with it. At the moment, wilting in the sun on Charlotte's doorstep, she felt the same. London was so large. If it had everything, getting your hands on any of it was another story. From afar, you imagined hopping on the tube and whizzing off to Fulham or Hampstead Heath, or wherever you wanted to go, and the distances were nothing. Then you arrived, and settled in, and you got tired of eeling your way through the crowds and waiting on stuck trains, and you probably ended up like the rest of the populace, letting years trickle past without visiting the National Gallery or your old friends who'd moved down to Richmond.

Gillian rang a second time. The cheese was going soft. This was not what was supposed to happen. She'd phoned on Sunday to confirm; surely Charlotte hadn't forgotten already? She bent down and peered through the letterbox, hoping no one was watching. She could see along the dim hallway to the doorways into the kitchen and the sitting room. There was no sign of Charlotte.

"Charlotte?" She called, sending her voice through the open slot in the door. What now? She could wait a little. Just in case. Just in case of what, she didn't know. She leaned against the doorway and looked absently at the garden. Charlotte could be inside, in a stupor. She could have gone to the shops. She might have had an earlier appointment and could even be stuck in the underground, right now, on a train taking a nap between stations, although this was improbable. It was far more likely that she was in the house.

Suddenly anxious, Gillian rang the bell for a third time and then, because there was nothing else to do, tried the door handle. The door was unlocked. Startled, she opened it and went in. The hall had the same smell as before, an ancient odour of habits, of long-unopened windows, of unwashed coffee cups and cigarette stubs. She left the door ajar and walked quickly towards the rear of the house, glancing through the doorways into the kitchen and the sitting room and the little downstairs loo. Nothing. She hurried up the stairs, calling Charlotte's name, rushing from room to room, half afraid of finding her. But Charlotte's bedroom and study and Olivia's old room were empty. No one was in the bath.

As Gillian started down the stairs again, the light from the open front door dimmed, and she heard footsteps come along the hallway.

"Charlotte?" she called, relieved and cross at the same time.

A woman with ginger hair stood at the bottom of the steps, holding a little dog so white it looked bleached.

"Who are you?" Gillian said.

"I might ask you the same question. I'm Mildred Smythe. Mrs. I live across the street. Taffy and I were passing by and saw you open the door and walk in. You'd looked through the letterbox first."

"I'm a friend of Charlotte's. Gillian Adams. I was supposed to meet her here, but she didn't answer the door, and I got worried."

"She's not at home?" The woman swivelled her head around, peering into the sitting room and up the staircase.

"I've looked up there."

"Perhaps she forgot."

"It's possible. But the door was unlocked. You didn't see her go out?"

"No. Taffy, we haven't seen her today, have we?"

The dog looked at Gillian with malice.

And you wouldn't tell me if you had, Gillian thought. You'd like to bite me instead, with your tiny teeth. "Well, it's kind of you to be concerned. I'll leave Charlotte a note."

She wanted the woman to leave. She felt certain Charlotte had never invited Mildred Smythe into her house. The woman was darting her eyes about as if it was her first opportunity for an inspection, looking at Charlotte's things with curiosity and distaste. Now she stepped towards the kitchen. Her nostrils flared. "There's a peculiar smell in here."

"It's cheese," Gillian said. "I brought some for Charlotte."

"In this heat? I should have thought fruit would be more—" Mrs. Smythe pushed past her and made a beeline for the table, which was gritty with sugar crystals. "Ants!" She swept the dirty room with a comprehensive glance. "And no wonder." Holding the dog under one arm, she stabbed at the ants with a thick forefinger, squashing them one by one.

Gillian blinked, dumbstruck.

Mrs. Smythe flicked a dead ant off her fingernail. "Poison, that's what's needed. And a good dose of soap and water."

Gillian found her voice. "I'm sure there's a bucket. Would you like to begin right away?"

Mrs. Smythe flushed. "You can't deny it's dirty, can you?" She pointed at the back door. "She might be in the garden. Have you looked there?"

"I haven't had the opportunity." Gillian marched past her towards the door. The light was brighter here than in the sitting room; the curtains were made of thin cotton. The back door wasn't quite closed. She pushed it and stepped through onto the little porch, Mrs. Smythe and the dog close behind her. Charlotte was lying at the bottom of the steps, on her face, her brilliant silk kimono hiked up nearly to her hips, an arm flung out, the palm reaching, as if she'd tried to break her fall.

"Charlotte!" Gillian stopped, shocked, and then stumbled down the steps. "Charlotte!" She bent down and called Charlotte's name again. Charlotte didn't stir. "Charlotte?" she whispered, and touched the back of her hand to Charlotte's cheek. The skin was cool, warmed only by the summer sun, not by living blood. Fat flies shot away and then buzzed in the air overhead. She leaned in close, her ear to Charlotte's lips, listening for breath. She felt for a pulse in the throat, but there was nothing at all, not the slightest movement. There was only an absence.

Behind her, Gillian heard a hissing intake of breath.

"Taffy! No!"

The little white dog wriggled out of Mildred Smythe's arms and landed on the ground splayfooted, yipping like an alarm gone haywire.

Charlotte's scarlet kimono blazed in the sunlight. A beetle emerged from beneath the rucked fabric, innocently traversing the pale, smooth white flesh of her thigh. Charlotte didn't notice. Her leg lay still, as insensible as polished marble. There was a smell in the air, a faint, meaty stink.

"Taffy! Oh dear," Mrs. Smythe said. The dog was going on and on. "Taffy. Quiet now."

Gillian brushed savagely at the beetle. Charlotte's head lay at the edge of the path, where an edging of brick was raised above the concrete slabs. A narrow trickle of dried blood ran from beneath her cheek to the crack between the pavement and the bricks. Her brown hair, streaked unevenly with gray, spilled over her neck and fell forward across her temple. Gillian lifted it. Charlotte's half-open eye was dull, the liquid shine of life already lost, time settling over it in a dusty shroud.

Yip!Yip!Yip! Taffy made a little dash, then stood braced, her mad black eyes staring at Charlotte.

"I'm going to phone," Gillian said, getting to her feet. "Take the dog away now, would you?"

"Taffy's upset," Mrs. Smythe said. She scooped the dog up and held it protectively against her bosom.

"I can see that." Gillian tried to keep her voice neutral. No point in being antagonistic; the gossip would be bad enough and would start the minute the creature was out of sight. "You should take her home."

Yip!Yip!

"Taffy!" Mrs. Smythe raised her voice to a honk. "You should have someone with you."

"The police will come quickly." As soon as Gillian said it, she regretted it. The bloody woman would dig in, now.

"Police?"

"They always come when there's a sudden death."

Yipyipyipyip! The dog was writhing, trying to get down.

"Aren't you going to ring for a doctor?"

"I'm afraid it's a bit late for that. Look, you've really got to go, you can't let the dog loose."

"Oh Taffy," Mrs. Smythe said. "You bad baby." But she capitulated.

Gillian herded her through the kitchen and into the hall. "You don't mind being left alone?"

For God's sake, get out of here, Gillian thought. Just get out.

She shut the door behind Mrs. Smythe and leaned her back against it. Charlotte was dead. She couldn't take it in. Charlotte was dead. She should call the police without delay. They would have to come. But she could wait a few minutes; there was no emergency, Charlotte couldn't be saved. Gillian walked clumsily down the hall and sank into Charlotte's chair in the sitting room. She breathed in and out, shallow breaths, feeling the air catching at the back of her throat, her lungs shutting down, her ribcage cramping around her heart. Charlotte was dead. There was a blankness to it. It was a wall. She tried to think about what must have happened. They'd talked only two days ago, she and Charlotte, and Charlotte had been expecting her. How long had she been lying there? Hours, Gillian thought. So many hours, hours when Gillian had been doing ordinary things like reading the paper and drinking coffee and walking to the underground. When she'd been making up silly newspaper headlines.

Gillian knew where the telephone was, but she went back to the front door first, to make sure she'd locked it. Then she retraced her journey through the kitchen and sat at the bottom of the back stairs, close to Charlotte. Charlotte lay exactly as she had been a few minutes earlier. She looked as if she could be sleeping there in the sun, her cheek against the warm pavement. I won't ever hear her voice again, Gillian thought. She controlled an impulse to adjust Charlotte's kimono. The police would be happier if the body hadn't been disturbed. Charlotte's legs were startlingly white, the long thighs soft and heavy, not the muscular dancer's legs she'd once had. Her ankles were swollen inside the wool socks. She'd been wearing a pair of backless slippers. One had come off and was lying upside-down on the grass.

Her vision blurred. For a split second, she saw Charlotte moving, her legs drawing under her as she prepared to sit up. She believed it for an instant and almost laughed with relief. Then she blinked. What she'd seen was only what she wished to see.

Charlotte could not be dead, but there she was. What could have happened? A stumble, coming down the steps? Charlotte had hit her head on the bricks. Had she lain here, unconscious? Or conscious but unable to move? Not that. Please don't let them tell me that, Gillian thought. Don't let them say she lay there helpless, that she couldn't crawl to the telephone or cry out to save herself.

What she ought to do was go and call the police, but she didn't want to. This had nothing to do with them. It had to do with herself and Charlotte. With Olivia, of course, and in some sense with Tom. With those who had loved Charlotte. Not with the police, who would come through like a piece of noisy machinery. The police would prod and poke at the body and then take it away to poke at it some more. Charlotte wouldn't let them in, if she had a choice.

And what had Charlotte wanted in the garden? She'd said they would sit out here, but where? On what? Perplexed, Gillian looked at the miniature wilderness that was Charlotte's back yard. It was as untidy as the front. Worse, really. There was more scope. High walls surrounded it, and huge, straggling vines clambered over the tops. The trees, unpruned, had shot up, towering above the box-like space. A dense tangle of branches squabbled for light, while thorny-kneed roses stood marooned in a patch of rank grass. Bindweed ramped over the shed. In the midst of the desolation, a metal table splattered with rust and bird droppings stood atilt, its feet buried in buttercups.

"I remember sitting in this garden," Gillian murmured, talking half to herself, half to Charlotte. "It used to be so pretty." She could remember the scent of nicotiana, the blossoms glowing in the dusk of late summer. They'd sat on the scrap of lawn, around the white table. Charlotte and Tom and Gillian. Edward sometimes, later on. There'd been a fountain on one wall, a marble goat's head, with sharp little horns and a jet of water falling from its mouth into a small basin. And when Olivia was small, she had an inflatable pool under the apple tree. She splashed in it naked and squirmed away like a fish when Charlotte wanted to put her to bed. Charlotte had chased her all around the garden and into the house, and they'd heard her giggles echoing down the stairs. There was no lawn left. The grass hadn't been trimmed for years. It had invaded the flower beds and stood tall and pale, heavy with seed.

She was struck by the quiet. The long row of gardens, back to back, was closed off from the streets by the houses and tall brick walls. She heard a bird fussing from branch to branch. There had once been the trickle and splash of the fountain, but there was no sound of water now. The trees had grown so big they completely obscured the rear of the house opposite, and Gillian could hardly see the windows of the houses on either side through the wild embroidery of vines. A little pool of sunshine still lay in the lap of the garden, surrounded by green shadow.

Gillian stood up, and her eye caught a flash of white in the tall weeds beyond Charlotte's body. She couldn't quite see what it was. She walked around Charlotte and stepped cautiously from the path into the grass. A white and green plastic bottle lay on its side, only a few feet from Charlotte's outstretched hand. The colours were bright, so it hadn't been out in the sun for long. She touched it with the toe of her shoe. It had weight. A spatter of green powder showed pale and dry against the duller green of dandelion leaves. Flash, Gillian saw on the label. Scouring powder. Gillian could picture the bottle arcing away into the grass as Charlotte lost her balance and flung out an arm to save herself.

Hadn't the fountain been on the wall just beyond the roses? Gillian peered through the ragged foliage and found the basin.

It was dry and filled with leaves. A fat black spider hung between the goat's horns, devouring a fly. The goat's blind marble eyes seemed to stare, as if there were another world, past or future, into which it could see.

Charlotte lay still, in the irrevocable present. Gillian bent over and pulled the kimono down over her naked thighs. It was all she could do. She straightened up, walked back up the steps and through the kitchen to the telephone. Then she sat in Charlotte's chair, listening for the sound of the police arriving.

The constable was young. He hunkered down, felt for a pulse, listened for breath. "You've touched her?"

"Her face, her hand. I haven't moved her."

"How long have you been here?"

"Not long. Half an hour?"

"She's a friend of yours, then?"

"For thirty years." What could that possibly mean to this boy in his new uniform, a child who hadn't yet been alive for thirty years?

"And you found her lying here?"

"A neighbour and I found her."

"A neighbour?" The constable's eyes scanned the garden, lighting on the shed, as if the neighbour might be concealed there.

"I sent her off. Her dog wouldn't stop barking."

"What's her name?"

"Mildred Smythe. And the dog is called Taffy."

He made a note in his book and checked his watch. "Thank you. Now, why don't you go fix yourself a nice cup of tea? The surgeon will be here soon."

She didn't want tea. Tea wouldn't do a damn thing for her. But it wasn't this young squire of the city's fault if Charlotte was dead, or if nobody had paid attention to what was happening to her while she was still alive. It wasn't his fault if nothing was done until she was dead, when everything that didn't matter would be done carefully and correctly. The constable meant well, and he had a job to do. Tea. Well, when in England.

Did Charlotte have tea? She rummaged in the cupboards and found a tin of Twinings Earl Grey with a drift of powdery tea leaves at the bottom. She rinsed out the teapot and put the kettle on. By the time it was ready, the surgeon had arrived. And more police, including a sergeant. The sergeant was middle-aged, sandy-haired, with blue eyes, deep crows' feet, and transparent eyebrows.

"How did you get in?" he asked.

"The door was unlocked."

"But it was closed?"

"It was closed. I opened it and went in after ringing the bell several times. Charlotte was expecting me, and I was worried, so when she didn't answer I tried the door and called her name. I was looking for her in the house when a neighbour came in. She said Charlotte might be in the garden. I opened the back door, which wasn't locked either, and then we found her."

"This neighbour, Mrs., um, Mildred Smythe, she suggested that you look in the garden?"

"Yes."

"And you found everything as it is now?"

"Yes."

"You didn't touch her?"

"I touched her. I didn't move her." Gillian turned her palms upward in her lap and looked down at them, as if they could speak for her. "When I touched her, I knew."

"Knew what?"

"That she was dead, of course." His questions sounded nonsensical; it was like being at the Mad Hatter's tea-party. She held herself still and remained polite with difficulty.

"Were there any signs of disturbance in the house? Did you notice anything missing?"

"No, the house looked about the same as last week."

"Then what did you do?"

"I got rid of the neighbour."

"And why was that, Dr. Adams?"

"Her dog was barking its fool head off, and I didn't think she should be in the house. She was rude. I resented the way she walked in. You may think that's a bit rich, since I'd just done it myself, but I was Charlotte's friend, and she was expecting me."

"You don't think she was expecting Mrs. Smythe?"

"No. Mrs. Smythe was prying."

The sergeant frowned. "Into what?"

"Into whatever she could find. The situation. Something to gossip about."

"All right. Now. The woman in the garden is Charlotte Minter Douglas? And she's the owner of the house?"

"Yes. She's lived here for years."

"You're old friends, I understand. What can you tell me about her?"

"What do you want to know?"

"Family? Did anyone else live here?"

"Charlotte lives here alone. She was divorced six or seven years ago. Her husband's—former husband's—name is Thomas Bening. He still lives in London, he's married to someone else now. He has a company, I think it's called Innova. Charlotte also has a daughter. Olivia Douglas-Bening. She's twenty-three. She's not in London at the moment, she's in Morocco. I don't know how to find her. I assume her father does."

"That's all right. I'm sure we can locate her. Charlotte Douglas was expecting you, you said?"

"Yes."

"When did you last speak to her?"

"Sunday morning, not more than forty-eight hours ago. I tried to phone this morning, but the answering machine was on."

"She sounded all right on Sunday morning? Her usual self?"

"More or less."

The sergeant gave her a sharp look. "Can you explain that?"

Gillian had both hands wrapped around her mug of tea. The liquid had no flavour, but the hot china was an anchor in reality. "The autopsy will tell you. Charlotte drank. Rather a lot. Too much. Her usual self was variable, according to how much she'd already consumed."

"I see."

"She also had difficulty walking. I don't know why. Pain, I think."

"She told you that?"

"I've seen her recently. Last week. It was hard for her to climb the stairs."

"Well." The sergeant made a note. "We'll see what the surgeon says, but, as you seem to know, there will have to be an autopsy. It's routine in these circumstances. It's what you call a sudden death."

"Yes," Gillian said. "Sudden."

"It's a shock, isn't it?"

It was a simple human statement, and Gillian was grateful. Her eyes stung.

The sergeant waited a moment. "It's an unfortunate accident, I expect. But we'll need to ascertain the cause of death. The autopsy should clear things up. It may have been her heart, you know," he added kindly. He rose. "We have your address and telephone number in Pimlico. You're a resident of London?"

"Yes." She was a resident of London now, but it seemed strange to assent. Admitting it to a police officer was like making it official.

Kevin wedged his big shoulders into a phone booth and dialled. The phone rang at the other end, and an answering machine repeated the number aloud. He listened to the beep and the silence that followed. He listened for her voice.

Sometimes it came to him over the phone; the machine would be on, but she would talk to him, he could hear her saying his name. He could see her, she was only wearing a skimpy little T-shirt. She smiled; her hair was loose. His lips moved; he muttered under his breath. When the answering machine disconnected, he dialled the number again. The machine beeped.

A paunchy, middle-aged man with a briefcase appeared outside the booth and glanced in. He stood waiting; after Kevin had dialled several times, the older man tapped on the glass, frowning. Kevin ignored him. He dialled once more, jabbing at the numbers. The man outside tapped again, loudly. Kevin shoved the door open.

"Piss off, yer bastard."

The paunchy man looked at his face, turned and walked hastily away. Kevin saw him stop a little way off and glance back. He stuck his head out of the booth again. The man retreated.

Kevin dialled the number once more. It was no good. He'd lost Olivia now. She'd gone away. He scowled at the receiver. Maybe she hadn't been in the flat at all, it could be a trick. She'd recorded her voice or something. She would know how to do that, she was an actress. She could be somewhere else, with her boyfriend. The word rang in his head. Boyfriend. Boyfriend, a sodding boyfriend. But the flatmate he'd talked to, she could've been lying, the cow. Everyone lied to him. Even his Mum lied, telling him she hadn't got money when her bag was stuffed with ten-pound notes. He knew they lied, so they couldn't get away with it. He caught them out.

It was true that Olivia had gone off, though. She'd gone on location with Bobby Carr. There was absolute proof, in the magazine. And Bobby Carr could be her boyfriend. Kevin unfolded the creased and dog-eared copy of *Screen*, the shine of the pages dulled with fingermarks. He studied the photographs, biting his lip. Olivia Bening. It said she was on location in Morocco. In the Sahara Desert. She was right next to Carr, he might even be touching her, you couldn't see, they didn't want you to see. Poxy bastard. Everybody knew what film actors got up to. Olivia was supposed to be with *him*, Kevin. She wasn't to go off without asking. She knew that, because he'd told her.

Screen didn't say when she was coming back, but she was in London, he knew it, he could feel it. He had to speak to her, tell her she wasn't to make any more films. What if she was with Bobby right now, laughing because she thought he didn't know? He dialled the number again. "I know you're back, you bitch," he hissed into the phone. "I know where you went." Olivia's answering machine beeped. He banged the plastic receiver against the phone box until it cracked.

A constable drove Gillian back to the flat. As soon as she'd closed the door and was alone inside, she wanted to leave. It wasn't like being at home, it was like being sad in a hotel room. She fled, without knowing where she wanted to go, only that she wanted to be alone. Speaking to the police had exhausted her reserve of good behaviour. Without intent, she found herself at the end of Claverton Street, breasting the wash of diesel fumes that flowed beside the Thames. The dead hulk of the Battersea Power Station loured on the opposite bank. She walked along to the Pimlico Gardens, a dull little park between the rivers of traffic and water. The shade was deep under the plane trees. At the far end there was a marble statue of William Huskisson, who'd been squashed by a train in 1830. Not a soul sat on the benches. Some imbecile had cemented a course of concrete blocks to the top of the old Victorian wall so that it was now too high to lean on. To see the width of the river, she had to stand on tiptoe.

The water glittered darkly in the hazy sunlight, and a cool scent of mossy stone drifted up from the embankment. She wouldn't want to swim in it, but the Thames was clean enough for fish, now, an astonishing reversal of centuries of reckless abuse. When she'd first come to London, the river had barely begun to recover, and a hundred years earlier, it had been worse than dead, it had been putrescent. In the summer of the Great Stink, a blazing hot summer like this one, Gladstone and Disraeli had rushed, gagging, from rooms in the Parliament Buildings with windows overlooking the river—a 'Stygian pool reeking with ineffable and intolerable horrors'. People walking over Westminster bridge breathed through handkerchiefs, and passengers on steamers retched as the paddles churned up lumps of sewage. Obstinately, Londoners piped their waste into the river, tipped in their rubbish and the poisonous effluents from tanneries and the filth from knackers' yards. Then they proceeded to turn around and drink the water. No wonder cholera had run rampant. Oily and thick, reeking in the noses of watermen, the Thames had killed hundreds. It might as well have been called the Styx.

If you drained the river now, what would you find? Roman coins and gangsters' guns? A string of little sailboats was moored at a dock below the wall where Gillian stood, their stays tinkling in the faint breeze like windchimes. Across the river, a barge loaded with bright yellow containers lay at anchor. But nothing moved on the water. London had once been the greatest port in the world. She tried to picture how busy the river had been then: the thousands of lighters skating over the water like beetles, the hundreds of colliers at anchor, the men scrambling to fill the coal merchants' barges, the wherries skipping back and forth from bank to bank, ferrying passengers across. The smelly old river had been lined with breweries and flour mills, sugar refineries and shipyards, and enormous docks—the East India Dock, the West India Dock, St Katherine's—crammed with ships carrying tea and wine and grain and cotton. Now the river wound its way through miles of silent warehouses and desolate wharves, past blocks of flats with water views, its reaches blank and quiet. No longer a sewer or a highway, it offered its placid width as a palliative to the jangled citizens of the electronic age. Here, for once, there was no blare of traffic, there were no glassy new towers going up, no mobile phones ringing. The eye could rest gratefully on empty space.

Charlotte, Gillian thought. Charlotte. My mother is dead, and now Charlotte. Would there be a rain of frogs next, or locust swarms? Boils? Plague? Plague was the most likely possibility, what with the stocks of deadly microbes governments were said to be hoarding.

Charlotte. She could not take it in. The shared past had been a tent they could crawl into, where they could retell their stories of themselves. Even in the recent, difficult years, Gillian hadn't believed they would lose that, had assumed that Charlotte would be there until the end, an obscure, shared end that one didn't contemplate. And now she was gone, vanished forever, into the dark. Why? Where had she gone, the old Charlotte Gillian had loved, the Charlotte who had listened to anyone's tales of woe, who had charmed and befriended, who had loved dinner parties and ridiculous expeditions, who had charged at her own fears and ridden them down? Charlotte could still have had a life—twenty years, thirty. Why hadn't she? It was an absurd question, Gillian knew it, but it drummed in her brain like the pulse thudding in her wrists and neck. To ask why was to presume an answer, and there was none.

The reality of it was as raw now as when she'd found Charlotte's body in the garden. A few hours made no difference. She knew, in her bones, that her mother was dead, knew it most days, that is; she'd faced it over and over in the past few months. But she still wasn't used to it; she could feel the thought come like a blow sometimes, as if a stranger had thrown a knife and hit her in the back, right behind the heart. It would take time to accustom herself to this death, too.

A seagull screeched overhead. Behind her, the traffic hurtled along Grosvenor Road, the ground thrumming faintly. She contemplated the statue of William Huskisson.

It wasn't very good. He could be anybody, in his standard-issue toga. She'd looked him up, once. He'd been a member of cabinet. His wife had given the statue to Lloyd's, who'd presented it to the London County Council. Lloyd's, she suspected, had been eager to be rid of it. The Council had probably looked at it and said, 'Oh Lord'. They'd put it where they thought no one would notice.

Below the tarred walkway where she stood, the water slid opaquely past, carrying its load of silt, with infinite patience carving the land out from under her feet. A branch floated past, a single green leaf raised above the water like a sail. She followed it with her eye as far as she could, not wanting to lose it on the confused brightness of the water's surface. She strained after it until it blinked and vanished at the edge of sight.

The traffic hummed on, relentless. Nothing would stop, or even slow down, for a death. She would forget, part of the time. But Charlotte would not come back, and it would not be all right.

Late that afternoon, at the end of her last day of work on *Rough Diamonds*, Olivia took the underground back to St. Paul's and walked downhill to Raymond's flat. She wasn't in the mood for a party, but she had to go. It would be a promotional scrum, packed with actors and agents and producers and publicity people. There would be a certain number of men who would look at her like a piece of meat, like something they might cut a steak from. In return, she would imagine them struck blind by a vengeful goddess. Thwock. Staggering, with arrows in both eyes. She would have to circulate, and smile until her face ached, while people drank too much, when she would rather stay home and eat fish and chips and think about Nicky's film. Or watch something on TV. Anything. A documentary on the spiny anteater.

But today had been an easier day than Sunday or Monday: she'd been able to attend an afternoon dance class; she'd spent a free fifteen minutes looking at listings of flats for rent and tried again to ring her mother. Her part in the production was finished, now. She was glad, and a bit deflated, and relieved to have Nicky's project to wrestle with. Already, since dinner with Nicky last night, the atmosphere of the sordid little house in Acton was vivid in her mind, although she hadn't seen it yet.

They'd talked about risk. In Nicky's film, the character Olivia was playing took a lot of risks, some of which made little sense to her. "She throws herself at things," Nicky'd said. "She's always rescuing a child from a burning house." Olivia had taken that away with her; it had given her the key to imagining a body for the character, what she looked like, and how she would move. She'd been excited all evening and all day; she'd read the script many times, but now she could place herself inside it, feel the dimensions of its reality.

Once or twice, she'd been tempted to ask Nicky's advice about Johnny, but she'd already known what it would be. For one thing, Nicky wasn't that keen on Raymond. For another, Nicky's own high-voltage affairs never lasted very long; she liked the intensity of the first few months, but as soon as any relationship threatened to settle into predictability, she began to be bored by the same quirks that had formerly charmed her, and they rapidly declined into fatal flaws. Despite these sudden onsets of disillusion she was smitten with a frequency that she made her own wry jokes about, and she liked to proclaim that women should be wild in their twenties or they'd be full of regrets later. Olivia's caution she regarded as a waste of time. "How much can you learn from balancing?" she'd asked Olivia after a few pints. "You have to fall."

Olivia had never been wild and had no wish to be wild in just the way Nicky was, but something new had happened to her when she saw Johnny outside the Roma. Now, walking through the churchyard, she was thinking about Eugene, her gentle musician boyfriend, the one before Raymond. So shy, he'd mumbled anything he said to her. Beautiful sounds came out of his trumpet, heartbreaking, mournful, tender notes. All that feeling, and none of it could ever escape from him in the shape of words. It had been months before they'd gone to bed together, and when they did it was tentative and clumsy. Affectionate, but for her without desire. She could have refused, but she'd thought perhaps she might learn to feel more. Some women, she'd heard them say so, didn't respond at first but did later, when they got used to sex, or understood their bodies better. For her, it hadn't changed.

Not with Raymond, either, though he was certainly more experienced and less shy than Eugene. He seemed to know what he was doing, but it was all very contained; Raymond would be embarrassed by too much emotion or naked appetite. Raymond in bed was chaste, like his designs. Sometimes, during sex, a wistful mood, or even a depression, passed over her like a cloud; or it was as if she weren't there: what was happening was happening to someone else, while she went away or merely stopped existing. She didn't investigate this feeling, or absence of feeling. Raymond wouldn't ask for what she couldn't give; she wouldn't be vulnerable; disaster couldn't happen.

At the same time, she wondered whether other people exaggerated what they felt. It would be a way to show off. But she believed what Nicky said about herself. She was different, Olivia had decided, a little envious but also relieved. That had been before Saturday, before meeting Johnny. Now she wasn't so sure. She laughed in pure amazement. Cupid's dart. It really could pierce you. A single look, and you felt yourself change. Her heart, during the anguished probings of drama school, had been defiantly mute, refusing to say anything about love. At the approach of strangers, it went into hiding. Now, without warning, it appeared and opened itself, as if it had been waiting. She was frightened, but she couldn't say exactly why. Nothing was in the order it was in before.

Though she hadn't asked for advice, the dinner with Nicky had perhaps had an effect, or else she'd been feeling carefree this afternoon because the shoot was finished. When Johnny called, she'd agreed to go out with him. She looked at her watch—that had been an hour ago. It had been easy to say yes. She could have invited him to escort her to the party this evening, but she'd chosen not to. It would be a crush, and people who knew Raymond would see them there. Instead, she'd said she would meet him tomorrow after her rehearsal.

The desire to flee hadn't left her; she'd been almost overwhelmed by it the instant she'd said yes. She could leave a message at the club, say she had to cancel. Lisa, she thought. I don't want to hurt Lisa. And in a sudden glimpse of the subtle interpenetrations of intention, it struck her that friendship could serve as an excuse to run away. Panic could dress as loyalty. Momentarily, she was lost in a chaotic universe of human behaviour where moral choices couldn't be made, could never be separated from hidden layers of self-interest. Philosophers had theories about all that, she supposed. She let the vision slip away. You couldn't decide anything if you started worrying that whatever you did you were fooling yourself. She'd said yes. In her own mind, she'd passed through a border. Or gone over a brink. Maybe, like Nicky said, you had to fall.

Olivia's handbag beeped at her as she stood waiting to cross the street, caught in a swell of office workers streaming homeward.

"Olivia! It's Lisa."

"Oh, hi."

"Bad news, luv. Kevin. You told me to call you. I checked the answering machine, and he's been ringing up again. He left a message, he says he knows you're back in London. I've got it on the tape."

The light changed and Olivia was jostled by people moving past her into the crossing. She hardly noticed. "Oh God, Lisa. When? Did he say anything else?"

"Today, while I was out. I thought I'd better tell you right away."

"He said he knows I'm back, that's the message?"

"He sounds furious. What a wally. Who does he think he is?"

"I wish I knew." Olivia pressed the phone to her ear, to shut out the street noise. "Tell me exactly."

"I know you're back, you bitch. I know where you went," Lisa's voice hissed at her.

"Oh my God. He knows?"

"He knows you're in London, that's all. But he'll give up soon, Olivia, he has to. This is so stupid, how long can he carry on, right? Look, you have to believe that it'll be okay."

"What difference will that make?"

"You have to believe it, or you'll panic," Lisa said, with unexpected insight. "Remember, he doesn't have a clue where you are."

"But you told him I moved. He's looking for me, I know it." Olivia scanned the faces close to her, then she crossed the street, hurrying, wanting to be already at home, locked in, invisible.

"He'll never find you. London's too big. You're a needle in a bloody haystack, and he's still calling the flat, so he doesn't know anything. He's a moron. Listen, don't sit at home brooding. Are you working this weekend? Why don't we go out, or is that when you're in Paris?" Lisa asked.

"Paris, oh God, I don't know. Raymond might have to postpone his flight, and Nicky wants to change her schedule; she can borrow the lights she needs on Sunday. Let me ring you, I have so much to do—bloody flat hunting, and I've absolutely got to see Mummy. I'd like to go to Fulham tomorrow; I've been trying to ring her."

Olivia hurried along Upper Thames Street, holding her key in her hand. She should have taken a taxi. Kevin's message frightened her so much she wanted to break into a run. Every male figure in the distance was starting to look like him, she was in a city of multiplying Kevins, as if she was hallucinating. Fear rose in a wave each time her mind superimposed him; then the image of Kevin dissolved, only to fasten itself to another shape in the distance.

A man was leaving the building, a stranger; he smiled and held the door for her, and she wanted to cry out, "Don't! Don't let people in." Someone might hold the door for Kevin, too, and then Kevin would be inside. The lift was waiting. She rode up four floors, her heart thumping.

Only a few months ago, she hadn't known his name, wasn't aware of his existence. Even now, she didn't know exactly how he had found her. He'd seen her in a movie, she knew that. *Karma Kids*. It had played in London in the spring. Then he'd discovered her coffee bar.

The Chagga, across the street from the flat she'd shared with Lisa, had been a habit. A latte and a joke with Bibi, at the beginning of the day, whatever time the day began. She and Lisa went together when they weren't on conflicting schedules. It was like living in Paris; every day, you went downstairs and there was your café, you stopped in and had a coffee and said hello, and then the day had begun. Her morning ritual, a little piece of life that Kevin had stolen from her.

The morning in April when she'd first seen him, she'd had no idea. The day seemed ordinary. She was alone. It was the end of Bibi's rush hour; there wasn't a queue, but the tables were full. Olivia sat on a stool at the counter and waited for Bibi to make her a latte. Then she noticed a man with a crew cut standing outside, staring in at her through the glass. He was big and rough looking, in his twenties. She was accustomed to being looked at by men in public places and practised at ignoring them. But there was something unwaveringly intent about him that she didn't understand. In drama school, she'd studied body language and the communication of emotion, and, in any case, interpreting the looks and stares of strangers was an urban survival skill. At twenty-three, she'd already had nine years of being challenged, hated, invited, dismissed, assessed and admired by men who'd seen her only for a fleeting moment in a public place. But the man's rigid expression, his transfixed stare, were unnerving.

She thought of leaving, but she would have to walk right past him. It seemed safer to stay inside and wait for him to go away. Bibi fixed her a latte without asking, and they exchanged a few words, probably about the showery weather. Abruptly, the man left the window and shambled in through the open door. Olivia kept her face turned away, but he came directly across the room and stood next to her. He smelled rank and sweaty.

"You're Olivia Bening," he said, in a voice cracked with nervous excitement.

She opened her bag to pay Bibi for the coffee, not looking at him.

"I saw you in that film, *Karma Kids*. You're Olivia."

He was leaning over her, much too close, a goblin grin stretching his mouth wide. His pale eyes glittered, inches from her face. "I'm Kevin."

She slid off the stool, backing away.

"Excuse me," Bibi said, sharp, trying to intervene.

The man ignored her. "I know you," he said to Olivia, as she fled towards the door, stumbling over a chair leg in her haste. "I'm Kevin," he said. "Wait."

"Leave me alone." She kept walking, willing herself not to run.

He followed her outside. "But you're Olivia Bening," he insisted.

His hand reached out. "Go away," Olivia said loudly. "I don't know you." Heads turned. She rushed up the street, hearing a commotion behind her as Bibi came steaming out of the coffee bar. She shouted at the man. Olivia glanced back. He hadn't followed her. He stood, his arms hanging; people were staring at him. He looked disoriented, like an actor on stage who'd forgotten his lines, what scene he was playing.

She'd hoped it was over, then. All day, she'd quivered with fear and repulsion whenever she thought of him looming over her, his face breathing into hers. But she'd told herself it was just a weird urban moment, that she'd never see him again.

For a week, she avoided the coffee bar. Then she resumed her former pattern, except that she went with Lisa, not alone. She scanned the street the first three times and saw nothing to alarm her. She'd begun to relax when she saw him for the second time at the window of the Chagga. The same eyes, peering in. She had to stifle a scream. Lisa saw him, too, and ran after her as she scrambled for the door before he could corner her. "Bugger off," Lisa hissed at him, grabbing Olivia's arm. He stepped back a pace, but he didn't go away. He stood there watching while they walked very fast up the street in the direction of the tube stop.

After that, Olivia wondered if he'd been watching for her every day and had only missed her because her schedule shifted about. She began to check the street from the flat window as soon as she woke up, and again when she was dressed, and again before she went out. She was keeping watch from behind the curtain, brushing her hair with angry, nervous little strokes, when she spotted him prowling along the pavement, sidling up to the window of the Chagga. He peeked in and turned about and looked straight at the door of her block of flats. It was then that she realised that the coffee bar was no longer the problem. He'd found out where she lived.

Olivia felt the lift slowing. It stopped; the door slid quietly back. Slinging her bag over her left shoulder, out of her way, she listened, then peered up and down the corridor before stepping out. It was empty. No one was there. She let her breath out, suddenly aware that she'd been holding it. In seconds, she was inside Raymond's flat with the door bolted.

It was a relief to be here, with the video entryphone and the porter downstairs, no name on the bell, no phone listed under Bening. To go back to Lisa's flat every day wasn't possible any more—it had made her sick, knowing he might be watching any time she came home, knowing the calls would be on the answering machine.

She couldn't remember exactly when the phone calls had started. Silent calls, just the sound of someone breathing and listening. She knew who it was. After a few days, she stopped picking up the phone. But he kept calling her, filling up the tape on the answering machine with his silences and his whispers. Now and then she listened, but she could rarely hear the words he said. During one week in June, he rang up twenty times a day. She choked with nausea at the sound of the ringing phone. She relied on her mobile; he didn't know that number.

He'd tried sending her presents. One morning, six roses were delivered to the flat, with a card from Kevin. She threw them away. Then it was chocolates. She refused to allow deliveries to the flat unless she knew the sender. After that, single roses began appearing at the front door of the building. She cowered in the flat, feeling trapped, examining the street for endless minutes before daring to go out. It wasn't because he accosted her; he never touched her and rarely spoke a word. But he spied on her. He wanted something from her. She could feel his wanting like cold breath from a dark tunnel. His presence infuriated her and knotted her stomach with fear. Twice, near the end of June, he saw her come out and followed her when she walked to the tube stop. She kept her curtains closed, she took cabs. In her mind, the city became an alien terrain. She was aware of doorways and corners, of windows, shadows, stairwells. Like a fugitive, she maneuvered, mapping every step, evading her pursuer.

In Morocco, she'd been able to forget about Kevin, but now she was back. The sitting room of Raymond's flat was stuffy and quiet. She opened the balcony doors and kicked off her shoes. She checked the video screen and the windows that opened on to the courtyard. Nothing. No one.

He sounded angry, Lisa said. What would he do? He said he knew where she went; if he didn't mean Raymond's flat, he must mean filming in Morocco. Was he angry at her because she'd gone away, or because Lisa said she had a boyfriend? Or both? Did he think he owned her? That was ridiculous. She'd never even talked to him, except to tell him to leave her alone.

The phone in her bag rang. She jumped and then fumbled for it.

"Hello?"

"Olivia, you're back in London?"

"Oh, hi Daddy, yes, I'm back," Olivia said. "How are things?"

"Where are you?"

"I just got home. To Raymond's flat, I mean. I've been working all day."

"Olivia, I'm dreadfully sorry. I have some very sad news about your mother."

4

Gillian finished her second gin and tonic. She'd found the box with her photograph albums and was looking at the pictures she and Charlotte had taken on a spring holiday in France. Charlotte, in profile, sitting on a stone wall in a long leather skirt, one leg crossed over the other. Charlotte, not yet thirty. She held a cigarette between long, elegant fingers and admired the view.

The phone was ringing.

Edward said, "It's just as hot in Liverpool and Manchester, in case you were wondering. Gillian?"

"Charlotte's dead."

"Are you—Charlotte? But you were going to see her today. Charlotte? Good God."

She began to cry, though she hadn't meant to. "My old friend Charlotte."

"When?"

"I don't know. Yesterday, I guess. She was dead in her back yard. Lying there. Not cold, because the sun was so warm, but just lying there, with a beetle crawling down her leg."

"You mean *you* found her?"

"Yes, when I went to her house this morning."

"Oh, Gilly, that's awful."

"I keep wondering how long she was there. Whether she was alive and only died because she was alone. I wish you were here."

"So do I. It goes to show one should never accept invitations to these blasted conferences in the first place. But what happened to her? Do you know?"

"I think she stumbled on the steps and fell. I don't know why. They think it happened yesterday."

"And she was alone, so no one knew."

"Yes."

"Did you ring the police?"

"Yes, of course."

"And?"

"Don't worry, they were perfectly correct. But it's not what you need, just at that moment, is it? A load of strangers, a team with a mission? You just want to be left alone."

"What did they tell you? What did the surgeon say?"

"Not much. Not to me. He said she'd hit her head on the brick edge of the walkway. I guess she might have been drinking, or she might have had a heart attack, as the sergeant so tactfully suggested."

"What's his name, the sergeant?"

"Hardwick. Nice blue eyes and no eyebrows."

The two drinks she'd had seemed to have gone down like water, with no numbing effect. The image of Charlotte's bright red kimono kept appearing in her mind's eye as if a flashbulb were going off and lighting it up.

"I'll talk to him," Edward said.

"I didn't mention you."

"I'll give him a ring. They'll take particular care."

"She was so alone, out in the garden. It's not fair, it's such a stupid ending. Oh, Edward, I know I sound like a child. Why would I ever expect it to be fair? I should be thinking of all the babies who die before they're a year old. Et cetera. But I don't care, I expected Charlotte to live a long while yet, and now I feel she's been cheated. We should all have the vote, all have enough to eat, all live to be eighty-five."

"We're still working on voting and eating. But poor Charlotte. How did you find her? Get into the house, that is?"

"The door wasn't locked. I was worried when she didn't answer the bell. She has a neighbour who must be the rudest woman I've ever met. She saw me open the door and walked right in herself, with a dog, and without knocking. Being nosey, I think. Then we found Charlotte, and the dog started yapping its head off. The woman was avid. I almost had to push her out the door—she would have stayed there and let the bloody dog bark all day."

"Was she a friend of Charlotte's?"

"She didn't claim to be, and I'd bet my shipping bill Charlotte detested her. The house is properly locked now, though. The police found Charlotte's keys in the kitchen. I guess they'll give them to Olivia. She may not even know about Charlotte yet. They'll have to phone Tom, so he can tell her, and let them know where she is."

"At least the poor child wasn't the one to find her mother."

"I wish I'd gotten there sooner. I'm haunted by the idea that Charlotte was lying in the garden helpless, when she might have been saved."

"You don't know that. She could have died instantly, without even knowing she fell."

"I hope so. Talk to me about something else. Anything ordinary. How was the train?"

"Late. Packed. Hordes of people, all of them ringing someone to say they were on the train and it was late. I shifted a load of email. And this afternoon I jumped through a series of bureaucratic hoops in Liverpool only to find that chummy was rushed to hospital early this morning. If I'm lucky, I may have a chance to see him on Friday. Now I'm in my hotel room, my back aches, and there's nothing on the box except an episode of *The Sweeney*."

"I used to love that show."

"You should watch it now. You won't believe how silly their hair looks. I have an entire day of meetings tomorrow. This isn't what I pictured when I was young and ambitious and wanted to make DI in record time."

"What did you picture?"

"It's hard to say, exactly. When you're new at the job, you do the dogwork, and you're always second-guessing your superior officers, thinking how you'd run the investigation yourself. From that perspective, the higher-ups have the interesting decisions to make."

"And you do, don't you?"

"Yes, but that's the salary without tax. The tax is, I'm wasting my days in conference rooms in hideous hotels. Not doing, sitting about."

"You could get yourself busted back to sergeant."

"I'm giving it serious thought. Do you remember the bank robbery I told you about? The one that happened when I was still in school?"

"When you watched the detectives at the crime scene?"

"Yes. They'd cordoned off the pavement, but we could see into the bank when they were taking the photos and gathering the bits of evidence. There was something fascinating in that, the idea that those men could sort out what happened, even without witnesses. I thought that's what the job was all about, being a bloody fool teenager at the time."

"You still wouldn't choose differently, would you?"

"No, but I'd be warier."

"Who wouldn't? Is there anyone at the conference you'll be pleased to see?"

"Fox Hardy. We're having dinner tomorrow night. The one saving grace. Listen, are you going to be all right?"

"Yes, I'll be all right. I'll topple into bed in a few minutes and wake up feeling rotten. I'll still be alive. It appalls me."

"What does?"

"That Charlotte's dead and I'll still be alive."

"You musn't feel like that."

"But I do. You know, I understand suttee better than I used to."

"What?"

"I don't mean it's okay. I'm not saying widows ought to immolate themselves on their husbands' funeral pyres. If it's such a terrific idea, then widowers should have to do it too. But I used to see it purely politically, and now I can feel the emotion it plugs into. It's just that there's nothing else you can do that expresses the loss. If you don't do it, if you go on living, you'll forget the dead. You can't think about them every minute. And death is such an insult. It feels like another insult to forget, even for a second."

"You can't help it."

"That's exactly my point."

"How else could it be?"

"I know. I just can't accept it at the moment. There's nothing for you to worry about—I'm not going to set fire to the flat. It cost too much." Finally, she could feel the gin taking hold, dulling the edge of the pain. "I can't tell you how much I'll miss her. But does that mean I'm feeling sorry for her, or am I just feeling sorry for myself? I can't really tell the difference."

She hadn't eaten anything since breakfast, and she wasn't hungry at all, but she was abruptly, devastatingly weary. "I'll go to bed now. Call me tomorrow, all right?"

"Of course. I'll ring first thing in the morning."

But in the morning Gillian woke late with a throbbing head and limbs stuffed with sand. She was vaguely conscious of the sound of the phone, burring insistently, a long way away. She rolled over and thrashed her way through layers of sleep and groped for the receiver. Fumbling, she dropped it, and, as she leaned over to pick it up, she remembered that Charlotte was dead. She'd been dreaming about Charlotte. The caller was gone. Probably Edward. He'd left the number of his hotel, but it was in the sitting room. She had a guilty feeling that the phone had been ringing earlier, too, though that might have been a dream.

It was the first time she'd spent a night alone in the new flat. She'd taken one of the sleeping pills she used for jet lag because she hadn't wanted to wake in the middle of the night thinking of Charlotte. Now she had no idea what time it was; the day was bright outside, and she'd neglected to turn off the bedside lamp. Whatever the time, there was no reason to get up. She would rather sleep for the rest of the day. But sleep, of course, was over for the present. She opened her eyes and gazed blankly at the walls, as bare as those in a cell.

For some reason, she found herself thinking of the year Olivia was born. Maybe because she'd stayed in a bare room, then, too, in Charlotte's house in Fulham. Charlotte, on maternity leave, was blissfully happy. Nothing bothered her, except when the baby cried, which seemed to be only when she was hungry. It was the oddest Christmas. There were no streetlights in London and hardly any heat, and bombs kept going off in cinemas and shops. The oil embargo was on, and coal miners protesting. What she remembered was the strange darkness of the streets, and people waiting on platforms for hours for trains that never came. Charlotte's house was freezing. Charlotte joked about it; she couldn't have cared less, except when there wasn't enough hot water. Even then, she grumbled cheerfully and said they would manage. "Two inches of bathwater, dear, even for hygiene-crazed Americans. It's the Dunkirk spirit."

Charlotte had been in her element, then. Elbowing her way through crowded shops, peering at the shelves in the smoky twilight of kerosene lamps, squeezing into the candlelit, defiantly raucous pubs. Charlotte had her baby, and the city was under seige, of a sort. Daily life was an unfolding drama, everyone a hero. Gillian had never seen her so happy.

"You love this, don't you?" Gillian said. Charlotte was smiling and waving at two glaziers expertly shifting a large, heavy rectangle of window glass.

"Of course I bloody love it. Look at the people, they're marvellous. Stuff the IRA. I wish I'd lived here during the Blitz. Not with a baby, though."

Charlotte had been born during the war, but in Leeds, not in London.

"How could my mother leave me?" she asked Gillian one day, holding Olivia in her arms. "I understand it less than ever. How could she bear it? I couldn't leave this child, it would be like tearing my heart out of my body. How could she do it? I was five years old, and she went to Australia and never came back." She looked down at the baby. "It seems impossible."

"Have you ever tried to find her?"

"I don't want to find her."

"She might answer your question."

"I don't want to hear her lies. She never even sent me a letter! Not a single word, not even a postcard. The only truth could be, she didn't love me. She's not going to say that, and I don't want to hear it."

Olivia was swathed in layers of blankets, only her small, pink face exposed to the wintry air in the sitting room. Charlotte cooed. "Mummy wouldn't do that to you. Nooo, Mummy wouldn't go to Australia. Mummy wouldn't go to the end of the town, not like silly old James James Morrison Morrison's mother."

"Are you and Tom all right?" Gillian asked. Tom hadn't been home much over the holidays; he worked long hours, even at Christmas.

"Perfectly, considering this wasn't his idea. He doesn't change nappies, but never mind. Oh Gillian, this is bliss. I could move to the country and bake bread and have a dozen children."

But she hadn't. Olivia had been the only one.

The phone was ringing again. This time, Gillian snagged the receiver in time. She peered at Edward's clock. It was after ten.

"Gillian? This is Tom," the voice said. "Tom Bening."

She recognised the peaty baritone voice instantly.

"Hello, Tom."

"I had to ring you. About Charlotte, of course. The police came round."

"I can hardly believe she's dead."

"You found her, I understand. I'm sorry. That must have been a shock."

"It was."

"She was in the back garden?"

"By the steps. I'd spoken to her on Sunday."

"I suppose we should have been prepared—the way she was living, something of the sort was in the cards," Tom rumbled. "Still. It's a shame. Awful for Olivia. I saw her last night."

"Oh, she's back in London, then. Is she all right?"

"She was terribly upset when I told her. This morning she sounded tired, but she was calm. I suppose it's sunk in, a little. When did you last see her?"

"Several years ago. I haven't had many chances since she stopped living in Fulham."

"I see." He paused. "She wants to talk to you about things. I'm sorry, Gillian, it won't be easy, I know. You've been rather dropped in the middle of this. Are you here for the summer, or on sabbatical leave?"

"Neither. I've moved to London."

"You have? I hadn't realised. That's splendid. Is Edward, er—?"

"Yes. We've got a flat together. Near the old one, but bigger."

"Good, good. Are you teaching here?"

"Not at the moment. I'm taking some time off. What are you doing these days? Charlotte said you have your own company now."

"Oh yes, no time off for me. I'm very excited about what we're doing, actually. You must come round sometime. I'll tell you about it."

"I gather you're married."

"Charlotte told you, I suppose. Yes, I've remarried. People do."

He sounded defensive, Gillian thought.

"My wife is having a baby," he added.

Gillian felt a spasm of resentment on Charlotte's behalf. It was so easy for men to remarry, to fill up their hearts with the children of younger wives.

Tom cleared his throat. "But Charlotte's dying like this, so suddenly, it's grim, isn't it? I feel my age, even if I'm not her husband any more. Look, Gillian, about the will, let me know if there's anything I can do to help. I can give you the name of a good solicitor."

"The will?"

"Yes, you're the executrix—you know that, surely?"

"What? But Tom, that arrangement was made years ago, when Olivia was a child, and Charlotte wanted me to be her guardian if you both died. Surely it's been changed?"

"Well, no, I'm afraid not. That is, the provision for a guardian has lapsed, of course, now that Olivia is an adult, but Charlotte's will still names you as executrix, or it did the last I knew. She told me so."

"Good grief. What was she thinking I'd do? Manage it from across the ocean? I would have had to hand over most of the work to someone else."

"I told her that. But she didn't want to alter it. Charlotte had her blind spots, you know. And then she always counted on you, Gillian. She said she knew you'd do the things that mattered."

Gillian sighed. "I suppose it can't be that complicated if it all goes to Olivia. Do you know where the will is?"

"No. Charlotte may still have a deed box tucked away somewhere. It used to be in one of the desk drawers, but it's been years since I was in the house. At one time she used a room upstairs as an office; you could look there."

"All right. I'm glad you let me know."

"I meant what I said earlier. Ring me if there's anything I can do."

"I will."

Tom Bening wasn't a person Gillian had expected to hear from again. When he'd walked out of the marriage, he'd walked out of an entire life, except for his job. His working life had always been separate; he'd said he saw more than enough of his colleagues without bringing them home to dinner, so his and Charlotte's mutual friends had been the people in Charlotte's world—journalists, film makers, and an eclectic assortment of Londoners she'd picked up when researching her productions. They were more entertaining than scientists, Tom claimed, but after he moved out, he never phoned them and he declined their invitations.

The divorce had been conducted with stony civility on his side and tears and panicky conciliation on Charlotte's. If it hadn't been for Olivia, Gillian had thought at the time, Charlotte would have given Tom everything, would have virtually thrust their joint assets into his arms, driven by a foolish hope that her self-abnegation would inspire Tom with renewed affection and bring him back to her. But if she wouldn't defend her own interests, she would protect her child. She wanted a stable environment for Olivia, and so she kept the house in Fulham. Tom had given her his share as part of the settlement.

This struck Gillian now, in her raw awareness of the value of London property, as extravagantly generous. Also somewhat out of character, according to her idea of Tom. It was always Charlotte who'd made grand gestures, and on occasion retracted them, too. However, Tom was already making rather a lot of money then and expected to make more. Perhaps he'd simply been paying off part of the sin of leaving, like buying indulgences from the church. He'd never asked for half the cottage, either, but it hadn't cost much, and Charlotte had paid for it with her own money. Gillian had been glad that Charlotte didn't have to leave her house, but she'd never had a chance to talk to Tom about the divorce; her only view had been from an angle over Charlotte's shoulder. Tom had shut her out, like all the other friends.

Slowly, Gillian sat up and swung her feet over the edge of the bed. She needed to pee, to wash, to have some coffee. The tedious wants of her body were becoming insistent. The will. Charlotte's will. She hadn't changed it. How odd. Or was it? Charlotte's will. Funny, she hadn't ever thought about the word that way, that the name of the document expressed a power of mind, a force of intention stronger than a wish. Her first reaction had been to recoil; she'd had enough of wills for the present. But now she was almost glad. It meant that she could do something for Charlotte.

She got up and went to the kitchen to plug in the kettle. The sunlight had a heartless brilliance. She felt ancient and heavy, like an old wooden gate sagging on its hinges. Even the bottoms of her feet ached as she walked barefoot across the tiles. While the kettle was heating, she washed her face, and then she got dressed, because it was the next thing. You followed these routines automatically, when they had no meaning, or you turned into Charlotte in her kimono, in a dark room. One foot in front of the other. She ran a comb through her hair, and the short curls lifted and sprang back. They were still more dark than silver.

It had been in her mind, yesterday, to face the boxes, while Edward was away, but that had been before she found Charlotte. Now she'd lost interest in them; maybe she should just send them all to Oxfam. Or put them on a barge on the Thames and set them on fire.

She hadn't seen Tom for eight years. What did he look like now? She tried to imagine a middle-aged Tom run to fat, with steel-gray hair, several chins and a rotund belly sleeked by expensive tailoring. Not likely. He'd been very handsome when Charlotte met him; now he'd be weathered and bony, with a thatch of whitening hair and a good baseline tennis game. Gillian wondered if Sibyl was a cook, and whether Tom cared. Charlotte had been superb, sophisticated but earthily sensual and unfussy. A genius in the kitchen. When she remembered Charlotte's dinner parties in the good years, Gillian felt that her personal civilization had lost a small but immeasurably precious piece. She'd seen an apron once, inscribed with a purported piece of wisdom about marriage: 'kissin' don't last, cookin' do.' But Tom had left Charlotte despite her cookin', and afterwards Charlotte had lost interest in food.

Gillian had seen them together not long before Tom had moved out. His manner had been immaculately opaque, but Charlotte had quivered like a wire about to snap. It was in the fall; she'd been in London for a week, at a conference, and had had only one evening free. Charlotte had phoned to invite her to dinner, without telling her anything was wrong. She'd gone on her own; Edward wasn't free—just as well, as things turned out.

It was Tom who'd opened the door when she rang the bell, and nothing in his manner had alerted her. It was only when she walked into the kitchen that she knew, when she saw Charlotte's eyes, huge and dark with fear. When she put her arms around Charlotte, Charlotte's shoulders trembled. Her face said: my life is coming apart, but don't ask any questions.

Gillian took that to mean, don't ask in front of Tom, and obediently chatted about her own affairs until Tom left the room to answer the phone. Charlotte dumped a heap of parsley on the cutting board and picked up a large wedge-shaped knife. She began chopping rapidly without looking up.

"Charlotte." Gillian touched her shoulder. "What in God's name is the matter?"

The knife kept moving up and down. "Thomas says he's leaving me," Charlotte hissed. Gillian saw a tear hit the cutting board. "I can't talk about it now." She scraped the heap of bright green fragments together and chopped faster, reducing them to a pulp. "Pretend you don't know."

The food was sublime. Charlotte had surpassed herself, producing roast pheasant and bread sauce—Charlotte made beautiful bread sauce, not the wallpaper paste kind—and an apple tart flavoured with Calvados. Olivia was out, so the three of them sat at the table in flickering candle light, drinking wine. Tom was jovial, praising the Gigondas Gillian had brought, ready to tell amusing anecdotes about the trials of starting his own company. They'd talked about the Berlin Wall. Checkpoint Charlie, Tom said, would soon be a tourist attraction. What else had they discussed, as they sat on and on, not meeting each other's eyes. Nothing personal, that was certain. Gillian had asked how Olivia was doing.

"Fine," Charlotte said. "She's studying for A levels." Charlotte was usually eager to talk about Olivia, but that night she didn't mention her again. She said very little on any subject and drank only one glass of wine. A few forkfuls of pheasant were all she managed to eat, but she kept offering Tom more food, until he refused with a hint of impatience. Then she winced as if he'd hit her.

Gillian was pained by the spectacle of Charlotte's humiliation, and by its futility. Charlotte believed she was on trial, that Tom was making his choice from moment to moment. She was terrified of making the smallest error, of saying a foolish word, of telling a story that bored him. She strained for perfection, as though she could save herself with the tender slices of pheasant, the soft breadcrumbs lapped with cream, the feathery pastry, the glistening spiral of apple slices. She saw her case hanging in the balance, to be lost or won by the smallest gesture, and she had absolutely every detail right. But looking at Tom, with his impenetrable eyes, his crisp haircut and the restive, fidgety movements of his hands, Gillian was certain the verdict was already in.

If he'd told Charlotte he wanted to leave, he'd doubtless been chewing on the idea for a while; people either slammed out or detached themselves by increments. An announcement like Tom's meant he'd thought silently about leaving, had turned the prospect over in his mind until it had the heft of reality. For how long had Charlotte been walking around, unknowing, while Tom glanced at her furtively and wondered whether to stay or go? Married people hid their thoughts of leaving; their plans ripened underground. Tom, with his broad, calm forehead and sceptical, heavy-lidded gray eyes, would have concealed whatever was in his mind better than most. He had a stern chin, and pink cheeks that invariably looked as if he'd been walking in a brisk wind, and his vigorous attention to his engineering work—his lab, his company—appeared to reduce the personal to a pleasantly-furnished corner of his life. The only outward sign of a change in him was the quantity of wine he drank.

Charlotte, however, looked older. She'd gained weight, and her face was creased with anxiety and distress. At the end of the evening, Gillian had gone back to Edward's flat in a lather of loyal indignation. She'd talked to Charlotte on the phone the next day, but, even with Tom off at work, Charlotte couldn't or wouldn't tell her much. She sounded depleted, after her effort to create the illusion of a normal evening.

"I don't know, Gillian. Thomas doesn't talk to me. He just says he can't stick it any more."

"Stick what?"

"It. Us. Me."

"The marriage? But why? Everything seems to have gone so well for the two of you."

"It used to. It doesn't any more. Nothing's been right for a year. We hardly speak, now. Only the same things you say to strangers. He's never home unless he has to be. I've begged him to change his mind, but he's implacable."

Gillian could believe that. There had always been something immovable in Tom's character. "What happened a year ago?"

There was a distinct pause. "Life's been hell since the accident," Charlotte said.

"You mean your car accident? What's that got to do with anything? It wasn't your fault."

"I tell myself it wasn't. But I keep thinking, what if I'd seen him a second earlier? What if I'd been going more slowly? What if, what if, what if?"

"Christ, Charlotte, Ralph Brody stepped into the road right under your wheels. You told me there were witnesses who said so."

"But he haunts me. It still gives me nightmares—I drive over him in my sleep and wake up crying."

"Oh, God. I guess it would, you were friends. How is he?"

"The same. They don't think it'll ever change. Don't ask me about him again."

"All right, but I don't see what the accident has to do with your marriage."

"I'll tell you. If Thomas is leaving me, I can't help feeling it's a judgement."

"Charlotte, that's crazy logic. You think you're being punished by God? By Tom? Why? A man doesn't leave his wife because of a stupid accident like that."

A few weeks later, Tom left. He'd found a flat. Charlotte offered him everything in the house, but he preferred to take nothing, apart from his clothes. He didn't even take his good turntable. "I'll buy CDs," he said.

For Gillian, his decision remained an enigma. Twenty years, she'd known him, but whatever had happened in that catastrophic year, he wouldn't tell. He severed himself from the friends who might ask.

There was the phone again.

"I rang earlier," Edward said.

"I was asleep."

"How are you?"

"Awake. I feel like hell. Tom phoned today. Charlotte's ex. Do you remember him?"

"Of course. He said the first little pig had the right idea after all, and someday we were going to build houses out of straw."

"I think he's figured out how to do it, and it's making him rich. But he told me today that I'm the executrix of Charlotte's will."

"You? Why?"

"She has no family, other than her daughter."

"It would have made more sense to leave it in the hands of a solicitor."

Gillian shrugged. "Tom said she counted on me."

"For what?"

"I don't know. Maybe she meant to change the will and simply didn't get around to it. That's common enough."

"You should get a solicitor. There's Godfrey Rule. He handled my father's affairs. He's very decent."

Gillian thought of her brother. He was still dealing with their mother's will; it would be months before the last documents were filed away. "Yes. It was such a relief to let Franklin do the paperwork for Estelle's. It's awful, blundering around the legal labyrinth. There's nothing cathartic or useful about it, it's like being stuck in one of Kafka's stories. You don't understand a word anyone says, and you keep going back for more photocopies."

"You'll like Godfrey. Did Tom have anything else to say?"

"I asked about Olivia. She's back; he saw her last night. He says she wants to talk to me. Edward, what am I going to say? It feels like having to talk to Mrs. Wayland."

"At least Olivia already knows the fact."

"You know, when Olivia was a little girl, I would have been glad to take care of her if something had happened to Charlotte and Tom. At least I think I would. I would have done anything for Charlotte, but it's hard to know, isn't it? When the chance seems so remote, I mean. I never really considered how it would affect my day-to-day existence. Olivia's all grown up now—she could be executrix herself. But I guess we instinctively select someone with more experience than people have at her age."

"It may be rather a lot of work, the house, especially."

"I don't mind. I'm not busy, and it will give me a chance to see a bit of Olivia. She'll probably call me soon. I could well be the only person Charlotte spoke to in the last days of her life."

"Oh, by the way, I've had a word with the sergeant you saw at the house. Hardwick. The autopsy should take place in a couple of days. I'll get a copy of the report."

"Good. I'd like to know exactly what happened to her. Not that it makes a blind bit of difference, so I don't know why I care, but I do."

"Hardwick says the neighbour, Mildred Smythe, told his constable that you were keen to hurry her off the premises."

"Too right, I was. I'd like to hurry her off the planet. I'm sure she can't imagine why."

"I don't think there was anything else. I'll have to go in a minute. By the way, remember Bertuca's pen?"

"The little copper?"

"That's the one. It's been kidnapped. Keith told me."

"Kidnapped?"

"Yes, the pen's been abducted, and the kidnappers left a menacing note, telling him not to call the police." Edward laughed. "It was made of words cut out with scissors and pasted together."

"That's funny."

"I hope Bertuca's laughing."

Pranks. Gillian hung up the phone. They were stupid, but so was worrying about her boxes, or travelling to Manchester for a conference you didn't want to be at. All the profligate usages of the days, as if they had no number.

She saw Olivia in the afternoon, at a flat on the river below St. Paul's. On the phone, Olivia had sounded shy and uncertain, but now she was composed.

"It's kind of you to come," she said politely.

"I wanted to." Gillian looked out at the view, which spanned two painted bridges and a rich slice of London's history. Boats full of tourists swished past. Across the water, Gillian could see the Globe Theatre and the mammoth Bankside power station, bathed in the aura of its imminent second coming as a mammoth art museum. "How lovely to be right on the river."

"This isn't my flat. It's my boyfriend's. Raymond's letting me use it while I'm hunting. You wouldn't believe how difficult it is, finding somewhere decent to live in London."

"Yes I would, Edward and I just moved."

"Edward. I remember him. Would you like something to drink? Coffee? Mineral water?"

There had been an awkward moment at the door, when Gillian hadn't been sure whether or not she ought to embrace Olivia. She'd seen quite a lot of her when she was an imperious and charming child, had read her stories and taken her out for treats. The memories of those occasions were doubtless more vivid to herself than to Olivia, who had been petted by many people. Charlotte had liked to refer to Gillian as an aunt, not having had any sisters. If Gillian had been a real aunt, she would certainly have kissed Olivia now, in recognition of the family tie, but the protocol for a stand-in aunt was not so clear. Love for the children of friends was an extension of the friendship, Gillian had reflected, hearing the voices of children from the playground in Warwick Square, on her way to this encounter with Olivia. It was deliberately lacking in discrimination when they were young. But when the children grew older, a quiet winnowing took place. You delighted in some of them, had your own conversations with them. Others gradually turned into people whom you saw only through the lens of their parents' pride or worry. You cared about their effect on your friends, but felt removed from the children themselves, though you didn't wound their parents' feelings by saying so.

Gillian had never lost her attachment to Olivia, and today, jolting eastward on the Circle Line, she'd been flooded with her old tenderness for Charlotte's child, for the baby in Charlotte's arms, for the girl who sat at the kitchen table drawing horses and telling Gillian their names. Nevertheless, a distance lay between them, and Gillian was preoccupied with how it might be crossed. The gap of years since she'd seen Olivia wasn't important. But earlier, before Olivia had left home, she'd turned away, abruptly withdrawing into a zone of wordless refusal. Or it had seemed abrupt to Gillian, who'd felt the difference from one London visit to the next. In November, she'd taken Olivia to a movie, and they'd had a tandoori dinner and a lively chat afterwards. By the following spring, Olivia had turned suddenly shy, and when Gillian saw her again in the autumn, she rebuffed invitations and stayed in her room or went out with friends her own age.

Charlotte talked about a phase, and in one sense she'd been right: Olivia had found her voice again; she'd become less timid and shy. But she was still remote, unreachable. After she moved out of the house, Gillian rarely saw her. It was some time before Gillian looked back and connected Olivia's retreat to the trouble between her parents. Then she remembered the evening that Charlotte hadn't wanted to talk about her. Perhaps the collapse of everything familiar and secure had driven Olivia away from the dangerous world of adults.

In any event, no assumptions could be made now about the imprint Gillian had left in the past, or what Olivia remembered. When Gillian knocked and Olivia opened the door, they both hesitated. Then Olivia stepped forward, gave Gillian a fleeting kiss and immediately retreated.

The coffee was good. Olivia sat on one of the leather sofas and sipped from a glass of Perrier. Gillian sat opposite, across a glass table. The flat reminded her of an expensive hotel. It was bland, assembled from a tasteful kit: glossy wooden floor, big mirrors bouncing back the river light, pale colours, artful arrangements of dried flowers in heavy glass vases.

Olivia's lime-green linen sun dress looked as cool as the sparkling water in her glass, and Gillian was struck anew by her resemblance to Tom. She was very fair; one of the things one noticed about England at first and then got used to was that so many people were fair-skinned and blond, or red-haired. Olivia was ash blonde, with a clear skin and cheekbones from Vogue. Like Tom, she had heavy-lidded gray eyes set wide apart and a round, firm chin. She also had his look of the favoured child, of genes that had been pampered for generations. She was tall, like both her parents, but Gillian couldn't see any resemblance of feature to Charlotte. What was touching was that Charlotte was there, too, in Olivia's gestures and in her expressions, the way she held her head and moved her mouth and frowned. She was wearing lipstick and jade earrings as well as the pretty dress, but her feet were shod in tatty old sandals, as if she'd started out with the idea that she ought to dress nicely but had given up before she finished.

"You look so much like your father," Gillian remarked.

"That's what Mummy always said."

"She was one of my dearest friends. I'll miss her terribly." This, Gillian thought, would give Olivia an opening to ask about Charlotte straight away, if that's what she needed.

"Yes, she always talked about you," Olivia said, and then, "Daddy says you're the executor of her will."

"That's what he told me. I haven't seen it. Tom thinks there might be a copy in the house, but I don't have the keys. The police have them."

"The house is mine; Mummy left it to me. You can have my keys."

"I thought you might want to come with me."

Olivia shifted her position on the sofa. "Do you need to go right away? I have a lot to do, filming, tomorrow and Friday. And I'm afraid I don't know where Mummy kept anything."

"I should go soon. There are things that need to be done. You don't have to come. I just thought—"

"To be honest, I'm dreading going to the house."

"Don't, then. But I'm going to have the lock changed; the police said the old lock's not up to much. I'll get you new keys."

"Can I sell it?"

"Not right away. There's all the legal nonsense to go through first."

"Oh. I'm looking for a flat right now, or it wouldn't matter."

"Perhaps you could borrow the money—a solicitor could advise you. I'll go to the house tomorrow and try to find the will."

Olivia got up and fetched her handbag which was lying on a chair near the door. She fished out a keyring and slipped off two keys.

"You probably ought to see the will, too, Olivia, but there's no hurry."

"Oh. Yes, all right." Olivia looked at her blankly. Then she said, "I'm sorry, I don't know anything about what I'm supposed to do. This, this is all so strange."

"There's no need for you to do anything. Not right away. And I'll have a solicitor to help me."

"A solicitor? I thought you were the executor. Mummy wouldn't want a stranger going through her things." Olivia's voice was suddenly thick with emotion, as though the image of a solicitor's cold fingers pawing through the drawers had made death more immediate.

"I can't do all the paperwork, but I'll go through the house myself, it won't be the solicitor," Gillian said.

"I can meet you tomorrow afternoon for a little while, I'll have time. If it would help." Olivia's voice wavered. "It's only—I can hardly believe she's not there. I don't want to."

Olivia turned her head towards the view, but Gillian didn't think she was seeing anything. Almost inaudibly, she said, "Was it bad, when you found her?"

Instantly, Gillian could see Charlotte's long, pale legs again, threaded with small blue veins, her twisted ankle, the scarlet silk kimono spread like a crushed flower.

"It was shocking. But it wasn't messy, if that's what you mean. It must have happened very suddenly. She looked peaceful," Gillian added. That wasn't perfectly true, but it was true enough.

Olivia looked relieved. "Why did she fall? I asked Daddy, and he said he didn't know."

"The surgeon who came didn't say. I don't think he could be sure."

"Where is she?"

"At the morgue. I'm afraid they have to do an autopsy, because they don't know why she died."

"They have to?"

"It's a legal requirement."

"She'd hate that," Olivia said in an appalled voice.

"Well, at least she won't know."

"Oh," Olivia said, and stopped.

Gillian could see it registering. Death was like a huge, invisible object: you couldn't observe it directly; you could only keep bumping into it.

"Was she drinking?" Olivia said abruptly, in a voice that told Gillian she was braced against the answer.

"If you really want to know, you can find out. There'll be a report."

"She drank every day, didn't she? She was an alcoholic. She said so."

"She was very unhappy," Gillian said.

"I know."

Gillian was silent. It might have been an awful burden to be Charlotte's child: the field of operation of such a will to perfection, and then the up-close observer of Charlotte's collapse. And yet, Olivia had been adored, protected, encouraged; everything children were supposed to need, she had received, in spades.

"I loved Charlotte, you know," Gillian said slowly. "For years and years and years. But I've found it very difficult to be her friend since she became so bitter. I'd be impatient, and then I'd try to atone for that by being more understanding. We'd have the same conversation over and over again, and nothing I ever said made any difference, really. I don't believe it did. Still, there would be days when she'd be almost her old self, full of mordant wit and funny stories and apt quotations. Then I'd remember all the other years, the years she lit up any room she was in. I used to think that Charlotte *had* to come back."

Olivia's eyes darkened. "It would have been different if Daddy hadn't left."

She sounded like a little girl now. Gillian recognised the feeling; it was how she'd felt when Estelle died: like a three-year-old lost in a park.

"I haven't seen her for weeks and weeks! I tried to ring her up twice to say I was back in London, but first I got her machine, and then nothing. I never talked to her. Today was my first free morning—I was planning to go see her before lunch, but when I got here after work yesterday, D-Daddy rang me."

"Don't feel bad," Gillian said, knowing it was useless. "Nobody expected this."

"Oh God, I need a fag." Olivia got up. "I don't smoke in the flat; Raymond won't have it." She stepped outside, onto the balcony. Gillian followed her out and they sat in two folding chairs under a white canvas umbrella. A packet of Dunhills was on the table, and a heaped ashtray. Olivia slipped on a pair of dark glasses.

"I've been smoking myself sick since Daddy came over last night," she said. "It's so stupid. I quit months ago. In Morocco, half the crew were smoking like chimneys, and I didn't start again."

"How's it going—you and acting?"

"My brilliant career? Absolutely fabulous. That's what I'm supposed to say. Actually, *Rough Diamonds* is the first work I've ever done for real money. I gave Mummy the script to read. She hated it. But she stopped going to films. It's sad, we used to go all the time, or rent videos. Remember? That's why I saw so many, especially the old ones. But she just stopped bothering. I thought she'd be happy that I wanted to work in film, but she wasn't very thrilled about me being an actress."

"She never said so to me. I think she wanted you to do whatever would make you happy."

"She wanted me to go to Cambridge or Oxford. So did Daddy."

"Well, yes, she did think you should have that."

"Because she didn't."

"Maybe, yes, probably you're right. But also so you would have it if you needed it. So many girls dream of being actresses."

"She's so damned pretty," Gillian remembered Charlotte saying when Olivia was barely fourteen. "Strangers turn in the street to look at her. I don't want her to think she can live on her looks. She ought to have something else to fall back on."

"She has a good brain, Charlotte."

"Fat lot of good that'll do if she doesn't use it!" Charlotte had retorted.

"I expect she was worried about how you'd survive—parents always worry about dreary things like money. It's in the job description. If you haven't been paid much until this film, how have you managed?" Gillian asked curiously, gazing across the river. The power station that would become a museum looked vast, almost as big as the Houses of Parliament.

She and Olivia were sitting high above the river, on the balcony of a big flat hedged about with security and furnished with Italian leather sofas. If she and Olivia had lunch at a nice restaurant, it would cost forty quid, and the restaurant would be packed with people prepared to pay that much. Where did all the money come from, she thought, with baffled amazement. The surfaces in the flat were slick with it, as though money were an oil that had been rubbed into everything. Tatty old corners of the city were buffed to a sheen. The river and the rivers of cars in the streets below glittered in the sun. From here, London seemed like some magical sheikdom, where money just fountained out of the ground.

"Waitressing. In a place called the Gaslight, because the tips were enormous. All the waitresses wear red and black lace corsets and fishnet stockings, and they all have to be entertainers, too. I did a dance routine; some of the other girls sang." Olivia rolled her eyes up. "Ugh. The pigs in that place—you wouldn't believe them. As soon as I signed the contract for *Rough Diamonds*, I quit."

Waitressing. Some things never changed, then. Charlotte hadn't ever mentioned the Gaslight, but perhaps Olivia hadn't told her exactly what sort of place it was. Charlotte would have worried. Where Olivia was concerned, she'd been a champion worrier, and what she'd wanted for Olivia had been what she hadn't had herself. Gillian remembered the fight over Olivia's French. It had been one of those sites on which the battle between parents and children is waged, like diets, tattoos, and television. Olivia loathed French, Charlotte was determined that she learn it. "Every day," Charlotte had said, "it's my will against hers. I'm exhausted. A half-hour with Olivia and French verbs is a thousand years in purgatory."

"Take her to Paris," had been Gillian's advice, the sole occasion on which she could recall successfully giving advice to any parent. "Take her shopping for clothes. Show her the Marais. Beautiful French boys lounging in cafés. Maybe she'll fall in love with it. You can't poke holes in her head and stuff French verbs in like slivers of garlic."

So Olivia had learned French, but she supported herself working as a waitress in a tacky bar anyhow. A draw.

"And now what?"

"Who knows? I'm lucky to have done this film; if it's popular, my whole life could change. But it won't open until Christmas."

The air was hazy. It had been hot in the underground. Gillian felt herself going limp, like a lettuce leaf on a buffet platter. The tide was out, exposing a strip of greasy brown muck beside the water. The skeleton of a boat lay below, its gray ribs half-buried in the ooze.

"When I first met your mother, she was no older than you are. I've been thinking how amazing that is." Who would Olivia be, in thirty years? A former ingenue, a character actress, a producer's ex-wife with grown children and a chunky divorce settlement?

"Back in the sixties. Mummy told me. You went to Greece, right?"

"We backpacked one summer. We went to Amsterdam and Paris and down through France and Yugoslavia to Greece. It was great, all of it, even when Charlotte had her passport stolen, because everyone was so nice about it and we met some Greek people and stayed at their house for three days. They wanted to know about the Beatles, and we sent them a record after we got back to England. *The Magical Mystery Tour* double EP—it was so appropriate."

"She still has that record—tons of scratchy old rock LPs."

Gillian wasn't surprised. Charlotte hoarded things. She wondered what Olivia would do with the records and Charlotte's other collections—her furniture, her prints, her books. What would *she* do, if Charlotte had left the contents of the house to her? She was relieved that it wasn't her dilemma.

"What did she say when you saw her last week?" Olivia asked.

"She thought I was insane to move to London, and she told me that Tom and Sybil were having a baby. She was in one her bleak moods, that day. But then she called me, and she'd cheered up. She was remembering old times, and she wanted to sit in the garden and chat."

"That's all?"

"No, she talked about what a lovely baby you were, and the cottage."

"The cottage?"

"How she never goes there any more."

"Oh."

"And when she called me, she talked about Beatrice Street and her first boyfriend. Freddie. We made a date for another visit. She said—she wanted us—you and me—to see each other."

"Yes, she said that to me before I went on location. She was glad you were moving here." Olivia stubbed out her cigarette. She looked wan. "I didn't sleep last night. Maybe I could, now."

"I'll go." Gillian thought Olivia looked too wrought up to sleep, but perhaps exhaustion would win out.

"I'll ring you," Olivia said at the door. "Tomorrow."

"Will you be all right?" Gillian couldn't help asking. Despite the view, the flat seemed bleak and lonely. "I can stay—"

Olivia shook her head. "No, thanks anyway." It was almost a whisper, the thinnest tissue of politeness over the need to close the door, to stop talking, to rest, to absorb what had already been said.

Gillian sat in the cool dimness of St Paul's, while the tourists shuffled up and down the aisles, and marvelled at how children could be swept into the howling tunnel of adolescence and walk out at the other end as adults. Olivia seemed very capable, more so than Gillian remembered herself being at that age, but Gillian had still been a student at twenty-three; an actress would require more nous to survive.

Tom had said Olivia was calm this morning; he'd talked to her on the phone. Gillian had seen that calm now and thought it lay only on the surface. Olivia was reserved and somewhat like her father; she certainly didn't take after Charlotte, who had been dramatic and volatile, but she wasn't placid, she was shocked and bitterly alone. As alone as Gillian had been when her own mother died, until her brother Franklin had arrived at the house. Never, in her whole life, had she been so grateful to have a brother. Tom ought to be with Olivia now, she thought, even if his new wife was about to have a baby. Some people had to lick their wounds in private, though, and perhaps Olivia was one of them.

The little shops in the arcade had closed for the night. The Chagga was closed; the pub was open. Wedges held the doors back, to let the evening air in. Light and noise spilled out. In the block of flats, the windows on the fourth floor were dark. Lisa clicked rapidly past the pub in her heels, carrying a Harvey Nichols bag with a new skirt and a pair of shoes in it, a straw handbag, and a boxed pizza from Antonio's, near the tube stop. She arrived at the front door of her building and fumbled for her keys.

From the entrance to the arcade, where he stood watching, Kevin saw her go in. She was alone. There was no sign of Olivia; he knew she wasn't in the flat, he'd been keeping it under observation. The curtains were closed, but he could tell when the lights were on; a glow came through the fabric, and the gap that was a dark, mysterious stripe during the day became a brilliant lopsided triangle of light. He'd sometimes seen Olivia at night, moving back and forth. She left the gap there on purpose, he'd thought, to tease him. But she wasn't there, now. Not at all. He'd waited all evening to see. The lights in the flat went on, but it was only the other girl, the bitch on the phone.

Olivia might be with her boyfriend. If she wasn't coming home, she might be with him, spending the night. But sometimes she was late. He would wait a little longer, and see. The glowing curtains were like a trick. If he hadn't been watching, he might have fallen for it, believing she was there now. He didn't like the other girl, the flatmate. She said Olivia was gone, but she was probably lying, to throw him off the scent, or just to play a game, to humiliate him. She didn't want him to find Olivia. She was trying to keep them apart. The woman in the coffee bar, too, she wouldn't let him wait for Olivia there, she said she'd ring the police. No one wanted him and Olivia to be together. But she was somewhere in London, he would find her.

From St Paul's, Gillian had taken the underground back to Pimlico. She changed her clothes and at seven left again to go to dinner. Edward's mother had chosen the restaurant, a long-established family-run bistro in South Kensington where she was still recognised by the staff, although she seldom dined out now.

"I hope you don't mind—perhaps you'd prefer to try one of the new places, but I'm comfortable in my rut."

"I like it. I don't want everything to look like a Matisse on a plate and be garnished with a sprig of grass and three pistachio nuts," Gillian said. "I hope the family has one of those 999-year leases."

"They own the building—bought it donkey's years ago. Before property in London was so dear."

The proprietor brought them two glasses of sherry. "It's a pleasure to see you here," he said, acknowledging Gillian with a friendly tilt of the head but reserving his smile for Delia. "It has been some time since we've seen you, madame. Your son will not be joining you this evening?"

"My son is away, so the mice will play," Delia replied. "Now, what do you recommend on this torrid evening?"

"The sole. It's particularly good, and cooked with a beurre blanc. You will not find it heavy, even in this tropical heat."

Delia glanced interrogatively at Gillian. "Would you like that, dear?"

"Yes, it sounds perfect." It was a relief not to have to choose, Gillian thought. She wasn't hungry.

"Two, then, thank you, Charles, and bring us a bottle of something nice to drink with it." Delia settled back in her chair.

She looked the same as she had for years, Gillian thought. Her hair had turned white early; it ruffed up around her face like a Colobus monkey's fur, an impression reinforced by her delicate bones and round brown eyes. She wore a blue linen skirt with a Liberty print shirt and little pearls in her ears, all as neat as a pin. She could walk across the Gobi Desert without getting dust on her espadrilles.

"How do you like the new flat?" Delia enquired.

"We were lucky to get it. I've shipped too many boxes, though. There's never going to be room for everything. I thought Edward would faint when he came home, but he's been heroically calm."

"You lived in a large house, didn't you?"

"A ridiculous house for one person. An old wooden house with four bedrooms. It had a fireplace and a stained glass window and a big front porch with carved brackets. There were fruit trees in the back yard."

"It sounds like a house in the country."

"Yes, it was like that. Shaggy, with lots of greenery around."

"And hard to part with, I should imagine."

"One makes choices."

"Mm." Delia sipped her sherry. "When I met Edward's father, I was engaged to someone else."

"Oh." Edward hadn't ever mentioned this, though he probably knew. He wouldn't have been curious about it, the old path his mother hadn't taken.

"I liked him very much, but when I met Hugo, I knew I couldn't go through with the engagement. I said I was desperately sorry, and he went off to the war. He had the most sublime Elizabethan house. I was mad to live in it, but there it was, I had to give it up and stay in London instead. The awful thing is, I still yearn after that house sometimes, and it wasn't even mine!" She laughed.

"Edward says you and Hugo were both in the war."

"Well, yes, but I only drove an ambulance for about sixteen months. Then my father had a heart attack, and I had to come home. I worked for the War Office, but I would rather have been driving. Hugo, of course, was in North Africa, and then Italy and France."

"What happened to the other man, the one you were engaged to first?"

"He was killed, poor lamb. Hugo was lucky, he was only wounded once. He had a good war, I suppose. But he lost several of his dearest friends—boys he'd gone to school with. And his parents' house was hit by a bomb during the Blitz. Fortunately, they weren't in it at the time, but when Hugo came home on leave I had to tell him, and then we went and looked. It was a dreadful blow to him. A great gaping hole in the street and heaps of bricks, no roof at all. The sitting room was like a stage—only three walls. I remember the wallpaper. It was dark red, with gold stripes."

"Edward told me he used to play in those bomb sites."

"All the children did. It was dangerous, but you couldn't keep them away. Now we've built so much rubbish I sometimes think we could do with a few more bombs."

The wine arrived. The waiter poured a little so Delia could taste it, but she declined. "If Charles chose it, it will be fine," she said.

When both glasses had been filled, she lifted hers. "Here's luck." There was bread on the table, in a white napkin, and butter, and a glass dish of olives.

Gillian wasn't hungry enough for bread, even with chilled curls of the best butter. She tasted her wine. It was a Sancerre, stony and clean. Her spirits lifted a little. She hadn't been at all in the mood for dining out and had wanted to cancel, but now she was here she was finding it soothing to listen to Edward's mother recall the events of half a century ago. The restaurant was so pleasant, she might almost be tempted by her sole when it came. She felt guilty. Charlotte was dead and she could think about how her wine tasted.

"Hugo and I used to drink Sancerre quite often," Delia said. "Some Frenchman he met during the war gave him a bottle; he sat in a stable and drank it with a hunk of dry bread. He always said it was the best bottle of wine he ever had."

"What did he say about losing his closest friends?"

"Oh, my dear, he never talked about that." Delia looked at her shrewdly. "Why do you ask?"

"Because I just lost one of mine."

"Ah. I thought you looked a little peaked, but it might have been this wretched heat. Who was it?"

"My friend Charlotte. I've known her ever since I first came to England."

"Charlotte Douglas? I met her once, didn't I? It was a long time ago. We talked about Covent Garden—she was there, at the march. She made a television program about it. What happened to her?"

"She fell down her back steps and hit her head."

"Oh, dear. What a pity."

"I don't know why, exactly. They're doing an autopsy to find out." Gillian sighed. "And I'm the executrix."

"When did she die?"

"Sometime on Monday afternoon, they believe. She was alone. I can't seem to take it in. I think about it all the time, but it keeps catching me unawares." To her horror, Gillian felt the pressure of tears at the back of her eyes. It wouldn't do to cry here.

"I think you should see Godfrey Rule," Delia said.

"Edward had the same idea."

"Yes, well, Godfrey was marvellous when Hugo died. He's very busy, but I'm sure he'd be glad—did Charlotte have any children?"

"One—Olivia. I saw her this afternoon. It was painful."

"Poor child."

"Yes, she's feeling lost. And guilty, because she hasn't seen her mother for weeks—she's been away. She and her father aren't close. He's remarried. Oh dear, grieving's hard. The things you haven't sorted out rise up and haunt you. She told me Charlotte didn't want her to be an actress, but really, all Charlotte asked was that she get a university degree first. She would have moved the moon for Olivia—"

"Children go their own way, these days."

"She wanted Olivia's life to be perfect."

"We all want that for our children."

"Not as much as Charlotte did. Charlotte's mother disappeared when she was five years old. If Charlotte was going to do anything in her life, she was going to be a good mother."

"She was devoted."

"That would be putting it mildly. But she's been hard to deal with in the past few years and she didn't like to leave the house; Olivia probably saw her less often than she might have otherwise. And now she's gone."

"How old is Olivia?"

"Twenty-three, almost twenty-four."

"We didn't see much of Edward when he was that age. He and Hugo—they couldn't be in the same room for five minutes without getting into a row. But later it was all right again. Twenty-three—one doesn't have much perspective on one's parents at that age."

"If you mean distance, yes, only time can give you that, or finding out what it was like to be their age when you're that age yourself. Olivia and Charlotte had rows, but they were extremely close when Olivia was young, and then Charlotte went to pieces. Maybe Olivia had to separate herself in order to grow up, or not to be engulfed by Charlotte's depressions. I don't know, how much can I say, when I've seen so little of what went on?"

"You're very fond of her, aren't you?"

"It came home to me today how attached I am. She's like part of my family. And now she's all I've got left of Charlotte."

"Hugo wanted a daughter, but they're trickier than sons, I think."

"Did he ever stop minding about Edward being a detective?" Gillian asked, a little recklessly. She'd never asked such a direct personal question before.

"Not precisely. Hugo would always have preferred that he go into the army. But in the end he was reconciled. Not at first. At the beginning, Hugo was absolutely furious, and he went about it quite the wrong way—tried to lay down the law. Goodness. I can remember them shouting at each other. We had no idea, you know, that Edward was serious. Hugo thought it was a boy's whim. I tried persuasion, but Edward had got his back up. They stopped speaking. It took Hugo ages to come round. He didn't approve of Edward's divorce, either. He said it was our own fault, for not sending Edward away to school—letting him go to a grammar school and mix with all sorts in the streets. Perhaps he was right. But you know dear, everything changed after the war. Nothing was ever the same again. Hugo couldn't understand that, didn't want to, really. I suppose he had an idea of what he'd fought for, and if all of that was going out of the window, then why had his friends given their lives? That's not what he said, of course, and even if he had, it would have made no sense to Edward, he was far too young." She looked out at the street on the other side of the glass. Two men in leather jackets and ponytails walked by together, Tweedledum and Tweedledee on their mobile phones. "England's such a different place, I hardly recognise it." She laughed again and said, in music hall Cockney, "'There's electric light naow and tellyphones.' I don't suppose you'd remember Gertrude Lawrence. She was marvellous."

"*Red Peppers*. My parents had a record they used to play. She says, 'And a little invention called moving pictures'."

"You do know it! 'Garbo for nine pence.' Closer to nine pounds, these days."

The waiter brought the sole and warned them that the plates were hot.

"Charlotte used to have her favourite haunts, but she told me they're all gone. It's lovely that this place is still here. Mmm. The fish is perfect. Do you still like living in London? After all the changes?"

"I don't like the traffic, I don't suppose anyone does. But I told you, dear, I have my little rut. I don't read the newspapers. If I've got John Eliot Gardiner and Charles, and the cats, I can't complain."

"I wish you'd met my mother."

"So do I, darling. She wrote me a very charming letter, once. Hugo finally stopped being silly about you—your being American—and you and Edward not being married. I invited her to stay, and she wrote back and said it would be lovely. But somehow it never happened."

Gillian looked at Delia, a little startled. 'Silly.' They were on their second glass of wine. Delia had never been so offhandedly candid. But of course they'd rarely spent more than an accidental few minutes alone together. In the years when Edward's father was alive, she'd used her charm to defuse the tensions between father and son. In mourning, she'd been brisk and matter-of-fact but had retreated into an arctic zone in which emotions were ice bound and barely visible. Now, at seventy-seven, she was on her own, and she seemed to have left the old constraints behind, in another life.

They finished their sole while it was hot.

"Tell me about Charlotte," Delia said. "Whatever you like."

"Charlotte was a dramatist. Whatever happened was awful or wonderful, or hilarious. Nothing was gray. People loved her for that—their own lives always seemed bigger and brighter when she was around. The footlights were turned up."

"Who brought her up?"

"Her grandmother, first. Her father was killed in the war. Then the grandmother died, and she was sent to live with some people named Arthur. They believed they meant well, I'm sure, but Mrs. Arthur was a rigid disciplinarian, and Charlotte was miserable. I guess that's why she couldn't ever say no to Olivia. Mr. Arthur was something in the navy, and he was almost never home. Charlotte said she thought Mrs. Arthur preferred it that way—it was tidier. Mrs. Arthur was always dusting and mopping, washing and ironing and polishing. She wanted things spotless, and the children were beaten if they got dirty. With a piece of rope. One of the children wet the bed and was beaten every morning. I remember when we talked about it—we were at the zoo, and Charlotte was looking at a monkey in a cage. It was all by itself in a corner, and it was pulling its own fur out. She said it was just like that living in Beatrice Street."

"There were other children?"

"Three other foster children. They were all tied to their beds at night and read the Bible twice a day."

Delia made a muffled exclamation. "What happened to Charlotte after that?"

"Charlotte left for London and never went back. She invented herself, that's what cities are for, isn't it? She had her career in television, and she married Tom, and had a baby and money and a little cottage, and everything most of us think we want. She was happy. Well, as happy as Charlotte could be. Now I think she was inconsolable."

The waiter poured more wine into Gillian's glass. Delia shook her head. "No more for me."

"It all came apart so fast, so completely. Tom left, and she went into a spiral like an airplane on fire. And now she's dead. I don't understand it."

"You never can, really. It doesn't matter how much you know."

Later, Gillian said, "It's so odd. When I met Charlotte, she was as anticlerical as you can get. A few years ago, she started going to church."

"What sort of church?"

"Catholic."

"That's not so bad, is it? She might have turned into a Moonie, or one of those channellers. I have a neighbour who talks incessantly with her dead husband. She even asks me if I wouldn't like a word with Hugo."

"Yikes. I never thought of that." It was an odd sort of comfort Delia offered, but it was effective.

"Would you like a sweet?"

"I'm sure they're wonderful. But it's so hot."

"Neither would I. Let's have a digestif, instead. Brandy?"

When Gillian got back to the flat, the phone was ringing.

"How was dinner?" Edward asked.

"Remarkable."

"Really?"

"Your mother told me more about your family than I've learned since I met you. How's the conference?"

"We had some chaps talking about geographical profiling this morning. What exactly did my mother tell you?"

"Oh, all about your father hating you being a detective, and not liking me being American, and not wanting to accept any changes in the world."

"Is that all?" Edward sounded relieved. "But you knew all that anyway."

"Sort of, but Delia and I have never spoken about any of it before. Do you know she has a neighbour who talks to the dead and asks her if she'd like to chat with Hugo?"

"You're joking." Edward laughed. "My father didn't even like using the telephone."

"She remembered Charlotte. It felt strange, having a nice dinner like that. There was a moment when I was going to cry, and I thought, I can't cry here, and then everything seemed absurd. A friend dies, and there are places where you're not supposed to cry."

"It would have been all right."

"It would not. It would have been making a fuss. What were you worried she'd tell me about?"

"I don't know. Embarrassing anecdotes. Parents are very unruly."

"Did you know she was engaged to someone else when she met your father? She broke off with him, and he went away and got killed."

"The chap with the house? We drove past it once, when I was still in my teens. I think it was in Dorset. It was bought by some rock star in the eighties. She read about it in a magazine. She wasn't half narked."

Olivia sat on the balcony of Raymond's flat. She was indistinctly aware of having sat there for a long time. Across the river, the lights were glowing and twinkling in the near-dark. Gillian had left her hours ago, and she hadn't done anything since except sit, smoking and drinking a bottle of white wine that had been in the fridge and watching the tourboats go stupidly back and forth on the river.

In the morning, before Gillian's visit, she'd talked to her father, who'd rung to ask how she was. Then she'd called Nicky and Lisa and Raymond. Lisa wanted to come over right away, but Olivia explained about Gillian and said she would ring back later if she wanted company. Lisa had two parents who still lived together in a suburb of Birmingham and didn't drink, except sherry at Christmas; in addition, she had four grandparents, a brother, a sister and cousins. No one in her immediate family had died, only a hamster. They crowded together during holidays, and Lisa came back from these occasions bursting with anecdotes about Aunt Linnie's mynah bird and the time Lisa's mother absentmindedly put chestnuts in the stuffing without shelling them first and they exploded inside the turkey. Charlotte's story was exotic to her, but it was like something she might have read in a history book at school. Olivia didn't ring back; Lisa was seldom quiet, and if she thought Olivia needed cheering up, she would natter endlessly.

Nicky would have been all right, Nicky was the only person Olivia wanted, but Nicky couldn't come, because her shoot was starting. Fifteen or twenty people were converging on the house in Acton, with the cameras, the lights, lengths of cable, sound equipment, props, a generator. Nicky had put her frenzied preparations on hold to listen on the phone and cancelled the rehearsal that evening, saying she had too many other things to do anyway. She offered to come to Raymond's flat when she was finished for the night, which might be at two or three in the morning, but Olivia said she would try to sleep. She knew Nicky would probably be working all night. They would see each other the next day. Olivia insisted she would come to the set, as planned.

"It'll be good for me to work, to think about something else."

"Is Raymond coming home?" Nicky asked.

"Maybe tomorrow, if he can manage it. I told him it was all right if he couldn't."

Raymond had been terribly sweet over an echoing connection; Olivia found herself telling him not to worry. If he dropped everything and rushed back to London, what could he do for her? He'd pace up and down fretting about the hundred things going wrong in his absence, the unanswered questions, the bad decisions. She'd called him because he was her boyfriend, but she hadn't felt comforted. There was a sense of constraint; she was reluctant to explain to him how her mother had died.

She should go inside and drink some water. Turning her head felt odd, like dragging a weight behind it. Oh dear, dizziness. She must be a bit drunk, and she didn't like being drunk. A long time ago, she'd tried it once, to see what it was like, and she'd loathed it. She squinted at the wine bottle. It was hard to see what was left in the dim light. She reached out and tilted it. More than half empty. And she hadn't eaten anything. She stood up, and the horizon line shifted alarmingly. Carrying her glass, she walked unsteadily toward the sliding door to the flat, misjudged the height of the sill, tripped and fell into the sitting room. This surprised her. She was strong and agile; she never fell. Numbly, she lay there, thinking that she should get up, but staying still because her head was spinning. When she tried to lift it, it seemed to swell, swaying like a water-filled balloon. Finally she sat, and then hauled herself up, clutching the doorjamb. Her phone was ringing. Someone was calling her. The phone was on the sofa. Still dazed by her hard landing on the floor, she lurched to the sofa and collapsed on the leather cushions. She picked up her phone.

"Hullo?" she said muzzily.

"Olivia? Is that you?"

"What?"

"What's wrong? Were you asleep?"

"Oh. Johnny." It was Wednesday; she'd said she'd meet him tonight. "I was going to get a glass of water." She looked about for the glass. Pieces of it were on the floor by the door. "I broke the glass."

"Are you all right?"

"Fine," she said automatically. Then, "No. I'm not."

"You don't sound good."

There was some dark liquid on the floor. But she'd been drinking white wine. Then she noticed that there was blood welling from a long gash on her right calf. "I'm bleeding," she said, surprised. "I've cut myself. Must've been the glass. It's not too bad. It doesn't hurt a bit." The blood was all over her leg. "I have to get a towel or something," she mumbled.

"Is anyone there with you?"

"No, nobody."

With difficulty, she clambered off the sofa and walked around the furniture towards the kitchen, clutching the phone in one hand. A fat cylinder of paper towels hung on a roller. She grabbed the end and pulled, and the towels spun wildly. A long, jointed tongue of white towel unfurled to the floor. "Dammit."

Johnny said something, but she didn't hear it. Tearing off a section of paper towels with one hand was impossible; the roll kept spinning. She sat on the tiles. A fast, bright trickle of blood was running from the cut. She put the phone down.

"What are you doing?" Johnny's voice said, from the floor. He sounded tinny and urgent.

"Stopping the bleeding." She made a wodge of paper towels and pressed on the gash in her leg.

"I can't hear you. The traffic."

"Wait a minute." She could press with one hand. She picked up the phone again. Slimily, it squirted out of her hand and fell back to the floor. Her palm was smeared with red. "Sorry. Dropped it. Bloody slippery."

"What happened to you? I thought you were at a rehearsal."

"Oh, Johnny. My mother died."

A siren shrilled somewhere close. The sound pulsed through the phone, then faded.

"You said she died? Your mum?"

"Daddy told me last night."

"But you shouldn't be all alone there. Why aren't you with your Dad tonight?"

"He's married. Going to have a baby any minute." She leaned her head wearily against a cupboard door. She saw a trail of her own glistening footprints leading into the kitchen. "What?" she said, realising Johnny was talking.

"Listen, I can be there in five minutes," he said clearly.

"Where are you?" she said, confused.

"In the car. What do you have there, an entryphone? What's the flat number?"

"Um, twenty. But—"

"I'm going to come and see if you're all right."

"I'm okay. I mean, you don't have to."

"Don't be daft." He was peremptory.

She stood up, and the room spun slowly about before settling down into its usual place. The phone had gone silent. "No," she said. "Everything's a mess." The mobile beeped at her. It had cut out; the battery pack was low again. Maybe it was defective; she was always having to recharge it. When she set the phone down, it clung stickily to her fingers. She wiped it patiently with a paper towel. Fuzzy white shreds cemented themselves to the plastic. She left the phone by the sink and detoured around the empty space in the middle of the kitchen, touching the edge of the counter for support, like a child learning to walk. Why was he coming to see her now? It was stupid idea, she thought. What could he do? Nobody could do anything.

She saw him on the video screen before he touched the button and pressed the buzzer to let him in. Then she unlocked the door of the flat and sat down on the floor. Blood was welling from the cut still, or again, but slowly. She had the paper towels in her hand. She turned them over until she found a clean patch and attended to the business of her leg.

When he came in, she smiled up in the general direction of his face. "The bleeding's stopped."

He knelt down. "Let me look."

She sat still.

"It's not too deep," he said.

"Only a flesh wound."

He looked at her face now. She couldn't get him into perfect focus. "I'll be all right in a minute." Concentrating, she stood up, swaying only a little. She put her hand out to the wall for support. "Too much wine," she said, apologetically.

"How much have you had?"

"Half a bottle."

"Not used to it, are you?" He sounded like a condescending older brother.

"No."

"You need coffee."

She walked carefully into the sitting room, feeling that she might topple over if she didn't sit down again soon. Her hands were covered with sticky brownish-red smears. She wanted to wash. Johnny was looking at the carnage: the trail of bloody footprints on the floor, the broken glass, and, outside on the balcony, the half-empty wine bottle and the ashtray full of cigarette ends. "Nice," he said. "The only thing missing is crime scene tape."

She sat on one of the dining chairs. It was much easier than standing. He disappeared into the kitchen; she heard the hollow noise of the kettle filling. She looked at her hands. The sounds—beans pattering into the grinder, the whump of the fridge door, were soothing. "Would you bring me a hand towel, a wet one?" she asked, accepting the situation.

He gave her wrung-out blue towel from the bathroom. It was warm. She wiped her palms and her fingers and then cleaned the blood off her calf and her ankle and the sole of her foot. It was already dark and dull. Blood was amazingly bright when it ran, a dazzling red. She'd cut her finger badly with a kitchen knife, ages ago, when she was twelve. The memory of the blood flowing down her hand was momentarily vivid. Mummy had been there, had said it would be all right.

She was clean, now, that was an improvement, but she was still feeling woozy, so she didn't move. It came to her that she should remember this, remember how she felt, in case she had to play someone who was drunk. She examined the feeling. It was like swinging too high, the giddiness, and then gravity hauling you backwards. She put her hands flat on the table, to stay level.

Johnny said, "There aren't any plasters in the bathroom."

She looked up. "Box with the cross on it in my kit," she said, through her fog. "Square blue case in the bedroom."

He vanished again, then came back with her miniature first aid box and set it on the table.

"Quite a travel kit. You have everything in there."

"In case I get lost in the desert."

He went away. Really, he was coming and going a lot. She was still in the green dress she'd been wearing all day; it was wrinkled; her lipstick had worn off, and she was holding the soggy towel. At any rate, Lisa couldn't accuse her of trying to seduce him.

He returned with a mug of black coffee. "Drink this."

She dropped the towel and took the cup from him with both hands. The hot liquid scalded her tongue but she drank. The heat felt good, going down her throat.

"Is Gina all right?" she said suddenly, the thought coming out of the blue. "The girl who was hit by a car? Did they take her home?"

"This morning. Drink."

Applying herself to the task, she swallowed another mouthful and then another, until without speaking again she'd emptied the mug. He took it away from her and brought a refill. She drank that more slowly, while some of the mist cleared from her brain. It seemed very odd that Johnny was here with her.

"How did you know where I was?" she asked, when she'd drunk about half the second cup.

"Andy told me. He heard you give the address to the taxi driver."

She puzzled over this for a minute and then remembered who Andy was. He'd got the taxi for her outside the club; he'd looked as if he could pick one up and carry it. "How did you get here so fast?"

"I was coming from the South Bank. I rang to see if you'd finished rehearsing. You were going to meet me, remember?"

"Yes." She drained the cup. "Some date, huh?"

He smiled at that. "I've had worse."

She opened the flat white box with the red cross on the lid and picked out some large plasters in sealed translucent packets. She was beginning to feel much better. "I'm going to tidy up," she said, rising. An arrow of pain went up her leg. She winced. "It hurts, now."

"Good."

She frowned at him. "Why?"

"Because it means you're sobering up. When I heard you on the phone, you sounded like you could bleed to death and not even notice."

She went into the bathroom and closed the door. Her face was pale and blotchy in the mirror, awful-looking, her hair rumpled. Her eyes were pink around the rims. She must have been crying earlier. She took her time, sitting on the edge of the tub, combing her hair and pressing a cold, wet cloth to her eyes, putting on some make-up. This calmed her.

She ripped the paper off one of the plasters, peeled the backing away and pressed it to her skin. It felt laborious, complicated. Her fingers were stupid. It was like trying to put on false eyelashes for the first time. When she was finished, she went back to the sitting room and found the sandals she'd been wearing earlier in the day. She surveyed herself briefly in the large mirror that hung opposite the sliding balcony doors. Better. She didn't feel like her usual self, but she looked all right, which helped.

She smelled toast. Johnny was in the kitchen, beating eggs and milk with a fork and tipping them into a frying pan. Lisa had once said Johnny could cook when he felt like it.

"You need to eat something," he announced.

"There's not much food here." But the eggs smelled good; she was hungry. "Can I help?"

"No, I don't want to drive you to the burn unit next."

"Very funny."

"Anyway, it's about ready."

Her leg hurt, standing, so she sat on the sofa, feeling spacey. River-cooled air drifted in through the doors.

"You look better now," he said, bringing the plates.

They ate their toast and eggs outside, in the dark, watching the lights of the cars flowing over Southwark Bridge. The buttery crunch of the toast, the smoothness of the eggs, occupied her. Their two chairs, low-slung canvas folding chairs with high backs, were side by side, facing the river. She finished the last corner of toast, leaned back and sighed, turning her head to face him. She felt enormously calm.

"What happened to her?" he asked.

"I don't know exactly. It could have been a heart attack. They found her in the garden."

"In London?"

"Fulham." The word sounded strange to her for a moment, like phlegm caught in her throat. "I grew up there. I thought I was going to see her today, but Daddy called me yesterday when I got home from work. The last time I saw her, we had a row about a script. It seems idiotic, now."

The water below them was crinkled, like tinfoil. The city hummed in the night.

"Did you know anything was wrong with her?"

"A few years ago, when I was still living at home, I used to be terrified that I'd come back and find her dead at the bottom of the stairs. She was drinking a lot. But she wasn't like that when I was a kid; she was different then. She had a job, but she still did everything else, like cook and sew dresses for me and read stories at night. I suppose she drank a bit then, too, but nobody noticed. But if she has, I don't know, heart problems, she's never said anything. Mummy didn't like doctors." She didn't mind what she told him. "Are your parents alive?"

"My mum is, absolutely. My father's dead."

"Oh. I'm sorry."

"It was a long time ago."

"When?"

"I was fourteen."

Johnny had left his jacket indoors. He went inside and came back with cigarettes. There were still a few left in the packet on the table. She shook one out and he lit it for her. He'd rolled up his sleeves when he'd cooked the eggs; she could see his strong wrists, the tendons and muscles of his forearms. A gold ring glinted in the dull light from the lamps inside. The smoke rose and vanished into the London haze. She felt slack, now, like a marionette with broken strings. If she could, she would rest her head on his shoulder and go to sleep. The thought was so seductive she felt her eyes closing. She forced herself awake.

"This is a nice flat," he said.

"It's not mine. It's Raymond's. Just for a few months. Then he's moving into a building he bought in Clerkenwell."

"You're not?"

"No. I'm just staying here for a few weeks while I look for my own flat." She didn't mention Kevin, because it would mean thinking about him. In the day since she'd learned of her mother's death, she hadn't left Raymond's flat, and Kevin had been banished from her mind. Now he hovered, a fugitive shape glimpsed at the rim of consciousness. She pushed him away. "Johnny, that fight at the club. Why did it happen?"

"Because Max brought Marie. He shouldn't have done that. Roy's jealous, and someone was bound to see Marie there and tell him."

"Lisa said you were angry."

"Max can handle himself; he used to be a boxer. But I don't want that kind of trouble at the club. Doesn't do it any good."

"I thought the doormen were supposed to screen people."

Johnny shrugged. "Connors isn't an ordinary punter; he's known around town as a tough bloke, with friends. The doormen wouldn't be keen to take him on. Max is a bloody idiot to fool about with Marie, and that's his business, but I can't be having brawls at the club, or a man like Connors holding a grudge." In the cigarette glow, she saw his brows draw together in a frown. "It's a headache. Max and I had a row, but we'll sort it."

"Marie must have been terrified."

"She knows Roy, she should have seen it coming."

"Men are mad."

Johnny's teeth gleamed. "And women aren't?"

"Not as mad as men."

"Everyone's raving mad. Especially in London."

Her left hand was resting on the wooden arm of the chair. He reached across the little distance and took it in his. For a minute or two, they said nothing.

Johnny tilted his head back, looking up. "I was on a boat once, at night. In the channel. You know how many stars there are, when you're out on the water? It's bloody amazing." He searched the pallid darkness. "You never see them here."

"I used to go to the country. You can see stars there."

"Where did you go?"

"Hampshire. My mother's cottage. I haven't been there in a long time."

"Why's that?"

"It's rented."

"But if it's yours, now, you can go if you like."

"No."

He got up and leaned on the railing, looking down, a dark silhouette against the flaring night. She felt drained of all emotion; it was odd to look at him now and remember the elation and panic she'd felt in the club, the days churned up with desire and ambivalence. She felt weightless, her head as hollow as a plastic doll's.

He threw his cigarette over the edge. "It's late."

Will-less, floating, she let herself be led indoors. It was going to happen, now, like going over a waterfall; there was no stopping it. She would observe the event from a great distance. It wouldn't matter. Nothing mattered when you were drifting like this, far away, your body hardly connected to your mind at all. Already she felt like a face on TV with the sound turned off.

They were in the sitting room. She stood, not moving, saying nothing. Waiting. There was a lamp on somewhere behind him, but the light seemed very dim. He stepped close to her and put his hands on her shoulders. She could feel the shape of each finger on her skin.

"You're asleep," he said.

It was true. She came a little awake, blinked, said his name.

"Johnny?" It came out in a croak.

His face was in shadow, his eyes like ink.

"You should go to bed."

"Yes." She didn't move; his hands were still holding her shoulders. He let them drop. "I think I remember the directions," she said, turning away at last.

In the bedroom, she pulled off her sandals, unzipped her dress and let it fall to the floor. Too stupified even to brush her teeth, she crawled between the sheets and muttered, "Good night," in case he was listening.

"I'll see you tomorrow," he said, sounding far away. She was asleep before the door opened and closed.

5

Olivia had given Gillian two keys, one for the front door and one for the back. The first one she tried fitted the lock on the front door and turned with a little jiggling. On Gillian's list of things to do this morning was to call a locksmith, since the house was now empty and unprotected. Standing in the gloomy hallway, she listened to the silence. An envelope lay on the floor, just inside the door. She bent down reluctantly, as if at the moment of touching it she would accept her responsibilities as Charlotte's executrix. But that was foolish. She'd accepted them already, when she took the keys from Olivia. The envelope was from Inwood's Wine Merchants, a bill, by the looks of it. She wouldn't open it yet.

She walked into the sitting room and pushed the curtains back. Dust shook itself from the folds, swam in the light. In the glare of the sunshine, the room looked like a stage on which the same play was always performed. Everything was where it had been the last time. The plate with its dried crusts was still on the floor. Olivia might be coming later in the day, and it would be better if she didn't see it. Gillian dropped the bill from Inwood's on the desk and carried the plate to the kitchen. Dirty coffee cups were jumbled on a counter speckled with greasy crumbs. In the sink, a small enamel pot contained a quantity of something as black and hard as lava. Fruit flies gleaned in a field of empty wine glasses. As Gillian approached, they rose and looped torpidly in the air above her head. It would be a simple thing to do, to clean the dishes. She would start with that.

The dishwasher had a rusty odour; Charlotte, Gillian guessed, rinsed her few dishes under the tap. She squirted some Fairy Liquid into the sink and put the glasses in to soak. Then she looked in the fridge. It wasn't too bad: brown stains and dry curls of onion skin on the solid shelf over the drawers, a few nodules strung along the wire racks like a handful of greasy beads. But no fur, no extra-planetary life forms. The fridge was almost empty. Her wedge of cheese lay untouched in its wrapping, and a loaf of unsliced bread was hard and light, like a styrofoam brick. There was little else, apart from a lump of butter in torn foil and two bottles of Muscadet. On the evidence, Charlotte ate nothing but toast. The milk was sour. In the vegetable drawer, Gillian found a few potatoes, pouchy and withered, the eyes sprouting, stubby root tips pushing blindly through the skin. They made her think of Charlotte lying on a slab in the morgue. The aroma of congealed Roquefort mingled queasily with the scent of decay. She poured the milk away and dumped everything else into an Inwood's plastic bag.

Disturbed by the potatoes, Gillian became determined that Olivia should not see dirty dishes or feel the crunch of crumbs under her shoes. She shouldn't smell wine dregs. In a burst of energy, she washed and rinsed the dishes, wiped out the fridge and swept the kitchen floor. She scrubbed the table clean of sugar and ashes and the brown rings of milky coffee stain. A silk scarf dangled over the back of one of the chairs; Charlotte didn't bother with accessories any more; perhaps it belonged to Olivia. Gillian left it. There was a bag of rubbish under the sink; she took it outside, after emptying the ashtrays. Charlotte's bins were in the tiny front yard. They looked quite at home next to the shabby lilac bush, Gillian thought, whereas the bins next door huddled like asylum seekers among clipped box hedges and terra cotta pots of trailing lobelia.

Inside, the smell of cigarettes was deep and rich, not like the thin odour that frets the clothes of non-smokers after a party. The curtains and carpets had been cured in tobacco smoke. Gillian went upstairs to see about opening some windows. She couldn't remember what the rooms had looked like when she'd rushed up on Tuesday, looking for Charlotte, but she knew the layout from previous visits—three bedrooms and a bathroom.

Here was Olivia's old room, where Gillian had slept during the Christmas when there was no heat, when Olivia was still a baby snuggled into a cradle beside Charlotte and Tom's bed. The window overlooked the back garden, half-visible through a screen of leaves. A branch squeaked against the glass as she raised the sash. Looking down, she could see the place where Charlotte had fallen.

When Gillian had first seen it, the garden had been full of mud and paving stones, not trees. The bedroom had white-painted plaster walls. There was nothing in the room then except a brass bed and a single chair. Later, it was a nursery, then a child's room crammed with toys and books, with stars on the ceiling that glowed in the dark, and stencilled vine leaves around the windowframe. Still later, Olivia and Charlotte put up wallpaper and hung a big oval mirror over the dressing table. The room, with its white cotton curtains and bedcover, was the same now as it had been just before Olivia stopped living at home, except that it was tidy. A dozen dolls reposed on the bed, propped against the pillows. Gillian opened the clothes cupboard. The laden hangers were jammed together, and the floor was a heap of battered shoes. On top lay a single bright pink platform sandal with a sole nearly two inches thick.

The room held the past like a cup. It was full; there was no space for the present. A dustcloth hung over the mirror. Gillian lifted it, half imagining that the glass beneath would reflect some other moment, would show her Charlotte long ago, perhaps, with a baby on her arm.

Charlotte's room—Charlotte and Tom's old bedroom—was at the front. The blinds were pulled tight, and the curtains drawn across. Gillian flicked the light switch on the wall and a floor lamp with a beaded chiffon shade came on. Torn shreds of chiffon hung like cobwebs. The bedcovers were rumpled, the quilt dragging on the floor. Drawers stood half-shut. Charlotte's dressing table was covered with jars and bottles and crumpled tissues. A paisley scarf was slung over the mirror.

Gillian crossed the room and pulled aside the curtains shrouding the windows. Sunlight lanced in, as if opening a wound. She shut the drawers and contemplated stripping the bed, then thought that a bare mattress would look cruelly efficient: a hospital bed between cases. She yanked the covers into something like order and spread the quilt over the top.

She looked at the books on the shelf by the bed. *Winnie the Pooh. The Wind in the Willows*, a pattern of willow leaves on the binding. *The Little Prince, The Secret Garden*. All the books Charlotte had bought for Olivia, the books she believed children should have, and that no one had given Charlotte when she was young. The summer after Tom left, she'd spent hours just sitting in the garden, sipping wine and reading them, one after another. She said she preferred Narnia to London.

Gillian gathered up the tissues and carried the wastebasket away. On her way to the stairs, she passed Charlotte's office. An old Mac was on the desk, along with an even older fax machine. A mountain of paper. Boxes of video tapes were stacked against one wall. Gillian paused to look. *London Album,* she read on several labels. The dates were from the early 1970s. She pulled out one cassette and examined it. Not a format that could be played on the VCR, alas.

The doorbell rang. It couldn't be Olivia; she hadn't called yet. A police officer? No reason she could think of. Mildred Smythe and darling wee Taffy?

It was a young man, delivering flowers. He looked at her, then his eyes went to the number above the door. "Olivia Bening? Is she here?"

Flowers. How kind, Gillian thought. I wonder who sent them. "Are those flowers for her?"

"Yeh."

"You can leave them, if you like, but I'm afraid she's not here."

"Oh." He frowned. He had a round head with hair shaved close to the scalp, light, almost colourless eyes, and a small triangle of dark beard at the tip of his chin, like a drip of dirty water. Big shoulders. He was funny looking; it wasn't so much the round, bristly head and the risible beard, as something about the eyes.

"It's OK, she'll get the flowers. Do you want me to sign for them?" As she said it, Gillian noticed that he had no clipboard, and there wasn't a van parked in the street in front of the house.

"Sign? I wanted to give them to her, like."

"Oh. You know her."

"Yeh, what'd you think?"

He was wearing a loose shirt that hung over floppy trousers. She should have realised. "I'm sorry. Her mother just died. I thought someone had sent flowers to the house."

"Her mum?" He stopped. Gillian saw him take it in. He must have known Charlotte; the news startled him.

"Yes, it was very sudden. Olivia's just come back to London."

"From Morocco."

"That's right."

"Is she here then?"

"Not at the moment."

"I thought she would be here," he said stubbornly. He looked over Gillian's head, into the house. "Staying, like. Where is she then?"

"I don't know," Gillian said, unwilling to offer any information about Raymond's flat. "I can give her a message when she calls." Instinct prompted her to be evasive. Ordinary urban caution, perhaps; she didn't know him from Adam.

"What happened to her mum?"

"An accident."

"Car?" he said, with quick curiosity.

"No. A fall." A car accident was a natural presumption, she supposed.

He looked down at the green cone of paper enclosing the flowers, wiping one palm on the fabric of his trousers and shifting his weight from foot to foot. "I got these."

"I'll tell Olivia. What's your name?"

"Kevin." He grinned awkwardly, an attempt to be ingratiating. "Look, can I come in, just for a minute?"

"I don't know—" Gillian hesitated. She was busy. Besides, it was Charlotte's house, and she felt an obligation to Charlotte's privacy.

"A note, innit? Can I just write something?"

"Yes, of course." It would be rude to refuse. He was an oaf; she felt a twinge of pity.

Gillian led him into the kitchen, thankful that she'd cleaned. His eyes darted everywhere, up the stairs and into the sitting room as they passed. She had a pen in her bag and gave it to him, then left him in the kitchen while she went to the sitting room for paper. She pulled open one drawer and then another.

When she got back to the kitchen, he was standing behind a chair, holding up the silk scarf that had been draped over the back.

"This is Olivia's," he said, looking at Gillian suspiciously.

"Oh. I thought it must be hers." She put out her hand for it. For a moment, she thought he was going to refuse to relinquish it. His arm jerked backward. Then he changed his mind and laid it over the chairback.

"I brought you some paper and an envelope. I'll put the flowers in water," she said shortly, and began to search the cupboards, hunting for a vase. He watched the doors opening and closing. She found a heavy ceramic jug and filled it with water.

He was unwrapping the flowers. Lilies, large white ones, their stamens heavy with pollen, a reek coming off them like spilt perfume in a suitcase.

She set the jug on the kitchen table. "Did you want to write a note?"

"Right." But instead of doing so, he placed the lily stalks one at a time in the jug, absorbed in minute adjustments to the way they stood. It was an odd spectacle, Gillian thought, this lout with his brutal haircut and ungainly posture and sloppy clothes, finicking with the lilies like a florist arranging a window display. Perhaps he was worried about what to write.

He picked up the pen and sat down but didn't touch the paper. Gillian meant to be silent, so that he would hurry, but, despite herself, she spoke. "Did you ever meet Charlotte?"

He didn't look up. "Yeh. Coupla times. She was famous, like. Something on telly."

"She produced a documentary programme. *London Album.*"

"Yeh." His tone was flat, affectless. He bent over the table and scribbled for a minute, folded the paper and inserted it in the envelope. Then he propped it against the jug. Gillian saw a look of satisfaction flit across his features. There was something sly about it, as if he had a secret that pleased him. He stood up.

"I'll make sure Olivia gets it," Gillian said, moving to the door of the kitchen. He made her uncomfortable; she was eager for him to go. As they started down the hall, his head turned, and his forward motion was sharply arrested. Gillian could almost hear a squeal of brakes. The light from the sitting room, where Gillian had pulled back the curtains, lit the hall indirectly. On the wall was a photograph Gillian hadn't noticed in the gloom preferred by Charlotte—a black and white portrait of Olivia. She looked about fourteen or fifteen, shy, thrillingly beautiful, achingly young. Kevin stared at it. His body was rigid and trembling; he was like a cat at a window seeing a bird outside. Then he was moving again, clumping along the hall towards the front door.

Gillian opened it for him. He went through it and down the steps as if he'd forgotten her existence. She stood and watched him disappear up the street, not happy that she'd permitted him to enter the house. She'd met plenty of lumpish youths in her years of teaching, boys who blundered through doors, who barely knew how to say hello or goodbye. They weren't like Kevin. There was something off about him. Wrong. She glanced at her watch and shut the door. It was time she got on with finding the will.

Olivia spent the first part of the morning rubbing at rust-coloured smudges on the floors and the counter in the kitchen. The flat embarrassed her when she woke up: the stains, like evidence of a crime. She felt guilty of criminal stupidity and cleaned in a penitential mood. It took a long time. The glazed wood wiped clear, but a print from the heel of her palm left a faint oval on the paint near the door, even after a scrubbing. She had a headache. The gash on her leg was tender, a long, narrow split in the skin, as if it had been laid open with a lash. Her body felt sluggish. Standing in the shower, she turned the hot tap off and let the freezing torrent shock her awake.

All that time, she didn't think about the previous day or evening, about her mother or about Johnny. She thought of herself as June, the character she would play in Nicky's script. June, cleaning up after her sister. The efficient, furious, desperate way she would scrub, as if scrubbing could save a life. At four, Olivia would arrive at the house in Acton; they would start. She would walk about the set first, touching everything, sensing the size of the space, how long it took to cross it, the feel of the floor under her feet.

Dressed in a T-shirt and soft, black cotton trousers, her hair pulled back in a clip, she distanced herself from the person she'd been the day before. Today, she had to be ready to work. She made more coffee and permitted herself to smoke a cigarette on the balcony. Her throat felt charred. She'd dreamed of her mother lying asleep in the garden. And of the accident, again, but she'd often had nightmares about it. This afternoon she would go home. She didn't want to see the empty house; it would bring her mother's death into sharp focus. But it felt like an obligation, an acknowledgement, something she had to do, because she hadn't been there for weeks. And it seemed selfish to leave Gillian alone with everything that needed to be done. I'll have to ask her what I should do, Olivia thought. Next week I should have some time.

She would go straight from Fulham to the set. Perhaps it would be helpful, seeing her mother's house, the empty chair, the books, the ashtrays still full of stubs. When, in Nicky's film, she had to go through her dead sister's things, she'd bring this experience with her, this knowledge.

Olivia had the thought and then was chilled by it. To be an observer of her own grief, to think that she could make use of it, what did that say about her?

Parts of the previous evening were hazy. She tried to remember the sequence from the beginning. She'd wanted water; there had been a phone call. Johnny. She saw herself sitting on the kitchen floor with a lot of paper towels. He'd made her drink coffee. She remembered the coffee quite clearly, and wiping the blood from her leg, and everything after that, but when she tried to go back and picture herself falling, it was like looking through glass blocks—seeing only light, and rippling patches of colour that refused to resolve into shapes. The moment when he'd walked through the door was there in her memory, but after that there was a missing piece of footage. Not a very long one, she guessed, but long enough to have made a complete prat of herself. She hugged her knees, her eyes closed, wanting to erase her embarrassment, to be invisible. Then this, too, felt self-indulgent. She'd been squiffy. Why make a fuss? It could be worse, after all; Jane Fonda in *The Morning After* had woken up with a dead man in her bed.

Heat radiated from the building surfaces; the sky was blank, the air gravid with moisture. She was sitting in the same chair, her hand resting in the same place it had been last night. The day blazed, and the other chair was empty, but she could close her eyes and feel what it had been like in the darkness, and the moment when he took her hand. All her emotions had seemed to speak through the touch of their palms. It had been like having a friend, like having Nicky there.

Back inside, she noticed that the red light on Raymond's phone was blinking. A call must have come in while she was in the shower. She listened to the message. Raymond. He was sorry, but he couldn't possibly return today, there was a crisis, there were delicate negotiations. He would be back as soon as possible; he'd booked a flight for Sunday. He asked her to ring him back.

The message ended. Olivia felt a rush of pure relief. Raymond's return had become a complication, and today she couldn't endure another complication. If he walked in the door now, she wouldn't know what to say or do. She was familiar with Raymond's reluctance to delegate. Lisa called him a Virgo Victim—meaning that he was fussy, perfectionist, convinced that everything would fall apart as soon as his back was turned. Olivia was usually more understanding, but now she felt a spurt of animosity. If he'd come home and found her after she fell, his idea of her would have been quite spoilt. He would have cleaned up the mess, no doubt, would have been concerned; she could imagine him making coffee for her. But she would have felt his disdain; there would have been no jokes, no sitting side by side in the dark talking about stars. She would have felt worse, not better. If he'd come home, she decided, it would have been the turning point, the scene she would think of when she explained to herself or Nicky, or perhaps someone else, why she and Raymond split up.

The top sheet on the notepad by the telephone had been folded back; a phone number was scrawled on the new sheet underneath. Nothing else, no message. She scrutinized the paper as if the writing might yield something besides a sequence of digits, but it was uninformative. She tore the sheet off the pad and tucked it in her bag and went to collect her mobile, which was in the kitchen. She touched it and hastily put it down again. The little phone was scaly and fuzzy, like strange insect. It was covered with dried shreds of bloody paper towel. Impatiently, she scoured it clean. She ought to have recharged it, too, but she was out of time, now.

Tom had said the will might be in Charlotte's desk, or in her office upstairs. Gillian decided to try the desk first. A heavy rolltop affair, with pigeonholes, it stood in a corner of the sitting room. Under the bill from Inwood's, which she'd dropped on top, was a large, discouraging heap of paper. In the light from the nearby front window, a fine powdering of blackish dust was visible on some of the lower layers.

Gillian lifted the Inwood's envelope and looked at what was underneath. At the top was another unopened envelope, this one from Inland Revenue. It looked menacing, she thought, but then envelopes from the tax office always did.

They made you wonder what you'd done without knowing it, like the sight of a police car in the rearview mirror. How long since Charlotte had done her taxes? She'd hated it always, and always cried when she went to see her accountant. She said he ought to charge double, for therapeutic as well as accounting services.

Beneath the threatening envelope were at least five inches of paper. The heap would make a fine bonfire. She poked at the top layers, finding a five-pound note and a notice from the borough council about recycling. She would have to go through the lot, but not today. Dismally, she began pulling open the drawers. Blue airmail stationery, the kind that folded twice and had three glued flaps that you had to slit with a letter opener. A box of carbon paper. Carbon paper! She hadn't seen a sheet of carbon paper for about fifteen years, or received a cc that actually was a carbon copy. Gillian knew a few people who still had typewriters, but they used photocopiers, not carbon paper. Charlotte was not one for clearing out.

The deed box was in the deep bottom drawer. Gillian lifted it out and noticed that her fingertips were already black with dust. She washed her hands in the kitchen and opened another window. The smell of the lilies was so strong it was oppressive. Then she opened the box, which contained several manila envelopes with red string fasteners. In the first, she found the deeds to the house and Charlotte's cottage. The second held several old passports, an international driver's licence from 1985, and Olivia's birth certificate. Charlotte's will was in the bottom envelope. Gillian was relieved, not as much by having found it without difficulty as by the evidence of order, of control, that the deedbox represented. Charlotte might not have known what day of the week it was, she may have been sozzled by noon, but she'd been able to keep track of these papers and ensure that she wouldn't leave chaos behind. There was a letter with the will, addressed to her, Gillian.

She sat in Charlotte's chair and opened the letter. The date on it was almost a year in the past.

Dear Gillian,

I'm of sound mind as I write this, though you have leave to wonder. I've made a new will, because Olivia is legally no longer a child. But I still want you to be executrix. Not to do the legal paperwork, you can pay a solicitor for that, it doesn't matter. What matters is the rest.

I want you to go through the house and help Olivia decide what to do. She has no idea what books and prints are worth. She'll need advice, or some spiv will offer her two hundred quid to clear out the house and she'll say yes. I don't want Tom mucking in, and I don't think she'd ask. Have you ever thought that when you're dead someone will sort through your drawers, will look at your letters and your underclothes? It makes me want to burn the house down when I go. Being of sound mind, as I said, I'm asking you to be executrix, instead.

Be Olivia's guardian angel, Gillian, please. She's not a child, but I don't want her to handle everything alone. I've left her the house, of course, and the money, whatever doesn't go to the taxman. I've never been any good with money, as you know. It's a miracle I'm not a bag lady. I'm well aware that most of my neighbours think I might as well be.

As for my body, what's left of it, I'm bloody well sick to death of having one. Remember how they told us in school that we were 98% water? That's what I feel like, sitting in the bath, an old bin liner full of water, bulgy and splitting at the seams. Everything aches, and I'm afraid of losing my mind. A few months ago, I went to church one Sunday and a woman I knew came up afterwards and said hello. To my complete horror, I found I couldn't talk at all. Couldn't make a sound come out. It lasted for what felt like hours but I suppose was about a minute. It was like trying to yell underwater. Rather terrifying. I've been waiting to see whether it would happen again. It hasn't, but a little bird tells me that this episode signifies nothing good. That's why I'm writing this letter.

If I had my druthers, I'd have a funeral pyre like Shelley, on the beach, with enormous logs. It would be grand, wouldn't it? You'd feel that life must have meant something after all if you could have a whacking great blaze up to the heavens, and not some oleaginous little man pressing a button and sliding you through purple rayon curtains. But if you burn me on the beach you'll go to prison, so you have my permission to let the undertakers do their job. No fuss, please. I should look decent if Olivia wants to see me, but no fancy coffin, and, for God's sake, no embalming. It's grotesque. I don't want a service. Just light a candle for me and scatter my ashes on the River Thames. Or whoever's ashes you get in the tacky little urn. Did you know the ashes are often not those of your own dear departed? After all, how would anyone tell the difference?

Gillian blinked and burst out laughing. That was Charlotte. The old Charlotte. Who else would joke about mixed-up ashes in a letter to her executrix? Charlotte had had a damn good time writing it; judging by the tone, she'd enjoyed writing this letter more than she'd enjoyed anything for years.

Take one of the botanical prints. My choice for you would be the traveller's joy, since you're always going back and forth, but choose whichever you like. I want to think of it hanging somewhere in your house.

There was one more paragraph.

Forgive me for putting you to so much trouble, and remember me kindly, if you can—think of us sitting under the trees in Provence, eating cherries. I still do, though it was a long, long time ago.

Your old friend, Charlotte

Gillian's eyes blurred. She got up to look at the print of traveller's joy. *Clematis vitalba*. Charlotte was asking for more than her help with the house; it seemed to Gillian that

Charlotte wanted Olivia to have somewhere to turn, apart from Tom, if she was in need. Gillian thought, I'll do whatever I can, whatever Olivia allows me to do. She read the letter again. Would Olivia know the story about Shelley's funeral pyre? She'd called; she would be arriving soon.

The will was signed and properly witnessed. It wasn't complicated. The house and contents went to Olivia, along with whatever financial assets survived death duties and probate fees and legal bills. But Charlotte had left the cottage and its furnishings to Iris Gill.

Iris Gill. How extraordinary. It had been a long time, years, but Gillian remembered her very well. She'd met Iris on several occasions in Hampshire, at the cottage. There had been dinners with Charlotte in London and a picnic, one summer. Iris Gill had been married to Ralph Brody. They'd been close friends of Charlotte's and Tom's, until the car accident. Until Charlotte had knocked Ralph down in the road between the cottage and the pub and had nearly killed him. Now she'd left Iris the cottage. How extraordinary.

Ralph, Gillian remembered, had been a handsome man with a monkeyish charm which he probably used to advantage in his antiques business. He had an eye for objects and a fund of stories; there was an amusing one about a recipe collection and finding Victorian love letters written in code by two lesbians. He was a good cook, and at the cottage he sometimes made repairs for Charlotte; once, when Gillian was visiting, the pipe beneath the kitchen sink sprang a leak, and Ralph came over from the cottage he and Iris were renting. Charlotte fluttered about the kitchen cooing encouragement while he lay on his back on the floor with his head under the sink.

Still, it had been Iris whom Gillian had liked. A small, sharp-featured woman, like a hawk. An artist. Absorbed in her work, she was less sociable than Ralph, but talked fluently when in company, her conversation laced with an incisive candour and an appreciation of the absurd.

In the months immediately following the accident, Charlotte had rarely referred to Ralph's medical condition and of Iris had only said she'd heard she was coping. Ralph had been in intensive care for weeks; after a while, he'd been sent to a rehabilitation centre. At that time, he could neither walk nor speak. Later still, he'd been transferred to a nursing home. Charlotte had told Gillian that, and then she'd stopped mentioning his name. Nor did she speak about Iris. Gillian, having once been warned off, never asked about them.

And now the will. After a breach of almost a decade, Charlotte had left the cottage to Iris Gill. There was no reference to Ralph. Perhaps he was dead, perhaps he and Iris were divorced. Gillian didn't know what had happened to him. Charlotte had often made impulsive gestures in her life, but giving the cottage to Iris was a choice she'd thought about. It must have meant a lot to her. Gillian hoped she'd discussed it with Olivia. And where was Iris? Still in London, most likely. Gillian would have to find her.

There would be a lot to do, Gillian knew that. Yet in another way she felt that there wasn't enough. The last will and testament of Charlotte Minter Douglas: no funeral, no complicated distribution of possessions, no gatherings of relations. Just Charlotte, erasing herself. 'Scatter my ashes on the River Thames.' It wasn't much, but at least there was something Charlotte had asked for, some small ritual the living could perform as an act of remembrance. Charlotte had wanted so much when she was young.

There was the doorbell. It had to be Olivia this time.

"I've found the will. It was in Charlotte's desk, just where Tom told me it ought to be," Gillian said, when they were in the sitting room. "So that's all right. Did you sleep?"

"Yes." Olivia stood in the middle of the room and removed her sunglasses. She looked quite different with her hair pulled back. Resolute, Gillian thought, ready to face the next thing.

"Have you read it?"

"It says she's left you the house and the money—if there is any. She doesn't know. Is the house paid off, did she tell you?"

"The mortgage? Yes, they were finished with that before Daddy left."

"Did she explain about the cottage?"

"Explain?"

"That she's left it to a friend, Iris Gill?"

"Oh. I know, yes, it's all right. I don't want it."

"Do you remember Iris?"

Olivia was looking at the room as if she hadn't been in it for a long time. The light coming in through the window was strange, after the years of closed curtains. She fiddled with her sunglasses. "I knew her when I was a child, when she and Mummy were friends. I haven't seen her for years."

"Charlotte hasn't mentioned her to me in ages. I wonder whether they've seen each other again. Do you know what became of Ralph Brody, in the end?"

Olivia shook her head.

"He was in a rehab centre and then a nursing home," Gillian said. "Did he ever recover?"

"I don't know." Olivia's voice was tight, clipping off the words.

Gillian dropped it. Charlotte's car accident was the last thing Olivia needed to be reminded of now that Charlotte was dead. "Anyway, I'll find Iris and let her know. Olivia, if there's any money, it'll be a while before you get it."

"It doesn't matter."

"Yes. Um, what about Charlotte? Do you want to see her?"

"See her? Her, her—no."

"Are you sure? It can help, sometimes."

"No." Olivia moved restlessly about the room, then stopped in front of the whatnot and studied the picture of herself and her parents. "Do we have to bury her?"

"Scatter her ashes in the river, she says." Gillian didn't mention Charlotte's comment about mixed-up ashes. If she were ever to show Olivia Charlotte's letter, it would be years from now.

"That's good." There was relief in Olivia's voice. "I don't like graves. I can't help thinking they're cold."

"Maybe Charlotte thought the same. She told me she wished she could have a gigantic funeral pyre, like Shelley's, on the beach. Do you know that story? Shelley was drowned off the coast of Italy, and his friends made a great ceremonial fire to burn his body. Byron was there."

"Byron?" Olivia looked interested. "Do you know about Byron? There's going to be a film of his life, and I might be offered a part in it. Teresa. Who's she? I was going to ask Mummy."

"I don't know, but Charlotte undoubtedly has a book here that will tell us. Shall we look?"

"Later." Olivia cast a rather despairing glance at the shelves of books. "I can't keep all these. I suppose I ought to. It's so hard to be in this room without her; she always sat here."

"I see her everywhere. She put so much of herself into this house. What about a cup of tea or coffee? I brought supplies."

"Tea would be nice. I'm tired, and I'm going to work in a little while." Olivia followed Gillian towards the kitchen. "What's that smell?"

The lilies stood on the table; their cloying, heavy odour filled the room despite the open window.

"Oh, the flowers," Gillian said. "Someone left those for you."

"Who?" Olivia's voice was so sharp Gillian was startled.

"A friend of yours, he says. His name's Kevin. He left a note."

"Kevin? Oh God." Olivia looked at the flowers as if they were a snake and might strike at her.

"What's the matter?" Gillian said. "Who is he?"

"He's a nutter."

"A—what do you mean?"

"He was always hanging about and ringing me. Sending flowers, leaving roses at the door. Then he started following me. That's why I moved."

"*That* guy? Oh no! Charlotte mentioned something about him."

"But he's never been here! How did he know I was coming?" Olivia's voice shook.

Gillian thought. "He didn't know. He asked if you were staying here, and he wanted to know where he could find you, but I didn't tell him. There was something weird about him; he bothered me. I didn't know why."

"He's barking mad, that's why."

"Does he know you?"

"No! I've only spoken to him once—to tell him to leave me alone."

"But he does know something about you. He says he's met Charlotte; he knew she was on television. He knew you were just back from Morocco."

"He can get that kind of information. From magazines, the internet, I don't know."

"Christ," Gillian said. "He was very plausible—about knowing you." She picked up the flowers. "I'll take these outside. And then let's have some tea and think about this."

"He wasn't in the house, was he?" Olivia looked ill.

"For a few minutes. I'm sorry. He came in to write a note. I thought it would be about your mother." Gillian held it out. "Do you want to open it?"

"Ugh, I don't want to touch it. Throw it away. He's a nutter."

"I think we should look at it."

"You do it, then."

Gillian tore the envelope and unfolded the paper. The writing was small, the letters tightly squeezed together. "Well, the note isn't about Charlotte. It's—here's what it says: 'Beware of the liars. They keep us apart. But I know how to find you'."

Olivia opened her bag, took out a cigarette and lit it with shaking fingers.

"This is an awfully strange note," Gillian said. "How long has he been bothering you?"

"Since April."

"God. Charlotte didn't tell me he was following you."

"She didn't know. I didn't tell her that part."

"What about the police?"

"I talked to them only a few weeks after it started. They were useless. You know what they said? 'Sorry, luv, we can't do anything until *he* does.' Until he breaks into the flat or something. They told me to let the answering machine take all my phone calls, and not to talk to him—that's the best they could do."

"Couldn't they at least speak to him? Give him a warning?"

"They said it's not always a good idea. Sometimes a warning just makes it worse. There's a new law; I saw it in the paper, it's supposed to be better, because stalking is an offence, now. But it doesn't help, they still won't do anything unless they see he's threatening me. If he's just leaving roses at the door, or watching me, it's like they're not interested. They don't understand how terrifying it is. It's like he's in a different reality. I tried to tell them that, and one of them told me to keep a diary. He seemed nice, and he said he'd talk to me again, but he's never rung back."

Gillian stared at the note. "Who are the liars? 'They keep us apart'—what's he talking about? It sounds paranoid."

"I don't know. That's what I mean—he's in a different reality."

"Are you keeping a diary?"

"I tried, for a few weeks. I wrote down how many times he rang up, all that. But then I went on location. And I moved. I had to get away from him."

"You went to Raymond's. Kevin doesn't know where you're living, that's why he turned up here."

"Lisa—my flatmate—told him I was moving in with my boyfriend."

"Maybe he thinks she's one of the 'liars'. You know, I don't think he was convinced I was telling the truth when I said you weren't here. This note is evidence. The court might think it was threatening, it's certainly creepy enough." The kettle was boiling; Gillian poured water over the tea. "What do you think triggered this mania? Charlotte said he was a fan."

"I was in a film that came out this spring, *The Karma Kids*, a story about some people who go to India looking for enlightenment and then try to bring a load of hash back and get into trouble. He saw it, he told me in April when he first started harassing me. The timing fits."

"What's the film like?"

"It's a character piece. Funny and sad. They kids aren't bad, just naive and a bit greedy. It's a road movie, in a way. The characters become enlightened, but not like they expected. It did okay on the festival circuit, and it played for weeks in London."

"You had a big part?"

"There are five leading parts. We're listed in alphabetical order in the credits. There isn't much violence or sex—it's not the kind of movie you'd think anybody would get all twisted about. But you never know. There's a scene where one of the blokes, who's desperate, tries to sell me to a man in Rajasthan. I escape, but I'm sort of a potential slave for one scene. Maybe a few perverts could get excited by that. Any nutter can go and see you, that's the problem. You wouldn't believe the weasels out there. They watch you, and it's not about the movie, it's something else to them. If they want to they can rent the video and watch you at home—you know, sit in the dark by themselves, have whatever fantasies they like, do whatever disgusting things they want to. And don't even ask about the websites."

"Ugh," Gillian said, wincing. That Olivia had been forced to become matter-of-fact about this appalled her. She read the note again. "Do you mind if I show this to Edward?"

"Do you think he can do something?"

"I don't know, but at least he won't just forget about it, like the dopey officer you talked to," Gillian said, wishing she could utter a few choice words to said officer. "I don't like the way Kevin came here. I don't like the way he says he knows how to find you. Is Raymond coming back soon?"

"Maybe Sunday. He never knows until he's boarding the plane."

"And Tom? Does he know about all this?"

"Daddy? No. I don't want to tell him. He can't protect me, can he? He'll only worry. And he's busy with Sibyl—she's having a baby."

"I think it would matter to him, to know." Gillian poured the tea. "If you're nervous alone at Raymond's, you can stay with us."

"Oh." Olivia looked surprised. She thought for a moment. "Thanks, but the security's good where I am. The trouble is, my schedule's hard for anyone normal to live with. It keeps shifting about, and I can be out really late. But it's sweet of you to ask me."

"The offer's open. Something could change."

"Yeh, totally, if Kevin finds Raymond's flat." Olivia had a hunted look. She stubbed out her cigarette and sniffed. "Why lilies? It's usually bloody roses." The odour still hung in the air.

After tea, Olivia went upstairs to inspect the contents of her room. She opened the cupboard and grimaced at the clothes and the mound of shoes. Then she sat on the bed. She looked very young. "I still know all their names," she said, looking at the dolls and animals. She picked up a battered cotton lamb with a pink felt tongue and cradled it against her cheek.

Gillian thought of her own museum of childhood, her old room, unchanged for decades, how necessary it felt to her now.

"Mummy covered up all the mirrors," Olivia said. "She didn't want to see herself by accident. Have you been in the loo up here? There's paper taped over the mirror. She used a little hand mirror to put on her make-up and then turned it face down."

"I didn't know that."

"You wouldn't, if you didn't go upstairs. She hated her body; she could be savage about it. She once said it was all fat and tendon, like a cheap cut of meat. At first, she used to uncover the mirrors before I came home, so I wouldn't know, but then she didn't bother any more. She still liked me to tell her when I was coming, though, so she could get ready. So she could put on a skirt instead of that tatty old kimono. Comb her hair."

"Poor Charlotte."

"Yes, but why couldn't she get over being left? Daddy isn't God."

"Because her mother ran away? Childhood wounds stay with you. Tom leaving must have felt like the same thing happening all over again, and she couldn't bear it. Abandonment."

"It always seems easier to understand other people's parents," Olivia said.

Gillian laughed a little. "Yes, they're not the Mum and Dad who fucked you up."

"Ugh, Larkin. Mummy quoted that a couple of times when we had a fight. I hate that poem. It's good, but it's so mean and hopeless."

"Do you want kids yourself?"

"If I'm married. I don't want to be a single mother."

"Makes sense. Though you can't predict what will happen."

"Husbands run off."

"Wives, too."

"I don't think I'm the running off type." Then she blushed.

Gillian let her glance shift to the green branches of the trees in the garden. She was curious but wasn't going to ask questions. Raymond, she suspected, had better look to his laurels. Olivia didn't choose to pursue the subject; she was getting up, still holding her lamb.

She went as far as the end of the hall, then stopped at the doorway to Charlotte's room. "She moved all those books in here after I left home. The books she used to read to me."

"They must have reminded her of the times when she was happiest."

"She did a lot for me. For Daddy, too. All that entertaining—and he'd just buy the wine and help clean up. But then she stopped working, and she hardly ever invited anyone here. I would come home, and she'd be sitting in that chair downstairs, or she'd be in bed. She thought if I didn't actually see her drinking I wouldn't know, but it was so obvious."

"It must have been difficult for both of you."

"You don't know anything about it."

It was like hearing an echo. Charlotte had used the exact same words the last time Gillian had seen her. Her voice had rasped with the years of smoking, and Olivia's was clear and resonant, but the words were identical, and the tone: curt, fuelled by a half-conscious anger. Charlotte had been angry at Gillian for prodding her about her health and for being happy with Edward, but she'd mainly been angry at Tom and herself. And Olivia? She was grieving, but she was angry at Charlotte for falling apart, and also a little at Gillian, because she thought Gillian was taking Charlotte's side.

"Sorry," she said in a muffled voice. "That was rude of me."

"But you're right, I don't know much," Gillian said. "I wish you could tell me—Charlotte never would. Once upon a time I used to think I knew Charlotte as well as it's possible to know anyone, but that was when she used to talk to me more. Before she was so unhappy. When things started to go wrong with Tom, she never told me about it. Of course, I wasn't in London most of the time, but I didn't realise what was happening until the end. I was hurt, actually; I thought she should have told me sooner." Gillian sighed. "But I can understand that she didn't because she was afraid to. Words are real—they make things happen."

Olivia pointed to the neatly made bed. "You know what I'm remembering right now? When I was little, she'd sometimes threaten to send me to Mrs. Arthur. She'd do it when I was rude and silly, but I always knew it wasn't a real threat. Later she told me about Beatrice Street, when I was eight or nine, and then my friends and I used to pretend we were orphans and had to live with horrible Mrs. Arthur. We'd come in here to play, we'd take turns being Mrs. Arthur and tieing the others to the bedposts. Mummy caught us at it and she didn't mind, she laughed. Isn't that amazing?"

"Yes, and it sounds like Charlotte."

Olivia looked down at the shabby stuffed animal still in her hand. "I used to feel safe in bed if I had my lamb. Will you think I've gone off my head if I take it with me?"

"Not at all. I just wish it had big sharp teeth."

At the bottom of the stairs, Olivia paused, glancing through the doorway into the kitchen. She noticed the square of rust and olive silk draped over the chair. "Oh. My scarf. I thought I'd lost it."

"Kevin recognised it. He wanted to take it away."

"He actually touched it?" She flinched. "Then I don't want to wear it."

Gillian was studying the photograph of Olivia. "That's a marvellous picture of you. I know I've seen it before."

"Iris Gill took it. She had it framed and gave it to Mummy and Daddy as a present. It used to hang upstairs, but Mummy moved it down here."

"Is Iris a photographer?" That didn't seem right.

"No, I think she's just good with a camera. She does some other kind of art."

"I like the portrait of you and your parents that's in the sitting room, too."

"Why don't you have it, then?"

"Are you sure you don't want it?"

"Mummy has lots of photos—they're mostly in albums, or in boxes somewhere. Take that one. You can have anything you like—books?"

"Some are valuable."

Olivia groaned. "I don't know which ones."

Gillian was cruising the shelves. "Here's a book about Byron." She pulled it out and looked at the list of illustrations. "And there's your Teresa. Countess Teresa Guiccioli. Byron's last mistress."

"Let me see." Olivia examined the drawing. "How old was she? I wonder what she was like. She looks tender, I like her mouth."

"Why don't you take the book with you and read about her?"

"I will. She's holding lilies of the valley. Are they symbolic?"

"No doubt."

Olivia turned the page for a moment. "Lady Byron. She looks clever and mean." Her expression was rapt. "I haven't had time to read the script yet, but looking at these pictures makes me want to read it right now." She glanced at her watch. "I should go. I'll ring for a taxi."

"There's no need for you to come back for a while, if you don't want to. The legal wheels have to turn before we can do anything."

"But I'll help you, if you'll tell me what I can do. Now that I've been here once, it'll be easier the next time." She looked uneasily towards the door. "Do you think Kevin will come back?"

"I really don't know. If he doesn't know where you are, he might keep returning to places he knows are connected with you, on the off chance. Let's hope not. Do you want a sandwich while you're waiting for the taxi? I brought one for each of us."

Gillian got out some clean plates and unwrapped the sandwiches. They sat down again at the table in the kitchen. Olivia bit into her grilled pepper and mozzarella. "Mmm. This is a lot better than the food on the set will be. You know, Mummy took me to films all the time, but you used to go with me, too. You took me to see *Le Rayon Vert* when it came out. And *A Room With a View*. I loved both of them." Olivia's eyes were suddenly bright. When the taxi came, she tucked the Byron book into her bag and gave Gillian a hug.

"Come and see me in Pimlico," Gillian said.

Olivia rang Johnny's number from the cab.

"Troy."

"It's me. Olivia. I called to say thank you." She was tense; she knew her voice sounded formal.

"How are you?"

"I'm fine. My leg hurts a bit, but I'm trying not to stand on it too much."

"What about your head?"

"It's miracle of modern pharmaceuticals." Now she sounded flippant. Why didn't she just say what had to be said? "Johnny, I feel like a prat. I don't drink a lot."

"I know. You're the mineral water girl."

"You were very nice to me."

"Ring me anytime for coffee and eggs," he said easily.

"I mean more than that." She wanted to describe what she meant, but she didn't know how. "You were elegant. Cary Grant couldn't have done it better."

That made him laugh. "I've had practice. Two sisters."

"You have sisters?" She was surprised. She hadn't imagined that.

"Pieces of work, both of them. I've scraped them off some floors you wouldn't even want to step on."

"They're younger than you."

"Of course. If they were older, they'd have told me to sod off. Where are you?"

"I've just been home, to my mother's house. I'm on my way to work, now. Nicky's film. I'll be working in Acton all evening."

"You've been home and now you're going to work? That doesn't sound easy."

"Working's better than not."

"Do you want to go out for Chinese food when you're through? I'll be at the club, you can call me. How do you get back?"

"There's a van. Yes, I'll ring if you don't mind if it's late. I'd love to have some Chinese food. What are you doing now?" she asked, curious.

"I'm in my office."

"What do you do there?"

"Answer the phone," he said. "I've got a band manager on the other line, so ring me, okay?"

"Yes."

"See you later."

Olivia put her phone away and leaned back in the cab, closing her eyes. Her mind was shooting ahead, past the hours of work, to the moment when she would see him. She couldn't allow that. She had to pull back, concentrate on what she was about to do. Mummy, the house, the flowers from Kevin, meeting Johnny, they would destroy her performance if she let her thoughts go rushing about like rabbits. In fifteen minutes, or even sooner, she'd be arriving at the set. Nicky would need her to be ready to work, to be far enough into June that every inflection and expression, each motion or decision to be still would be in character. They didn't have the money for retakes of every scene, not like Bobby's film. They would shoot fast, the hand-held camera would help; Nicky didn't want a lot of fancy angles, but the actors had to be on top form and able to improvise. Olivia took out the script, not to look at, she already knew it well; she held it in her hands to focus her thoughts.

6

Gillian took the will and Charlotte's letter and the note from Kevin back to Pimlico. Her thoughts were full of Olivia and Charlotte, Charlotte's will and her marriage and divorce. She was relieved that Olivia knew about the cottage and that it wasn't a bone of contention. But why wasn't she more attached to it? That was surprising, though perhaps Charlotte's disaster in the car had spoilt it for her as well as for Charlotte.

It had pained Olivia to be in the house, Gillian could see it. But she was more trusting than she'd been yesterday, more ready to say what she felt. It was a pity she was so distant from her father. To understand her was going to take time, but today Gillian was hopeful that the old bond of affection could be renewed, if she was patient. Whether Olivia would ever turn to Gillian, as Charlotte seemed to hope, or confide in her, was another question. The answer would depend on many things, not just trust, but whether Olivia opened up to anyone. Her father was an oyster, or had been when he'd been married to Charlotte. And Charlotte herself?

Charlotte had given the impression that she worried about everything out loud. She took you into her confidence; the fluctuating moods of everyday life, the minor pitfalls, the reverses, the absurdities that other people concealed or ignored, she paraded, and these vivid little displays made you feel that you knew her terribly well. Indeed, she'd told Gillian a great deal about her life. And yet, as Gillian had discovered when Charlotte's marriage collapsed without Charlotte having said a word until that awful dinner a few weeks before Tom left, she kept to herself what she feared most. Charlotte, at her core, had been consumed by terror. She awaited catastrophe, and her stories were all distractions from it.

That ghoulish crack about her body as a cheap cut of meat. That was Charlotte. Rather a fierce observation to fling at your daughter in the bloom of her youth, especially such a pretty daughter. It reminded Gillian of paintings she'd seen: knobbly crones in black huddled around a lush young beauty, cackling at her ignorance of fate, at their bitter knowledge that she too will soon wither. But Charlotte surely hadn't meant it that way, not consciously, at any rate.

"She did a lot for me," Olivia had said. True; she could also have said, simply, 'she did a lot,' and she'd have been right. Even before she met Tom, Charlotte had made a name for herself, and, happily married, she'd become an irresistible force. In the year after the wedding, Charlotte produced the first programmes in her successful *London Album* series, and the next year the series won an award, and her future in television was assured. Those were the days when everything seemed possible.

Charlotte and Tom bought the house in Fulham. For a while, Charlotte's domestic life—what Gillian saw of it on her more-or-less annual visits—was a maelstrom of renovations and dinner parties. From the moment the house was bought, Charlotte set to work to transform it, stripping floors and putting up Laura Ashley wallpaper, and stenciling a floral border in the hallway. She learned about furniture and china and collected Victorian tiles; she acquired a library of books on architectural styles, on carpets and silver marks and Wedgwood. A few years later, when the house was arranged to her liking, she bought the cottage and whizzed out of London on weekends to peel up mouldy sheets of linoleum and hunt for suitable furniture at auctions in country towns.

By that time, she had Olivia to look after, but Olivia hardly slowed her down. Olivia was fed and dressed and read to every night; she was taken to museums and theatres and cinemas and to the country for holidays. She had ballet and piano lessons. Her friends romped through the house.

Gillian remembered weekends in the country, at Charlotte's cottage, Charlotte cooking lavish breakfasts of eggs and ham and scones, and even more lavish dinners—jugged hare, pheasant, trifle, damson tart. At the cottage they sat on cushions Charlotte had made and picked the salad for lunch from Charlotte's garden. She knew the name of every wildflower they saw on their walks, the history of the local village, and the crops in the fields. She didn't keep chickens, but she knew the breeds and could tell you when you saw a Buff Orpington or an Andalusian.

"How on earth do you find the time for all this?" Gillian had asked, on being shown a dress Charlotte had made for Olivia's fourth birthday.

"I don't need much sleep, you know," Charlotte said. "I sew, I write, I read for hours in bed while Tom is dead to the world."

"But you were busy before you met him—how do you manage to lead two lives at once?"

Charlotte snorted. "Oh, in the old life I spent half the night in pubs."

Everyone had watched her programmes about rock concerts and strikes and protest marches and solstice festivals. She wore her hair cut short and stamped about in tall boots; she made another prize-winning program about raising daughters, and Olivia was seen on TV before she was five.

"I was lucky not to have been born earlier," Charlotte said, while she was working on that program. "Imagine me a hundred years ago: a bastard daughter, deserted by my mother, not tuppence to my name, raised by Bible-thumping foster parents. No chance would I have had. No bloody chance at all. I'd have been given a place as a maid, or been on the streets, unless some poor sod married me, and then

I'd have been trying to raise six children on the change from what he spent down the pub."

Who knows what goes on inside a marriage, Gillian thought. She remembered that Tom had a trick of treating Charlotte like a child, when he was tender or amused, and outside her areas of formidable competence, she flirted with childishness, making comical mistakes and letting him rescue her, as though he were the father she'd never had. This game, played straight through the years of high feminism, had irritated Gillian, but she'd believed Tom was a good match for Charlotte—her temperamental opposite, a choice that at the time seemed right, an unforced gesture towards life, towards happiness. He was an optimist whose experiences had by and large confirmed his inborn nature. He expected things to turn out well, and for him they usually did, his energies not being wasted on worry. Charlotte was attracted to this self-perpetuating confidence in the future; she attributed it to Tom's comfortable middle-class childhood, his competence at sport which had made him a popular child, his parents' stable marriage, his mother's unwavering love. "All that good food," she said, "and sensible conversation around the dinner table, and a Cambridge education regarded as a birthright." Later, she did her best to duplicate these conditions for Olivia.

Perhaps she'd felt that his optimism could bend her fate in a different direction, that catastrophe could be cheated. She'd known instantly that she wanted to marry him. Gillian still had her ecstatic letter, the one she'd written after meeting him at a wedding in Kent where everyone was barefoot and stoned. And Gillian had the snapshot she'd sent a couple of months later. It was in an album now, but at the time Gillian had inspected it as closely as a queen's councillor would have studied a miniature of a marriageable foreign prince. It had been taken outdoors, at a pub. Tom sat in a relaxed attitude, his shirt sleeves rolled up, his head tipped back a little as he laughed. Charlotte was next to him, leaning forward, both arms gesturing; she was saying whatever had made him laugh. The photograph was very pleasing. She'd stuck it on her fridge for a while and hoped Charlotte would be happy.

Gillian hadn't met Tom until the wedding, a more traditional affair than the one in Kent, shoes being worn, and champagne being offered rather than pre-rolled joints on a tray. There was no one to give the bride away, but Charlotte said it didn't matter, she wasn't anyone's property. She had no family, and she was buggered if she'd let her foster parents give her away. "I wouldn't let the Arthurs come to my funeral, never mind my wedding."

"What about your name?" Gillian had wanted to know. It had been a big issue then, women's last names and what to do about them when they got married. Gillian had heard women say they'd just as soon have their husband's name as their father's, since they were both men anyway, and it would be better for the children, and had heard other women who said they weren't giving up their own names and the children could hyphenate, and their children's children, faced with four names, would work it out. Charlotte said she was keeping her name, because it was established in the media. "And I can't stick Bening on with a hyphen, or people will think I'm putting on airs."

Gillian went away believing that Tom would be good for Charlotte. He was calm, where Charlotte was stormy; he admired her, he was charmed by her quicksilver intelligence. Whether Charlotte would be good for him, Gillian didn't concern herself with. Plainly, life had never dealt Tom the blows that had been Charlotte's share. In Gillian's view, he was lucky to get Charlotte, although Charlotte believed the opposite.

She adored Tom. "Tom is amazing," she would say, and launch into a recital of Tom's virtues. Gillian would change the subject, having heard the list before, but she enjoyed Tom's company. He was genial, attractive to women, funny, intelligent. There was nothing to dislike. Yet she could stay in the house in Fulham for a week and hardly feel she was any better acquainted with him at the end of it. He voted Labour, went to NHS doctors on principle, and swore his daughter would go to a comprehensive, though he later changed his mind. Gillian knew these things about him, and other things that Charlotte told her, she appreciated his dry wit. But Tom himself remained a mystery. She felt she didn't know him at all. Perhaps what she meant was that he never revealed a weakness.

And now, Charlotte didn't want Tom in the house when she was dead. Well, that was easy to understand; she wouldn't want to be exposed like that to the man who had left her. But what had driven them apart? Something had happened that Gillian didn't know. An affair, perhaps, though she rather thought Charlotte would have confided that, no matter how painful it was.

And why was the Hampshire property left to Iris Gill? Charlotte had stopped going to the cottage years ago, but she hadn't sold it. That was odd, wasn't it? She could have thought Olivia would want it when she grew older, and then changed her will when Olivia said no. But it was possible that she'd always intended it for Iris, since the car accident, as a kind of recompense.

Once, during the early eighties, when Gillian was on sabbatical leave in London and consequently saw a good deal of Charlotte, Charlotte had confessed to loneliness. She'd been married twelve years and was turning forty, slowing down a little. Tom never talked to her, she said. He worked long hours, ate a silent dinner and then read journals. She often felt too tired to give dinner parties, but she did it anyway, because only then did Tom talk. He brought work to the cottage, and sometimes Charlotte and Olivia went without him. She was drinking more, a few glasses of wine in the evening to assuage the loneliness. But how could she complain, she said. He was ambitious and competitive and intellectually absorbed; she admired those qualities in him.

Eight years later, when Tom left, she was devastated. For how long, Gillian wondered, had the marriage been losing its weight and momentum, while, externally, it appeared to bowl down a straight track into the future?

The house Nicky had chosen had no electricity and only one working cold water tap. The cable from the generator snaked up the steps and in through the front door. Wires were taped to the floors and strung along a passage to the toilet, which had a cracked seat but still flushed. However, a scene was being shot in the bathroom at the moment, so no one could use it. Before they started, Nicky had asked if anyone needed to, just like a parent with kids before a long car trip. Most of the windows in the house were broken, including the window of the room Olivia was in, which looked out on a square of concrete and overflowing rubbish bins. Nicky was thrilled with the place.

Olivia was in a small back room crammed with three grungy sofas, where actors and crew could sit when they weren't needed. Usually, the room had at least a couple of people in it, sprawled on the sofas or staring morosely at the stale biscuits and the freckles multiplying on the bananas. But one of the crew had gone to a twenty-four hour corner shop for cigarettes and sweets, and the rest were busy doing their jobs. Olivia was waiting, trying to stay focused on June, while the other two actors did the bathroom scene. A needle had fallen in the toilet and the junkie was yelling at June's sister. Olivia could hear their voices through the floor.

"Stupid cow."

"You bloody dropped it."

"Oh, my fault, is it? I swear to God you're a stupid cow."

By the time June made her entrance, her sister would have a black eye.

Olivia laid her palms against the wall and slid down until she was bent at a right angle, flattened her back, contracted her quadriceps, and pulled her hips away from her fingertips, lengthening her spine. Then she let her hands drop, resting her palms flat on the floor. Seven o'clock. She was alone, and the room was extraordinarily depressing. The ceiling was stained, and the floor was splintered and scarred. This wasn't much like the day she'd shot the kiss for *Rough Diamonds*, when she'd had her own dressing room, and people to refresh her make-up and organize her costumes and bring her cold drinks. It was almost embarrassing, the way they'd whisked about, escorting her on and off the set. The fuss had made her tense. She was more comfortable here, not in the hideous room, but with the people, with the crew and the actors hanging out and joking together, eating the same awful food. It was what she was used to.

Everyone had been kind; they knew about Charlotte. Olivia was familiar with the stop-stop-go rhythms of work on the set, but tonight she didn't want any lulls; her concentration was fragile. She lit another cigarette and counted how many she'd smoked. Twelve, now. Too many. She'd done all right until she'd seen the flowers from Kevin. It had been horrible, going home. The house so sad and grotesque, even with the kitchen cleaned up and the bed made. It reminded her of Charlotte's feeble efforts to clean when she knew Olivia was coming, only Gillian had done a better job. And the wallpaper, the shelves of books that Charlotte had stopped reading, the dark, unpolished furniture, they had all soaked up the sadness like tobacco smoke; the house was brown and oily with misery. Yet Olivia could remember when it hadn't been a dark house.

Mummy. It was so strange that she was gone. She'd always been there, even sitting in her chair with the sixth or seventh glass of wine, even snoring on her bed in the middle of the afternoon. She'd been there, a mother-shape, a figure blocking out the dark. The only one who loved you forever, no matter what. Now there was just a hole where she'd been, and hardly anyone would care. Gillian would, but who else? Not Daddy; he had another wife, a new baby coming. He'd left.

This house was miserable, too, but in a different way. Mummy's house was hers, top to bottom, but you couldn't tell who had lived here. The only traces left were scars and smudges, smears of filth on the walls. The subject of the film was not addiction, Nicky said, it was sisters. Sisters and loyalty and childhood roles that kept their grip. The script worked that way; it felt a bit like a war film, Olivia thought, about people in a foxhole. In the end, one of them was hit, but the film was not about bullets, it was all about what the people said to each other in the dark while they were stuck there. Still, what they said was different from what they would have said if they'd been somewhere else. So it couldn't help being about addiction. She and Nicky had been back and forth on that several times.

Olivia thought of Kevin at the front door of her mother's house, the big round head with the skull gleaming through the colourless bristles of hair, the heavy-shouldered way he stood, with his arms hanging long at his sides. He'd come to find her and when she wasn't there had made up a story to get inside. In her mind he filled the hallway, the big head turning this way and that like a robot's, tracking her, hunting for any piece of information that might lead him to where she was.

She hadn't told Nicky, there had been no chance to talk about it. Now she shuddered so hard her teeth chattered. He'd been inside her house. She felt like an animal in a narrowing chute, gates closing behind her, something unknown and terrible in front. She was sweating. Through the smell of cigarettes and greasy cardboard she caught a sour whiff of her own fear. Outside the window, a rat emerged from a hole in the concrete and ran furtively along the wall, disappearing behind the bins. She stared, wondering if she'd imagined it. Sooner or later, he would find her. She knew it. But what would he do? What did he imagine he wanted to do when he found her?

She curled up in one corner of a sofa, hiding her face in the cushions, her heart beating erratically, her breath short and jerky.

"Christ," Nicky said.

Olivia hadn't even heard her come in.

Nicky shut the door and put her arms around Olivia. "Sweetie," she said. "Sweetie."

Gradually, it got through, and Olivia slowed her breathing down and stopped crying. "I'm sorry, Nicky."

"Shh. What is it? Your mum?"

"Yes and everything. It's too much, I can't—Kevin was at my house today, he was looking for me. And it's so depressing in here, and I saw a rat."

"Yeh, the location's brilliant, they should stage *No Exit* here. Everybody's freaked; it's like the house is full of ghosts. Hang on, what did you say about Kevin? Kevin was in Fulham?"

"He left a weird note, it says he's going to find me."

"And then what?"

"It doesn't say."

"Most nutters don't do anything," Nicky said. "You know, physical."

"Where am I going to go if he finds Raymond's flat? I haven't had a chance to look yet."

"You can stay with me."

"Oh, Nicky." But Olivia knew she wouldn't feel safe there for long. If Kevin was making a map of her life, Nicky was too big a piece of it to miss. "It was so sad going home. But I'll be all right, now." She blew her nose and tried to grin. "Good practice for you, calming down your star, right? Part of the director's job."

"You're doing great work."

"Not without you."

The door banged open. "Where the hell's Nicky? Oh, sorry."

"It's okay," Olivia said. "Is Chris back from the shop yet? I would kill for chocolate."

In the evening, Gillian went to the take-away in Tachbrook Street and bought butter chicken and spinach panir, and some rice and naan. She wasn't hungry, but the spicy fragrances made it possible to eat. Dinner was never a problem any more. You could live off M&S and take-away and forget about cooking for weeks at a time. Elizabeth David might not approve, exactly, but as the Lenin of the English food revolution she'd have to be gratified by its runaway success. She should really have a monument in recognition of her achievement. They could put a bronze braid of garlic on the empty plinth in Trafalgar Square. Or a giant bottle of olive oil. B.E.—before Elizabeth—you could only find olive oil in Boots. Then again, a statue might be nice. Elizabeth in classical drapery, London's Athena. There weren't many statues of women. Boadicea, Florence Nightingale, and Queen Victoria, of course. Who else? Emmeline Pankhurst, that was good.

Gillian poured herself two fingers of whisky. She couldn't think of any more statues of women. You could certainly argue that Elizabeth David had had a more beneficial effect than some of the dead-and-gone generals who littered the capital. And why should William Huskisson have a statue while Elizabeth David didn't?

She was picking at her dinner when Edward called.

"I found the will. The house goes to Olivia, the cottage goes to Iris Gill, an old friend of Charlotte's who's an artist. That's pretty much it."

"Have you spoken to Godfrey Rule?"

"Briefly. He was very soothing. Just like a glass of whisky."

"That's why I wanted you to ring him."

"He was also useful—instantly, I mean. He knows who Iris Gill is. Knows her work. She's quite well established now. He's seen an ad recently in an art magazine, so he's going to let me know who her dealer is."

"Oh yes, Godfrey takes an interest in art. He likes to be up-to-the-minute, too. He'd have half a dead cow in his office if he could afford it, and if he wasn't afraid of losing most of his clients."

Gillian laughed. "He could have something made of elephant dung, if he didn't tell them what it was."

"Where's the fun in that? So you're going to contact Iris Gill?"

"Yes. Godfrey Rule will do the paperwork, and he's quite pleased to have the opportunity, because he'll meet her, but I wanted to talk to her first. She used to be close to Charlotte."

"Before the car accident."

"You remember it was her husband? I didn't think you'd ever met them."

"I didn't. It's the sort of thing that sticks in my copper's brain. And Charlotte's left her the cottage? That's interesting. Will she want it?"

"She can always sell. Oh, Edward, Olivia's going to sell the house."

"Did you expect her to live there?"

"No. But."

"You hate to see it go."

"There's something awfully sad about selling—all the work Charlotte put into it, and her wonderful little library, and the prints, and even the furniture. It all goes together, it's Charlotte. And now someone else will move in and re-do the house their way, and Olivia won't be able to keep all the things Charlotte collected. It feels like watching builders bury a bit of Roman wall under the footings for a new office tower. But I don't blame Olivia. She has to live her own life, not Charlotte's."

"What's she like?"

"Looks like Tom, and is composed like Tom. None of Charlotte's theatrics. But she's her mother's daughter, too. Vulnerable and high strung. I'm not seeing her in the best of circumstances, but I think she's more resilient than Charlotte—she should be, if a happy childhood makes a difference. You remember what a pretty child she was—you'll have to see her now, she's a real beauty. I hope this comedy she's just made doesn't turn her into an instant celebrity. She hasn't acquired the asbestos suit she'll need to wear. Oh, Edward, I've told her she can stay with us if she needs to. Sorry I didn't ask you first."

"By all means. Fill the flat with dazzling young blondes. I can always sleep at the nick. Is she by any chance bringing boxes?"

"Matching luggage, more like."

"Why would she need to stay with us? Just satisfy my curiosity on that point."

"Because an obsessed fan is bothering her. Following her about, sending her unwanted presents, that sort of thing. He showed up at Charlotte's house today."

"You saw him?"

"I didn't know that's who he was, at the time. He brought flowers for Olivia. He was unsettling. He said he was a friend of hers. There's a photograph of her in the hall; when he noticed it he really stared at it, and then he tried to pretend he wasn't interested."

"Has she talked to the police about him?"

"Yes. She said they weren't any use."

"Hmm. I wonder who she talked to. We've got a new law, if the man is harassing her, he can be arrested."

"She says he has to threaten her, or the police won't take an interest. What he mainly seems to do is call her incessantly and watch her. He's tried to give her flowers before."

"Does she feel threatened?"

"Very. She was so scared she took one of her stuffed animals with her for comfort. A lamb. I'd be frightened, too. I have a strange note the man left for her. I'll show it to you when you come back. She probably won't ask to stay, but I don't think she's comfortable with her father and his very pregnant wife, and I thought she should have a bolt-hole. She might feel safer with you sleeping in the next room. If you're ever planning to. Are you coming back tomorrow?"

"Yes, sixish."

"'Sixish?' What is 'ish'?"

"I'm travelling on British Rail. 'Ish' is anything from 6:05 to midnight. I'll do what everyone else on the train does and call you on my mobile if I'm going to be late."

"I'll be right here. The air's like lead. Maybe it's going to rain tonight."

"Every time I see you, you're starving," Johnny said, watching Olivia devour a plate of black bean sauce chicken.

"I don't eat much during the day. And after filming I'm either ravenous or my stomach's in a knot. Film work and a sane diet are two different planets."

It was after midnight, and they were sitting in the fluorescent glare of the Happy Luck Restaurant. Most of the tables were full, and bins of cutlery were crashing in the kitchen.

"What's the film about?"

"Two sisters. One dies of an overdose. I'm the other one—the rescuer. Except, of course, I can't save her. I end up with the baby, who's born addicted. It's called 'No Friend Like a Sister'. The place where we're shooting is horrible. There are rats."

Johnny grimaced. "Why do you want to do it?"

"Nicky's good," Olivia said, still eating. "She's my friend; it's a challenge."

"Rats? I think I'd draw the line at rats."

"Well, I don't have to sit on one. Not like the camels."

"Your agent should put a no livestock clause in your contracts."

"The next two films I have a chance at will probably have horses in them. I'm doomed."

"Do you ride?"

"I used to, a bit, in Hampshire." She changed the subject. "Poor Nicky, she's sleeping at the ratsnest tonight. She and the DOP. They have to guard the equipment."

"No budget for security?"

"No, it's bare bones. So different from Bobby's film—he didn't eat with the rest of us, you know, in the desert; he had his own chef and organic food flown in." She rolled her eyes. "Look, Nicky's put everything she has into this film. She's in hock to her eyeballs, even though we're all working for nothing and she managed to get the stock donated and borrow the lights. It's a short, not a feature; the shoot will be over within a week. I'd do it for her even if I didn't think it would be good."

"But you do. What comes next? After the rats?"

"I don't know yet. I've got a script about Byron to look at, but these deals are all air until you've got a signed contract. Maybe a movie for TV, Victorian romantic drama."

"Not my kind of film."

"No? What *is* your kind?"

Johnny grinned. "*Terminator.*"

"Very blokeish. What else?"

"*Terminator Two. Total Recall.*"

She laughed. "Stop it. You must like something besides Arnold Schwartznegger movies."

"Yeh, if the special effects are good."

"Aren't you laying it on a little thick?" She arranged her chopsticks neatly on her plate. "I suppose you never go to films with subtitles."

"If you're in one, I will."

"I'd like to be in an Eric Rohmer film just so you'd have to." She looked him with comical dismay. "If I was the boy, here, and you were the girl, you know what would happen now? I'd rant at you for the next three hours about film, and explain why you have to see an enormous list of movies from France and Japan and twenty other countries, you know, like Poland, and I'd tell you the names of directors you *can't* not know about, and actors, and cinematic influences. I wouldn't shut up, and you wouldn't tell me to bugger off, you'd be incredibly impressed and tomorrow you'd go to the video shop and take home whatever you could find that I mentioned so that the next time you saw me you could tell me yeh, yeh, yeh, it was great."

"You're very funny. Go ahead and rant."

"More? Not tonight. It's too late for the three-hour version."

But it was a quarter to two before Olivia looked at her watch and said she had to go because she was working again the next day.

"The car's just down the street."

When they were outside, Olivia said, "Hey! I felt a raindrop." She looked up. Orange-black clouds were hanging directly overhead. A gust of cool air smelling of earth blew past, lifting her hair. Thunder rumbled, and several more drops came down, hitting her shoulders and the pavement all around her.

People laughed and scurried for cover.

"We're going to get wet," Johnny said.

"I don't care."

Halfway to the car, the rain suddenly streamed down, soaking her T-shirt.

"Jesus," Johnny said. "Want my jacket?"

"No, it's heavenly." But in a few seconds the rain was icy on her face, falling like pellets. She glanced down as they ran. Her formerly white T-shirt was transparent and clinging to her skin.

The pavement darkened. They passed huddled figures in doorways. An awning sagged, and a sheet of water spilled at their feet. The road was painted with streaks of light. Then Johnny was opening the car door. She slid in, shivering, sending water droplets flying.

In the car, he shrugged his jacket off and draped it over her shoulders. The rain sluiced over the windows and drummed on the roof.

"Very sexy rain," Johnny said. "Come here." He put his arms around her under the jacket. "You're cold."

She felt his heart pounding against hers. "Not now."

Her hair was plastered to her head. Raindrops gleamed on his face. "You look like a mermaid," he said, and kissed her. The rain poured down like grain from a chute. The streets were empty.

"Don't," she said, after a minute, turning her face away. But her body yearned towards him, contradicting her.

"Why?" He turned her face back with his palm and kissed her again. She touched his hair, the wet nape of his neck, kissed him back with a fierce desire that had hidden itself and now sprang.

Overhead, the storm moved on, crossing London. People emerged from shelter, passed the fogged windows of the car. Water gurgled in the gutters. Finally, she pulled away; they were breathing like runners.

"But this is happening so fast."

"It doesn't seem fast to me."

"Five days!"

"Five minutes can feel like five years."

Johnny started the engine but let it idle while the windows cleared. A few lazy drops spattered the roof. She stared straight ahead, and then turned her gaze on him like a miner's lamp, trying to see into the darkness ahead. The atmosphere in the car thickened and deepened, piling up around her like snow.

In a film, say a Rohmer film, the camera would move in close. She could see it. Her skin would still be wet and gleaming, polished by the rain. Her face would be naked, everything she thought would be visible: *Yes or no? Oui or non? If she said no she would have to think about the same question again tomorrow; it wasn't going to go away or be easier to answer, and maybe it was absurd to be so nervous, lots of people fell in love, they felt passion and desire, they went to bed and it ended happily or if it didn't they survived and went on to whatever happened next. Why couldn't she? When was she ever going to, if not now? She couldn't decide. The impossibility of yes, the impossibility of no: they filled the universe.*

Rohmer would put all this on the screen. Her name would be Claire or Delphine. In a movement of pure delay, she reached into her bag for a cigarette. Her hand slid past the book on Byron and, groping, found her lamb, from her bedroom at home. She'd forgotten she had it with her. How stupid of her to have wanted it, how was a frayed cotton lamb made for her by her mother twenty years ago going to help? This is ridiculous, she thought, touching its nubbly texture with her fingertips. At the same time she remembered her room, her own bed, her mother carrying her to the window, waving to her father, who was in the garden planting a tree. "A quince tree," Charlotte said. "We'll dine on mince and slices of quince." How strange that she should think of that now. She must have been about five. It would be hard for Rohmer to put it in a movie.

She would remember this moment forever, she thought, whichever way it went. She'd remember the rain, and the lamb, and Johnny's arms holding her in the dark. Even though she'd never be in a Rohmer film. She closed her bag and left it on her lap; she really didn't want a cigarette right now.

Johnny's hand floated to her face, a mothwing brushing her cheek, her neck, the clammy cotton moulded to her arm.

"What do you want?" he said, finally. "I can take you home."

She could go back to the flat. She saw herself riding up in the lift, lying awake in Raymond's bed. "No. I want to be with you."

The car wheeled softly away from the curb. She tugged his jacket close around her shoulders, shivering a little. He drove west, following the rain.

7

Gillian stopped to admire the display in the fishmonger's window on the Fulham Road. It was artful, the fish arranged in a collage of textures and colours against a glittering ice ground. She passed a plant shop, the door flanked by bay trees, pruned foliage spiralling upward like green corkscrews. In this neighbourhood, even a res that wasn't very des would carry a hefty price tag. Charlotte's house had been neglected of late, but it had stripped pine floors, a major selling point judging by the number of times the phrase appeared in notices in estate agents' windows. It was in what the agents called a sought-after road. It will sell quickly, Gillian thought.

What sort of shops had been here in the seventies? Certainly not carphone dealerships and florists for voluptuaries. Vans hurtled past her, and a man with a briefcase bellowed into his phone while he was waiting to cross the street. Fulham had seemed further from the centre when Charlotte moved in, almost not London.

Inwood's Wine Merchants had a signboard propped by the door:

WE DONT SELL
milk phone cards papers
bread videos batteries
GO TO TESCO'S

Gillian wondered if people who would go into a wine merchant's to buy milk and batteries would read the sign.

It had been summertime when she took her first walk through London with Charlotte. Charlotte had been living in Notting Hill Gate, and they walked through Hyde Park and then to Sloane Square and down the King's Road to World's End. It was a Saturday afternoon. In the park, the smell of marijuana hung like skunk spray in the air. Couples smooched heedlessly, entwined on the warm grass. The King's Road was a vast party, everyone dressed up. Boys in velvet flares and ties five inches wide, creamy-skinned girls with wild hair and long, floating frocks. No country for old men.

This morning, Charlotte's little street was as quiet as the day before. A painter leaned against a ladder, smoking. The windows of the houses Gillian passed, close to the pavement, revealed rooms full of furniture and flowers, but no people. Some rooms opened into other rooms with windows facing the gardens; Gillian could see straight through the houses to the light falling on green leaves.

It was on other walks that Charlotte told her about Beatrice Street, about visiting her grandmother when she was dying, lying in bed and unable to speak. Charlotte said she could only remember the awful smell in the room. Her grandmother had been covered up to the chin, and her head on the pillow looked tiny, like an old doll's. Another time, Charlotte had talked about her mother and father.

"They hadn't known each other long. He went off, you know, after a leave, and he never came back. I don't even know what he looked like. We lived with my Nan in Leeds. She told me about my father being killed in the war. Then my mum, she went to Australia. It was always sunny there, my Nan said, and she could do better for herself than she could here. She was supposed to send for me when she was settled. Australia. It could have been the next town, for all I knew. She went away and never came back, and then my

Nan died, and I ended up with Mrs. Arthur, don't ask me why, I don't know. I hardly know anything about it."

"Did you ever think that your mother might have died—that she never wrote because she was dead?"

"I don't believe it. Listen, I never thought of this before, but my Nan could have told a white lie, about my father being killed."

"Why would she?"

"To protect me. My mum was out most evenings, before she went off. She might not have known who he was."

Charlotte had never searched the records; her parents were dead or had abandoned her, and, either way, she refused to investigate. Presumably Olivia would never know who her maternal grandparents had been. What had Charlotte's mother been like? She'd worked in a munitions plant during the war, that's all Gillian knew, and she hadn't been willing to go into service when jobs for girls were scarce afterwards. She'd gone to Australia to try her chances. A generation later, Charlotte had gone to London to do the same, though of course without leaving a child behind. Charlotte's mother had liked to go out in the evenings. Perhaps she'd had Charlotte very young.

Charlotte had liked going out, too, in the London of the Beatles and the Stones. It was funny that she hated London now, when there was so much about it that was reminiscent of that other time, the time when everyone's anthem was *Astral Weeks*. Charlotte once lived in the Dionysian city, Gillian thought now, and so did I. We stayed up all night listening to music and walked miles across the city at dawn and woke up in rooms we'd never seen before. Olivia and her friends must do more or less the same.

The air was much cooler after last night's rain, but it had been a long hike from Sloane Square and Gillian's feet were burning in her shoes like foil-wrapped potatoes. She had her key out, but when she reached Charlotte's front door she saw she wouldn't need it. The door wasn't shut. Not properly.

The lock had been pried loose. She stood on the step, looking down, and then pushed on the door with the flat of her hand. It swung inward. A lip of rainwater glistened on the floor just inside the threshold. She saw no footmarks. He'd come before the rain, then.

She knew who had been there. He'd come for the picture. He'd sneaked back in the dark and forced the door and taken the photograph of Olivia away. He was gone, now; if he were still in the house, waiting, the door would be closed.

A locksmith was meeting her this afternoon; perhaps if she'd had the job done yesterday, Kevin wouldn't have been able to break in. There was no way to know; he wasn't a common burglar, to be deflected by a better lock. He knew what he wanted; he might have brought tools.

Leaving the door ajar, Gillian walked down the hall. She'd shut the windows before leaving the previous day, and the air in the house was unrefreshed by the rain. Where Iris Gill's photograph of Olivia had hung there was now only a wall with a small hole. Even the hook was gone.

She walked into the sitting room and ran her eye over the books and pictures. She looked at the desk. The papers appeared undisturbed; there was still dust on the lower layers. The papers from the deed box were in Pimlico, of course. Kevin hadn't any interest in Charlotte's will, Gillian believed, but she was still glad that it hadn't been lying about. He'd had an odd flash of curiosity about her death. Perhaps if she'd moved the photograph, or taken it away? But then he might have ransacked the house, looking for it.

In the kitchen, she opened the back door, to let the tree-scented air from the garden in. She thought she could still smell the lilies, though she'd removed them to the furthest corner, by the shed. The jug was in the sink; the dishes were where she'd left them to dry. It was possible that he'd taken the picture and left.

She went back to shut the front door and saw Mrs. Smythe with Taffy on a lead. They were on the other side of the street, but they crossed.

"Back again?" Mrs. Smythe said, with what Gillian assumed was her usual tact.

"I'm waiting for a locksmith. There was a break-in last night."

"Really? They're not common in this street. Of course, most people are sensible and have alarms installed."

"Most people are away all day. Charlotte was at home. You didn't see anything last night, did you?"

"No, but Taffy barked at about eleven o'clock. And she never barks, do you my precious? So she probably heard something."

The dog that never barked in the night, Gillian thought. She imagined Mrs. Smythe in the witness stand, swearing that Taffy never barked at night, followed by six neighbours testifying as one to Taffy's incessant yapping. Mrs. Smythe's dog wasn't going to help Gillian find out when Kevin had been in the house.

"The thunder was dreadful, wasn't it? Taffy hid under the bedcovers, poor darling."

"I liked it," Gillian said.

Mrs. Smythe sniffed. "Well, the rain's good for the gardens. What are you going to do with the house?"

"That depends on Charlotte's daughter."

"We don't like noise, we're a quiet street."

"I'll be sure to tell her that."

"That chap who brought the flowers yesterday," Mrs. Smythe said. "Is he a friend of Charlotte's daughter?"

"No, I've seen him before."

Gillian was startled. "Here?"

"We were out for our bedtime walkies. He was loitering. Up to no good, perfectly obvious. Taffy didn't like him, either, she's a clever beast. I sent him off," she added, in a tone of satisfaction. "We don't want his sort hanging about. Did your burglar take anything valuable?"

"I haven't finished looking."

"If you'll take my advice," said Mrs. Smythe, "don't bother about the police. We had them in two years ago and they did nothing but track mud on the carpets."

She marched up the street and Taffy barked at the painter when they passed him.

Gillian went back inside and closed the door. She had to look upstairs, not that she would know with certainty whether anything was missing, but she ought to check. She looked down the hall at the flight of steps going up to the bedrooms. In a quarter of a century, Charlotte must have climbed them at least twenty-five thousand times, if not fifty. Before Gillian dealt with whatever she found upstairs, there was something else she wanted to do.

Charlotte's record albums were in the sitting room, with the record player. She had tapes, too, but she'd never shifted to CDs. Gillian went through the records and found *Sergeant Pepper* and put it on. She listened all the way through, not particularly annoyed by the crackling and hissing. Then she wanted to hear *Yesterday*, so she played it, and the song was over too quickly, so she played it again. She would have liked to listen to more records after that, but the locksmith was coming soon, so she needed to check the rooms upstairs and then start sorting through Charlotte's papers.

She went up and stopped at the door of Olivia's bedroom. When they'd been in it yesterday, the bed had been neatly made and all the dolls and animals arranged on the pillows. She remembered Olivia sitting there. Now the bed had been ripped apart, the covers flung back, dragging on the carpet. The bottom sheet was creased and scuffed with dirt. The dolls and animals had been knocked to the floor. Beside Gillian's feet, a gray plush elephant was lying on its back, staring at her with one eye. The cupboard door stood wide open, clothes and shoes spilling out. Drawers gaped.

Gillian didn't go in. She checked the other rooms and then went downstairs to the telephone. She called Olivia's number and left a message with the answering service. Then she called Detective Sergeant Hardwick.

He was in his office.

"This is Gillian Adams. We met on Tuesday, at Charlotte Douglas's house."

"Yes, of course. DCI Gisborne has been in touch with me this morning."

Good, Gillian thought. I'm glad that's fresh in your mind.

"What can I do for you?" the sergeant went on, affably.

"I'm at Charlotte's house now. Someone broke in last night."

"Anything missing?"

"A large photograph of Charlotte's daughter. Maybe more, I'm not sure. The point is, this wasn't an ordinary burglary. Charlotte's daughter's bedroom has been vandalised." If she'd been talking to Edward she would have said the room had been raped, but if she said that to Hardwick he would probably think she was hysterical. He would listen to her, she knew, because there had been a sudden death in the house, but she wanted him to see the room, right away. If he saw it, then maybe he, or someone, would take Olivia's stalker seriously.

"Vandalised?"

"The bed's been torn apart, things thrown all over the floor."

"Perhaps he was looking for something?"

"No, it's not like that. He was in her bed. I want you to come and look at it."

"I could send someone round this afternoon."

No. Not some young constable, with no experience and no power to commandeer resources. She wanted to mobilise the entire Met, but a detective sergeant would have to do for a start. "Edward told me to ask for you," she lied.

"Yes? Erm, I'm due at a meeting in Earl's Court in about two hours, but I could pop in."

"A man came to the house yesterday while I was here; I'm quite sure he's the one who broke in last night." Hardwick would be more interested if she could provide him with a suspect.

"Oh? What makes you think so?"

"He saw the picture that's been stolen; he was very strange about it." She wasn't going to mention stalking until Hardwick saw the room.

"A photograph is an unusual sort of theft. Can you give me a description of the man you saw yesterday?"

"Yes, a good one."

"I'll be round in about twenty minutes."

There were no spaces and Hardwick double-parked. He gave the door a cursory inspection. "Could have opened it with a stick of gum."

"The photograph was hanging there. It's a big one, not an object you could hide."

He followed her up the stairs. Then he stood in the doorway of the room for a minute or two, looking. "Was he expecting her to be here?" he said, looking at the dirty sheet, the pillow wedged against the headboard.

"I don't know. I told him she wouldn't be, but he might not have believed me. He's been stalking her since April; he suspects that people will lie to him about where she is."

"What do you mean, 'stalking'?"

"Calling her incessantly, following her, leaving flowers, that sort of thing. He brought flowers yesterday."

"Has she reported this chap before?"

"Yes, but she was told nothing could be done about him."

Hardwick lifted an eyebrow. "Describe him."

"Tall, big shoulders, round head. Caucasian. Very short hair like bristles, little beard at the bottom of his chin, sloppy clothes, strange manner."

"How old?"

"Twenties. I think she's in danger."

"Mmm. You have a name?"

"Kevin. She doesn't know his last name. She's scared of him. I would be." Gillian caught sight of a bit of rust-coloured silk tangled in the bedclothes. It was torn. "Her scarf. It was downstairs yesterday. He knew it was hers, he picked it up."

The detective sergeant was unclipping a phone from his belt. "We'll try to get some prints. And I'll need to talk to her about what she's reported previously." They went downstairs. "Where are the flowers he brought?"

"I threw them into the garden yesterday."

He went down the back steps ahead of her and stepped on the place where Charlotte's body had been lying when Gillian found her. Gillian walked in the long grass instead. They waded through the weeds to the end wall.

"Over there," she said, pointing to the wilted lilies. The white petals sagged, splaying limply from the stiff stalk. They were stained with yellow pollen.

Hardwick sniffed the air. "Fair knock you down, wouldn't they, when they were fresh? Bloody funeral flowers."

Gillian swallowed. "He used to bring roses, Olivia said."

In the middle of the morning, Olivia was lying propped on one elbow looking at Johnny's face, a few inches from her own. His left hand rested on her right hip. They hadn't been awake long.

"Do you have to go anywhere?"

"Not till noon."

"Good." His hand slid up, curved around her breast.

She closed her eyes for a moment, then opened them and moved his hand back to her hip. "Tell me the name of a movie you like that doesn't have Arnold Schwartznegger in it."

He laughed and moved his hand again and then kissed her for a long time. When he finally stopped she said breathily, "Name one movie," but his mouth was on her throat now, and then her nipple, so he didn't answer. His skin tasted of salt, of the warm London summer. His hand slid between her thighs and she said, "One movie!" and then he rolled on top of her and said, "Anything by Eric Rohmer," and she squealed "What?!" and laughed and then wasn't interested in the answer for a while.

Afterwards, she said, "Rohmer! What made you say that?"

"Last night you said you wanted to be in one of his films."

"I see. Total recall." She let her eyes wander over the unfamiliar room. She'd noticed nothing the night before except the deep softness of the carpet under her bare toes. Now she saw that the carpet was a dark maroon colour, and so were the curtains. The room was uncluttered. On the wall was a large colour photograph of several balls on a pool table. The green felt filled the picture to the edges, so it wasn't possible to know how the balls lay in relation to the pockets. They appeared suspended against the green like a constellation in a green sky. She remembered her indecision of the night before. Right now, in the pure morning light, everything seemed very simple.

"Coffee?"

"Oooh, yes."

She sat in the bed wearing one of his T-shirts and sipped her coffee. "No one in the world knows where I am," she said dreamily.

"What are your working hours today?"

"We start at two." She looked down at her cup. "I've got to go to Raymond's, first, for a change of clothes."

"Yeh, the rain." Johnny lit a cigarette. "When does he get back?"

"Sunday." Jesus, she thought. She would rather jump out of a window than go to bed with Raymond Sunday night. "I'll go straight from there to the set."

"I can pick you up tonight, when you're finished."

"But it's way out in Acton, and I'll be terribly late."

"I like driving late at night."

"Really? It would be nice." Raymond had never offered to pick her up at a remote location in the middle of the night.

"Then I'll be there. I'll abduct you."

She laughed. "And drag me off to your cave?"

"After I spear a lamb tikka or two."

Later, when she was dressed, she went into the sitting room for the first time. It had big windows, a gas fire, a sound system and a large TV, plus a couple of shelves of video tapes.

"Hmph," she said, after reading all the titles. "No Rohmer. You have good taste in gangster films, though."

Olivia took the Central Line to the station in North Acton and then waited for the van to pick her up.

It was Nicky at the wheel. "I needed to get out of there for a few minutes," she said. She gave Olivia an appraising look. "Okay, what's happened to you?"

Olivia was wearing a dress instead of trousers; the cut on her calf was healing, but still pink. "You mean my leg? I told you I fell on some glass."

"Not your leg, my dear twit. Yesterday you were miserable. Today you're different. You've got a glow, I know it when I see it."

Olivia flushed. "I've met someone."

"A man? You're having me on." Nicky stared. "No, you're not."

"And last night I didn't go home."

"Who is he?"

"I shouldn't tell you."

"Why? Is he a married Tory politician?"

"Because he was going out with Lisa, and she doesn't know yet."

"Blimey! You mean it's Johnny Troy?" Nicky chortled. "I don't believe it."

"You know him?"

"Not carnally. I wouldn't mind, though."

"Huh." Olivia started to smile. "Hands off, Nicky, or you're dead."

"Oh, I am? Roger, I copy. When did you meet him?"

"Last Saturday. Anyhow, what don't you believe?"

"That you did it! You're so careful about men. Did you fall for those smouldering brown eyes?"

"Oh shut up, Nicky, yes. But he's also been incredibly sweet to me."

"Sweet?"

"My life hasn't been a romantic comedy for the past week."

"True. Jeez, look at you. All tied up with pink ribbon."

"I'm gone, Nicky. In at the deep end."

"It's so funny, you've never—"

"Never what?" She knew, but she wanted to hear what Nicky would say.

"You know, leapt into bed with some pea-brained bloke because he has beautiful eyes and you both like the same bands."

"He's not pea brained."

"Okay, okay, but you know bloody well what I mean."

"You're the one who said about Raymond that, quote, I shouldn't waste my youth. And I have to fall, blah blah, et cetera."

"But Johnny's not even your type."

"Wrong. I love him." A flash from the morning in bed made Olivia shut her eyes for a second. "I nearly fell over when I found out who he was."

"You're going to have to tell me the whole story—dialogue, locations, the lot."

"I will. It's been almost scary."

"Scary?"

"Sex. Wanting it like that." Olivia took a breath. "Having it like that."

Nicky laughed. "Sweetie, you've won the lottery."

"It's never happened to me before."

"And it scares you?"

"I think something bad will happen."

"Why?"

"It's just a feeling I have."

"It sounds like you mean if you have too many orgasms God will be angry."

"Maybe he will. Don't make fun of me, Nicks."

"Sorry, but that's idiotic, you know."

"I can't help it."

"Where did all your guilt come from? If it worked that way, I'd be a pillar of salt already."

"Who says God makes the same rules for everybody?"

"Does he love you?"

"Johnny, or God? I can't really tell. He wants me. He certainly knows how to court me. And the way he looks at me sometimes....If he says he'll ring, then he does. He's never like, well maybe." Olivia held up her hands like the paired pages of a book, then let them fall. "He reads me. It's like everything I'm feeling is stamped on my forehead, but I don't know what *he's* thinking. He talks to me, mind. He's funny, he says sweet things in a teasing way."

"Men," Nicky said.

Olivia looked down at her bare calf, the healing cut. "I don't know if I could hurt him. Not that I want to, I just mean if he loved me it would be possible."

Nicky nodded ruefully. "Easy."

"This morning, when I said I had to go to Raymond's flat for some clothes, he asked when Raymond was coming back and then didn't say anything."

"Raymond, oops. Yeh, what about him?"

"I have to move out of the flat. Whatever happens with Johnny."

"About bloody time."

"I may borrow your sofa for a few nights."

"It's yours, lumps and all. Johnny's got a history with women, you know that, right?"

"I'd have to be an idiot not to."

"If he hurts you, I'll have him topped."

"Well, if he does, it won't be right away." Olivia looked glumly at Nicky. "I'm the one who'll be hurting people. Raymond and Lisa. I have to tell Lisa. I didn't before last night because I didn't know whether anything would happen—whether I'd have the nerve to go through with it. What do you know about his history?"

"Just dirt from one of his ex-girlfriends. She went around with him a couple of years ago. It lasted for six months, he even took her to Grand Cayman for a holiday. But she didn't see him all the time—he had other girls. A serial polygamist, she said. Commitment wasn't in the frame. She had some brilliant Saturday nights, though."

"Maybe that's what I need, for a change."

"Bollocks. Don't put on that front for me. I know you."

"No you don't, this is the new Olivia. Bad case of *l'amour fou*."

"Uh oh, French phrases. The girl's gaga. Huh. You and Johnny Troy. You think you can handle that much fire power?"

"Nickee!"

"Are you seeing him tonight?"

"He's going to abduct me when we're finished," Olivia said primly.

Nicky hooted. "Stealing the virgin priestess from the temple of cinema?" She rolled to a stop in front of the house. "Okay, you've taken my mind off the film for five whole minutes. I can go back in there and act like a sane maniac. Now it's your turn. Don't think about him for the next twelve hours. We have work to do, woman."

"Six fifty-two," Gillian said when Edward walked in on Friday evening. "You're early."

"I thought I was late."

"I told myself you wouldn't be here until seven-thirty at the soonest, otherwise I would have been pacing up and down or composing shocked and appalled letters about the train service."

"Are you glad to see me?"

"No, it's a gun in my pocket."

He set down his bag and kissed her. "Any blondes on the premises?"

"Not at the moment. Hungry?"

"Famished. There wasn't anything on the train."

"You're in luck," Gillian said. "I hoped you might be home for dinner, so I went to the fishmonger in Fulham Road; the window rates three stars from Michelin. There will be highly-sought-after scallops, followed by a well-presented garden salad."

"Have you been reading restaurant menus?"

"Estate agents' notices."

"Charlotte's house?"

"What else? You don't think I want to move again, do you? The magic fish would be fed up with me, and we'd wake up back in your hovel."

He drank a glass of water standing at the sink and then went to wash his face. When he came back she opened a bottle of white wine and poured a glass for him. "Sancerre. I had some with Delia, and yesterday I bought six bottles."

"That's a good sign. It's nice to be back."

"What about Liverpool? Did you see the man you wanted?"

"A waste of time. He wouldn't say a word, but I had to try."

In the sitting room, Edward saw a nest of paper. "Charlotte's?"

"Yes, putting things in order for the solicitor. It's tempting to tip the whole desk into a plastic bag and hand it to him."

"And Olivia? What about the fellow who brought the flowers?"

"That's what I want to tell you about. He broke into the house last night."

The phone rang, and Gillian picked it up. "Oh, Olivia." She put her hand over the mouthpiece and said to Edward, "She doesn't know."

"I'm sorry I didn't ring earlier," Olivia said. "I got your message, but I've been busy. I'm at work now, but they don't need me for a bit."

"Oh, well, I phoned because something's happened. It's rather upsetting, maybe you don't want to hear about it at work, but you need to know."

"Is it about Mummy?"

"No, no, not Charlotte. It's Kevin. He broke into the house last night."

"Oh God."

"Yes, I know. The lock wasn't very strong. I've had it replaced now, but I suspect he won't come back. He stole the photograph of you, the one Iris Gill took."

"He broke in to steal that?" Olivia sounded bewildered.

Gillian stood holding the phone, looking at Edward. "Yes, but that's not all. I'm sorry, I hate to tell you this. He went into your room—left it in a mess." She could hear Olivia's sharp intake of breath. "He tore the bed apart and threw things on the floor. I thought you had to know, it seems so hostile and violent." Silence. "Olivia?"

"I feel sick."

"Me too. I've had the police in. They took prints, maybe they'll find out who he is."

"What would he do that for?"

"Maybe he was angry that you weren't there. Are you all right? How are you getting home later?"

"Someone's picking me up. I'm not staying at Raymond's tonight, I won't be alone."

"That's good. I'm worried about this. Can we talk tomorrow? The police will want to speak to you, too."

"Yes, okay." Olivia's voice was hard to hear. "I have to go. I'll ring you."

Gillian put down the phone. She was still holding her glass, the wine untasted. "The poor kid. Now you know what I was going to tell you."

"You toned it down for her, didn't you?"

"How did you know?"

"I could see on your face that it was worse than what you were saying."

"The feeling of it. The violation. He was *in* the bed, and it was such an innocent little room, with the dolls and the pillows."

"You said you had the police in. Hardwick came?"

"I used your name so he wouldn't send a me a rookie."

"Good. I'll ring him."

"What about Kevin? Can they put him away for a long time?"

"If they can tie the break-in to a previous pattern of harassment? He could be inside for years. Did you say he'd left a note for her?"

"I've got it." Gillian fetched the envelope and unfolded the note.

"You didn't give it to Hardwick when you saw him today?"

"It was here. I didn't expect to see him."

"Defence will challenge it. Evidence not in secure custody. Et cetera."

"Nuts. I can testify that I gave him the paper and the envelope, that I saw him write it and put it on the table and I opened it myself. And that I read these very words."

Edward looked at the note without touching it. "'They keep us apart.' Who are 'they'?"

"Her friends? Her boyfriend? Hobgoblins? I think he was waiting for her in the house last night."

"I don't like the sound of it at all. Look, the phone calls you told me about, they can be a serious offence on their own, if a reasonable person would feel threatened. The law recognises that, even if the officer she spoke to doesn't know it. Perhaps she misunderstood him, but he could have made a mistake. It takes a while for anything new to penetrate the reptilian brain of the Met."

"There'll be a record of her complaint, at least."

"And the calls can be traced."

"I'm so glad you're back."

He followed her into the kitchen. "I'm giving up conferences. They can fire me. I want to come home every night to Sancerre and well-presented scallops."

"Or highly-sought-after M&S spiced aubergine thingummy."

"If I can have it with you."

"Oh, I'm quite well presented for my age." She dropped a lump of butter into a skillet and turned a low flame on.

"You should have moved to London a long time ago." He set down his wine glass and embraced her.

"Yes, we could have bought a larger flat."

A minute went by, and then the distinct odour of browning butter rose from the pan.

"Help! The butter. You're famished, you said. We'll talk while I cook."

"Then let me give you the latest newsflash about the kidnapped pen. They sent Bertuca a photo today—the pen's taped to the front page of the *Daily Mail*, to prove they've got it and it's still alive. Even Nick had to laugh."

Olivia changed back into her dress and waited near the front door when she was ready to go. The street was sunk in a deep night silence. It was nearly three. Nicky linked arms with her.

"Tired?"

"Knackered."

"Me too. I'm sorry it took so long, but we're finished with this creepy place. He's on his way?"

Olivia nodded.

"Kevin in your room, that's so sick and weird. I'm glad you'll be with Johnny; if it was me, I wouldn't spend a night alone until they put that bloke away. You're talking to the police tomorrow?"

"And Lisa. It'll be a fabulous day."

"Have a nice lie in first." Nicky assessed Olivia's blue dress. "Good outfit for an abductee. You could pass for Little Bo Peep."

"I feel more like Dorothy. I'm not in Kansas any more."

"You forgot Toto."

Olivia pulled her lamb out of her bag.

"What's that?"

"Mummy made him for me."

"Hey, he's sweet. What about your mum? Is there going to be a funeral?"

"She didn't want one."

"What, then?"

"I don't *know*, Nicky. I can't deal with it right now. I have to think about moving, I have to worry about Kevin. Gillian will help me decide what to do. Do me a favour, shut up about funerals."

"Hey," Nicky said gently. "Hey. It's going to be all right."

Olivia tucked her lamb away. Lights scythed down the dark street.

"Here comes Mr. Wonderful," Nicky murmured, grinning. "If you ever get bored with him, let me know."

"Yeh," Olivia retorted. "He'll be too old to do it. And so will you."

The car stopped, and Johnny leaned across and opened the door. Olivia walked towards it, every detail of the scene sharp to her senses: the flat roofline of the industrial buildings across the road, their blank, unlit windows, the dim glow of the car's interior, two gleaming cat's eyes under Nicky's van. She heard the click of her own heels hitting the uneven blocks of concrete paving, muffled voices from within the house.

She slid into the seat, and Johnny kissed her. She kissed him back, the sweetness of it touching her everywhere, like being dipped in sugar. After a moment, she opened her eyes and looked through the car window and thought she saw a shape, the form of a man, standing a little distance away, watching. She jumped and pulled away, staring out into the dark.

"Someone's there."

Johnny turned and they both peered down the shadowy street, but now she saw no one. The murmur of voices was suddenly louder; figures appeared in the doorway of the house; the cat's eyes had gone. The shape, if there had been a shape, had vanished into the night. "Maybe I imagined it. Let's go." As the car moved down the street, she kept looking through the rear window.

"You're jumpy," Johnny said. "What's wrong?"

"I thought I saw Kevin. You don't know about him," she said rapidly, trying not to sound as panicked as she felt. "He's not a boyfriend, I don't even know his last name."

"What's he done to you?"

"He won't leave me alone."

"Hang on, Lisa said something—was he always ringing you up?"

"I know that doesn't sound terrible, but it was. Like someone drilling a hole in my head and I couldn't get him off me. And he watched me all the time. Now it's worse; I moved, and he's angry. He's looking for me; he went to Mummy's house. Yesterday he left a weird note, and then last night he broke in."

"To the house? You know it was him?"

"Who else would steal a photo of me? And he trashed my room."

In the highway glare, she saw Johnny's look of disbelief. "That's..." He broke off. "He's a real nutter, then."

They were on the Westway, now, the road empty in front of them. The twinkling labyrinth of London extended to the horizons. As the car surged forward, she rolled the window down to feel its power bursting through the wall of air. Her hair whipped around her head, the light poles flew backward. She breathed in the rushing wind and wished the car could lift off the ground, could glide over London like a silent spaceship. She wanted to drive to the end of the world. Far ahead on the Marylebone Road, emerald traffic lights changed to topaz, then ruby. The rubies zoomed towards them.

Johnny eased his foot off the accelerator.

"You need to find out who he is."

"The police took prints today." The bed. She couldn't even say it.

"They'd better take him away in a padded van. What are you doing to protect yourself?"

"What I can. I moved, I take cabs at night—"

"If he's a nutter, that's not enough."

"What do I have to do? Leave London until they arrest him?"

"Maybe."

"I have work to do. Nicky's film—she can't cancel everything because a man's harassing me."

"Don't be daft, Olivia. If he knows where you're working—besides, they'll probably nick him in a few days."

"I'll think about it. He just broke in last night, I didn't know until a few hours ago."

"Are you sure you saw him when I picked you up?"

She closed her eyes from sheer exhaustion. "No, I'm not. I see him behind every lamp post, now."

Johnny was quiet. He reached out and touched her shoulder. "I'm sorry, Olivia. I just want you to be safe."

"Let's talk about it tomorrow."

8

When Olivia woke on Saturday, the bed was empty. Yawning sleepily, she stayed where she was; they'd been up until six, and now she had no desire to do anything other than continue to lie there like a sultan's favourite. She ought to have jewels and feathers and silk bed curtains. She shut her eyes again and drifted into a fantasy in which she was locked in the flat with Johnny for some long but unspecified period of time, all of which they spent in bed, except for some hours when he would need to go out, for reasons also unspecified, during which she would luxuriate in longing for him to come back. She would never go anywhere; Hollywood producers would beg and plead, leaving frantic messages, and she would put them off.

Johnny came into the bedroom with a white towel wrapped around his waist, his hair wet and slick against his head. She smiled at him, remembering the rain. He sat on the bed.

"I have to go to the club in a little while," he said regretfully. "Don't look at me like that."

"Like what?"

"You know what. There's coffee, if you want some. Listen, Andy's going to drive you today."

"Andy? Where?"

"Wherever you need to go, until five or six, when I can meet you. Remember Andy, he got the cab for you when you left the club?"

"Yes, but why would he drive me anywhere?"

"Because I asked him to."

Olivia was taken aback. "That's very nice, but did it ever occur to you to talk to me about this first?"

"You were asleep. I don't want you going anywhere alone, not until this Kevin bloke is sorted."

"*You* don't want. What about me? Don't I have a say?"

"I'm trying to protect you. He might do anything."

"Is this the way you always do things? You just decide, and the world says yessir?"

"Either that or it says sod off," Johnny said, looking amused.

"Well sod off, then."

"You're pissed? Don't you think it's a good idea? I've got to work today, and Andy's a tough bugger."

"I know it's a good idea."

"Then what's your problem?"

"Jesus. Your sisters must have wanted to shoot you."

"Yeh, but they always missed."

Olivia jumped out of bed, no longer in a languorous mood. "I'm going to take a shower." She shut the bathroom door and fumed.

Then she thought about what she had to do: call Gillian and talk to the police about Kevin; go and collect her clothes from Raymond's flat. He was coming back tomorrow; she couldn't wait any longer. She supposed she would leave them at Nicky's. It wouldn't be very convenient, if she was spending frequent nights here in Johnny's flat. The problem of not having her own flat suddenly seemed acute. Not that she had nowhere to go, but she didn't want to flounce off after a quarrel and sleep on anyone's sofa, not even Nicky's. She wanted to flounce off home, where she could kick the furniture if she felt like it. She wanted him to be the one to wake up with all his clothes somewhere else, at least sometimes. She wanted her own territory.

Andy looked like a bouncer. Kevin wouldn't go near her if she had Andy for a minder. Andy worked at the club, she guessed. She would be safe. Obviously it mattered to Johnny that she be safe. She felt a little sorry for her outburst, he was going to a lot of trouble. But he could have asked her first. When she came out, she was still in two minds. Her gait was a touch stately as she entered the sitting room with her mug of coffee. Johnny was smoking and reading figures on the screen of his laptop.

"What are you doing today?" he said, his eyes still on the screen. He spoke as if she hadn't stalked out of the bedroom.

"I have to go to Raymond's flat and collect my clothes," she said neutrally. "I can't stay there any more."

Johnny looked up.

"He wouldn't understand my need to sleep on the sofa. I'll take my things to Nicky's; I'll have time to hunt for a flat next week. Thank you for asking Andy to drive me," she added politely.

He grinned. "You're sexy when you're angry."

She set her mug down on the coffee table with a snap. "Did you say that just to annoy me?"

"I said it because it's true. Come over here."

"Is that an order?"

"It's an invitation."

"No thank you." She gave him a slitty-eyed look and sat on the far end of the sofa.

"A command?"

"Huh."

"Is this mutiny?"

"No!" she exploded. "You're not the effing captain of the effing boat!"

The next moment they were wrestling on the sofa and laughing. He had to struggle to pin her. "Oof," he grunted, surprised. "You're strong."

She was panting. "Terminator Three."

"You can stay with me, while you're flat-hunting," he said. "If you'd like to. Bring your clothes here."

She stared at him, surprised in her turn.

"If you want to be in London, this is about as safe as you'll find. They wouldn't let the prime minister in here without ringing upstairs to see if he was expected."

"I don't know. I'm used to having my own digs."

"So am I, but, Olivia, the more you move about, the more chances you give him. If he knew where you were filming last night, he can find out where your friends live. It's Saturday, I have to be at the club tonight, are you coming with me?"

"Yes."

"Why don't you bring your gear here, then? For the weekend, anyway. The coast might be clear by Monday."

"All right. The weekend."

"So, where else are you going today, besides Raymond's?"

"I have to ring that police officer. And tell Lisa. About us, I mean." She flushed slightly. "That we're going out. She's my friend, I have to."

"It wasn't ever serious, she knew that."

"Not for you."

"You're saying it was for her? I didn't think so."

"Well, she'll be absolutely furious. So would I."

"What can you say? These things happen."

"I can say I'm sorry." But if she wasn't sorry it happened, was her regret about Lisa mere hypocrisy? Lisa might think so. Olivia only knew she had to speak to her. 'I'm going out with him,' she could say, or, 'I've spent two nights in his flat.' 'I'm in love with him.'

He still had her pinned to the sofa, after their wrestling match. She felt his weight, his warm breath. He was so beautiful she wanted to kiss him all over, his eyelids, the back of his neck, the arches of his feet. His gaze poured down into hers. "Oh," she said, burning, pressing upward as if she could leave the shape of her body imprinted on his. "I want you."

The brown eyes moved closer. There was a glint in them. "Is that an order?"

The entryphone buzzed.

"Damn, that's Andy." He went to answer it. "He'll take you anywhere you need to go; he'll wait for you. You ring him on your mobile when you're ready to leave. If you're at Raymond's, ring from the flat and then wait for him to come up and fetch you. Right? You understand?"

"Okay, Johnny." She was listening to him but still distracted by desire.

"Andy's good; you'll be all right. If I didn't trust him, I wouldn't let you go with him. Ready?"

She straightened her dress.

Iris Gill's studio was in Underwood Street, in Hackney, just beyond the edge of Islington. Gillian walked up from the Old Street tube stop, past Moorfields Eye Hospital and a cluster of shabby men selling bicycle tyres and gears and unpromising bits of plumbing. She passed two tiny galleries and then found the entrance to Iris's building. In the vestibule, the tiles were cracked and dirty. A motor scooter was attached by a heavy chain and a lock to a thick bolt in the wall. Above it, a sign with a red arrow directed her up a long, dark flight of stairs to Mad Cow Studios. The door at the top was painted red. Gillian knocked and waited. A bolt slid back, metal scraping metal.

The woman who opened the door scrutinized her casually. "Yeh?"

She was in her twenties, dressed in black jeans that were cut off high up on her rounded thighs, and a pink T-shirt. She had a mobile phone hooked to her belt, her hair was orange, and she had a nose ring, an eyebrow ring, and at least six earrings. She reminded Gillian of some of her former students.

"I'm Gillian. I spoke to Iris on the phone earlier."

She let Gillian in and shut the door again. It clunked solidly into place. "My name's Kattie, I'm Iris's assistant."

Gillian found herself in a long, narrow space with white-painted brick walls and a high, uninsulated metal roof. At the top of the walls, steel struts bridged the empty air. Above them, the gray, corrugated roofing rose steeply towards a row of glass panes running most of the length of the roofpeak. The room was flooded with daylight. The exposed pipes were painted white, and a space heater hung in one corner. The high, narrow bareness of the studio reminded Gillian of a country church. This room would be as cold in winter, and the space heater would roar like a train in a tunnel.

A flabby sofa and a couple of low-slung chairs were grouped around a square table, but the rest was studio space. The air smelled, not unpleasantly, of glue and paint. A long worktable stood under the skylights.

"Iris is just washing her hands, she'll be out in a minute," Kattie said. "Would you like some tea?"

Across the back was a newish wall. There was probably some newish plumbing behind it.

"Thank you," Gillian said, thinking tea might be a lubricant, if one was needed.

A ceiling fan rotated lazily, stirring the air. The studio was warm, but not stifling. She moved over to the long table. A heap of naked dolls was piled up at one end, sexless baby dolls made of rubbery plastic, with chubby feet and round bellies and wide eyes. They had pink skin and blond or red curls, or brown skin with fuzzy black curls, their eyes were blue or brown. The middle of the table was crowded with mounds of unspun wool and fabric, needles, brushes, and tubes of glue and paint. At the farther end, a phalanx of dolls stood in close, neat rows. These dolls were naked, like the others, but they had been transformed. The heads had been removed and replaced by handsewn sheep's heads. Beside the table was a wire mesh box of decapitated dolls heads, as if a toy guillotine had been at work. Blue and brown eyes stared randomly out through the mesh, or at the distant roof.

"That piece is called *Dollies,*" Kattie said. She nodded at a ten-foot stack of glittering hexagons at the far end of the room. "And that's *Chimera.* Iris has a show next month."

Iris chose that moment to appear from behind the wall. She was recognisably the woman Gillian had met on half a dozen occasions, but she'd altered. Gillian had an impression that she was smaller and darker: more concentrated, a more powerful essence of her former self. Her wild hair was dyed a purplish-brown and caught in a clip, and she was wearing a black collarless shirt, loose black trousers made of some soft, dull material, maroon lipstick and maroon sandals.

She held out her hand. "Iris Gill. I remember you. Especially at the picnic we had with Charlotte on Primrose Hill. Nice of you to come. Has Kattie offered you tea? Kattie, is that package of slides ready?"

Kattie was murmuring into her mobile. "Yeh, I'm going to take off, now, if that bolshie machine will let me. I'll bring back some more film, and the wire." She clattered down the stairs, and Gillian heard the whine of a motor starting.

Iris emptied the boiling kettle and brought the tea to the table in a blue china pot with two mugs.

"You have a show soon, Kattie said."

"Next month. Anthony Reece. He's been my dealer for the past twelve years."

"This seems like a pretty good place to work," Gillian said.

"It's much better than anything I've had before. Supposedly I've got it until 2010, but of course I could lose it sooner."

"Why? Don't you have a lease?"

"It's not like that. My rent is subsidised by a group called Space—it's a charity. I could never afford this, otherwise. Space holds the lease from the owner—if they renegotiated, I wouldn't have any rights."

"But why would they?"

"The owner could offer them money to break the lease—money they could use to lease something else. Then I'd be out. The area's changing. Spitalfields, Shoreditch, everything's being bought up, bit by bit, and redeveloped. I know dozens of artists who've been booted out of studio spaces. The old warehouses are very nice when they're renovated. I wish I'd had a bit of money a few years ago, I could have bought something then, and now it's all too pricey. But you came to talk about Charlotte. It was rather a blow when you told me she was dead. We were close friends for a long time."

"She used to mention you often, in the days when she wrote letters."

"Did you still go and see her, in the past few years, that is? I knew some people she was friends with, but they gave up."

"Whenever I was in London. It could be difficult, visiting her. She was so ferociously unhappy."

"About Tom?"

"He's what she'd talk about. And her childhood, sometimes."

"The monstrous Mrs. Arthur, with her locked doors and ever-ready enemas. I think if Charlotte had believed in hell, there would have been a sign, 'Beatrice Street,' over the front entrance."

"Charlotte started going to church a few years ago."

"Charlotte? She *hated* the church." Iris sipped her tea, a pained look on her expressive face. "Well, if it helped. What's happened to Olivia?"

"She's grown up, living on her own, now. She's a film actress."

"Good for her. She had that idea when I still knew her. And she was lovely, you couldn't take a bad picture of her."

"I saw the marvellous one you took when she was a teenager—the one you gave to Charlotte."

"I remember. I took it in Charlotte's garden, in June. A couple of months before the car accident."

Iris's tone was matter-of-fact. They hadn't referred to the accident on the phone. Gillian had spoken cautiously of

Charlotte's death, not knowing what sort of reaction there might be. She'd had no idea how Iris felt about Charlotte, or whether there had been a renewal of the old friendship between them. It was quickly obvious that there had been nothing of the kind; nonetheless, Iris had sounded sad as well as surprised by Gillian's news, and had been more than willing to see her.

"I never managed to get to Hampshire that summer," she was saying now. "I had two classes to teach and a show deadline; but I went to see Charlotte for lunch in Fulham. For some reason, I had my camera with me. You knew Olivia as a child—she was a bewitching hoyden, with Charlotte wrapped around her little finger. What happens to girls in their teens?"

It was a rhetorical question.

"She was fourteen and suddenly shy and looked like a baby giraffe—that Modigliani neck and legs up to her shoulders and she'd peep at you from behind the blonde hair as if you were the first human being she'd ever seen. I don't take that sort of photograph often, but it was a moment—you see something that's vanishing in front of your eyes. Charlotte persuaded her to let me shoot a roll. I gave the best photograph to Charlotte, and she loved it. But then there was the accident, and we didn't see each other any more."

"Yes, I wasn't sure how you'd feel when I phoned you."

"Oh, it wasn't my choice, you know, that Charlotte and I never spoke after that."

"It wasn't? She would never say what happened, so I just assumed—"

"That I couldn't forgive her? I could have, eventually, but she wouldn't permit it."

"Oh." This threw a different light on the gift of the cottage; it made more sense, if Iris had reached out to Charlotte. "I'm sorry, I don't know what happened to Ralph afterwards," Gillian said uncomfortably. "In the long term. Charlotte wouldn't talk about him."

"He came out of the coma, but there was no point—he'd lost his memory and speech, and he was incontinent and in a wheelchair. They tried everything they could, but it was hopeless. I went to see him every day, at first, and then every week for a year. He didn't recognise me once."

"Is he still alive?"

"No. He died six months ago. He never knew a thing after the accident—he'd have been better off dying in the road."

"What a dreadful story."

"It is dreadful. If he'd just died, it would have been a simple tragedy, but to have it drag on for eight years, what was once a man reduced to that—to a digestive tract—well, it was horrible. I had to stop visiting."

"What happened to you, Iris? To your life?"

"I got on with it. I had no choice. And I was lucky—I had something to do. Have you been married?"

"Not legally, but I'm living with Edward now."

"I was married to Ralph for six years—I don't count the years after the accident. I got married at thirty-eight because I wanted a child. We didn't have one, but Ralph and I did all right. We were a good match. He liked to cook, I didn't. He could fix the plumbing and charm the bank manager—I'm too impatient. And he had an antiques business, he filled our flat with lovely old pieces. He adored going to openings—the theatre of it, having a cosy little gossip afterwards. We had a life, and I could get on with my work. So when he left me, as you might say, for the nursing home, I missed him badly. Things fell apart for a bit. I was skint—couldn't afford the flat without Ralph's income, though he never made a lot of money. I had to give it up and find another, *and* cheap studio space. Prices in London had gone mad—I couldn't find anything. I worked in four different studios in as many years. Have you been in Spitalfields market? They shut it down as a fruit and vegetable market and for a couple of years they rented out the spaces underneath to artists. *Under* the market. Rooms with wooden walls the stall owners had used for storage. No ventilation and everything smelled of bananas. I still walk past bananas in a shop and feel ill. Two quid per square foot, I think it was. Artists go anywhere that's cheap.

"If I'd had a child, I don't know what I would have done. Things got better, though. It's odd, but all the time I was married to Ralph, I never sold any work. I had some shows, a couple of small catalogues, but I paid my way by teaching. Then, eighteen months after the accident, my dealer suddenly says now my work is much stronger, now he can see where I was going. He sold several pieces very quickly, and a year after that he put a new piece into the Banker Prize competition, and I won."

She poured more tea.

"Congratulations, Iris. It was a long haul."

"Yes, an 'overnight success' after twenty-five years of hard work. I bought a lease on a little flat near Hoxton Square. I can walk here from there. And since the prize, my work's been selling fairly well, so I can afford to have this space to myself and hire Kattie part-time. It's fine, I'm all right. I missed Ralph at first, but I'm used to being alone again now. Perhaps I'm better off. I've wondered, if I hadn't lost him, maybe my work wouldn't have developed in the same way. Poor Ralph is dead, but my problem is simple: keeping up with the rent. I still don't own a square inch of London. When my lease is up, God knows what will happen."

"I told you on the phone that Charlotte had left you something in her will. It's a substantial legacy, actually. She's left you the cottage in Hampshire."

Iris was dumbstruck. "The cottage?" she finally said.

"To you. Iris Gill. Cottage and contents. It's rented right now."

"What about Olivia?"

"She says she knows, and it's fine."

"But it must be worth a fair bit, and she used to go there as a child."

"She doesn't want it."

"Goodness. I certainly did, when we used to rent in Hampshire. I would have bought one like it if I could."

"Then Charlotte did the right thing. You own something, now."

"If only it was that easy!" Iris looked distressed. "I don't know whether I ought to accept it."

"Why not, if she wanted you to have it?"

"She's trying to make it up to me—for Ralph. She doesn't owe me that."

"Maybe she's just saying something about you and her, not about him."

Iris paused, sipping her tea. "Ralph. It was pitiful. When he died at the end of January I felt hopeless—didn't work for weeks. But I don't blame Charlotte for the accident. I did at first, but I know that road, it's a bad corner. The witnesses said he walked right in front of her. She wasn't found to be at fault." Iris stopped. Then she went on. "And, well, I knew Ralph. He was never a look-both-ways sort. He'd had a few. He was erratic—way up or in a funk. When he was up, he rushed at things. That's why he never made much money in the antiques trade. He'd see something he had to have, and he'd pay too high a price for it, just to know he'd got it. But when he was down, he went into himself, stopped noticing things. He'd been in a terrible funk all that week. I never knew why.

"Poor Charlotte. I tried to see her after Ralph was in the nursing home, after I'd stopped hoping he'd recover, but she wouldn't talk to me. She couldn't face me, I think. Such a pity, we'd been friends for so long, we could have patched it up somehow. I tried twice, and then I gave it up. Somebody told me she'd started drinking heavily and wasn't working any more. I thought of trying to do something about it, but I was frantic then, just keeping my head above water. I left it. And now she's dead. What a pity."

"That's how I feel, that I should have done more, and now it's too late. But for heaven's sake, she gave you the cottage because she loved you, and you need it. It's a gift of the heart. Take it and feel blessed."

"Perhaps I should. I'll have to get used to the idea. Why didn't she leave it to you? You've been her friend, all this time."

"I have a refuge—my mother's house."

"In America?"

"Near New York. It's home, Iris, nothing could replace it."

"Home? That's a concept I've lost along the way."

Gillian had finished her tea. "The solicitor knows your work; he'll be elated by the opportunity to meet you. May I go and look at the boxes, Iris? Kattie said that piece is called *Chimera*."

"Go ahead. There are five pieces in the show—these two, and three called *Metamorphosis*; they're not here—they take up too much space."

A bank of hexagonal wooden boxes, each about a foot in diameter, made a hive-shaped honeycomb. Each hexagon was faced with polished brass and lined with straw, and each contained a large, shining egg, about the size of an ostrich egg. Gillian walked closer. The eggs looked like real gold, solid and weighty; they were gilded, not painted. Several had hatched; the cracked shells had fallen back and revealed what was being born: a cock with a serpent's tail, a fish with feathers instead of fins, and a chicken with a chicken-shaped body that, instead of feathers, was covered with densely-packed kernels of corn. The head was pecking at the body, trying to eat the kernels that were its own skin. All the hatchlings were larger than the eggs and were finely detailed, jewelled and glittering. The fish had iridescent feathers and real fish scales glued to its fabric body.

"Fabergé mutations," Gillian said.

"That's one aspect of it. We're so rich, we play with our genes like czars. It's about other things, too, but I'd rather let people look. If I talk, the words are confining—they shut off what people might think of themselves."

There were rows of photographs taped to the wall.

"They aren't part of the show. I take photographs when I'm thinking about a piece; I like to have them up while I'm working."

"I'd love to see the show—can you give me a card with the dates?"

"Come to the private view, if you like." Iris went to a table in the back corner heaped with books and files. She came back with a card and a big manila envelope. "Some photographs I took at the cottage. I thought I might do a piece about it—funny—I was going to go back to see how the landscape's changed—so I brought these to the studio."

They sat on the sofa side by side and Gillian looked through the pile of a dozen large prints.

"These were taken a decade ago," Iris said.

There was the cottage, exactly as Gillian remembered it, the little wooden gate, the delphiniums, the big garden with the tomato plants at the back. Now the fields rolling up from the road, and a barn in the distance. Now Charlotte, her arms full of flowers. Tom and Ralph; she recognised Ralph, too, lugging a sideboard through the front door. Tom and Ralph doing something to the roof, Olivia lying on the grass, absorbed in a book. Then a photograph of a picnic lunch. Everyone on the grass. Tom and Charlotte, Olivia, Ralph and a boy.

"Who's the boy, Iris?" Gillian asked, staring at the black and white image.

"That's Ralph's son. Ralph was married to someone else before he met me. He had a child."

"What was his name?"

"Kevin."

The likeness seemed to leap into focus as Gillian heard the name. She kept studying the photograph, but she'd known subconsciously when she asked who the boy was. This was the man who had come to the house with flowers for Olivia. Or rather, that man was this boy, grown older.

"Did he come to Charlotte's cottage often?"

"Hardly ever. We weren't staying there; we were renting nearby, and he wasn't with us many weekends. I'm afraid Ralph didn't fight very hard for time with him, and Kevin resented me, so I didn't particularly want him hanging about. We took him to visit Charlotte and Tom once, I think, when we had the picnic. And Ralph may have dragged him along during that last summer when I wasn't going down at all. Why?"

"Oh dear. I saw him at Charlotte's house in Fulham a couple of days ago. He brought flowers."

"Flowers for Charlotte?" Iris said, astonished.

"For Olivia. Who says she doesn't know him—I guess she doesn't remember meeting him at the cottage."

"Why should she? She hardly saw him. And he was very quiet. A strange boy. He struck me as being a bit disturbed, but Ralph wouldn't hear of it. I don't see Kevin any more. He came to my studio once, a space I had a few years ago, and asked for money. I wouldn't give him any, and he stole a camera and some tools. Tools I couldn't afford to lose. He was into drugs then, I could tell because he was twitchy and snivelly in that way they get. He denied it, of course, but I wouldn't let him in the next time, and he hasn't come back. I'd rather he didn't. He's big, and he has an unpredictable temper. Why do you want to know about him? I don't mind telling you, I'm sure you have a reason for asking, but I'd like to know what it is."

"He seems to be obsessed with Olivia. He's been pestering her, and it's becoming frightening. Do you know where he lives?"

"No." Iris looked sceptical. "The last I knew, he was living in a squat east of Bethnal Green and worked as a courier once in a while. He was close to his mother; she'd know. What do you mean, obsessed?"

"Endless phone calls, flowers, following her. That sort of thing."

"Stalking her? Are you sure it's Kevin?"

Gillian looked down at the photograph. "It's the same head. He said his name was Kevin. I'm pretty sure he broke into Charlotte's house Thursday night."

"If he knew it was empty, it wouldn't surprise me. What's that got to do with Olivia?"

"The photograph you took was stolen. I watched him looking at it earlier in the day, when he brought the flowers."

"The portrait?" Iris said, shocked. "But why did he go to Fulham in the first place?"

"Looking for Olivia, I believe. She's moved out of her flat to avoid him. It's worse than that. Whoever broke in tore her bedroom apart. Didn't touch the rest of the house."

Iris got up and walked agitatedly back and forth. "But God alive, that's demented."

"You said he had an unpredictable temper. Is that what you meant by disturbed?"

"Partly. I was really thinking of his fantasy life. He used to make up stories about himself, and he wouldn't have them contradicted. Ralph used to laugh it off and say he was a dreamer and would grow out of it, but I thought it was more serious. He'd get violently angry if you didn't believe him. I think his mother tried to do something about it; I didn't have any say."

"Did he blame Charlotte for what happened to his father?"

"He was furious that she got off. But he didn't have a happy relationship with Ralph. I expect we're all to blame for that, his mother included. Have you seen the police?"

"They came and took prints on Thursday, that's all I can tell you. We should call them."

"Oh, damn. Gillian, I always knew there was something the matter with him, but I had no *idea*. It's not as though I caught him torturing cats." She took the photograph from Gillian and looked at it, still disbelieving. "I was even surprised that he didn't do better at university. He was good at maths and science, but he never finished his first year."

"The police will need to see that photograph. I don't know who will call you, but DS Hardwick was my contact in Fulham."

"What about Olivia?"

"She's coming to visit me later this afternoon, I'll tell her."

"How bizarre that he should suddenly fasten on Olivia."

"He saw her in a film."

"And remembered her?"

"I don't know, but he tracked her down."

"A girl he can't have met more than two or three times, years ago. I hope he's not taking a belated revenge on Charlotte—for the accident."

"Oh." Gillian was startled. "His father died, and that might have set him off?"

Iris shrugged helplessly. "A guess. I haven't had time to think."

"Roses at her door? Constant phone calls? If he wants revenge, he's got that buried under other feelings, don't you think?"

"Yes. I'll say this, the Kevin I knew was clueless about girls. Wouldn't know how to talk to her. A porn consumer, I'd bet on it. Where is Olivia staying now?"

"In her boyfriend's flat. Kevin hasn't found it. I'm concerned about what might happen if he does."

They looked at each other, imagining the same scene.

"May I use your phone?" Gillian said. She dialled Hardwick's number and left a message.

Iris had walked over to her work table and was looking down at the box of dolls' heads. "Stalking," she said thoughtfully. "I once fancied a married man, a long time ago. I couldn't sleep for wanting him. I used to walk more than a mile across London to go and stand outside his house at night and stare at the windows, imagining what he was doing inside. If anyone had found out, I would have been mortified, but I kept going. Went out half the nights for over a week, until I got hold of myself. I suppose it could have come under the definition of stalking. Sex can be a demon."

"But can you imagine us without it? We humans?"

"Well, I do without, now. I don't give a damn any more; it's all pond life to me. You?"

"If I didn't give a damn, I wouldn't have moved to London." Gillian smiled. "May I bring Edward to the private view?"

"Will he be interested?"

"I won't have to blackmail him. He took his mother to see *Sensation* when she wanted to go."

"That Damien. Nobody can ignore him; that's his biggest asset. Of course, bring Edward along. And I'll ring you after I see the police."

Andy had instructions. He drove Olivia to Raymond's flat but didn't wait in the car while she went in. He double parked and escorted her to the door of the flat and looked in all the rooms before he left her. They had no conversation.

"You need me to stay while you pack?" he asked, having completed his tour of inspection.

"No, Andy, thanks."

"Call my mobile when you're ready," he said, and silently left.

She stood in the middle of the sitting room, feeling paralysed, DS Hardwick's warning still whirling around her brain. She'd spent nearly two hours at the police station in Fulham Road. DS Hardwick had asked her endless questions; they'd been over the whole story, from the coffee bar to her possibly hallucinatory sighting of Kevin at the film set in Acton. She'd told Hardwick every detail she could remember about the calls, the flowers, the terrible morning when Kevin almost followed her down the steps at the tube stop and then melted away when she spoke to a constable on the beat. Hardwick had asked her to put a date to it if she could, as the PC should have a note in his book. He seemed to be taking the matter seriously. In fact, he'd given her a fright.

"Miss Bening," he said at the end of the interview, sitting up and leaning towards her, his pale, almost invisible eyebrows drawing together, his forehead wrinkling up with concern, "This is important. You must let us know without delay if you see him again. I hope it won't take long to pick him up, but until we do you'll need to be very careful. Don't give him any opportunity to approach you. There's an escalating pattern of behaviour here, you understand?"

Escalating pattern, escalating pattern. That meant Kevin might do something violent next time he saw her. And they still hadn't discovered who he was. She was glad to be relieved of Andy's company for a little while; his silence made her nervous. But now she almost wished she'd asked him to stay, because being alone in the flat was making her nervous, too.

She picked up a few scattered possessions in the sitting room. The sooner she was packed, the sooner she could leave. The flat was in perfect order, tidy, dusted, the cushions plumped. Only her palm print on the wall, so faint that it wouldn't be noticed by anyone else, remained as a trace of the crime scene of Wednesday night. For a moment, she was disconcerted to see the dishes she'd washed put away and the bedcovers as smooth as a skating rink. Then she remembered that the maid came on Fridays.

In the bedroom, Olivia changed from her dress and sandals into a T-shirt and black linen trousers. The air in the flat was stuffy, but she didn't want to open the doors; she felt safer with everything closed. She clipped her hair at the nape of her neck and dug out a pair of sturdy black leather shoes to wear when she was carrying her bags. She didn't put them on; she would be cooler in bare feet.

Diving under the bed, she dragged out her two large travelling bags, remembering that she had some clothes at the cleaners, as well. Perhaps she'd leave them there; she would rather not take up a lot of space in Johnny's flat. He probably hadn't realized, when he said she could bring her clothes, that she had everything she'd taken to Morocco as well as her London gear.

She finished one case, shut it and lugged it into the sitting room. Then she started on the second, larger bag. Her heavy square blue travel kit only needed the top tray repacked, and she could stuff any extra items into her knapsack. The things at Raymond's weren't a problem. It was what she still had at Lisa's that she was worried about. What would she do if Lisa refused to store anything for her? Which Lisa might well do. After hearing about Johnny, Lisa might throw her clothes in the street.

Olivia unclipped a skirt from its hanger and looked guiltily and a little mournfully at the neat row of Raymond's jackets. She had to tell Lisa today. She'd spent two nights at Johnny's flat, now, and if they went to the club together, someone Lisa knew would see them. Olivia didn't want her to find out that way. The skirt was stained; it would have to be cleaned. Laying it to one side, Olivia eyed Raymond's phone next to the bed. She should call right away; Lisa would be awake now, and she might be going out later.

"Olivia! I wondered when you would ring. I've been leaving messages. How are you? Have you gone back to work?"

"It seemed like the best thing to do."

"Yeh, you don't want to be alone. Is Raymond home?"

"Not yet. I was in Acton until three in the morning, anyhow."

"How did it go?"

"Nicky's happy with what we did. It was exhausting, I'm half dead. Will you be home later? Like in an hour? I want to grab a few things I need, and we could talk."

"No problem. I'm not going anywhere until five. Hey, I heard a brilliant band last night. Total funky Afro-Brazilian boogie music, and a gorgeous bloke playing Hawaiian guitar. The Big Kahuna, you have to hear him. My inner bitch jumped right out."

Lisa must be having a good weekend, Olivia thought. For a moment she wished they could go out together, have a quiet drink in a pub instead of meeting at the flat, but it wouldn't be the right way to tell her. If Lisa wanted to cry, she shouldn't have to do it in front of an audience.

Olivia plunked herself on the corner of the bed and rehearsed various opening lines—'I'm leaving Raymond.' No, too gutless; they would talk about him, it would be friendly, and then when they got to the point Lisa would feel deceived. 'I've fallen in love.' Then Lisa would ask who she was in love with, and she would say his name. It was possible, but it sounded too dramatic. Olivia groaned. Once you started analysing dialogue as though you were going to play a role, you became hypersensitive to every possible nuance. Then you overinterpreted and nothing seemed right. It would be better to wait until she saw Lisa and then improvise.

As she was getting up, she heard a noise. It sounded like the front door being opened. Raymond wasn't due back until tomorrow. Andy was supposed to wait for her to ring him. She froze. Kevin. Escalating pattern. Maybe she hadn't bolted the door. He knew she was here; someone had let him in downstairs. She spun around, looking for a place to hide. No, if he'd been lurking, he'd have seen her arrive, he'd know she was in the flat. He'd find her. She needed a weapon.

Another sound. The door quietly closing. Now footsteps in the hallway. Oh God, why hadn't she asked Andy to stay? A heavy Swedish crystal vase filled with dried flowers stood on a chest of drawers. She snatched the flowers and threw them on the floor and picked up the vase by the neck. He was moving slowly, but she could hear him in the sitting room. Crossing the bedroom soundlessly in her bare feet, she squeezed behind the door and raised the vase over her shoulder.

The footsteps passed the kitchen and came down the little corridor towards her.

"Olivia?" Raymond's voice said. "Are you here?"

Olivia stepped out from behind the door. "Jesus Christ," she gasped. "You scared me half to death."

He eyed the vase as she lowered it. "This is a charming welcome home gesture."

"I thought you were coming tomorrow."

"I caught an earlier flight. I just—"

Her heart was still pounding. "You should have let me know."

"I'm sorry I scared you. Are you going to put that lethal weapon down?"

She put the vase back on the chest of drawers and bent to gather up the dried flowers. Her hands were shaking.

"Here, give them to me," he said, and laid them carefully beside the vase. "Who did you think it was?"

"Raymond, you've been away. You don't know what's been going on. That nutter who was bothering me, he's gone berserk. He broke into my mother's house, I've had to see the police, they think he's dangerous."

"Good God. Olivia, my poor darling."

He put his arms around her, and she let him hold her for a moment. Her body was still quivering. He patted her gently. "There." He was going to kiss her.

She broke away. "Don't. I—look, I'm sorry, I, I was packing."

He looked at the luggage. "Oh. I saw your case in the sitting room; I thought you'd brought more clothes. You've found a flat already?" He looked deeply fatigued. His eyes were pouchy, and the lower half of his face seemed to sag into his collar. She felt sad.

"No."

"But you're not staying?"

"No. I've met someone else."

"Ah. I really have been away." He walked heavily into the sitting room and sat down on the sofa. His suit was creased with travel. He shut his eyes for a few seconds. She stood at a little distance, looking at him doubtfully. He rubbed a hand across his brow and cheeks, and then opened his eyes again and crossed an ankle over his knee.

"Well, it was bound to happen. I always knew some hot young director or irresistible actor would steal you away. Which is it?"

She didn't answer.

"It's not your co-star is it? Bobby Carr?"

"God, no."

"Oh, that's good. I shouldn't have liked imagining you with him." His voice had a hospital nurse briskness.

"I'm sorry. I didn't mean to hurt you," she said.

"But you must. My dear, I've seen this coming."

"You don't have to be so bloody nice about it."

"Oh, yes I do. It's the only way I can maintain a shred of dignity as I am unceremoniously ushered out of your life."

"Raymond."

"Don't look tragic. I'm not going to die of a broken heart, I'm too busy. Olivia, I've been away so much, I'm surprised you've put up with me. But I do regret not coming back as soon as your mother died."

"It's all right, I know you couldn't."

"But you might like someone who could, I think. In my own defence, I can only say I never complained about your schedule. And I never asked questions about what you got up to when I was away."

"Nothing, not until now."

"Let's have a drink, my dear. Stiff upper lip, all that. I want you to say nice things about me when you've gone."

"You're making me feel awful."

"Splendid. I don't think there's any champagne, is there? Will sherry do?" He heaved himself up and went to the cupboard where the bottles were kept. "I hope the flat's been useful."

"It's been perfect. I don't think Kevin's even found it yet."

"Oh. You know, I'd forgotten about him for a moment. Are the police doing anything?"

"They're doing what they can. They haven't arrested him, they're looking."

He handed her a glass of sherry. "And you're not going to tell me who Mr. Right is?"

"You don't know him."

"You could tell me his name. You could tell me when you met." For the first time, there was an edge of anger in his voice.

"There's no point. It would be over even if I hadn't met him."

He contemplated her, his eyes narrowing. "You've changed, haven't you?" Then he shifted his gaze and cleared his throat. "I daresay you've been through a lot, while I was away. I was looking forward to Paris, you know. I'll miss you." He clinked his glass against hers. "*La princesse lointaine.* Here's luck."

"Oh Raymond, this is sad. I'm sorry to go."

"You'd better finish your packing. It's close in here, do you mind if I open the door?" He walked to the sliding door, unlatched it and pushed it back. Then he stood with his back to her, looking out at the long, winding frieze of the south bank, the bridges, the towers, the wide band of water reflecting the sky with its bloom of summer haze.

As Olivia went down in the lift, crowded in with Andy's bulk and her various bags, she wondered how much she'd really known about Raymond. She couldn't have predicted his behaviour; had she known she would see him today, she would have been prepared for sarcasm. Not this light touch, for she knew he was hurting.

Andy put her bags in the back of the Jeep. She gave him Lisa's address, and he eased wordlessly into the traffic. After a few minutes he delved into a pocket and extracted a packet of Silk Cut. Silently, he offered her one. She took it and thanked him, grateful for a glimpse of humanity as well as for the nicotine. She'd had two cigarettes after the interview with Hardwick. Not bad for the sort of day she was having.

They arrived at the flat without any further exchanges. He parked on a double yellow line and walked her to the front door of the building. She still had her keys to the flat.

"I'll be okay, now," Olivia said to Andy.

"I'm going up in the lift with you."

"But—"

"You don't want me in the lift, you talk to Johnny about it. When you're in the flat, I leave."

Olivia gave up. Arguing with Andy would be like trying to dent a boulder by banging her head on it. She hoped Lisa wouldn't guess the truth the minute she saw him.

She pressed the buzzer in the hall rather than letting herself in with the key, since she didn't live in the flat any more. Lisa opened the door wide without looking to see who it was. She never used the chain. "Hullo, Olivia. I thought it was you." She looked at Olivia's escort, surprised. "Andy! What are you doing here?" Her eyes turned hopefully to the lift, as though Johnny might step out.

"It's because of Kevin," Olivia said quickly. "I'll explain. Andy, I'll be down in a little while."

"Use the mobile," he said.

She went inside with Lisa and closed the door.

"What's going on?" Lisa demanded.

"Kevin broke into Mummy's house. The police are after him, now, but they haven't caught him yet. Lisa, he's been in my room. In my bed! Andy's my minder. I need one."

"How did you get him, did you ask Max?"

"Max?"

"He works for Max. You know, he's muscle."

"Johnny arranged it. Listen Lisa, I have to tell you something right now. I'm going out with Johnny."

"You and Johnny?" Lisa looked stunned. "Going out? Are you joking?"

"I wouldn't do that."

"I don't believe it."

"It's true."

"What do you mean, going out?" Lisa said, as if there might be an innocent version.

"I stayed in his flat last night."

That got through.

"In Johnny's flat? Jesus Christ, you twenty-four carat bitch."

"I'm sorry."

"Sorry? You cow."

"I really am sorry."

"Well, fuck you. FUCK YOU!"

The words hit Olivia like stones. "Go ahead, you can say anything you like, I came here because I didn't want you to find out some other way."

"How bloody sweet of you. How well bleedin' brought up. You were my friend! You knew how I felt about him!"

"But you knew he wasn't serious. You told me that. You knew he was going out with other women."

"At least they weren't my goddam friends."

"I can't help it."

"Shut up, that's not true."

"Yes it is. Oh God." Olivia sighed. "Maybe it isn't, but I swear it feels true."

"Goddammit. Why did I ask you to go with us? I must have been insane. But you had a *boyfriend*. Yeh, what about Raymond? Does he know?"

"I told him today."

"Doing a tour, are you? Saves time."

"Lisa!"

Lisa snatched a cigarette from the table and lit it. "How did Raymond take the news?"

"He was very sweet. Nicer than he sometimes was when we were together. I don't know why."

"What did you say? Thanks for the flat, darling, I'm off with my friend's boyfriend? Did you and Johnny have a good laugh, first?"

"I don't think this is funny. I feel bad."

"You take my boyfriend and *you* feel bad? That's a bit rich."

"Well, I've told you." Olivia didn't know what else to say. She turned towards the door.

"Hang on, when did this happen? At the Paradise? How did he get your number? You gave it to him, didn't you?"

Olivia nodded.

"And then we left in the cab together and, God, I asked you if you liked him. I didn't have a clue. We were talking, and you were already planning to go behind my back."

"I wasn't planning! It wasn't like that."

"I'll bloody bet."

There was a silence. Olivia fumbled in her bag for a cigarette. She'd run out. Lisa walked to the window, where she stood with her back turned to Olivia. "You should go now."

"Lisa."

"You're going to say 'can't we be friends'. Cow."

"I don't blame you for being angry." Olivia felt a jolt of anger herself. "But you know what? In my shoes you would have done the same thing."

"That's it, that's bloody it!" Lisa shouted. "Get out. And don't think you can leave your rubbish here because you've paid the rent."

"Okay, I'll come back for it next week."

"Get out of here!"

Olivia went blindly to the door. She pressed the bell for the lift and went down in it hardly knowing where she was. Bitch. Cow. Lisa hated her. Without thinking, she walked through the lobby, pushed the door open and was in the street. It was only when she was outside that she remembered she was supposed to call Andy on the mobile. He'd moved the Jeep. It was gone.

She reached into her bag and fished out her phone and tapped in the number.

"Yeh?"

"Andy? Listen, I forgot to phone from Lisa's flat, I'm—" The connection died. "Andy? Andy? Are you there?" Nothing. Christ, the battery was really gone. She tried again. "Andy, I'm in the street—" The phone died again. She turned it off. There was no point in calling a third time. She didn't know where he was, but he knew she was waiting for him now. He'd come.

She wondered whether she ought to go back inside and wait in the lobby. It might be wiser. She turned around and rooted for the key again, but then she saw something lying in the corner of the recessed entrance. It was in the same place that Kevin had once left roses for her. It seemed familiar. She stared at it. A doll's body, a cotton body with sewn-on black cloth shoes, a blue and white checked pinafore, and bare, pink cotton arms. She recognized it, although it had no head. "Sally," she whimpered.

No one had told her he'd taken a doll, but how would they know? A wisp of stuffing poked up from the neck of the tiny dress. She couldn't see the head anywhere. Just the body. Had it been there a few minutes ago when she went in with Andy? Had she looked?

She couldn't stay by the door, near it. She turned and ran. The traffic was thin; she dodged across the road, running towards the coffee bar. She would wait there, with Bibi; she could watch for the Jeep through the window. The street was too dangerous, too open. At least Bibi knew her, and she would feel safer indoors, out of view. There might be other people inside, at the tables. Kevin wouldn't look for her in the coffee bar any more; she hadn't been inside it since April.

She got to the far side of the road and paused to look back, hoping to spot Andy's Jeep. It was nowhere to be seen. But suddenly, as her eyes swept up and down the street, she saw Kevin. For a second, she didn't believe it, thought she was imagining him again. She wasn't. He was only twenty yards away, standing as though riveted to the ground by the sight of her. She turned, she was almost at the door of the coffee bar. As she ran, she saw him lurch into motion, flapping towards her like a monstrous bird of prey in his baggy shirt. He side-swiped a slow-moving fat couple, knocking them off balance. She heard a squeal of brakes in the road as she dived through the door.

Bibi looked up from her stool at the cash register. There was only one customer, a little man in shirtsleeves hunched over his coffee and a foreign newspaper.

"That loony, he's chasing me," Olivia panted. "Is there a way out?"

Bibi stood up. "Yes, but only into the courtyard." She hurried around the counter. "I'll lock the door."

Olivia ran to the curtained opening at the rear of the bar. Behind it was a dim room, crowded with furniture. An old woman and a small round-eyed child stared at her. She heard the front door of the bar crash open and looked desperately for a place to hide. As she plunged up a flight of narrow stairs, the sound of Bibi's voice followed her, shouting in the coffee bar. The stairs were dark. At the landing, there was a door, but it was locked. She raced up the next flight, her breath coming in gasps, and arrived at another door. She wrenched it open and stumbled into a big room, lit by skylights. A dozen women were sitting at sewing machines at two long tables. They looked up at her, startled, and then several began talking at once in high, frightened voices, like birds. They weren't speaking English. A baby started to cry.

Olivia looked wildly around, hoping for another exit, but saw only windows. She heard feet pounding up the stairs. Along one side of the room was a row of big ironing boards, like a barricade, at which several young women were standing. They'd been pressing the garments that were being sewn, but now they gawked at her. She leapt behind them as the door was flung open again and Kevin charged into the room. A woman wailed, a high-pitched cry of terror. "I'm calling the police," Bibi shrieked from downstairs. "The police I am calling!"

"Get away from me," Olivia shouted.

"I know what you're doing," Kevin hissed, his chest heaving, his breath noisy. He was poised on the balls of his feet, the blood pulsing in his neck, his eyes white around the irises. The sewing machine women shrank away, huddling towards the windows at the front. He was between Olivia and the door to the stairs. "I know. You can't fool me."

"What? Leave me alone," she cried. The woman beside her, who'd been pressing the seams of a silk jacket, dropped her iron and stumbled backwards, tripping on the cord, yanking it from a tangle of wiring on the floor. A woman at the far end of the room rocked her baby and moaned, and out of the corner of her eye, Olivia saw another sink to her knees.

Kevin didn't even glance in their direction. "Where were you?" he grated. "Where?"

"You're mad. You only saw me in a film. I've never even talked to you."

"Liar," he shouted her down. "You've been with him. You think I'm stupid, but I'm not. Little whore."

The baby howled, the mother was trying to shush it. The iron was burning the jacket sleeve; Olivia could smell the smoking threads. The room was as hot and bright as a film stage. Sweat ran down her neck. He was moving towards her, now. He was only ten feet away, eight, circling the flimsy barricade; in seconds he'd be close enough to reach out and touch her. She grabbed the iron by its handle and, using all the strength of her dancer's muscles, vaulted over the board and launched herself at him, screaming, aiming the iron straight at the bare triangle of flesh below the open shirt collar. She hit him with all the force of her leap, feeling the jar of the impact as the metal slammed into flesh and bone. He staggered backwards and went down, and she dropped the iron. Crashing to the floor, he scrabbled frantically at his throat, where the iron had got caught inside the shirt. Tears streamed out of his eyes. He was yowling. Her momentum carried her past him as he fell, and she landed on her feet. There was a smell of scorched flesh and hair. He flung the iron away and rolled to his feet, but she was already at the door. She belted down the two flights of steps. The skinny little man had fled. Bibi was standing by the door of the coffee bar, wringing her hands. "The police, they're not here yet. Bastards."

Olivia hurtled past her and darted out into the open street. He would be down the stairs and after her in a minute. A small crowd stood mesmerized on the pavement; a siren was shrilling in the distance. She kept running, looking for Andy, weaving past pedestrians. Kevin burst out of the coffee bar. Then she saw the Jeep, cruising slowly, and she dashed straight into the road, yelling more loudly than she'd ever known she could yell. The Jeep shot towards her. Kevin headed for her at a dead run. There was blood all over his shirt. As Andy stood on the brakes, the Jeep's door flew open and she crammed herself in, head and legs and feet in a ball, and they were moving again before the door swung inward. Andy reached across and slammed it shut. She lay against the seat, gulping air.

He drove fast, cornering like a racing driver as he made a left at the first intersection. Once out of sight of Lisa's street, he instantly slowed, blending into the ordinary traffic.

"JesusJesusJesus," she said, staring-eyed.

Andy turned his head. "Looks like you popped him good."

"I burnt him," she gasped. "With an iron."

"Burnt him? That's a good one." He drove silently for a few minutes while she caught her breath. Then he said, "Next time, use the mobile."

"I'm sorry, I was upset."

"You get hurt, Johnny won't be happy. Then Max won't be happy. Use the mobile."

"It was my fault." She was flooded with adrenalin. "But next time I'm going to break that bastard's goddam legs. God, give us a fag, Andy, please."

The car rolled smoothly through the traffic. Andy passed her the cigarettes and drove on without speaking. He was grinning to himself, the first smile she'd seen on his usually blank face.

"What are you smiling at?"

He chortled. "You. Look like a china doll, but you hit the target like a cruise missile. That bloke, he got barbequed. Barbequed!" He wagged his head up and down. "You're in the movies, right? Gonna be a star, gonna need your own driver. Call me."

"Okay Andy, no problem." She laughed. "Hollywood will be hammering on the door any day now."

The cigarette seemed to burn down to the filter in seconds. She stubbed it out and immediately wanted another. She stared unseeingly at the streets as Andy wove through the traffic. As the adrenalin drained away, she felt profoundly exhausted. What did women who were stalked do? How did they live through the days, keep going, remain vigilant? How did they stay alive? Even the Queen had found a strange man in her bedroom in the middle of the night, right inside Buckingham Palace. Olivia knew she'd made a mistake, leaving Lisa's flat by herself, but that wasn't the lesson, she thought wearily. The lesson was that nobody could guarantee her safety if Kevin meant to kill her. How long could this go on? Wanting to hide, all she could do was put her sunglasses on. As the elation of survival faded, she could feel the fear seeping in again, turning her body cold.

Gillian had said she'd be home after four and Olivia could stop in any time. Now, entering the quiet grid of streets behind Victoria, Olivia felt like a bird flying over a flood, longing for a drifting rooftop or the high branches of a tree to land on and rest.

Andy walked up the stairs with her and waited until Gillian opened the door. "Cheers," he said, and left. Johnny would pick her up later.

"Have you hired a bodyguard?" Gillian asked, watching Andy's two hundred and fifty pounds of muscle amble towards the stairwell.

"Sort of."

"I'm glad. Come on in, the place is a mess, though. I've been unpacking."

Olivia followed her past a stack of empty cardboard boxes in the hall. In the sitting room, a fan swished the air about. Pictures leaned against the walls and a side table was piled with china. White tissue paper was mounded here and there like the remnants of melting snow. Gillian's face was pink.

"What I want is some iced tea," Gillian said. She swept tissue paper off the sofa. "Sit down. You look wiped out."

Olivia sank gratefully onto the cushions. She took her sunglasses off and fished around in her bag and pulled out her mobile. "The battery's dead. I need to recharge it."

Gillian looked at her, started to say something, and stopped. "You'd probably rather have your tea hot, wouldn't you?"

Olivia nodded; she felt almost catatonic now. Her head leaned against the sofa back, and her eyes closed; she heard Gillian going away.

When Gillian peeped into the sitting room several minutes later, Olivia was fast asleep, her knees drawn up, her arms tucked under her, wrists crossed, her body rolled into a little ball like a hedgehog without spines. Gillian tiptoed past her and carried a glass of iced tea into the bedroom, where she shook out and refolded a heap of clothes on the bed. From time to time she looked at the photograph of Olivia and Charlotte and Tom that now stood on a little table, while she thought about the sleeping girl in the next room.

"Gillian?" Olivia's voice murmured.

Gillian went back to the sitting room.

"How long have I been sleeping?"

"Almost half an hour. Want some tea, now?"

"Yes, please." Olivia looked embarrassed. "I'm sorry. I had no idea I was going to do that."

"You must have needed it."

"I felt like a dead person. I almost was."

"The kettle's hot, it will only take a second to boil." Gillian whisked into the kitchen to fetch the tray, which she set on the coffee table in front of Olivia. She sat down. "Do you want to tell me?"

"Kevin came after me. He chased me into a coffee bar and up two flights of stairs. He was like a crazed animal."

"When? How on earth did you get away from him?"

"Just now, before I came here. I hit him with a hot iron, and he fell down. So I ran past him and got out."

"My God, Olivia. Good for you."

"Yeh, I felt fabulous for about ten minutes. Olivia, Queen of the Jungle. I could do anything—I was awesome. Then I crashed. Now all I can think of is that he'll try again."

"But where was that great hulking bodyguard?"

"I was supposed to use my phone, I wasn't thinking." Olivia was tearing into the cheese and biscuits like a starving stray.

"Did the police come?"

"Bibi called them from the coffee bar, so they must have, but I was in the car and out of there."

"So you don't know yet if they caught him."

"I doubt it. He was in the street—he'd be gone."

"I've found out who he is."

Olivia's head came up. "Who? How do you know?"

"I went to see Iris Gill today."

"Iris! What—"

"Kevin is her stepson."

Olivia's knife clattered to the plate. A piece of cheese dropped to the carpet. The blood sank away from her skin, leaving her pale as a lily. "Who?" Her voice was a mere breath.

"He's Ralph Brody's son. I've given you a nasty jolt. I'm sorry."

"Jesus," Olivia said and then was silent.

"I saw a photograph of him. Taken a few years ago, but I recognised his face. Iris was showing me pictures she took at the cottage. She said Kevin was only at the cottage once or twice, but you're in the photograph, too, so you must have met him, even if you don't remember him."

"I don't remember him at all." Olivia's voice was almost inaudible.

"Unfortunately, it seems he didn't forget you."

"I thought he'd only seen me in a film."

"Maybe it reminded him. Iris said he's always been strange. Disturbed, she thought. Living in a fantasy world. He was taking drugs, too, I don't know what, but he stole things from her, so she doesn't see him any more."

"Is, is his f-father still alive?"

"No. He died six months ago, in the nursing home."

Olivia burst into tears. Gillian put her arms around her. "What is it?"

Olivia shook her head, rocking back and forth and sobbing. "Nothing. I didn't know. It's all too horrible," she said, when she could speak.

"No wonder, what you've just been through. But the police will be able to find Kevin, now. It should be easy. They'll use Iris's photograph if he's on the run. I've already talked to Hardwick."

Olivia bent her head and covered her face with her hands. Gillian looked away, out of the window, and saw Edward crossing the street.

"Edward will be here in a couple of minutes. You haven't seen him since you were a girl, have you?"

Olivia was still pale. "No. Can I go wash my face?"

"Of course."

"I don't want to talk to him about it. Please? I can't bear any more right now. I'll just cry if I have to talk about it again. I had two hours with Hardwick this morning."

"Olivia, it's not Edward's case. He won't badger you, I promise. He'll want to know what happened, and I'll tell him, if you'd rather. But you're going to have to report that Kevin attacked you."

"I will, I'll do it later. They know already, Bibi rang them from the coffee bar."

"They'll still need your statement."

Gillian heard Edward's key turn in the lock. Olivia scurried into the bathroom. Gillian was absently rearranging the biscuits when Edward came into the room.

"You've been unpacking," he said, looking at the tissue paper everywhere.

"Detective. Olivia's here. We've just had tea."

"How is she?"

"I'll tell you later. She's had a traumatic experience. Did you get my message? Have you spoken to Hardwick in the past couple of hours? We know who Kevin is, now."

"The son of the chap Charlotte hit with the car. Olivia knows? Hardwick's keeping me informed. He said you saw a photograph."

"What's he doing about it?"

"Checking addresses. They've got one near Bethnal Green, but Brody's shifted about since then. They've also got the mother's name, from Iris Gill. And they'll circulate the photograph if they need to."

"Ralph Brody's dead, Iris said."

Olivia emerged from the bathroom, looking subdued.

"It's been a long time," Edward said. "I'm sorry about your mother."

"Thank you. I remember you at our house. You were sitting in the garden. It was in the summer."

"At a dinner party, I expect. They were wonderful, Charlotte's dinners."

"Can I ask you something? Gillian said they had to do an autopsy." She hesitated. "Do you know if they've finished yet?"

"Actually, I saw the report today," Edward said gently. "Massive cerebral haemorrhage. It would have killed her outright."

"You mean she wouldn't know?"

"Maybe she was aware. I don't suppose anyone could be certain. But she wouldn't have had time to suffer."

Gillian let out the breath she'd been holding. "Well thank God for that."

Olivia nodded. "Thank you," she said to Edward in a small, formal voice, "I wanted to know."

She said she wouldn't have another cup of tea. Retrieving her phone, she excused herself and dialled a number. "It's me. Oh, you've been ringing. Yes, I'm in Pimlico. He gave you the address?" Her voice went higher. "I had to recharge the battery, it was completely.... Yes, it's only one floor up." She put the phone away again. "He was calling me and getting my answering service. He says he's close by, he'll be here in a few minutes."

"I'm glad you have an escort," Edward said.

Olivia flashed a glance at Gillian. "Sergeant Hardwick said I should be careful."

"Kevin Brody," Edward said. "Is there anything you can remember about him that might help?"

"Nothing," Olivia said. "I don't even remember meeting him. Will you find him soon?"

"I hope so. But please do be careful. Whatever you do, don't leave doors unlocked and don't open your door unless you know who it is. I'm sure you're aware, but it's easy to forget."

"I know," Olivia said.

When the car pulled up outside, Gillian saw a dark-haired man at the wheel. He had a phone in his hand.

"That's him," Olivia said. Her phone beeped. "Yes, I'm ready."

He got out of the car and glanced up and then moved swiftly out of Gillian's line of vision. The buzzer went. She embraced Olivia; Olivia's body felt as taut as a wire. They said goodbye, and Olivia ran down the stairs to meet her escort.

"Johnny," Gillian heard.

"Are you all right?"

Gillian thought, oh, it's like that. She shut the door and nipped back to the sitting room. Johnny and Olivia emerged, his arm around her shoulder. They walked across the street together, and he opened the door for her. Then he slung himself into the driver's seat. The car roared away.

"Olivia has a new lover," Gillian said. "His name is Johnny and he looks like a Renaissance portrait come to life. Giorgione, maybe. Goodness, she's been staying in Raymond's flat, I wonder what she's doing about that now. We didn't even talk about it."

"What was it you were going to tell me?"

"She ran into Kevin this afternoon. He attacked her." She repeated Olivia's story, and Edward asked several rapid-fire questions she couldn't answer. "I didn't interrogate her," Gillian said, after the third one. "She was a wreck."

"I should think so. But an iron, of all things!" Edward said. "She's got pluck, that girl. Quick wits, too."

"I guess there's a little sweat shop over the coffee bar."

"Has she reported the assault?"

"The owner of the coffee bar called the police. Olivia came straight here, in the car. You should see the bruiser who came to the door with her, he's like a rhinoceros."

"She could have telephoned from here."

"But she was overwhelmed. She literally collapsed on the sofa, and she'd barely had time to tell me the story when I saw you coming. She said she couldn't bear any more questions now. She had two hours with Hardwick today, for Pete's sake, and then the assault."

"But don't you see? The officers who responded to the call from the coffee bar won't know this incident is connected to the break-in at Charlotte's house or to Olivia's previous complaints. Hardwick—the chaps who are already looking for Kevin—need to know."

"Oh. That didn't occur to me."

"You had enough to think about," Edward said. "But the Met is an octopus, and none of its arms knows what the other arms are doing."

"I told her the police would need her statement—she'll do it. She just needs a minute to breathe. Listen, it was awful when I told her about Kevin. I think his identity is almost as shocking to Olivia as being attacked."

"Why?"

"Because of the car accident, I guess. It was a horror for Charlotte, Olivia must have felt it. The name Brody would bring all that back. She turned white when I told her who he was."

"But she doesn't remember him."

"Maybe not, but she cried when I told her Ralph was dead."

"I'm going to call Hardwick right now. They'll step up the search."

Edward went to the phone. "About Charlotte," he said, waiting as it rang. "I spoke to the pathologist. He said it was a clot like a football. And it was probably a mercy. He found cancer in one of her lungs."

As soon as the car was moving, Johnny said, "I saw Andy. What the hell were you doing? Why didn't you call him from the flat?"

"Johnny—"

"I told you what to do! I know how to handle security because of the club. I get it all sorted, and you ignore me! You walk into the flipping street."

"I forgot."

"You forgot. It's a simple thing! Use the phone! End of story!" He shot through an orange light and tore past a lumbering bus.

"Don't."

"You just walked out into the fucking street! You didn't even listen to me." He jockeyed around a tradesman's van that was double parked.

"I did. I was upset because I saw Lisa."

"All you had to do was use the phone! Is that so hard?" The tires squealed. "You could have been killed!"

"Big deal. I'll be killed anyway if you keep driving like this."

He hit the steering wheel with his fist. "I know how to bloody drive. You were supposed to wait for Andy."

Suddenly she was boiling mad. "I made a mistake. I'm not used to it—having to think about security every minute," she yelled. "Why should I be? Why should I? All I did was forget and act like a normal person. I can't help that."

"Then don't go out," he bellowed.

"Oh, brilliant," she said hysterically. "I can go into purdah in your flat."

"Yeh. Not a bad idea. I've got your clothes." He turned towards her, the fire gone out of his eyes, but it was too late.

"Forget it. I'm not going to your flat. Take me to Nicky's."

"Don't be daft," he said.

"And *don't* tell me not to be daft! You haven't got a clue what happened to me today, not a bloody clue! Except you know I was scared witless and nearly raped or killed, and what do you do? You tear a strip off me."

"Olivia—"

"Shut up and don't talk to me. You're a brute. Oh right, totally charming as long as everything is exactly how you want it, then you dispense your favours, but let anybody step out of line for one second, and you're Saddam bloody Hussein. Take me to Nicky's."

"I thought you were staying with me."

"Well I'm not. You can't force me to."

"Force you? What are you—"

She cut him off. "Leave it out. You know what happened to me today? I spent two hours with the police. Then I saw Raymond. Yes, he came back while I was packing. How do you think *that* felt? Then I lost one of my best friends. And then I go outside and I find Sally, one of my own dolls, with her head ripped off. And then Kevin—and that's not even all of it. And you! You know what you do? You bloody stomp all over me with jackboots. Brilliant. I don't want to be with you."

She stopped, her whole body shaking with emotion. She groped for a cigarette, snapped the first one in two, managed to get the second one to her mouth but couldn't get it lit. Johnny lit one and offered it to her. She ignored it.

He wasn't driving fast any more. "Take the bloody cigarette," he said quietly.

"No. I don't want anything from you. Just drive me to Nicky's or I'll get out and walk."

"All right! I'll take you there, if that's what you want."

She lit her cigarette; she could feel the ache of tears starting in her eyes and forced them back. Johnny's face was grim.

Nicky lived in one of the seedier streets of Paddington; it wasn't very far. When they got there, he said, "I want to tell you something."

"Don't. I don't want to know. I can't bear one more thing right now. Nothing."

"I'm sorry."

"Fine."

She had a key; they went up in the lift with her bags, and she banged on Nicky's door before opening it. "Nicky, it's me."

Nicky came to the door, and her eyebrows went up. "I thought you weren't coming tonight," she said. Then she saw Johnny and the suitcases. "Oh. Change of plan."

Olivia marched into the little sitting room carrying her knapsack and her travel kit, and Johnny put down the other two cases. "Olivia," he said. She held up her palm, as if to ward off anything he might say. "I'll call you in the morning, then." He nodded to Nicky and left.

Nicky bolted the door. Olivia threw herself down on the sofa. "Oh God, Nicky," she groaned.

"What?"

Olivia's face was buried in the cushions. "Men *suck*."

Nicky hooted. "Stop the presses! This just in from Olivia Bening."

"They do."

"Men suck and the world is round." Nicky had a bottle of wine open, and she fetched another glass. "Last time I saw you, sweetie, you were being abducted. What the hell happened?"

Olivia sat up and took the wine Nicky poured for her. She reached for a cigarette from Nicky's open packet. "So much. Johnny's only part of it."

Nicky inspected her. "You're shattered. It's not just a row, is it? I'll tell you one thing, though. I saw the look on his face just now. You can hurt him."

9

Gillian was out buying the Sunday papers when the call came. She was tired, having lain awake half the night worrying about Olivia. When she got back, Edward said, "They've picked up Kevin Brody. Very early this morning."

"They have? Oh thank God. Where? How did they find him?"

"At his mother's. He was asleep. He'd told her some story about burning himself, and she hauled him to a local clinic. He didn't want to go—afraid we might trace him, I expect—but he wanted the painkillers. They made him groggy."

"Poor woman. It must have been awful for her when the police showed up."

"Hardwick says she didn't seem terribly surprised."

"Does Olivia know?"

"He's left a message—she's not answering yet this morning. Where is she?"

"With Johnny, I guess. Or Nicky—the friend she's making a film with. It doesn't matter, does it? She's safe now."

"We need her statement about the assault as soon as possible."

"Why wasn't Kevin's mother surprised? Has he been in trouble before?"

"With the police? I don't know, but she told Hardwick she hadn't believed his story about the burn. She didn't try to get the truth out of him, she said, because it was never any use. I'm going to visit her early this afternoon."

"Why isn't Hardwick doing that?"

"He's been at work since Friday morning."

Gillian felt light-headed with relief. Her fatigue retreated in a rush of exhilaration. She threw her arms around Edward. "I'm so happy. Olivia's all right, she doesn't have to be afraid any more."

"Hardwick's quite pleased as well. A good night's work."

"Do you want a real Sunday breakfast? Sausages? Eggs on toast? I could eat a moose."

In Paddington, Olivia was drinking coffee and listening to her messages.

"Nicky," she squealed. A roaring clatter came from the tiny kitchen, where Nicky was pushing carrots and sticks of celery into a juicer, her health counter-offensive to the junk food she ate while she was working. Olivia pranced in. "They've got Kevin."

"Never!"

"There's a message from the police."

Nicky threw a carrot in the air and caught it. "They've arrested him?"

Olivia played the message again. "Yes, early this morning. I'm free, Nicky! I can go to any coffee bar I like. I can walk home! I can answer the phone!" She jigged up and down. "You know how it feels? It's like exercising with ankle weights and then taking them off. I feel weird and light, like gravity's let go of me. If I jump, I'll bang my head on the ceiling. What time is it? I should tell Johnny."

"Wait for him to call you."

"Why? Whatever he said yesterday, he deserves to know I'm safe."

"Eejit. Listen to me. Let him sweat. He acted like a schmuck."

"Yes, but—"

"Remember the self-help book we said we'd write last night about women and men? The bestseller? Advice for Betty and Bob? Well, what does Betty do now? She doesn't bloody ring Bob."

"Betty and Bob have been under stress," Olivia said. "Especially Betty."

"Are you making excuses for him?"

"Nicky, yesterday was the worst day of my entire life. It's been horrible since I got back to London. Mummy's dead. She died and I couldn't even go home without Kevin being there, stinking up the house with his lilies so I could hardly breathe, and leaving me insane messages. He's destroyed my room—the one Mummy and I decorated together. I don't ever want to see it again. And yesterday was an absolute nightmare. It's been like meeting Johnny in the middle of a war, like the Nazis are invading. But they've arrested Kevin, now. The war's over. Life can be normal, that's all I'm saying."

Nicky handed her a glass of juice. "Like when packages are just packages, and if the phone rings it's only some wally wanting you to work for nothing."

"Exactly. I need to feel grounded. I've got to find a flat; ever since I left Lisa's, I've been living out of suitcases. It's beginning to drive me potty. And I want to get things sorted with Johnny. After that, there's Mummy—the house—I've got to make some decisions and help Gillian." Olivia stopped, grimacing. "But the police need me to make a statement right away. The first thing I have to do is go and talk to them."

"You can do that this morning," Nicky said. "It'll take ages to set up in here."

"I thought you had a lot of furniture to move."

"Six of the crew are coming. It'll be like the underground at rush hour."

In the afternoon, a scene was going to be shot in Nicky's flat. A scene in which Olivia, as June, had a confrontation with her sister over money missing from their mother's house. A silent search, then accusations, lies, and a handbag spilling all over the floor. A little mirror breaking. It would take most of the day to set up the scene, film it, and clean up, if nothing went wrong.

"I almost wish you'd tell me you're desperate, I've got to stay here and help. I'm sick and tired of Kevin. I don't want to think about him, or talk to the police. And I don't want to go to court and be bullied by lawyers."

"I know," Nicky said. "But you'll do it, and then he'll be in prison and you won't have to think about him any more."

"Until he gets out again."

"Don't say that."

"No, best not to. I'll ring the police back this minute. When they're finished with me, I'll call Johnny."

"If it was down to me, I'd still say let him ring you. With those alpha types, you have to hold your ground."

Olivia rolled her eyes. "'All About Alphas,' by Nicky Chandler, coming soon to a cinema near you."

The intercom buzzed.

"That'll be the crew arriving," Nicky said. "You'd better get out of here."

"This flat looks like a trailer park after a tornado," Gillian said, looking at the newspapers and torn fragments of bubble-pack and an assortment of homeless objects.

"Do you want a hand with the books?" Edward asked.

"I don't think there's enough shelf space."

"Then we'll stop when there isn't any more."

"I should put the china away first. I unpacked it, and now it's all over the table."

"Tell me where you'd like it to go."

"I don't know. That's why I haven't put it away. Where do *you* want it to go?"

"Anywhere, so long as it's not back in a box."

"Fat lot of help you are."

"My mother has a china cabinet she tried to foist on me a few years ago. It's very nice, but I didn't have any use for a china cabinet. Why don't I ring her and ask for it? She'll be delighted."

"Perfect. Do you know anyone who has a large hole they'd like to fill with tissue paper?"

For an hour, they unpacked books, Edward carrying the boxes and slitting them open, both of them lifting the books out. "I dusted them all when I packed," Gillian said, looking at her hands. "What will happen to Kevin Brody?"

"That depends. Will the court find him guilty? Not guilty but insane? We don't know what to do with stalkers. There are men kept under lock and key who are probably harmless, and God knows we set some of them free and they murder their wives the next day. What do we have to go on? Psychiatric opinions. Might do as well with palm readers."

The phone rang.

"I'll get it," Edward said. "And I'll put the kettle on. I could do with a cup of tea."

Gillian washed her hands and then went to the bedroom to comb her hair, feeling disheveled by the work of unpacking. She looked at the photograph of Charlotte and Tom and Olivia. Charlotte's youthful zest and astringency looked back. Charlotte was like a bird that had flown into a plate glass window, Gillian thought. But had the glass been invisible, or had she been attacking her own reflection?

She could hear Edward on the telephone. Whoever had called was telling him something at length. Unaccountably depressed, Gillian drifted back to the smaller bedroom and sat on the floor hugging her knees and staring at her boxes.

"Moving's harder than I thought," she said, when Edward came back.

"We'll be finished soon."

"I don't mean the labour. That's just work. I mean what happens when you dismantle your life. You take it to pieces and pack it up as if you can reassemble it somewhere else.

But when you take it to pieces everything comes into question. It must feel like this, only worse, to lose your religion."

"You're not wishing you hadn't moved, are you?"

"No. Don't think that. I want to be here, and I can feel life starting. With Olivia, with your mother, with meeting Iris again. With having things to do for Charlotte. But it's still difficult—the problem of meaning cropping up. Ordinarily, you can keep it buried. You live a pattern, and the pattern keeps you occupied. You don't have to invent."

"It's Sunday," Edward said. "We should go to a pub this afternoon when I get back. Sit in the garden and drink beer."

"That's your solution to the vacuum in my soul? Beer?"

"You can't drink beer at a pub on Sunday afternoon and have an existential crisis at the same time."

Gillian got to her feet. "You're wasted at the Yard, you are. You should wear a loin cloth and sit on top of a mountain in India."

"By the way, that was Hardwick ringing again. He's seen Olivia, he took a statement from her. She was at the station all morning. He's more than satisfied. He's going home to sleep now—he'll be off for a few days."

Olivia was driven back to Nicky's by a woman PC. The interview had been an ordeal, repeating the details of the assault over and over, her terror and confusion vivid in her mind again. She'd been very tense, but now it was better. She dialled Nicky's number.

"I'm on my way back in a car; the traffic's not bad, I should only be a few minutes."

"A few minutes is good. By the way, Bob called."

"Bob?" Olivia was at a loss.

"Wanted to speak to Betty."

"Oh. *That* Bob. When? What did you say?"

"A couple of hours ago. I gave him the good news. I said you were at the police station and that he couldn't talk to you this afternoon because you had to work," Nicky said severely.

"The two of you in the same room would be like two Siamese fighting fish in a tank." Olivia became aware of the PC listening. "Bye, Nicky, I'll be there."

It was Sunday afternoon. She could go for a walk in Hyde Park; she could even lie on the grass and shut her eyes. No need to watch the crowds, looking for the round head, the strange eyes that were always looking for her. She could stroll along the Serpentine holding hands with Johnny, instead, watching birds and boats and clouds. She could go back to Nicky's flat and not wonder whether Kevin had discovered the address, she could stop imagining she saw him every time some man with big shoulders loomed in the distance. She smiled at the PC. "Nice day."

"Smashing. You're in films, right? Anything I would have seen?"

"I don't know. *Karma Kids*? It had a good run in London."

"Nope, sorry."

"Well, I just shot a film with Bobby Carr."

"Never! Bobby Carr? Oh, he's so-o-o gorgeous. What's he like? Does he look the same in real life?"

"You mean are the abs real? They're real, and he's not a dwarf."

"What's he like to work with?"

"Very professional."

"Oh," the PC breathed, "I've had dreams about Bobby. He must be such a ride. What's the name of it, the film?"

"*Rough Diamonds*."

"Ooh, right, I'll go see it." She giggled. "Wait till I tell them. The whole nick will go."

Olivia smiled and made some suitable response. Nicky had told Johnny about Kevin's arrest. He wouldn't be worrying about her. That was good; she couldn't possibly talk to him now, not with the PC listening, and she couldn't think about calling him while she was working, or she'd lose her concentration on the part. She'd ring as soon as the shoot was over.

Angela Brody's kitchen, like the rest of the flat, was small but tidy. Edward sat with the cup of tea she'd poured. She wasn't hostile, but she was wary, dubious about his sympathy. As well she might be, he acknowledged. He felt pity for her, but the reasons for his visit were practical.

"Yes, I've lived here a good many years. Since I was divorced. It's never gone bad, like some council estates. I bought this flat when Mrs. Thatcher said we could."

"So Kevin grew up here."

"Yes."

"What was he like, when he was a little boy?"

"Why do you want to know? Why should I tell you? You're not going to be of much use to him, are you?"

Edward looked at her gray hair, her sad and anxious eyes, the bitter lines carved deep between her brows and bracketing her lips. "It may be better that he's in custody now—less likely to harm anyone, or himself."

She looked sceptical. "He should have his medications."

"What medications?"

"I don't have a right to know, do I? I'm only his mother. I've only taken care of him since he was a baby."

"Who's the doctor?"

"Dr. Paul. G.R. Paul." She grimaced. "He's a psychiatrist. Can he visit Kevin, where he is?"

"That can be arranged. Has Kevin been seeing him?"

"No, he stopped. Wouldn't take the drugs, either, didn't like them. There's nothing I could do about it, he won't listen to me."

"It's common, I think, with some medications. Patients don't like the effects."

"They should bloody *have* to take them. I've been terrified about him, and now look what's happened. I know what you lot say he's done, but is it his fault? No one can help him unless he gives his permission. Don't tell me that's not daft."

"It must have been a shock, when the police came this morning."

"Not really. Kevin came in all bloody, I knew something bad had happened." She stirred her tea but didn't drink. "I had a terrible time when he was born. Sometimes I wonder if he wasn't damaged. I saw a program on the telly about it."

"What about Kevin's father, Mrs. Brody? You know the girl that Kevin attacked was the daughter of the woman who hit his father with the car a decade ago?"

"They told me. I don't have anything to say about it. Ralph and I were divorced a long time before that."

"Was Kevin upset about the accident?"

"I suppose anyone would be. We didn't talk about his father."

"Not even then?"

"Not really."

"But he saw him regularly?"

"Sometimes. Ralph wasn't that keen, even after he married again. And Kevin would come home angry; he would sit and brood. They didn't get on." She stood up abruptly and began to fold a basket of laundry that she'd set down on the counter when he arrived. She turned her back to him. "What does it matter now. He's dead."

Edward thought, there's something about his father she doesn't want to say.

"What's going to happen?" she asked.

"To Kevin? A psychiatric evaluation, first. What were the grounds for your divorce, Mrs. Brody?"

She rounded on him. "That's not your business."

"Anything to do with Kevin is our business right now."

"I suppose you'll go poking your nose in, asking people questions."

"It's the job. I'm not enjoying this."

"Aren't you? Why are you a policeman then?"

Nice return. He smiled a little. "When I started, I thought a good detective solved problems."

"And what do you think now?"

"That we clean up messes, often messes that need not have been made."

"Well, a mess is what Kevin's got himself into, I've no quarrel with that. But it's a bit late in the day to be talking of cleaning up." She folded a towel in half and half again, and laid it down. "Ralph gave me a divorce after I came home and caught him in bed with someone. I knew he had a bit on the side, but walking in on it was something different. It didn't come out in court, but people knew."

"Did Kevin know?"

"Not that I found them like that, no. Just that there'd been women. I told him they were tarts."

At six o'clock, they'd finished the shoot, except for packing up the equipment and moving the furniture back to its usual arrangement. The room was stifling, even after all the lights had been turned off. Most of the crew were guzzling beer. Olivia turned her phone on and dialled Johnny's number.

"We're done," she said. There were five people talking at once in the sitting room; she put a hand over her other ear. "What?" She squeezed past, into the bedroom. Her suitcases were imprisoned behind a pile of furniture. "Yes, isn't it? Nicky said she told you." She wouldn't be able to take a shower, and she would just have to wear the skirt that she'd put on in the morning when she went to the police station. "I want to see you too. No, don't come and fetch me. It's pandemonium, and it's hotter than the desert in here, because of the lights. The crew'll be here for ages, I doubt they'll even start cleaning up for a while. Everybody's knackered. Nicky doesn't need me. I'd like to go somewhere cool and quiet. Where are you?" A burst of raucous laughter came from the sitting room. She kicked the door shut and then she could hear him.

"At the club. We had an electrical problem last night. Some lights blew. A short, we had to tear a huge hole in the wall to find it. We're just closing it up now."

"I'll take the tube."

"Are you sure? I can meet you somewhere near Nicky's."

"It's fine. Johnny, I'm dying to walk to the tube station just like anyone else. I haven't been able to do that for weeks."

In Soho the streets were packed. Olivia zig-zagged her way through the churning mass of people, wondering how many of them were Londoners. She heard French and German and American voices, as well as accents from Jamaica and Pakistan. She caught snatches of languages she didn't recognize. The smell of frying chips came at her, a little wave, and then something more pungent, onions and spices. Crowds oozed out of the pubs, happy at the end of the day, in the warmth of the summer evening. Music blared from shop doorways. London, she thought, rejoicing. Her city. It *was* hers again, now. London, Lon-don, it sounded like a heartbeat.

The Paradise Club was in a nondescript brick building, the entrance easy to miss, with the unlit neon palm tree merely a dark squiggle on the wall. She pressed the buzzer and heard Johnny's voice over the intercom. "I'll come down." A moment, then the lock snapped back and the door swung wide. It was dark in the stairwell; they stood in the open doorway, the evening sun slanting in.

"Hi," he said. He was wearing a black T-shirt and jeans and his arms were streaked with soot and chalky white dust. It was the first time she'd seen him looking tired.

She heard voices from the room above.

"They'll be gone in a minute."

He shut the door and they climbed the stairs without speaking. The room looked huge in the dim light, an enormous cavern, the walls disappearing upward into gloom. At the far end, working lights illuminated the repaired wall. Two men stood in front of it, throwing elongated shadows on the white surface.

She perched on a stool at the bar and studied the room, curious to see it with the magic turned off. No band playing, no sparkling, swirling lights, the glowing green snake a colourless tube dangling overhead. No monkey behind the bar. Only the faint scent of gardenias conjured the memory of enchantment. Here and there a metallic glint reflected a stray beam from the working lights, hinting at the dazzle that could be created with switches. She didn't know how to begin, but it was Johnny's problem, she decided. She'd made the journey here, the next move was his. She lit a cigarette and crossed her legs and waited.

The men picked up their tool boxes and left. She heard their footsteps echoing in the stairwell and then the soft thud of the door closing. Johnny went behind the bar to wash his hands.

"Would you like a drink?" he said.

"Why not?"

"I'll need some light." He walked to an electrical panel and flipped a switch. The pink neon stars came on overhead. Behind the bar, the ranks of bottles winked and flashed. She saw herself in the mirror, sitting at the long empty counter. Behind the stars was blackness, like outer space. He came back and leaned on the bar, facing her. He seemed to have forgotten that he'd offered her a drink.

"All I could think was, if you'd called Andy from the flat you would have been all right."

"I know. That's what you said."

"What I said. I was a bastard. You should throw your drink in my face."

"If I'd had one yesterday, I might have thrown it at you."

"Or hit me with a brick. That's what I needed."

"I thought I never wanted to see you again."

"I knew that when I left you at Nicky's. I sat in the car telling myself what a stupid bastard I was."

"You were so furious with me."

"Andy said you'd come down to the street without calling him on the mobile. He saw you running into the road—I went spare when he told me. I kept seeing it, I kept thinking what might have happened. Anything." He stopped.

"Johnny—"

"I know. I shouldn't have taken it out on you. Christ." He suddenly turned and walked away, out from behind the bar. She watched him uncertainly, but he'd only gone to fetch his cigarettes from a table. "I'm surprised you're here," he said, from that distance.

"We were both crazy yesterday."

"I didn't even let you tell me what happened."

"I'll tell you now."

He was coming back, this time to her side of the bar.

"Listen," she said. "What I said yesterday, that you're only nice when you have everything your way, it's not true. I know it isn't. And maybe you saved my life—by asking Andy to drive me. What if I'd gone to Lisa's in a taxi instead of with Andy?"

A ghost of a smile flickered at the corners of Johnny's mouth. "I don't know, you might have kicked Kevin's arse. From what Andy told me, you've got more bottle than most blokes."

"I think I used every bit of it when Kevin chased me upstairs."

He stood beside her, very near. "I was afraid he'd find you again. I must have dialled your number ten times in the middle of the night, but I didn't let it ring."

She turned her head away and saw the blur of movement in the mirror behind the bar; their reflections swam in the dusk. "What were you going to say?"

His arms closed around her. His voice murmured in her ear. "Sorry I was such a git."

She lifted her eyes to look into his face. "Johnny, I love you."

"I love you."

In the mirror, the two indistinct figures glimmered and dissolved into one. The neon stars shone on.

"Wasn't I going to buy you a drink?"

"Yes, I could murder anything cold. Can I have a martini?" She'd never ordered one, but she liked the shape of the glasses.

"Olive or twist?"

"Olive."

He set a martini glass on the counter. "We could go to the Roma for dinner."

"I'd like that." She watched him mix the drink, swirling the gin and vermouth in a little pitcher of ice. He moved deftly, his hands seemed to know where everything was. He tilted the pitcher and the clear, slightly oily liquid slowly filled the glass. A delicate veil of moisture formed on the outside.

"Were you ever a bartender?"

"Yeh. It was the year *Tequila Sunrise* came out, and everybody wanted to order one. I can still remember how to make them, if you ever have the urge." He was pouring Jack Daniels into a whisky glass for himself.

"Robert Towne wrote the script. He's brilliant. Did you like it?"

"It was pretty good." He lit a cigarette and passed it to her. She took it, thinking of the one she'd refused when they'd been shouting at each other in the car. *I don't want anything from you.* The opposite was true.

That had been yesterday. Yesterday she'd been running from Kevin. She'd had a minder. "Who's Andy?"

"He works for Max."

"He's strange—he hardly said a word to me all day, and then he laughed about the iron."

"Yeh, Andy was very impressed. He's had lots of experience in security work. He's been a body guard for pop stars, that's why I asked him—he knows what he's doing. Max has a firm of doormen; Andy helps run it."

"Max." Involuntarily, her eyes went to the far end of the bar where the fight had taken place. "Have you talked to him?"

"I've known Max too long, since we were kids. I can't stay pissed at him. He's a madman. He does things that make me want to kill him, but if I ever needed anything—help, money, whatever, he'd be right there. He was there when my Dad died." Johnny shrugged. "You'll see what he's like. Max is a gambler; he goes for married women and likes to play with his money at casinos. He wins more than he loses. When he wins big, he can't spend the money fast enough. Anything he does, he's over the top. He gave me a coat once—Hugo Boss. Said I needed it. You don't refuse Max when he's in those moods. See what I mean?"

She sipped her martini. It stung her tongue, but she liked it. "This is good. If that monkey was here, I'd give him a taste."

"Bert? He'd finish the glass. He's a soak, that monkey. Never pays, either." They both laughed.

"I have a clean shirt in the back."

She drank some more. "I'll come with you, I haven't seen the back."

"It's a tip."

She followed him through the door and saw a round table and some sagging chairs. There were empty glasses on the table, and ashtrays loaded with cigarette butts. There was a dartboard. A small fridge hummed. The room had a shabby, comfortable backstage feel that was familiar to her. A radio had been left on low; she could hear Billie Holiday singing "I Only Have Eyes For You." Johnny went through another door, into a tidier room with a desk and a couple of leather chairs. A fresh white shirt hung on the back of the door.

"Your office."

"Like the view?"

A small window was coated with soot on the outside; it looked across a narrow space at another dirty window.

The message light was blinking on his desk phone, but he ignored it. He stripped off his T-shirt. "How was the filming today?"

"It's an emotional scene. It builds to a screaming argument. Suppose we're having a big row. We start here." She held her hand below hip level, palm facing the floor. "And end here." She raised her hand above her head. "Then we crash to the bottom. Way up and then way down. You run through that from start to finish several times, and then you stop and wait, and then you jump in, right near the climax, and do that part again, for a reaction shot. And stop and wait and do it again for a close-up, and so on. You turn on and off like a tap, and each time it has to be at the right emotional pitch." The daylight was fading. She stood at the dirty window, looking out. "It's a family row; I don't have any sisters, so I thought about my parents fighting, how that felt to me."

In the middle of the night, Olivia woke with a cry from a nightmare. It was a dream of suffocating she'd had in the past. A great weight pressed down on her until she couldn't breathe, and then she would wake, gasping, kicking at the sheet. She hadn't had the dream for a while, but now that it had come back, she remembered it.

"What is it?" Johnny said, coming awake.

"Bad dream."

"Anyone would have them, after what you've been through." She fell asleep again, nestled close.

The next morning, she forgot about the dream and got up and drank her coffee and went off to a dance class and then to work. When she woke up with Johnny and walked down the street to the underground, it felt like the first day of a new life. When Kevin came into her mind, she pictured a rubbish bin, put him in it and shut the lid. But in the back of her mind fugitive images floated, evanescent, nameless shadows. That night she woke twice, muffling her cries, from the same dream.

"Iztabout Kevin?" Johnny mumbled, half asleep.

"It'll fade, I suppose." It was hard to close her eyes. She lay staring into the dark.

They finished Nicky's film the next day and Johnny said they should have the wrap party at the Paradise Club, so they planned that for Friday. Olivia stopped at Nicky's for fresh clothes and then returned to Johnny's. Tomorrow was Wednesday, she would spend it searching for her own flat. She was reading the book about Byron. Teresa would be a good role, one she could play. If she got it, she would look at sketches, portraits of Italian women of the period, see how they stood, what sort of clothes they wore. She would read Teresa's book, of course, and Byron's poetry. Mary Shelley, reading ghost stories with Byron on the shores of Lake Geneva and writing *Frankenstein*, was extraordinary, and Teresa wasn't. But Teresa was captivating, and she was loving and giving. Olivia tried to imagine what it would have been like to have the most famous poet in the world erupt into her life when she was only nineteen and newly married. Teresa survived, she noticed. Years later, after her husband and the poet were both dead, she married again, a Frenchman who took delight in introducing her as Byron's former mistress.

She liked thinking about Teresa because Teresa was in the future. So was a new flat. Olivia told herself she was moving forward, that Kevin was an episode she had survived, and after the court case he would be gone. Erased from her life. In the meantime, she'd clean up the loose ends: collect her bits and pieces from Lisa's flat and quit smoking again.

But when she woke from her nightmares she was afraid to fall asleep again. She would dream she was suffocating, and then about the accident. In her accident dream, she was driving, and it was her mother who fell under the wheels. Johnny found her in the sitting room at 3:30 in the morning.

"What are you doing?"

"Watching a video." She was curled on the sofa in her dressing gown. He stood in the doorway. "You're watching *The Godfather*?"

"It's a good movie. I've seen it three times. Brando's great, the way he talks with those cotton wads in his cheeks. When the producer saw the rushes he yelled, 'Is this movie gonna have subtitles?'"

"I mean why are you watching it now? Kind of late, innit?"

"I was dreaming again, so I don't want to sleep." Don Corleone was at the fruit stand, the oranges were glowing like jewels. "The colour in this film is amazing. It's so dark, and when it's light, it's like they dipped the film stock in melted butter."

"You can't stay awake forever."

"I can try. Maybe I'll be so tired I won't dream."

"You're going to watch the rest of the movie?"

She nodded. He sat down and after a few minutes lit a cigarette and smoked it, watching the flickering light on her face. On the screen, the wrapped package arrived. Luca Brasi was sleeping with the fishes. Olivia glanced sideways at Johnny now and then.

"You don't have to stay up with me," she said. "I'm fine as long as I'm awake."

"Olivia, I'm not surprised you're having these nightmares after what Kevin did to you, but there's something else going on, isn't there? Why are you so upset that you met him a long time ago? When you told me about that, it seemed like the worst part of it for you."

She flicked a look at him and then turned her eyes back to the TV screen. Paulie was being shot in the car, by the side of the road. Clemenza took a leak in the reeds. In the far distance, the Statue of Liberty was bright against the sky.

"You hardly knew him, right?" Johnny said. "I know his parents were friends of your parents, but you haven't seen them for years."

"His father and stepmother."

"Right, whatever. But why does it matter so much?"

"I don't know if I can tell you. I've never talked to anyone about it."

"Maybe you should."

"*Leave the gun. Take the cannolli.*"

"Pass me a fag?"

He gave her one and lit it, and she held his hand and stared at the movie.

"I don't mean you should tell me," Johnny said. "Just someone."

Clemenza was cooking for the men. Kay told Michael Corleone she loved him. Now Michael was in front of the hospital. Pretty soon he would shoot Sollozzo and the cop, and then he'd be in Sicily, where he'd meet the girl.

"Have you ever been to Italy?" Olivia asked.

"No. I'd like to go. My mother's Italian."

"What part of Italy is she from?"

"Not Sicily. A little village in the hills above La Spezia. North of Pisa. She still has family there. You never talked to Nicky?"

"No, Johnny, I just wanted to forget it. I did pretty well, I hardly ever thought about it, and I totally forgot Kevin existed. Until all this happened."

"If we're going to watch the rest of this film, I'm going to get a drink. Want one?"

He poured neat whisky for himself and brought her a glass of wine.

"I like this part, on the hospital steps, with the cigarette," she said. "It's so simple. Michael's hands don't shake, that's all you need to see."

But her own were shaking. She couldn't follow the movie any more. The image of Kevin bursting into the upstairs room, snarling, shouting, kept superimposing itself. 'I know! Liar! Little whore!' Coming at her until she had to hit him. And behind that image, seen as if through a veil, the other one, the man looming over her, the feel of the gearshift poking into her back, the smell of wet grass outside and something flowering in the hedge, darkness, a huge moon with a silver-edged band of cloud, a stifling closeness, pain.

She didn't look at Johnny. Smoking helped, it gave her something to do. "I don't want to have secrets from you."

"It doesn't matter."

"Yes it does, it does to me."

She took a careful sip of wine, holding the glass with both hands. Then she set it down; she kept her face turned towards the screen. "We used to go to Hampshire, I told you that, remember? Mummy bought a cottage there, and we went all the time when I was a child. I loved it. Iris Gill was an old friend of Mummy's; she used to visit a lot. Then she married this man, R-Ra—" She couldn't get the name out. She inhaled slowly, held her breath, let it out gently. She could control her speech; she'd learned how. Then she tried again. "She married Ralph B-Brody. Kevin's father. He'd been married before. They rented a cottage near Mummy's and they were in and out of each other's kitchens the whole time. Very cosy. He knew a lot about antiques, and he and Mummy used to go to the estate sales. Everybody liked him, and he was nice to me. He had a friend with horses and took me there sometimes so I could ride. Mummy hadn't any brothers or sisters, and she thought he was like an uncle for me.

"So anyway, when I was fourteen, he started flirting with me. I was flattered. He was nice looking and sophisticated, and I was young, I'd never been out on a date, I'd only just got breasts, they were little, like lemons. I'd been calling him Uncle Ralph, and he made me call him Ralph. It was a kind of game for a while. I was embarrassed, but he only did it when we were alone. And then one night, my parents were out at a dinner party near Winchester. He'd come down from London without Iris, and he walked in the door and told me he was going to drive me to the top of a hill, to see this fabulous view by moonlight. And when we got there—"

She stopped.

"He raped you?" Johnny said.

She tapped her cigarette nervously on the ashtray. "If you say rape, people think it means using force, physical force. Mummy and Daddy said it was rape when they found out, but it wasn't that kind, not exactly. I mean, I didn't want to do it; I liked it at first when he kissed me, but then I was shocked. Scared rigid. He kind of coaxed me and kept putting his hands under my clothes, and he wouldn't drive home, he just kept on at me, you know? He kept kissing me and touching me and leaning on me, and it was like I couldn't breathe."

Olivia felt her throat closing, a constriction in her chest. She jerked her attention to the screen.

"*Stand him up straight.*" The big Irish police captain punched Michael Corleone in the face. Thunder rolled. Tires screeched. She breathed through her nose and then picked up the glass of wine and took a tiny sip.

"In the end, I let him. It was weird, I didn't know what else to do, I only thought, if I let him, then I can go home. It hurt, but it wasn't violent, I think he tried not to hurt me. He made me promise not to tell, and I didn't want to anyway, I was embarrassed, and I thought it was over. But he kept coming back. It went on for half the summer, he'd corner me when Mummy wasn't there and tell me he loved me and he'd die if he couldn't have me. Then he'd drag me off to the barn where he stored some antiques."

"Jesus Christ," Johnny muttered. "I could kill him."

"You don't have to. He's dead. Maybe that's why I can talk about it now. Gillian told me he's dead. It was such a relief that I cried. Yet he's been in a nursing home, there's no way he could have hurt me again." She remembered the pain, now, the numbness like a halo around it. "What I hate is, I didn't want him to do it, but I didn't stop him. I'm sure I could have, because he wasn't holding me down with a knife or anything like that. It makes me sick. He said it was my fault, because I had some kind of power over him."

"Your fault? And you were fourteen?"

"You don't know how he used to look at me. His face—it frightened me, it was like he was drowning." Olivia stubbed out her cigarette and reached for another. Johnny lit it for her, but she watched the flame, not meeting his eyes.

"What about his wife? Where was she?"

"She wasn't there. I don't think she went to the cottage once that summer."

"Olivia. Listen, love—"

She fastened her gaze on the bright blur of the screen, her face half turned away from him. "Don't say anything yet. I'm not finished." The wine glass chattered against the table as she set it down.

He reached for her hand. "You can tell me the rest another time."

"No. I have to say it now, then it'll be over." She took a gasping breath, like a person looking down the sheer side of a building and imagining falling from the window. "The other thing is, he was reckless. He'd invent reasons to take me away, like the riding, or he'd say he wanted help moving things in the barn. Mummy got suspicious, and she walked in when he had me half undressed, and there was a huge, ghastly scene. So then she told Daddy, and Daddy wanted to go to the police. Have Ralph Brody charged with rape. I said no. I absolutely couldn't face that—the police, going to court, the lawyers. His lawyers would say awful things to me, with everyone staring and talking about it. I didn't want anyone to know. I said I'd deny anything ever happened. Mummy took my side, and Daddy went into a towering rage. We went back to London, and all I can remember is them not speaking for days, and Daddy trying to convince me I should do it so Ralph Brody wouldn't get off scot free."

There were tears on her face. "We wouldn't have gone back to the cottage at all, but it was near the end of the summer and there are things you have to do, so Mummy went down without Daddy. I didn't want to go, but I thought it would be worse to stay in London, where Daddy would get at me, so I went. We were going to sleep one night and drive back to London first thing in the morning. Ralph was actually in the garden next to our cottage when we got there, and I just about died on the spot, but when he saw our car he rushed off. I don't know what he was doing there, maybe just mooning about. Mummy and I cleaned up—there was a bit of a mess because we'd left in a hurry the last time. And in the evening, Mummy drove to the off licence to buy some wine, and Ralph walked in front of the car, and she hit him."

"She ran him down?"

"Not on purpose. She told me he walked right under her wheels. There were witnesses there, they said it wasn't her fault—she couldn't have missed him." The pale light of the TV flashed and faded in the dark room. Olivia's face was stark, remembering. "She said perhaps he meant her to do it."

"But he didn't die?"

"They saved his life. In hospital—he was there a long time. Mummy was beside herself. He couldn't talk, or recognize anybody. So he went into a nursing home. Mummy started drinking quite a bit. I felt like everything was my fault—I didn't want anyone else to know what had happened. Mummy said no one had to know. She said going to court was like being raped again. But then she cried a lot and stopped working, and she and Daddy had rows and then didn't talk at all, and nothing was all right, and Daddy left."

She took a deep, ragged breath. The dawn light was turning the sky pale. China doll, she thought. Andy had said she looked like a china doll. That's how she felt, as if she might topple over and shatter. The story still had the power to make her despise herself. She turned to Johnny and buried her face in his shoulder.

They said nothing for long minutes. Olivia felt the tension gradually leaving her body. She'd blanked out the film, but now its sounds began to reach her again. The noise of a subway train grew loud, screeched to a halt. There were gunshots. Loud. Michael at the restaurant.

"It wasn't your fault," Johnny said.

"When Gillian told me who Kevin was, it all came back. His father." She lifted her head and looked at him. "All that."

He kissed her. "It wasn't your fault."

He held her as if they were on a wet deck in a pitching sea. She let her head drop to his shoulder again. After a while she heaved a deep sigh and said, "I'm glad I told you. I feel better." She looked at the screen. There were the beautiful dry hills of Sicily and the little white town. "Do you still love me?"

"Daft question. Come back to bed."

In bed, she wrapped her legs around him fiercely. This. Now. This tenderness and burning desire a cauterization of every wound.

In the morning, they took a shower together, soaping each other and laughing.

Olivia looked at flats all day. None of them matched their inviting descriptions, none was what she wanted. At a quarter to four, she emerged from viewing the last of the day's possibilities and walked along the wide, ugly thoroughfare at Notting Hill Gate, feeling the dejection that sets in after a cycle of expectations and disappointments. Her phone shrilled in her shoulder bag.

"Olivia?"

The voice on the phone was barely audible over the traffic gunning away from a light. "Is that you, Lisa?"

"Yeh, it's me."

"Oh. Hi. I'm sorry, I can hardly hear you. I know I should come and fetch my things—I've been all over London today looking for a flat."

"Yeh, well, can you come and talk?"

"Of course. When?"

"Now?"

Olivia looked at her watch. "I suppose I could. I'm not far, only at Notting Hill Gate. Lisa, you sound upset."

"No, I'm not upset. Please."

"I'm on my way." Olivia rang Johnny.

"Found anything yet?" he asked.

"Not a prayer. Maybe tomorrow. I'll be later than I thought, Lisa just called, she asked me to come to the flat."

"After what she said the last time?"

"Maybe she wants to talk about it. I don't know, but if she was still angry enough to chop me in little bits she would have done it on the phone, she wouldn't have asked me to come and see her."

"Fair enough. When can you meet me?"

"In a couple of hours. I'll need to change after flogging all over the city. What are we doing later?"

"I'm at the club, now. I'll need to be here tonight for a bit, want to come and dance?"

"Will the monkey be there?"

He laughed. "Lots of them. But don't fall for Bert, he's no good."

When she arrived at Lisa's block of flats, she scrabbled in her bag and realised the keys were in a different one. She glanced apprehensively into the corner where she'd seen her doll lying on the ground, but saw nothing threatening, only a torn and crumpled piece of foil wrapping. The police had the doll; Hardwick had shown it to her, and, wincing, she'd identified Sally. The two fat people moving slowly along the pavement, the ones Kevin had barged into when he chased her, had seen her come out of Lisa's block, seen her turn and run. So the police had searched the entrance and found the doll. The couple had still been on the pavement when she came running out of the coffee bar again, with Kevin in hot pursuit. They would be witnesses. Bibi, too. Olivia thought she would stop in and see Bibi, if she had time, ask her what had happened when the police came. She buzzed Lisa's flat, and Lisa's voice came over the intercom. "Yeh?"

"Olivia. I'm here."

Lisa buzzed her in. Maybe what Olivia had told her last time, about Kevin breaking into the house, had finally made Lisa exercise a little caution. Olivia waited for the lift and then went up to the fourth floor and knocked at the door of the flat.

Lisa said, "Is that you?"

"It's me."

The chain rattled. Olivia hesitated. Something was wrong. Lisa was standing almost out of sight behind the door. The tiny vestibule, which opened straight into the sitting room, seemed darker than usual. Olivia took one step forward, and then in a searing flash of instinct gasped and tried to jump back into the corridor. Her retreat came an instant too late. Lisa was knocked to the floor and Kevin's long arm shot out. He clamped his fingers on Olivia's upper arm in a painful grip and yanked her inside. She screamed. He slammed the door shut and covered her mouth with his other hand. She bit him and he let go and she opened her mouth and screamed again, louder, piercing the walls. He clouted her hard on the side of the head, and she staggered.

"Shut up," he yelled.

"I'm sorry," Lisa whispered, from the floor. Her face was swollen and bruised. "He's got a knife."

"Shut up. Bitch," Kevin said. His fingers dug into Olivia's arm. She was dazed, her ears ringing from the blow, but she tried to pull away. He twisted her arm behind her back and frog-marched her further into the room. The curtains had been dragged across the windows. "I'm smart, see. Don't know where to find you, but I know what to do, I come here. Have your little flatmate bring you. I knew you'd have a mobile, she could call you." He was talking fast, almost stuttering, the words spurting, running together. She could feel the heat of his body and smell his pungent sweat; his voice was high and tight, only a few inches from her ear.

Olivia saw Lisa's phone on the table next to an empty plastic carton of take-away noodles and a squashed paper bag. She could taste blood in her mouth; the side of her head was throbbing. Her hands and feet were icy cold and her heart was trying to vault out of her chest and into the street. Kevin was shouting at her.

"You think I'm locked up, like. Don't you? I'm safely stowed and you can do what the fuck you please. You think I'm never getting out, right?" He jerked her arm until she thought her bones would snap. "Right?"

She shook her head.

He sniggered. "You were wrong. They let me out."

"The judge?"

"The police."

"Nobody told me," she said blankly.

"Shame, innit," Kevin broke into a high-pitched giggle. "You would've brought that bloke with you. That big bloke. Is he the one you're with now?" Abruptly, he spun her about and shook her violently. "Slut."

Lisa was still near the door. She rolled over, got unsteadily to her feet and lurched at the handle. Kevin's head slewed towards her, and he momentarily let his hold on Olivia loosen. She wrenched out of his grasp and sprinted for the exit. The handle was turning, Lisa was pulling, Olivia could see a crack, an opening. Kevin threw himself at the door, slamming it shut once more. A violent thrust of his elbow sent Lisa sprawling again. He shoved Olivia into the wall and bolted the door. She aimed a kick at his midriff that would have doubled him over, but he twisted away and it glanced off his ribcage. He grunted and grabbed her by the throat. They wrestled across the room, crashing into one of the wooden chairs by the table. Lisa shrieked. He hurled Olivia at the sofa that stood in front of the windows. She landed and it tipped backwards, thudding against the wall. Grunting, she scrambled up, grabbing a curtain for balance. The broad swath of fabric came down with a ripping noise, covering her head and arms and legs. The sofa rocked back onto its four feet, and she thrashed out from under the curtain.

"Shut it," he barked at Lisa.

Olivia gathered herself, panting, her eyes darting, looking for something to hit him with.

"Stay there. Don't move," Kevin was shouting orders at her. He had one arm around Lisa's neck, now, and with the other he reached behind him and pulled a knife from his belt.

Lisa gave a little moan.

"Stay still or I'll cut her," Kevin said. Olivia froze.

Everything had been moving at lightning speed, with deafening noise. Now the room was suddenly quiet.

"Enough of this shit." Kevin held the knife close to Lisa's throat, then in front of her eyes. "Look at it." She looked, blindly. Then he let her go but stayed close, close enough to use the knife. "Pick up the chair," he said. Lisa moved hesitantly to the ladder-back chair that had been knocked over and set it on its legs. "Pick it up. Right. Carry it." He pointed to the corner of the room at the other end of the bank of windows, farthest from the door. She walked in front of him. He held the knife high, poised, ready.

Olivia's mind was racing. The seconds slowed down, stretching like minutes, time inflating as the world contracted to this single room, to this space within four walls in which a knife moved. It glittered, holding her eyes. The periphery—the telephone call, her doubt on the threshold, the other rooms in the flat, the street, the hallway outside the door—receded to the far rim of consciousness; her senses were alert to Kevin's every motion, the entire force of her mind was focused on the man, the knife, on what to do to stay alive.

Johnny, she thought, fleetingly. He would call. He would come when there was no answer. But that would be hours from now. He wouldn't even be sure she was here, and she might be dead by then. She couldn't warn him; Johnny couldn't help her. She let go of him. The police, they were her only hope, even if it was their fault Kevin had escaped. She had to find a way to let them know.

Her eyes flicked from the knife to Lisa's mobile on the table. Her own was in her bag, on the floor. What did he want, she thought wildly. To murder her? Not only that, or he could have done it already. If he wanted to kill her, he wanted something else, too. What? He'd liked telling her he'd used Lisa to lure her here. He was gleeful that he'd gotten out of custody and she didn't know—he'd laughed. He wanted her to be afraid, but also to think he was clever, to admire him. *I'm smart, see. Slut. Liar.* He'd called her a liar last time. What had she lied about? She'd never talked to him. *You've been with him,* he'd said in the room over the Chagga. Who? Who was he talking about? Johnny? Was that why he'd attacked her?

She had to get her hands on the phone, think of some way to use it. Not yet, if she reached for it now, he'd stab Lisa or smash the phone to pieces. He had to be calmer; he was like a bomb, any sudden motion might make him go off.

"Stop there," he said to Lisa. She stopped, as if in a children's game.

"Sit."

She put the chair down and sat on it. Kevin touched the point of the knife to her throat, under the left ear. Olivia saw a drop of blood form, like a red pearl. "Don't move, don't even scratch your arse," he said. Lisa sat like a mannequin in a window. Her face was puffy on one side, the other eye was wide and terrified. He stared at her twitchily. "You deserve what you got."

She made a tiny noise, a mew, through her closed lips.

"Shut up."

Next to Lisa was a shelf with her CD player and two little speakers. Kevin knocked a speaker to the carpet and ripped the wire loose.

Olivia watched him. Lisa's phone was out of her reach. He was going to use the wire to tie Lisa up. Olivia's mind raced in a maze, dashing down blind alleyways. She tried to guess at his next moves, what his plan might be. His motions were jerky, his breath coming fast; he looked scared.

Would Kevin let her use the phone for any reason? Only if there was a scene he wanted to play out and he believed someone was coming, someone who would interrupt, who wouldn't go away. Andy. He'd seen Andy driving the Jeep. If she said Andy was coming to fetch her, Kevin might believe that. But it wouldn't help, she thought. She couldn't ring the police, pretending it was Andy. She had to be careful, she'd have only one chance. If she tried to trick Kevin and bungled it, she'd be dead.

Lisa's hands were behind her back, now, he had the knife in his teeth. He was looping the wire around her wrists and the cross rail at the back of the chair. His eyes swooped back and forth between the wire and Olivia.

She didn't dare stir from the sofa. Her legs and arms were shaking; she fought for control. Her throat ached where he'd grabbed it with his big hands. His fingers were thick and strong. She would have bruises there. Everywhere. Find out what he wants, she told herself. Play a part. You know this set, every inch. It's yours. The flat is your friend. Just focus on him, let him tell you his story, what he's thinking. Play the role. Play it to his cues. Ignore Lisa, he's not here for her. Show him you're not fighting him. Be calm, so he doesn't use the knife just because he's nervous. He's crazy with tension, you can see it in every move. Watch his body language. He'll telegraph what he's thinking.

He'd got Lisa's hands tied to the chair. "Keep your mouth shut or I'll shut it," he snarled. He was coming back across the room, treading heavily. He was big but clumsy.

"How did you escape from the police?" Olivia asked, letting a hint of awe creep into her voice. She sat very still, eyes looking straight into his, her hands in her lap, palms up. Harmless. He was still gripping the knife tightly, ready for any move she might make.

"Coppers are stupid." He stopped a few feet from her. A sly expression flitted across his face.

"Yeh," she said. "A load of wallies. Did you fool them?"

His lips stretched in a brief grin. "They fooled themselves, innit?" He glared at her. "You burnt me, you nasty bitch. Look." He tore violently at his shirt buttons, and she saw a huge bandage on his chest. It was dirty, and the hairs curling up from its top edge at his throat were crusted with dried blood. "I had to see a doctor."

"I never wanted to hurt you," she said.

"You shouldn't've done that." A vein was throbbing in his neck. "Now it might be your turn." The knife quivered, but he didn't step closer.

Her stomach flip-flopped. She fastened on the word 'might'. Did he want to play with her fear? He'd hurt her already, but that was when she was fighting to get away. Now he had her cornered. What would he do? He hadn't done it yet, so maybe he didn't know, hadn't made up his mind. He wasn't confident, she could see that, not like a serial killer, with a history of killing, the knowledge that he could do it. Kevin couldn't be one of them, he couldn't be, Hardwick said they didn't have his fingerprints in the police computer.

"I never wanted to hurt you," she repeated.

"You lied," he said accusingly. "You knew me."

"What?"

"In the coffee bar."

She was bewildered. "You chased me."

"I mean the first time," he said, exasperated.

"I d-didn't, I didn't recognize you."

He rocked on his feet, gripping the knife so tightly his knuckles bulged, bloodless. "I knew you right off."

She said nothing, focused on control of her body, on not showing fear. *You knew me*. He must mean from the cottage. Her knees were clamped together to keep them from trembling. Ralph Brody was dead now. He was dead. That was over.

"You talked to me," Kevin said. "On the phone. Why did you stop?"

"What? I never talked to you."

"You talked to me," he hissed. "Don't lie."

Oh God, she thought, he's in another world. It's all turned around in his head.

"You bloody left without telling me, didn't you? You can't deny it. I saw you in *Screen*."

"I was on location, Kevin. I was only making a film. Working."

"Film." His voice went up an octave. "You think that's fine then?" Then he laughed. "Yeh, I saw you in that film, *Karma Kids*, your name in the credits, but I didn't need that. I knew you. Olivia Bening. You kissed one of those bastards, didn't you, but the other one was going to sell you. He knew what you were. A slut."

"Do you mean the girl I was playing?" Was he confusing her with the character? Olivia felt lost. That girl wasn't a slut, either. "I don't understand."

"You shouldn't be in any films. You're in another one with Bobby Carr."

"It's only work, Kevin. My job."

"I've seen you with him," he said, his tone shifting. There was something sly in his eyes again, as if he was laying a trap.

Let him give the cues. "Seen me?"

"You can't fool me."

"What?"

"About him. Your boyfriend. You can't lie to me. I saw you in the magazine."

"What? In *Screen*?"

"You were smiling at him. He was touching you."

"BOBBY? Jesus Christ, Kevin, you think Bobby Carr's my boyfriend? He's an actor. I don't even like him."

"You're lying."

"I promise I'm not," she said, her voice vibrant with sincerity.

Kevin stared at her. The hand holding the knife dropped a few inches. He wanted to believe her. She could see it in his eyes, in the way his shoulders sagged. If he really thought

Bobby Carr was her boyfriend, he might kill her, but he didn't want that. He wanted her to deny it.

"Swear to God?"

"I swear to God."

He looked dumbly at her, as if he'd lost the thread, as if he didn't know what to do next. Then he cut the air with a downward jab of the knife.

"Who *is* your boyfriend then? The one in the car?"

Christ, she thought desperately. Does he mean Johnny? "Car?"

"The wanker driving the fucking Jeep."

Andy! Now, this was her chance. "Kevin, listen. He's not a boyfriend. He's a minder."

Kevin gaped. "You've never got a minder."

"Yes I do, because of co-starring in the Bobby Carr film." This was ridiculous, no one at her level would have a minder, but she didn't think he would know much about film budgets or security. "He's a chauffeur, but he's a minder, of course that's what he is, that's why he's so big and tough."

"What you got a minder for?"

"The producer set it up; it wasn't my idea. Kevin, he's coming to fetch me soon. I'm supposed to go to a reception for the press."

He took a half-step closer to her. "He can't."

"He is. He drives me everywhere. It's his job to look after me."

"No." He was quivering, his nostrils flaring, eyes darting to the window. Then he gave a derisive snort. "He can't get in. He'll go away."

"If I change my plans, I'm supposed to let him know. He won't go away."

"Shit!" Kevin blurted. He whirled about to look at Lisa. "You didn't tell me she had a minder."

"She didn't know. His name is Edward." Olivia jumped in before Lisa could say a word. "I'll have to tell him not to come." She made her voice concerned, earnest. "You saw him, Kevin. A couple of doors won't stop him."

"I can." He made a little pass in the air with the knife.

"But Kevin, you don't want to have to do that, do you? He's *not* my boyfriend. Let me ring him."

"Fuck, then who *is* your boyfriend? *Who*?" He screeched the word. "She said you had one, it's true, innit? You went off, she said you were moving in with him. You weren't home. Who is he?" The knife waved wildly.

She held herself still and somewhere within she found a calm, dignified tone. She used it, her heart in her mouth. "Nobody, Kevin. And I'm not a slut."

"She said it." Kevin jerked his knife hand towards Lisa. "She said you had a boyfriend."

Lisa's lips were swollen. They moved, she mumbled something and shook her head.

"Shut up. Stupid cow." Kevin scowled.

"She told you that so you'd stop ringing up so much," Olivia said. "She was only tired of the phone."

He looked back and forth between them, assailed by doubt. The knife wavered. "She didn't want us to be together," he blurted. He swung back to Olivia. "Why do you want to ring him? Is it a trick?"

She fixed her gaze on him, widening her eyes and making her voice gentle and coaxing. She tilted her head up at him and opened her palms. She was in the part, now, she believed her own words. "Because I don't want anyone to get hurt. You want to talk to me, don't you, Kevin? You don't want to hurt me. I truly believe you don't." She paused, held it. "But Edward won't understand that."

Kevin stared at her. His breath hissed in and out, his face contorted in an agony of indecision.

"He'll force his way in, something terrible will happen." She looked intently at Kevin, her big gray eyes appealing.

"Okay," he said finally. "You can tell him not to come. But don't try to say anything else, or you're dead. Her too." He shot a vicious sideways glance at Lisa.

"I know the number. Edward's wife may answer the phone," Olivia said. "She's like his despatcher. If she does, I'll give her the message. She'll see to it."

"He's married? How will I know it's her?"

"Her name's Gillian. She'll say it." Olivia's heart stopped. What if Gillian had told him her name, when he came to the house?

"Give me the number. I'll dial."

She'd rung Gillian only yesterday; she remembered the number. Please let someone answer, Olivia prayed. Please. She couldn't think what else to do. Lisa probably thought she was mad, but she mustn't look at Lisa. Kevin would get paranoid, think they were plotting.

Kevin picked up Lisa's phone in his left hand, keeping the knife in his right. The phone was tiny in his broad palm, like a beetle helpless on its back. He pressed the buttons with his thumb and then held the phone to his ear. His eyes went to the window again, raking the street, looking for the Jeep.

He yanked the phone away from his head as if it were hot. "It's some bleeding Paki. A curry house or something, for Chrissake." He waved the phone at her. "What are you playing at?"

"Wrong number," Olivia said. "Please."

"This is bollocks." He frowned and slowly pressed the numbers again. Then he clamped the phone to his ear. Olivia held her breath. Five seconds went by, seven, eight. She felt her throat closing; if he gave her the phone, she wouldn't be able to speak. His face changed, the line was being picked up at the other end. He listened a moment; she heard faint sounds, too brief to be a recorded message. He held the phone in mid-air, then he thrust it into her hand and stood over her, his jaw muscles grinding, his eyes drilling into hers.

"Hello?" Gillian's voice said into the silence. It was louder than usual, questioning. She was wondering why no one had spoken.

"Gillian, this is Olivia Bening." Olivia spoke flatly and rapidly, not wanting to let Gillian say anything. "Edward was supposed to pick me up at Lisa's flat in Bayswater this afternoon; I asked him to come before five, but I want to cancel that. I won't be at the reception; I don't know when I'll be leaving here. Tell him not to come till I call, have you got that? Thanks so much, you're a dear." She pressed the button to end the call and held out the phone to Kevin, her hand open, palm up. "That's done it. He won't come, now, he'll wait for a call."

Kevin's body was still rigid with suspicion, his breath coming fast and shallow. He closed his fist around the phone and stuffed it into his pocket.

"That's better, isn't it?" Olivia said with inane cheerfulness. "Now we can relax. You know what? I'm dying for a fag."

"Yeh," he said. He patted his breast pocket vaguely.

"I have cigarettes in my bag," Olivia said, pointing to the floor.

He let her pick it up and made her turn it upside-down and dump the contents on the sofa. He took her mobile; now he had hers and Lisa's. She moved slowly, placidly, nothing quick and jerky. He mustn't think she would try anything with the hot cigarette end or the matches. What was Gillian doing? She had to know something was wrong. Olivia shook some cigarettes part way out of the packet and held them out. Her hand was steady. "Can we all have one? Can I give one to Lisa, too? Would you let me do that, Kevin?" Let him feel like king of the castle now.

He took the cigarettes and matches from her. "Don't move."

"I won't, Kevin. I want you to talk to me." She wouldn't move, she was going to wait while they smoked cigarettes together. Unless he got angry again. With his attention off her for a moment, she was almost giddy with relief. Kevin had been angry about Bobby, because of the photo in *Screen*. He'd broken into the house before Johnny picked her up in Acton. He couldn't have seen her with Johnny in the car, or he wouldn't be asking her all these questions. He'd know her boyfriend wasn't Bobby or Andy. She must have imagined seeing Kevin that night, in the dark.

He stuck a lit cigarette between Lisa's lips but didn't untie her hands. Lisa cringed away from him but pinched the cigarette between her lips, cocking her head to keep the smoke out of her eyes.

Unless he was playing a game, planning to catch her in a lie. The thought momentarily paralysed Olivia. She could be misreading him. If it was a game, there was no way she could win. He would just spin it out until he was tired of it. Then he'd tell her he'd seen her in the car with Johnny, and he'd kill her. She pushed the thought away. She'd done the best she could.

In the middle of the room, he stood still, checking the street briefly. He seemed satisfied by what he saw, or didn't see. The Jeep, not showing up. He lit two more cigarettes. Then he picked up the second wooden chair and planted it close to Olivia. He gave her a cigarette and sat down, the knife in his right hand, resting on his thigh.

"I knew I'd find you," he said. "Like I said in the note."

Gillian stood stock still, looking at the phone. Olivia's message made no sense. Edward to go to Lisa's flat? Tell him not to come? Why wouldn't Olivia ring him at the Yard? Why would she say 'Olivia Bening' like that, and call her a dear? Talk about Edward as if she employed him? Gillian thought about it for thirty seconds and then rang Edward's mobile, for once feeling grateful to the tyrannical little object.

"Gisborne."

"Where are you?"

"At the morgue."

Edward was at the same morgue, as it happened, where the autopsy on Charlotte had been performed. However, he was there for an unrelated case. The room hadn't changed during the quarter-century or so he'd periodically visited it. The long table with the drainage holes placed centrally under the light, the small dissection table, the scales suspended from a pole in one corner, with the round white-faced measure above, hanging there like a pasteboard moon, the tank for fluids, the porcelain sinks at the back, were all exactly the same. It was a barren and ugly room, like many he spent his time in, but its familiarity was oddly comforting. He'd finally worked out that it reminded him of his childhood, which seemed absurd, even macabre, but the association had nothing to do with the room's purpose, only with its period fixtures and utilitarian plainness. It was like the London kitchens of the 1950s, cramped, inconvenient, cheerless, and worn with decades of use.

He was used to what happened in the room, but not indifferent. The procedure followed a routine, more or less the same each time, yet each occasion had its particulars and peculiarities. Twice, in the first years that he'd attended post-mortems, he'd had to leave the room. Once because the putrid reek of the two-week old corpse had made him sick, and once because the body being dissected was that of a five-year-old child who had been tortured and mutilated by its own parents. The toneless recital of the damage, measured and numbered and catalogued while a secretary had sat taking notes, had been unbearable to listen to.

Now, when he heard Gillian's voice, he excused himself and stepped outside into the hall.

"Edward, I've just had the strangest phone call. Were you supposed to go to Bayswater to fetch Olivia this afternoon?"

"Olivia? No, what's up?"

"I don't know, but I'm sure she's in trouble. I know this is probably absurd, but they haven't let Kevin Brody loose, have they?"

"I should damn well hope not. He's being held without bail." He could hear Gillian's anxiety. What phone call was she talking about? "Why do you think she's in trouble?"

"Because what she said doesn't make any sense. She called me a couple of minutes ago. There was a long pause before she came on the line, as if someone else might have dialled the number and listened before giving her the phone, and she talked very fast and then hung up without letting me say a word. She said you were supposed to pick her up at Lisa's flat in Bayswater before five, but she didn't know when she'd be leaving. She said 'tell him not to come, have you got that?' Edward, if she's trapped there—"

"It sounds very odd, I must say," he said calmly. "Let me ring the nick. I'll find out and call you as soon as I know anything. We can send a car in any case, but if there's a chance it's Brody we'll handle it differently."

He poked his head into the room and nodded at Hilary. She moved quickly into the hall. "Something may have come up," he said. "Tell Keith we might have to leave him here and then join me at the car." Hardwick said Olivia had a good head on her shoulders. If she'd made an outlandish call to Gillian, something was probably amiss. It was in Edward's mind that her first complaints about Kevin Brody hadn't been taken seriously enough. Though it hardly seemed possible that Brody was the problem now, Edward was eager to rule him out. He wanted to hear that Brody was safely housed. He walked rapidly along the hospital corridor.

Gillian paced up and down in the flat for twenty-five minutes, glaring at the phone, willing it to ring. For crying out loud, she thought, what's taking so long?

When it rang, she snatched it.

"Complete cock-up," Edward said tersely.

"He's out?"

"Earlier today."

"Did they notify her?"

"I haven't got that far, but presumably not."

"Christ, then she's probably a hostage, now. She wouldn't have had any warning. How *could* they have let him out?"

"Mix-up in the paperwork, that's all I can tell you at present. Believe me, everyone's scrambling. I'm going to Bayswater myself, I'll ring you as soon as I can."

"I'll get a taxi. I want to be there when she comes out." If, she thought but didn't say.

"It may be over before you arrive."

"I can't sit here on my hands."

"All right, I'll be in the Rover somewhere nearby. It's not my operation, but I'll have a radio link, we'll know what's happening."

Lisa dropped the end of her cigarette. It rolled away and lay burning the carpet. She would have to move, along with her chair, to reach it with her shoe. She looked nervously at Kevin and sat still. Kevin watched as a little burn mark appeared in the pile.

"Put it out, for Chrissake. Stupid cow."

Lisa squirmed in the chair and reached it with her toe.

"I brought flowers for you," he said to Olivia. "Lilies."

"It was a mistake, what happened at my mother's house, right? You were just upset because I wasn't there. I understand that."

"She told me lies—" he said, looking balefully at Lisa.

"Never mind. It doesn't matter now," Olivia said hastily. She slid another cigarette from her packet and lit it. She held it out to him. "Here, let's have another fag."

"I could've hurt you."

"But you didn't. So it's all right."

"I had a plan." He leaned closer, sucking the smoke in, exhaling right in her face. She needed all her self-control not to wrench herself upward off the sofa and stampede towards the bolted door. The smoke stung her eyes, but he didn't notice. She didn't want him edging nearer. He might touch her, and she didn't know what would happen if he touched her. She had to distract him, now, use up the time. He trusted her for the moment; his anger had switched to Lisa, the liar who kept them apart.

"Kevin, listen. I'm hungry."

"You can eat."

"There's nothing in the flat—we only eat M&S and take-away. Can we order a pizza or something?"

"No."

"But I'm starving, aren't you? You can order it yourself—we have menus. Indian, Chinese, fried chicken, whatever you want. You must be hungry, too."

He scowled. "Too risky." He pulled away a little, irritated.

"What would you have if you could order anything you wanted? I think I'd go for a pizza with olives and mushrooms and anchovies," she said dreamily.

"No bloody anchovies. They taste rotten."

"What do you like?"

"Lots of cheese, pepperoni. No vegetarian rubbish."

"You choose, then. There's a good place down the street."

"No." He brooded, frowning and biting his lip. "That woman at the house, she said your mum's dead. Is it true?"

"Yes, Kevin, my mother's dead. She had a blood clot."

"My dad's dead too. Croaked in the nursing home. But she killed him."

Olivia said nothing.

Kevin glowered. "I don't give a toss. My mum, she caught him fooling around, she said. She wasn't having it. He buggered off, didn't he? Didn't give a fuck about me, only his sluts."

Olivia felt faint. She didn't want to listen. She was losing her precarious hold on herself, on the situation. When were the police going to come? They were taking too long. It seemed like hours since she'd rung Gillian. Kevin was banging on about his father and Iris. What a bitch Iris was. His father, his father. Why didn't he shut up?

She jumped. A telephone was bleeping. Her phone, in Kevin's pocket. Jesus. He fumbled, pulling out Lisa's. Olivia's was still ringing shrilly. "Shit," he said, jamming Lisa's into a different pocket. Now he had Olivia's tiny mobile in his hand. The answering service would cut in after four rings. Was it Johnny? The police? She tried to look unconcerned.

"Who is it?" Kevin asked, suspicious.

"I don't know. It could be my agent, or the publicity people, wondering where I am." Don't let him answer, she prayed.

"I'm not letting you talk to them." With an air of taking command, he switched the phone off. Then, as if it had rung a bell in his brain, he suddenly said, "But where were you? When I went to your house? You never told me."

Christ, he was back at that again. "I was filming, Kevin. Sometimes I work all night. Remember? I was working. Not with Bobby Carr," she added hastily.

"No more films."

What did he mean? That she wouldn't make any films because she'd be dead? Her eyes dropped to the knife and slid away. No. It was quiet, he wasn't thinking about it now. She had to keep him busy, keep making the time pass.

"You want to talk about the movies, Kevin? Tell me. We can talk about anything you want. But you know what? I'm really, really hungry."

"I'm hungry, too," he said irritably. "But I'm not a bloody fool."

"No, you can do it because you're smart."

He paused. He liked that.

"You'll think of the right thing."

"Yeh?" He stood up, his darting glance checking the door, the windows, Lisa. Thinking about food made him restless.

He paced back and forth, weighing the options. "The delivery."

"You can just buzz him in, Kevin. He won't know anything."

"No. I'd have to open the door."

"Only for a second."

"Not a fucking chance."

"I have money, he can keep the change. What could I do, Kevin? Scream? What good would that do? You could kill me and be gone before the police got here. But I don't believe you want to." He stopped in front of her. She made herself lean forward a little, locking eyes with him. "I know you don't. I'm going to trust you, and I'm not going to scream. I'm perishing. I haven't had a bite since breakfast. Can't we please have something to eat? Then we can talk all night if you like."

Edward's Rover was parked around the corner, in Queen's Road, out of sight of Lisa's block of flats. He sat alone, a tiny microphone fitted to his ear, a personal radio, and the Rover's set that connected him to headquarters. He was listening, by turns, to all three. He was still angry, but the anger was pushed down, out of the way, while he focused his attention on what was happening around the corner. Hardwick, he thought, poor sod. Goes home for a well-deserved rest and he's hardly turned his back when the silly buggers let Brody out. Bloody paperwork. Edward fumed, and then listened again. He kept an eye on the street, in case Gillian appeared. She should be arriving any minute, unless the traffic was heavier than usual. Would it be worse or better for her to be here, if the worst happened? He wouldn't think about that.

An area car had not been sent flashing and blaring to Lisa's flat. It had been deemed better to approach quietly. Edward was aware, though he couldn't see him from the Rover, that an officer had crept onto the roof of the building opposite

Lisa's and was observing and reporting on the progress of events inside the flat. Poor Hardwick, Edward thought again. Belting all the way up from Morden.

He saw Gillian in the rearview mirror, hurrying along the pavement, looking for him, her face drawn with anxiety. She spotted the Rover and sped up. He gestured, listening to the earpiece, and she slid into the passenger seat.

"It's Brody," he said.

"What's happened?"

"Nothing, yet."

"Where's Hilary?"

"At the intersection. They're going to re-route the traffic, and keep the pedestrians back."

Gillian's eyes widened. "Will they have to shoot?"

"Brody's in the flat," he said. "We've got an officer on the roof opposite, with binoculars."

"What can he see?"

"Brody with a large knife, looks like a hunting knife, and two young women, blondes. Must be Olivia and Lisa. They're both alive. One's sitting on a chair; she's got her hands behind her back, probably tied, she's not moving them. The man's not paying much attention to her, he's talking to the other woman."

"Edward! She called me almost an hour ago. What if he suddenly goes berserk? Can you stop him?"

"If they have a sharpshooter in position, and the hostages aren't in the way. He could have a gun, too, we don't know. It's dangerous, there are people everywhere."

"Does Kevin know the police are here?"

"Doesn't look as if he's twigged. They're trying to stay out of sight until the AFOs are in position."

"AFOs?"

"Authorised firearms officers. Brody's not being immediately threatening, so the inspector will try to bring in more resources—AFOs, a negotiating team. There's no team immediately available, though. It all depends on how much time we have, what opportunities arise. The inspector will clear the street, if he can, *if* he has time. Empty the flats on Lisa's floor. There's an ambulance standing by. But anything could break at any moment. They'll probably try to telephone Brody in the flat. There's a Trojan unit that could go in through the back; they have carbines."

"Jesus. How long do we wait?"

"Until the men are deployed or something breaks." He held his hand up, listening to the earpiece. "A report's come through, screams heard in the building at four o'clock—whoever called in waited more than forty minutes before deciding they might not have been part of a television program."

Gillian looked at her watch. "And then it took another forty to connect that report to this incident."

"Modern communications." He listened again. "Shots are moving into position. That means they'll try to get Brody on the phone in a few minutes."

Gillian gripped the edge of the seat. It was unbearable, sitting here unable to see anything or do anything. A minute went by, then two, then four.

"Something's up," Edward said, then, "I don't believe it."

"What?" Gillian said, agonised.

"Brody's ordered pizza! An officer's just stopped the delivery vehicle."

"PIZZA! How can he?"

"He must think he's got complete control of the situation. Pizza! Bloody cheek! They won't wait for negotiators now, this is a chance that can't be passed up." He listened to the earpiece and snorted. "He'll get his olive and pepperoni. Free delivery."

Olivia was doubtful that the pizza had been a good idea. Kevin had been calm until he rang with the order, but now he was agitated again, dangerous, prowling back and forth, his eyes bright and sharp, darting everywhere, from her to Lisa to the door. Where were the police? Maybe help was never going to come. Perhaps Gillian hadn't understood, or she couldn't reach Edward, or Sergeant Hardwick, or anyone who would have a clue what she was on about. Olivia kept her back to the window. She didn't dare look out, in case Kevin suspected something. Almost all of his attention was riveted on the door, now, on planning how he would open it, on the moment when the delivery would arrive. He'd thought of a plan, but he hadn't told her what it was, he'd just taken her money.

Lisa was rigid and silent in her chair, not wanting to attract his attention. She blinked, and Olivia saw two tears roll down her face. How was this going to finish? Maybe it would have been better not to ring the police, not to call anyone, just to talk to him. Perhaps she could still persuade him to let her go, she almost thought she could manage it. He was torn. But she couldn't take the chance, and anyway it was too late. She'd called. Part of him didn't want to hurt her, she could see it. That saner part would sit here and talk to her and, possibly after a long time, would get tired, would want to give in. But there was the other half, that didn't trust her, that kept asking questions and getting angry and jealous. He was afraid of hurting her, but afraid she would walk away and laugh. Which side would win? He'd hate feeling like a fool, he might start to let her go and then kill her because she'd almost gotten away. At any minute he could flip back to believing she was a slut who'd betrayed him. He kept asking where she'd been. The night he'd torn her bed to pieces was her first night with Johnny. Kevin couldn't know that, but he had an uncanny instinct about the question. Despite his distraction with the pizza, she grew more afraid as the seconds, the minutes, ticked by.

She had to play to his belief in her, keep him off boyfriends, not let him rant about his father. But if he thought he was her boyfriend, where would that lead? Did he have any lucid moments when he knew what was really happening?

When he knew he'd done something completely mad? Maybe before he'd chased her, she thought. But not here, not now.

Lisa sniffed.

"I don't trust her," he said abruptly, pointing the knife in her direction. "Find a gag."

Olivia's eyes went to Lisa's horrified ones. "She won't make a noise."

"Bloody right she won't."

"He's nervous," Edward said. "He's got a gag on the woman in the chair, now."

"Which one is she?"

"Lisa. She has to be. He spends most of the time talking to the other one. An armed team's going in through the rear, then one chap goes in the front with the pizza. Christ, I hope Brody doesn't get cold feet when the buzzer goes."

"I need a piece of paper," Kevin ordered.

Olivia tore a sheet out of her little daybook and handed it to him. He took the paper and hunkered down by the door. It slid easily beneath. Quickly, he pulled it back, then he sidled to the window and stood behind the piece of the curtain that was still hanging, peering down, his mind on the street again. The buzzer sounded, loud and startling. Kevin's body tensed, curving into a fighter's crouch. He stared out and down, his head craning. "Don't move," he muttered to Olivia, and stalked silently to the vestibule.

Edward swore softly. "Brody's looking out of the window. Should have been doing that earlier. He might have clocked our chaps getting into position."

"What about the officer with the binoculars? What does he say?"

"He's ducked down, says he can't see anything. They're keeping the traffic back, now."

The buzzer sounded again. Kevin stood, hovering, still undecided. Olivia turned her head and risked a cautious glance outside and saw the pizza delivery car double parked below. The entry to the block of flats was recessed, invisible. There was no traffic now, no cars going by. No pedestrians on the opposite pavement. But it must be near six, people should be coming home from work. Hope flared, she felt it like a sudden pain, the longing to live, to walk outside in the sun, to see Johnny again. Only hours ago, she'd been free, she'd talked to him. Only last night she'd lain naked in his arms. The memory of it touched her briefly. She looked down at the floor to hide her face and prayed that Kevin wouldn't notice the silence. He might not be aware of the time. It felt as if they'd been cooped up in the flat for days.

He lifted the intercom phone.

"Yeh?"

He pressed the buzzer. "Lie down on the floor," he said to Olivia. "Where he can't see you."

She lay full length on the floor, her heart hammering against her ribs, every muscle braced for whatever might come.

"And don't make a sound, or I'll kill you."

"Okay," she whispered.

He folded the paper around the twenty-pound note. Then he stood behind the door, waiting. Olivia thought she could hear the creak of the lift coming up. Kevin held the knife at his side, out of sight. She heard footsteps in the hallway outside the flat. Then a firm rap on the door.

"Who's there?" Kevin said, his voice cracking.

"Pizza delivery."

He slid the folded paper under the door; Olivia heard a dry whisper as it went over the sill. "Leave it. Money's there."

"Right-o, guv. Cheers." It was absolutely silent in the flat. Olivia heard a light tap as the pizza box was laid on the floor of the hall. Then footsteps retreating and the lift door closing, the machinery clunking and humming as it started back to the street floor.

Seconds went by. The clunking stopped. Kevin was listening. The hall was dead quiet. Olivia could see only part of the vestibule. She heard Kevin drag the bolt back, and then the click of the lock. He'd slid the chain into place; it clinked.

"What's happening, for God's sake?" Gillian said.

"They're inside, I don't know," Edward said. He gripped her hand.

Kevin opened the door and peered through the three-inch gap allowed by the chain. Olivia could see nothing. Suddenly there was a jarring thud, as the door slammed violently against the light brass links.

Olivia heard a shout. "Armed Police!"

In one jump she was on her feet. Kevin spun around, his mouth wide open in a snarl, the knife raised. "You bloody bitch!" he screamed. "*Cunt!*" She grabbed the empty wooden chair and held it up like a shield. The chain snapped and the door burst open with a crash. Men stormed through it, fanning out, filling the room, their feet booming on the floor, eyes flaring, huge gun barrels pointing. "Drop the knife," a voice was shouting. Kevin was rushing at her, unstoppable. Then there was an enormous bang, and he staggered heavily against the upraised chair. She saw the knife sail past her, glittering in the air. Blood splattered. Kevin fell almost on top of her and a chair leg rapped her sharply on the head like a constable's nightstick. She felt herself falling, and everything went black.

"They've shot him," Edward said.

"What about her?"

"Hang on, yes, she's alive, both the hostages are alive. Let's go." He leapt out of the Rover and they ran towards the corner, where he flashed his card at the officer keeping pedestrians back. As they sprinted, police cars filled the street. An ambulance slid past them.

When Olivia came gradually to consciousness, she was on a stretcher. A door opened and she was carried outside. She had a blurred sense of a crowd, faces she didn't know. A forest fire was burning inside her head. Red and blue lights were flashing. The stretcher swayed and jerked. She couldn't remember what had happened after the door crashed open. Suddenly, close to her, a familiar face.

"Gillian," she formed the word but no sound came out. The men were lifting the stretcher into an opening. "Don't go," she tried to say, but she couldn't hear herself.

"I'm coming with you," Gillian said, and climbed in. "You'll be fine, everything's all right, they said you just got a rap on the head. It's all right, Olivia, he's dead."

Dead. Olivia closed her eyes. She heard the noise of an engine starting, and felt movement. She opened her eyes again. Gillian was still there.

"Lisa's okay, she's only in shock. Your father will meet us at the emergency ward. It's all over, Olivia."

"Johnny," she said, through a fiery wall.

"Of course. I'll call as soon as we get there." Gillian realised she didn't know his last name. "Where can I ring him?"

"Paradise Club," Olivia whispered.

"Brilliant club," the ambulance attendant said. "Zombie Kiss plays there. You need a mobile? Use mine." He unclipped his phone and handed it to Gillian. Olivia closed her eyes again. Everything was a glaring haze, it was too noisy, her head hurt. The world faded out.

"When can I see her?" Tom said.

"In a few minutes," the nurse replied.

"Concussion," Tom said to Gillian, "but the X-rays show no fracture."

Gillian had heard the doctor too, but she simply nodded agreement. Tom seemed somewhat concussed himself. "She'll be all right," he repeated. He paced back and forth. "I had no notion she was being stalked. Dear God, she should have told me."

"She thought it would only worry you," Gillian said.

"I'm her father!"

He was much the same man Gillian remembered: tall, rangy, fair-haired. The bones were sharper under the skin, the hair thinning. He was drier and leaner, silvered over, like salt-rimed shingles on a seaside cottage. In appearance, he was what she had expected. But he was shaken now; she'd never seen him like this, nakedly emotional, off balance, speaking without thought.

"You knew, you might have told me!"

"I thought it was up to her."

He slumped into a chair. "Kevin Brody!" he said blackly, as if a pit had opened in front of him.

"It was a real shock to her."

"Christ, yes."

Gillian looked at him.

"Kevin Brody's father raped her when she was fourteen. One of our best friends."

"My God," Gillian said, and was silent. "Was that down in Hampshire?" she said at last.

He nodded, his hands gripping his knees, white-knuckled.

"Charlotte never told me."

"Olivia didn't want anyone to know. Christ, I would have told everyone, I would have stood with a sign in front of Ralph Brody's bleeding shop, 'Don't Buy From Rapists'. But Charlotte wasn't having it. Olivia refused to go to the police, and Charlotte backed her up, she said a court case would be like another rape. I didn't agree. I wanted to haul that sonofabitch in front of a judge and watch him writhe."

"I can't believe she never told me."

"She didn't even tell Iris. And Ralph was Iris's husband! So no one could be told. Then Charlotte went down to the cottage again and hit him with the car. He was in a coma, we didn't know what would happen."

For a moment, Gillian couldn't take it in. The accident that summer. Nothing was the same afterwards, Charlotte said. When her marriage broke up, she called it a judgement. Gillian looked hesitantly at Tom, wondering what he would say next. "That was awful. I remember," she murmured.

"It was worse than you knew."

"Because of Olivia."

"Yes."

"But it *was* an accident. The witnesses—"

"Eyewitnesses. They never know what they've seen."

"You don't think it was an accident?"

He smiled grimly. "Yes I do, but was it an unavoidable accident? I don't know. I never will. I'm not sure Charlotte knew. But if it had been me driving, I think there could have been a split second to hit the brake when I wouldn't have, and it might have made all the difference."

Gillian contemplated this. Finally she said, "Well, you can't have wished Ralph Brody a worse punishment."

"No. But I wanted Olivia to brave it out in court. What's to stop men like him doing that to children if no one goes to the police?"

"Yes, but you're not a fourteen-year-old girl who's going to be publicly humiliated and accused of leading him on."

"That's what Charlotte said. One of her television programmes was about women who took rapists to court. What happened could be brutal, she told me. It could make the experience worse for Olivia. Charlotte knew much more about it than I did: conviction rates, the rubbish that gets printed in the papers about the victims. She was closer to Olivia; she'd always made the important decisions about her. We fought and I lost. I was afraid of hurting my daughter. Afraid she'd hate me." His eyes were wet.

"There's no reason to believe that if you'd won you'd have prevented this." Gillian nodded at the doorway through which Olivia had been carried.

"He might have seen them." Tom had his head down, he was speaking to the tops of his shoes. "It's possible. Ralph brought him along one weekend that summer, before we found out what was going on. He might have spied on them in the barn."

"Barn?"

"Ralph rented it for his bloody antiques."

"Oh." Gillian felt queasy. The boy. Even if he hadn't spied on his father and Olivia, he could have sensed something. He might have read an expression on Ralph's face, or a furtive movement. Or shadows on a wall. Children were acute about such things, whether they knew it consciously or not. The way Kevin had stared at Iris's lovely portrait—it had been made that same year, when Olivia was fourteen. He'd ripped it off the wall, taken it. The police had found it in his dank little room: on the wall, still in its frame, but the glass was smashed. He'd had to have it, but what conflicting emotions had stirred in him, when he saw it?

"Why?" Tom groaned. "Why would he want to hurt her? My little girl."

"I don't know, Tom, he probably didn't know himself. Iris said he had a fantasy life that he could hardly tell from reality. He'd met Olivia, and she was in magazines, on movie screens. She was his biggest fantasy. When reality intruded, he blamed people for keeping them apart, but then what? She left the flat and he heard she had a boyfriend. He couldn't live with the contradiction."

"Christ, I'm glad they're dead. Father and son," Tom said. He had a blank look, the expression of a man confronted by something beyond the world as he had accepted it.

"And Iris was never told what Ralph did?"

"After the accident, it was impossible. What was Charlotte going to say? 'Ralph raped our daughter but I didn't hit him on purpose?' She could hardly tell Iris on condition that Iris be silent. The whole story would have come out. I didn't know what to do. I thought of speaking to Iris myself; it seemed wrong to keep silent. But, Charlotte would have felt utterly betrayed if I'd spoken, and so would Olivia. It was a terrible dilemma for me. I felt I was in a false position."

"And not just with Iris."

"Charlotte and I couldn't agree. She never had much use for the rulebook, you know. We didn't tell anyone, and in the end there wasn't any point, was there? Ralph never recovered, so why torment Iris? Why go through all that? Enough damage had been done. We only knew it later, though—how badly it would turn out for him."

"Charlotte never recovered, either, did she?"

"She couldn't forgive herself. She'd been such a superb mother, it was what meant most to her of all her accomplishments, of everything she'd done. Then she let Ralph into our lives. That's how she put it. She couldn't forgive herself for not seeing what he was, for not protecting Olivia. She said being a bad mother must be in her blood. It was beyond reason. She spent every night flaying herself alive."

"Is that why you left?"

"She wouldn't get over it. She seemed to think it would be morally culpable ever to get over it. It was better to drink."

"Christ, what a smash-up."

Tom looked at her bleakly. "It was my fault, too. And now this."

"Olivia will be all right, Tom."

"Will she?" He ran his hands through his hair and sat up, squaring his shoulders. "Yes. Yes, of course she will. She has to be." His glance moved from the doorway to the clock and back. He cleared his throat. "How's Edward?"

"Fine. He should be here soon. He stayed at the scene."

"Did he have some part in saving her life?"

"He found out Kevin had been mistakenly released and put things in motion."

"I must thank him. Will you come to dinner one night? Both of you? I seem to remember that Edward was seldom available."

"Oh, he's quite human about taking time off, these days. He has a different perspective. Time has a way of doing that to us, don't you find? Speaking of which, Tom, would you know where to reach any of Charlotte's former colleagues? I've had an idea about *London Album*. Charlotte still has all the tapes, but I'll bet the TV station doesn't. They rarely thought of saving programmes then, or of keeping archives. The tapes at Charlotte's are in an outdated format, but they can be transferred. I'd like to make an effort to save them. They're a terrific chunk of London's history. Lots of people would love to see them again. It would be a good legacy."

"I think I could dig up the right names. We'll talk about it when you come to dinner. It's a spendid idea."

"When's the baby due?"

"Any day. It's a boy, Sibyl asked."

"What will you call him?"

"Richard. My father's name."

The nurse came back. "You may see your daughter now."

In the middle of the evening, Olivia opened her eyes. She was lying flat on her back in a strange room. A high ceiling, dim light. A big round electric clock on the wall. Where was she? She had a headache. She closed her eyes again.

"Are you awake?" Johnny's voice murmured from close by.

She was. Her eyes flew open. She tried to turn her head, but her muscles were stiff and sore. He leaned down and his lips lightly brushed hers.

"Hullo, love," he said.

She was safe, she remembered now. Kevin was dead. Gillian said so. Her father said so. Consciousness came with a rush. Her whole body ached. There was a bar at the end of the bed. Something was taped to her arm. She'd never been in a hospital bed. She had a white plastic name bracelet on her wrist. It was like the movies.

"How do you feel?"

She looked up at Johnny. He was really there. The memory of being trapped in the flat came to her. She didn't want to think about it or talk about it now. Tomorrow, maybe. Tomorrow she could tell him how she'd held on to the thought of him while she lay face down on the floor, listening to the eerie silence outside and the creak of the lift coming up, wondering if she would still be alive in five minutes.

He sat beside the bed. The hospital room was dusky and quiet and they seemed to be alone. Then she heard footsteps coming down the corridor.

"Johnny," she said in a husky whisper. Her lips, her face muscles, felt strange, as if she hadn't spoken in weeks. It was a relief that sound came out. "Is the nurse going to come and say you have to leave?"

"No. I'm staying."

"That's good." She lay still, contented. Her right arm rested on top of the sheet. He stroked it gently and raised it to his face and kissed the palm. "We were going to dance," she said, remembering.

"The club will be there tomorrow. Bert says hello."

She turned her face carefully towards him. She was very sleepy again. "Kiss me goodnight. Violins. Dissolve. Credits."

Epilogue

Gillian sat curled on the sofa in the sitting room of the flat in Pimlico, holding a gin and tonic. "I hope they let Olivia out tomorrow. I'd feel like bundling myself into a blanket and spending the night on a bench there, except that I know Johnny's staying."

Edward stood with his back to her, looking out at the dark street, moodily jingling the coins in his pocket.

"The hospital has some sort of policy about overnight visitors—family members only. They were being a bit starchy, but he wasn't going to let any bureaucratic nonsense get in his way. He sugared the nurse, it was a treat to see. She was blushing and bridling and dashing off to find him a cot."

"Mmm."

"Tom's invited us to dinner, after the baby's born. Would you like to go?"

He didn't reply.

"Why does it feel as if I'm talking to the sofa cushions? Edward?"

"What?" he snapped.

"You're in a foul mood, aren't you? Olivia's all right. That's what matters."

"It never should have happened. We cocked it up twice! First no one listened to her, and then we opened the bloody door and let Kevin Brody walk out!"

"The rescue worked. She's safe."

"And a man's dead. It shouldn't have been necessary. You should have heard Hardwick when he arrived at the scene. Think of it: he has to go and explain to Angela Brody. She thought Kevin needed help, she said. Help! Some help he got from us. We had Kevin Brody and we let him slip away. Doesn't encourage faith in the system, does it?"

"But Olivia's alive. Christ, I can hardly believe it about Ralph Brody. The fourteen-year-old daughter of his friends."

"It wasn't the first time."

"What?"

"Angela Brody wouldn't tell me, but she caught him in bed with the daughter of neighbours."

"How old was she?"

"Fifteen."

"Is she all right?"

"Appears to be. Married, children, all that."

"That's good." She thought of the girl's parents, and Angela Brody. Tom. Charlotte. But her relief about Olivia overrode all other feelings. "Listen, Edward, it's finished now. Olivia is alive. You helped to save her."

"She saved herself. From what Lisa said, Olivia deserves an Oscar. That phone call to you. The pizza. I don't know what the Met deserves," he said bad temperedly.

"The officer who dressed up as the delivery boy could get best supporting actor."

"He did all right. He'll be in all the papers."

"Hmm. This gin and tonic's quite nice, you know. It may lack the magical properties of beer in a pub on Sunday afternoon, but it has a soothing effect. I'm afraid we don't have any scallops. Would you settle for M&S-whatzit-pierce-plastic-with-fork-heat-fifteen-minutes? Or shall we skip dinner and drink up all the Sancerre?"

"You're humouring me. It won't work."

"You'd rather be cross as a bear?"

"For a few minutes."

"Fine. Tell me when the few minutes are up." She took her drink and went to stand on the little balcony, breathing the night air. Lights were on in the flats across the road. A taxi let two people out and they climbed the steps to a door and went inside. The little yellow lamp on the roof of the taxi buzzed away like a firefly. Near an open window, someone was playing the piano, a Chopin nocturne.

Edward came out and stood silently beside her.

"How's your snit doing?"

"Three's a crowd."

"Especially on this balcony. You haven't told me whether there've been any developments in the case of the kidnapped pen."

"I'm glad you asked. The pen has a light. They sent Bertuca an envelope with the bulb in it. The note said if he didn't pay, they'd take out the cartridge and send him the ink."

She laughed. The pianist began to play the nocturne over again. All about her, under and over and through the notes, she could hear London, its millions being born and living and dying, an ocean of humanity, sounding an ocean's muffled, ceaseless, distant roar.

ALSO AVAILABLE

OLD WOUNDS

A Gillian Adams Mystery

by Nora Kelly

ISBN: 0-7434-9818-6

Historian Gillian Adams drops both her academic career in Vancouver and her plans to spend her sabbatical in London with policeman/lover Edward in order to return to her childhood home up the Hudson, and care for her aging mother, whose heart is giving out.

Gillian keeps her brain working with a light guest-lecturer load at sleepy rural Stanton College, a campus that seems serene—but is soon unsettled by the murder of a student on a lonely stretch of road....

To receive a catalog of other Poisoned Pen Press titles,
please contact us in one of the following ways:

Phone: 1-800-421-3976
Facsimile: 1-480-949-1707
Email: info@poisonedpenpress.com
Website: www.poisonedpenpress.com

Poisoned Pen Press
6962 E. First Ave. Ste. 103
Scottsdale, AZ 85251